FROM TEMPTATION TO TWINS

BY
BARBARA DUNLOP

Our policy is to use papers that are natural, renewable and recyclable products and made from wood grown in sustainable forests. The logging and manufacturing processes conform to the legal environmental regulations of the country of origin.

Printed and bound in Spain
by CPI, Barcelona

MILLS & BOON

First Published in Great Britain 2017
By Mills & Boon, an imprint of HarperCollins*Publishers*
1 London Bridge Street, London, SE1 9GF

© 2017 Barbara Dunlop

ISBN: 978-0-263-92832-7

51-0817

Our polic   is to use papers that are natural, renewable and recyclable
products a   forests. The logging   and
manufact   mental regulation   of
the count

Printed a
by CPI, B

For Mom

One

Here Comes Trouble

The man all but filled the open doorway of the dilapidated Whiskey Bay Crab Shack. His feet were planted apart, his broad shoulders squared and his no-nonsense chin was tipped up in a challenge.

"Is this supposed to be a joke?" he asked, his deep voice booming through the old brick building.

Jules Parker recognized him right away. She'd expected their paths would cross, but she hadn't expected open hostility—interesting. She hopped down from where she was kneeling on the dusty old bar and stripped off her leather work gloves.

"I don't know, Caleb," she answered as she sauntered toward him, tucking the gloves into the back pocket of her faded jeans. "Is there something funny about dismantling shelves?"

He squinted at her. "You're Juliet Parker?"

"You don't recognize me?"

He held out a level hand, moving it up and down, judging the distance to the ground. "Last time I saw you, you were—"

"Fifteen years old."

"Shorter. And you had freckles."

She couldn't help but smile at that. "Okay."

That was nine years ago. Did he think she wouldn't have changed?

His gray eyes hardened. "What are you doing?"

She pointed over her shoulder with her thumb. "Like I said, dismantling the bar shelves."

"I mean, what are you doing *here*?"

"In Whiskey Bay?" She and her younger sister, Melissa, had arrived yesterday, having planned their return for over a year.

"In the Crab Shack."

"I own the Crab Shack." At least, she owned half of the Crab Shack. Melissa was her partner.

He pulled a piece of paper from his back pocket, brandishing it in his fist. "You *extended* the business license."

"Uh-huh." The fact clearly upset him, though she wasn't sure why.

"And you *extended* the noncompete clause."

"Uh-huh," she said again. The noncompete was part of the original license. Everything had been extended.

He took a step forward, all but looming over her, and she was reminded of why she'd had a schoolgirl crush on him. He was all male then, and he was all male now—hot, sexy and incredibly good-looking.

"What is it you want?" he asked in that low, gravelly voice.

She didn't understand the question, but she wasn't about to back down. She squared her shoulders. "How do you mean?"

"Are you playing stupid?"

"I'm not playing at anything. What's *your* game, Caleb? Because I've got work to do here."

He glared at her for a couple of beats. "Do you want money? Is that it? Are you looking for a payout?"

She took a stab at answering. "The Crab Shack's not for sale. We're reopening."

The Whiskey Bay Crab Shack was her grandfather's legacy. It was hers and Melissa's dream, and also her death-bed promise to the grandpa she adored. Her father hated the idea of the family returning to Whiskey Bay, but Jules wasn't thinking about that today.

Caleb's gaze covered the room, seeming to dismiss it. "We both know that's not happening."

"We do?"

"You're starting to annoy me, Juliet."

"It's Jules. And you're starting to annoy me, too." His voice rose in obvious frustration. "Are you telling me it's not about *this*?"

She looked to where he was pointing out the window.

"What?" she asked, confused.

"This." He headed out the door.

Curious, she followed and saw the Whiskey Bay Marina. It looked much as it always had, although the caliber of vessel berthed there had gone up. The pier was lined with sleek, modern yachts. Beyond the marina, in what had always been raw land, there were two semitrailers with a front-end loader and a bulldozer, plus a couple of pickup trucks.

Whatever was being built there likely wouldn't be as attractive as the natural shoreline, but it was far enough away that it shouldn't bother their patrons after they reopened. To the south of the Crab Shack, it was all natural vistas. The signature, soaring cliffs of Whiskey Bay were covered in west coast cedars and wax-leafed salal shrubs. Nobody could build on the south side. It was all cliffs and boulders.

Jules made a mental note to focus the views on the south side.

"I don't think that's going to bother us too much," she said.

Caleb's stunned expression was interrupted by Melissa's arrival in their mini pickup truck.

"Hello," Melissa sang out as she exited from the driver's side, a couple of hardware store bags in her arms and a bright smile on her face.

"Do you remember Caleb Watford?" Jules asked.

"Not really." Melissa set the bags down on the deck and held out her hand. "I remember the Parkers hate the Watfords."

Jules knew she shouldn't smile at her sister's blunt statement. But the revelation couldn't come as any surprise to Caleb. The feud between their grandfathers and fathers was well-known. It was the likely reason Caleb was being so obnoxious. He didn't want the Parkers back in Whiskey Bay. Well, that was too bad.

Caleb accepted Melissa's hand. "Either you two are the best actors in the world…"

Melissa gave Jules a confused glance.

"Don't look at me," Jules said. "I haven't the slightest idea what he's talking about. But he's ticked off about something."

"You see that?" Caleb pointed again.

Melissa shaded her eyes. "Looks like a bulldozer."

"It's my bulldozer."

"Congratulations…?" Melissa offered hesitantly, her confusion obvious.

"Do you two have any idea what I do?" he asked.

"No," Jules answered.

She knew the Watfords were rich. They owned one of three mansions set along the cliffs of Whiskey Bay. Besides the mansion, the only other house on the bay was the Parkers'. It was just a regular little old house. Her grandfather had lived there for nearly seventy years before he'd passed away.

"Do you drive a bulldozer?" Melissa asked.

"Seriously?" Jules asked her sister, finding it impossible to imagine Caleb as a heavy equipment operator. "The Watfords are mega wealthy."

"He could still drive a bulldozer," Melissa said. "Maybe he likes driving a bulldozer."

"Rich guys don't drive bulldozers."

Jules pictured Caleb behind a big desk in an opulent office. No, that wasn't quite right. Presiding over a construction site, maybe? He could be an architect.

"Have you ever seen *Construction Vacation*?" Melissa asked.

"The TV show?"

"Yeah. All kinds of guys, rich, poor, whatever. They come on the show and play with heavy equipment. They like it. It's a thing."

"Well, maybe on a lark—"

"Stop!" Caleb all but shouted.

Melissa drew back, clearly shocked.

"He's been like this ever since he showed up," Jules said.

"Like a bear with a hangnail," Melissa muttered.

"I don't think that's a metaphor," Jules said. "Bears have claws."

Caleb was glancing back and forth between them. His skin tone seemed to have gone a little darker. Jules decided it might be good to let him speak.

"I own and manage the Neo chain of seafood restaurants. That—" he stabbed his finger in the direction of the bull-dozer "—will be the newest location."

Both women looked along the shore, and Jules realized why Caleb was so annoyed.

"Oh," Melissa said, pausing for a short beat. "Except you can't build it now because of the noncompete clause in our business license."

"It was *supposed* to expire on Wednesday," he said.

"I saw that when we renewed."

"Now I get it," Jules said to him. "I can see why you'd be disappointed."

"Disappointed?" Caleb caught the beer Matt Emerson tossed him from the wet bar at opposite side of the marina's sundeck. "I'm a million dollars into the project, and she thinks I'm *disappointed*?"

"You're not?" TJ Bauer asked evenly as he popped the top of his own beer.

The three men were on the deck that sat atop the Whiskey Bay Marina office building. A quarter moon rose in the starlit sky, while the lights of the pier reflected off the foamy water eddying between the white yachts.

Caleb shot TJ a glower.

"Do you think this is about your dad?" Matt asked.

"Or your grandfather," TJ added, bracing his butt against the rail. "This could be your chickens coming home to roost."

"They're not my chickens," Caleb said.

"Does *she* know that?" Matt asked.

Caleb couldn't believe Jules was capable of executing such a nefarious revenge plan.

"Are you suggesting she figured out that I was planning to build a Neo location at Whiskey Bay, waited until the last possible moment, the fortieth anniversary of their grandfather's business license, to extend the noncompete clause and shut down my project so I'd lose a fortune, in retaliation for the actions of my father and grandfather?"

"It would earn her a significant score on the evil-genius meter," TJ said.

"Your ancestors were pretty evil to her ancestors," Matt said.

Caleb didn't disagree with that. His grandfather had stolen away the woman Felix Parker loved, while his father had ruined Roland Parker's best chance at a college education.

There wasn't a lot about either man that made Caleb proud. "I didn't do a thing to the Parkers."

"Did you mention that to Jules?" Matt asked.

"She's sticking to her story—that she had no idea I wanted to build a restaurant of my own."

"Maybe she didn't," TJ said. "You know, this wouldn't be the worst time in the world to take on investors."

"This would absolutely be the worst time in the world to take on investors." Caleb had heard the pitch from TJ before.

"One phone call to my clients, Caleb. And seventeen Neo locations across the US could become forty Neo locations around the world. A million-dollar loss here would be insignificant."

"Read my lips," Caleb said. "I'm not interested."

TJ shrugged. "Can't blame a guy for trying."

"Then call her bluff," Matt said, crossing the deck and dropping into one of the padded chairs surrounding a gas fire pit.

"She's not bluffing," Caleb pointed out. "She already extended the noncompete clause."

"I mean pretend you believe her. That she's only after her own business interests, and this isn't some warped revenge against your family. See if she'll be reasonable about coexisting."

TJ moved to another of the chairs. "I see where he's going. Explain to her how Neo and the Crab Shack can both succeed. If she's not out to harm you, then she should be willing to discuss it."

"They serve different market niches." Caleb sat down, thinking there might be merit to the strategy. "And where they overlap, one could be a draw for the other."

"Cross-promotion," TJ said.

"I'd be willing to push some customers her way."

"Maybe don't make yourself sound so arrogant," Matt said. "I don't think women like that."

"Aren't you supposed to be the big expert on women?" TJ asked Caleb.

"Jules isn't a woman," Caleb said. But even as he spoke, he envisioned her sparkling blue eyes, her billowy wheat-blond hair and her full red lips. Jules was all woman, and that just made things more complicated.

"I mean," he continued. "She's not a woman in the way you're thinking about women. Not that she's not good-looking, she is. Anybody would tell you that. But that's irrelevant. It's irrelevant to the situation. I'm not trying to date her. I'm trying to do business with her."

"Uh-oh," Matt said to TJ.

"That's trouble," TJ said to Matt.

"It's not like that," Caleb said. "The last time I saw her she was fifteen."

TJ grinned. "And that was a logical comeback to *what*?"

"She was a kid. She was my neighbor. And now she's a thorn in my side. This has nothing to do with, you know, our recent discussions about the two of you getting back into the dating pool. How's that going, by the way?"

Both men grinned at him. "You think we're going to let you change the subject that easily?"

"Either of you dating?" Caleb asked. "Are you? Because I had a date last weekend."

Matt had just made it through a bitter divorce, and TJ had just passed the two-year anniversary of his wife's death. Both had committed to living Caleb's bachelor lifestyle for the next year. And Caleb had committed to helping them achieve it.

"Hey, Matt?" came a female voice from below on the pier.

"Speaking of women..." TJ said, interest perking up in his voice.

"Speaking of *not* women." Matt muttered under his breath as he rose to his feet.

"Who is she?" TJ asked, standing to look over the rail.

"My mechanic." Matt raised his voice. "Hi, Tasha. What's going on?"

"I don't like the sound of MK's backup engine. Can I have a day to tear it down?"

Through the rails, Caleb could see a slender woman in a T-shirt and cargo pants. She wore a pair of leather work boots. And she had a ponytail sticking out of the back of her tattered baseball cap.

"It's booked out starting Sunday."

"That gives me all day tomorrow," Tasha called back.

"Perfect. I'll make sure she's ready."

"Thanks, Tasha."

"*That's* your mechanic?" TJ asked as he watched the young woman walk away.

"You want to date my mechanic?" Matt asked.

"She's pretty cute."

Matt laughed. "She's tough as nails. I wouldn't recommend her as a starting point."

"You calling dibs?"

"Fill your boots, brother. She'll eat you for lunch."

Caleb couldn't help but grin. "Should we go into the city and hit a club tomorrow night?"

Whiskey Bay was less than two hours from the nightlife of Olympia and it sounded like TJ and Matt could use a little push into the social scene. Caleb would be more than happy to forget his own problems for an evening.

"I'm in," said Matt.

"Sounds great," said TJ.

Caleb finished his beer. "In that case, I'm going home to strategize." He rose. "I like your idea to test Jules's sincerity. I'll do it in the morning."

"Good luck," Matt called.

Caleb took the stairs to the pier then left the lights of the marina behind him on the walk home.

Whiskey Bay was characterized by stunning steep cliffs. There was very little land at sea level, just an acre or so under the marina and another parcel of a similar size where Caleb intended to build Neo. The Crab Shack was located on a rocky spit of land to the south of the marina. It had been closed now for more than ten years, since Felix Parker had grown too old to run it.

Four houses sat on the steep rise of the cliff. Matt's was directly above the marina. TJ's was a few hundred yards to the south, then came the Parkers' small house, with Caleb's house last.

Back in the '50s, his grandfather had built a small place similar to the Parkers'. But while the Parker place had remained intact, the Watfords had rebuilt numerous times.

After his grandfather's death Caleb had bought the house from the rest of the family, gradually renovating it to make it his own.

There was a path halfway up the cliff that connected the four houses. Caleb, Matt and TJ had installed solar lights a few years back, so walking after dark was easy. Caleb had passed below the Parker house thousands of times. But in the five years since Felix Parker had moved to a care home, there'd never been a light on there.

Tonight, it was lit. Caleb could see it in the distance, filtered by the spreading branches of cedar trees. As he grew closer, the deck came into view, and he had a sudden memory of a teenage Jules. It had to have been her last summer visiting her grandfather. She'd been dancing on the deck. Dressed in cutoff shorts and a striped tank top, her hair up in a messy knot, she was dancing like nobody was watching.

He could see her freckles. That's how he'd remembered she'd had freckles. The sunlight had glowed against her blond hair and her creamy skin. She'd been far too beautiful, and far too young. He'd felt guilty for even looking at her back then. He'd been twenty-one, building his first Neo restaurant in San Francisco.

"Spying on us?" Jules suddenly appeared on the trail in front of him.

"On my way home," he answered, quickly pulling himself back to the present.

She wasn't wearing cutoffs, and no tight striped tank top either. Thank goodness. Although her blue jeans and cropped white T-shirt weren't exactly saving his sanity. In fact, it was worse, because she was all grown up now.

"You're standing still," she pointed out.

He went with a partial truth. "I'm not used to seeing lights on in your house."

She glanced up at the deck. "I guess it's been a while."

"Quite a few years." He gazed at her profile. She was

quite astonishingly gorgeous. He couldn't remember ever meeting a woman so beautiful.

"Did you know your family sent flowers?" she asked. "When my grandfather died."

"I did." It had been Caleb who'd arranged it.

"Sent my dad off the deep end, I tell you."

Caleb felt a twinge of regret. "I hadn't thought of that."

She turned to look at him again. "So it was you?"

"Was that a test?"

"I was curious. It didn't make sense that your dad would have sent them."

"No, it wouldn't." Caleb's father had once been arrested because of an altercation with Jules's father, Roland. Caleb had never heard all the details, but his father had often railed about the overreaction of the authorities, and how it was Felix Parker's fault they were called in the first place.

"He might have sent a brass band," Jules mused.

"I don't know what to say to that." Caleb wondered if she was looking for an apology.

"It was a joke."

"Okay. It seemed a little…"

"Inappropriate? To acknowledge your father might have wished my grandfather dead?" She shrugged her slim shoulders. "We can pretend if you want."

"I meant to joke about your grandfather's death at all."

"He was ninety. He wouldn't mind. In fact, I think he'd like it. You're still mad at me, aren't you?" She tipped her head to one side.

Heck, yes, he was still mad at her. But he was also massively attracted to her. Gazing at her in the dim glow of the trail light, anger was a pretty difficult emotion to dredge up.

"We can pretend I'm not," he said.

She smiled, and his chest contracted. "You *do* have a sense of humor."

He didn't smile back. He hadn't been joking. He was perfectly prepared to pretend he wasn't angry with her.

She stepped unexpectedly closer. "I used to have such a crush on you."

He stopped breathing.

"I have no idea why," she continued. "I barely knew you. Only from afar. But you were older, and it was summer, and I was nearly sixteen. And I'm sure it didn't hurt that our families were feuding. Nothing like the Montagues and the Capulets, or the Jets and the Sharks, to get a young girl's heart going. It's kind of funny now that you—" She blinked at him. "Caleb?"

He couldn't kiss her. He couldn't. He could not…

"Caleb?"

There was no way she was doing this by accident. She had to guess what it would do to him, to any mortal man. She truly was an evil genius.

"You know exactly what you're doing, don't you?" he managed to force out, annoyance in his tone.

She searched his expression. "What am I doing?"

The woman deserved an acting award.

"Putting me off balance," he said. "Dancing around on your balcony, tight shorts, tight shirt—"

"What? Dancing where?"

"You're twenty-four years old."

"I know that."

"You're standing out here in the woods, alone, telling a grown man that you once had a crush on him."

Her expression fell, and she took a step back. "I thought it was a sweet story."

His voice came out strangled. *"Sweet?"*

"Okay, and a little embarrassing. I wanted to open up. I was trying to get you to like me."

He closed his eyes for a long moment. He couldn't let himself believe that. He couldn't let her get under his skin. He didn't know what to do with this, what to do with her, how to put her in any kind of context. "I'm not going to like you."

"But—"

"You should go."

"Go?" She actually sounded hurt.

"I think we're on two completely different wavelengths."

She didn't answer. The woods around him fell silent.

He opened his eyes to find her gone. He breathed a sigh of relief. Then the relief turned into regret as he second-guessed himself. He could usually read the signs with women—tell the difference between flirting and an innocent conversation. With Jules, he couldn't.

"You told him you'd had a crush on him?" Melissa asked from the bottom of the stepladder the next day.

Jules removed the next in a cluster of '50s movie star portraits that hung on a wall of the restaurant. "I was trying to… I don't know." She'd had more than a few hours to regret her words.

"Did you not think it would sound flirty?"

Jules handed the portrait of Grace Kelly down to Melissa and reached for Elizabeth Taylor. "I didn't mean for it to be flirty."

"It was flirty."

"I realize that *now*."

"What were you thinking *then*?"

"That it would be charming. I was being open and honest, sharing a slightly embarrassing story. I thought it might make me seem human."

"He knows you're human."

"In the end it was just humiliating." Jules handed down the Elizabeth Taylor.

"So, you learned something." Melissa crossed the room to set the portraits in a cardboard box on the bar.

"I learned that he has zero interest in flirting with me."

"I was thinking maybe a broader point about relationships, time and place, and appropriate comments."

Jules climbed down and moved the ladder, settling it

into place where she could read the next three portraits. "Oh, that. No."

Melissa grinned. "Tell me more about the crush. I wish you'd told me about it back then."

"You were too young."

"It still would have been exciting."

It had certainly been exciting for Jules. "I was fifteen. He was tall, and he shaved, and he lived in a mansion on the hill. And I was fresh out of grade nine English class. Between the Brontë sisters and Shakespeare, I spun a pretty interesting fantasy."

"I don't even remember him from back then."

"That's because you were only twelve."

"What I remember most is Grandma's hot chocolate. It was so nice, coming here, spending time with her, especially after Mom died."

"I miss them both."

Melissa gave Jules's arm a squeeze. "Me, too. But I don't miss the squirrels waking us up in the morning."

Jules handed Audrey Hepburn to Melissa. "I hated those squirrels."

"You really should have thought of that before we moved back here. They're going to wake us up every morning."

"Do you think we could livetrap them, relocate them like they do with bears?"

"I don't see why not."

Jules thought about it for a moment as she handed down Jayne Mansfield. "I wonder what we'd need for bait."

"Going fishing?" The sound of Caleb's voice startled her, and she swayed, grabbing the top of the ladder to steady herself.

"Whoa." Caleb surged toward her.

"Steady girl," Melissa said.

"I'm fine." Jules regained her balance.

She focused on his forehead instead of meeting his eyes.

She'd pretend nothing awkward had happened last night. Hopefully, he'd play along and they could both ignore it.

"Should you be up on that ladder?" he asked.

"I was fine until you scared me." Jules turned back to her work and reached for Doris Day.

"You were talking about fishing?"

"We were?" Jules couldn't figure out why he thought that.

"You said we needed bait," Melissa put in.

"Matt can take you fishing," Caleb said. He was hovering beside Melissa, looking like he wanted to take over the operation. "Do you need a hand with that?"

"Why are you suddenly being nice?" Jules asked as she handed over the next portrait.

She'd prefer it if they were cordial to each other. But after their argument yesterday and their encounter last night, she'd expected him to avoid her, not to drop by and pretend they were friends.

"I'm not being nice," he said.

"Who's Matt?" Melissa asked as she crossed the room with Doris in her hands.

"He owns the marina." Caleb took over from Melissa and braced both sides of the ladder.

"All those yachts?" Melissa asked.

"He has a charter service."

"Out of our price range," Jules put in. She could only imagine the exorbitant cost of renting one of the lavish-looking yachts.

"He won't charge you."

Jules took a step lower on the ladder, expecting Caleb to move back and give her room. "We're not going fishing."

"Let's not be hasty," Melissa said.

"I can set it up." Caleb didn't move.

Jules turned before she took another step down. Deciding she'd prefer to face him while edging into his space.

"We're far too busy to fish," she said, meeting him at eye level.

"Exactly how long would we need for a trip like that?" Melissa asked.

"How are you not suspicious of this?" Jules spoke to Melissa but kept her gaze locked on Caleb. "An enemy bearing gifts?"

"I'm not your enemy." Caleb's deep voice seemed to rumble through her. There was a challenge in his gray eyes. One more step down, and she'd practically be in his arms.

She wasn't going to be the one to back down. She took the final step. "So why are you here?"

"I wanted to talk to you."

"About what?" She told herself to ignore the sizzle of arousal that skipped across her skin. He was a great-looking guy, and she had some emotional baggage where it came to him. But she could handle it. She could easily handle it.

He drew a deep breath, his broad chest expanding. A few more inches and they would be touching. She wondered how he'd handle that. She should make it happen and find out.

"The contractor's here," Melissa said, as a vehicle engine sounded outside in the parking lot.

"You need me?" Jules made to move, thinking she'd probably just been saved from…something with Caleb.

"Nope. I'll just show him around," Melissa said and headed for the door.

"We don't need to be competitors." Caleb firmed his stance as he spoke to Jules.

"We're not competitors." She wondered how long he intended to keep her trapped. She eased slightly forward to test his boundaries. "I have a noncompete agreement, so you can't build Neo."

Caleb leaned in himself, as if he could read her thoughts. "Neo's not your competition."

"I know it's not. Because it doesn't exist."

"I mean, if it did exist. We'd cater to a different clientele."

"The Crab Shack caters to seafood eaters. What does Neo do?"

"Neo's high-end. The Crab Shack is casual."

"What makes you say that?"

He seemed surprised by her words. He glanced around the building, taking in the aging brick, the torn linoleum and the rustic wood beams. "It's humble, basic, kitschy. Don't get me wrong—"

"How could I take that wrong?" She crossed her arms, and her elbows touched his chest. She tipped her head, re-capturing his gaze and letting her annoyance tighten her expression.

"If you *were* to go high-end," he said.

She waited. She couldn't believe he hadn't backed off yet.

Instead, he increased the connection between them, his chest pressing along the length of her forearms. It was a firm chest, a sexy chest and an amazing chest. For a second, she lost her train of thought.

"If you were to go high-end," he said. "We'd be comple-mentary. We could feed customers to each other. You've seen it, a restaurant district or an auto mall. We could be-come a seafood restaurant cluster—*the* place to go in greater Olympia for terrific seafood."

"That's pretty good."

"So you're interested?"

"No."

"Why not?"

"It's a pretty good argument, Caleb. It's not true, but A for ingenuity."

Something flashed in his eyes. It was either admiration or annoyance, maybe a bit of both. "There are examples of it all over the world."

"Neo's a nationally known and renowned chain. You'd annihilate the Crab Shack."

Melissa's and the contractor's voices were muffled as they talked outside on the deck.

"You're not going to agree to this, are you?" Caleb asked.

"No."

"We're not going to be friendly?"

"I'm afraid not."

"Okay." He nodded. He let go of the ladder and rocked back, breaking their contact. "I guess I'll go back to my corner and come out swinging."

She wasn't disappointed, she told herself. And she definitely didn't miss his touch.

"But first," he said, surprising her by reaching back to cup her cheek with his palm. "Since I probably can't make the situation much worse…"

His intent was clear. She told herself to say no, to turn her head, to step sideways. There was nothing stopping her. She was free to move and shut this down.

But she didn't. Instead, she surrendered to nine years of fantasy and parted her lips as he closed the space between them.

Two

Before his lips even touched Jules's, Caleb knew he was making a huge mistake. He also knew he didn't care.

He'd lain awake half the night thinking about her, picturing her on the trail outside her house, reliving her saying she'd had a crush on him. He should have kissed her right then. Any other man would have kissed her right then.

Now her cheek was soft against his palm, warm and smooth. He edged his fingers into her silky hair, and his lips finally covered hers. He kept the kiss soft. He wanted to devour her, but he didn't want to scare her, and he sure didn't want her to push him away.

Her lips softened. They parted. He firmed his grip, anchoring her mouth to his, while his free hand went around her waist. Desire pulsed through his body, arousal awakening his senses. He gave in to temptation and touched his tongue to hers.

She moaned, and his arm wound around her, bringing their bodies flush together. He deepened the kiss, bending her slightly backward. His body temperature rose, and he could feel the pulse of the ocean, or maybe it was the beat of his heart.

Melissa's voice penetrated from outside, saying something about the roof. Her footsteps sounded on the deck. A man's voice rose in response to her question.

Jules's hands went to Caleb's shoulders, and she gave the slightest push.

He reacted immediately, pulling back, her flushed cheeks coming into focus, along with her swollen lips and glazed blue eyes.

He wanted it again. He wanted more. He absolutely did not want to stop.

"I've made it worse," he said, half to himself.

"We can't do that," she said, obviously voicing her own train of thought.

"No kidding."

"I can't trust you."

"You could have said no." This wasn't all on him.

Her smile looked self-conscious. "I know. I'm talking about more than just the kiss."

"Tell me why?" He didn't know why he cared, but he did.

"Why I can't trust you?"

"Yes."

She thought about it for a moment. "I can't trust you, because I can't trust you."

He wasn't buying it. "That's a circular argument. You're too smart for that."

"Okay," she said, drawing back against the ladder. "I can't trust you because you're a Watford."

He knew he should walk away, but his feet stayed stubbornly still. "You barely know me."

"I know your family."

"That's not the same thing."

"I know you want me to compromise my interests."

"Not really," he said.

She cocked her head and sent him a frown of disbelief.

"Only a little bit," he amended. "But it'll work in the long run. I know it'll work in the long run. For both of us."

"Are you lying to yourself or just to me?"

"I'm not lying."

"You definitely inherited it," she said, apparently growing tired of waiting for him to back off. She slipped sideways, putting some distance between them.

"Inherited what?" He watched her go with regret.

"The gift of persuasion. Just like your father and grandfather, you're confident in your ability to talk your way out of or into anything."

Caleb wasn't like his father or his grandfather. At least he didn't want to be like them. He tried very hard to mitigate his father's character traits in himself. For the most part, he thought he succeeded.

"That's not fair," he said.

"Fair?" She gave a light laugh. "A Watford talking about fair? Let me add to that. A Watford talking about fair while he tries to talk a Parker out of something?"

Caleb knew he'd lost this round. There was no way she was going to listen to reason. At least not right now. The kiss had been a colossal error.

Then again, it was a fantastic kiss. He couldn't bring himself to regret it. If that kiss was the biggest mistake he made today, it was going to be a good day.

"No comeback?" she asked. "Come on, Caleb. You're disappointing me."

"Is there anything I can say to change your opinion?"

"Uh, no."

"Then is there any chance you'll go out with me?"

The question seemed to take her aback, and it took her a second to respond. "You mean like on a date?"

"Yeah. You and me. Dinner, dancing, whatever." He wasn't exactly sure how they'd separate their personal attraction from their business interests, but he was more than willing to give it a try.

"Is that a joke? Are you trying to put me off balance?"

"Yes, I'm trying to put you off balance." He took a couple of steps toward her. "But no, it's not a joke. There's obviously an attraction between us."

"We have nothing in common."

"I like kissing you." And he was pretty confident that she liked kissing him.

Her expression didn't soften at all. "I bet you like kissing a whole lot of women."

Not as much as he liked kissing her. But the accusation was fundamentally true. And he didn't want to lie to her. "I suppose I do."

"Then take one of *them* out on a date."

"I'd rather take you."

"You're too much."

"You're stubborn."

"Give the man a gold star."

The answer surprised him. "You admit to being stubborn?"

"Oh, yes." She jabbed her finger against his chest. "And you ain't seen nothin' yet."

He trapped her hand, holding it against his heart. "Fightin' words?"

"You said it yourself. We're both going back to our corners now to come out swinging."

Her eyes were alight, her cheeks still flushed, her lips were still swollen from his kisses, and he could see a little pulse at the base of her neck. She was the sexiest woman on the planet.

"Don't you dare," she said, snatching her hand from his grip.

He couldn't help but grin. "I'm not going to kiss you again."

"You better not."

"I'll make you a deal."

She shook her head.

"Not a business deal. A personal deal. Next time, you have to be the one to kiss me." Even as he said the words, he feared he was making a mistake.

She might never decide to kiss him. But he had no choice. He couldn't take the chance of misreading her signals.

Melissa bounced through the doorway, enthusiasm in her expression and in her tone. "Jules, this is Noah Glover. He's offered to help us with the renovation."

Jules expression immediately neutralized, erasing their

kiss, their argument and everything else. Noah Glover had walked in, and she'd given him a brilliant smile that made Caleb jealous.

Noah was tall and brawny, with an unshaven face and a shaggy haircut. He looked like the kind of guy who worked all day out in the weather.

Jules smoothly closed the space between them. "Nice to meet you, Noah."

They shook, and Caleb felt another shot of jealousy. He gave himself a ruthless shake. It was one thing to want to kiss her, even hold her, even strip her naked and make love to her—which he did. But it was something else altogether to be jealous of a man shaking her hand. He wasn't about to let that happen.

"I hope Melissa warned you we're on a tight budget," Jules said to Noah. "We want to do as much of the work as we can ourselves."

"I can work with a budget," Noah said. "And as much work as you're willing to do is fine with me."

"That sounds perfect." She was still shaking his hand.

That was it? The entire interview? They were going to hire the guy right here and now? What about reference checks?

Caleb stepped up and stuck out his own hand. "Caleb Watford. I'm a neighbor." He wanted this Noah guy to know he couldn't simply stride in and take advantage of Jules and Melissa.

"Nice to meet you," Noah said.

His grip was firm. Of course his grip was firm. He was a carpenter. But Caleb was no slouch. From what he could see, they were about the same height. Caleb could bench press one-eighty, but Noah had a lot more calluses.

"And our sworn enemy," Jules said.

Caleb slid her a look of annoyance. Did she have no idea that he was trying to help?

"What happened while I was gone?" Melissa asked, glancing from one to the other.

"Nothing," Jules said quickly. "Well, more of the same."

"I'm happy to get started tomorrow," Noah said to the women. "If you pull together your budget, I'll get going on some estimates, and we can see what we have for options."

His voice was deep. Caleb wasn't crazy to learn that. He'd heard women liked men with deep voices. It was supposed to instill a sense of confidence. He didn't want Jules feeling overconfident with this stranger.

Caleb had never heard of Noah Glover. Was he local to the Whiskey Bay area? Was he passing through? His truck outside was old and battered, and he wasn't exactly a poster child for professionalism. Caleb was definitely going to check him out.

"I'm up for that," Melissa said. "I'm excited to get started."

Noah gave her a nod. "Until tomorrow, then." He gave a parting smile to Jules before he left the building.

"He really seems to know what he's doing," Melissa said as she watched him leave.

"You just met him," Caleb said.

Both women looked at him in surprise.

"How can you judge his competency?" Caleb doubted either Jules or Melissa had any expertise in construction.

"He seemed open and straightforward," Melissa said. "Talked in plain language. He came highly recommended."

"Did you check his reviews?" Caleb asked.

"Melissa has a business degree," Jules said.

That was news to Caleb. He didn't know why it surprised him.

"Of course I checked his reviews," Melissa said. "I am aware of the internet."

Caleb wasn't sure whether to backpedal or press forward. "I only meant…"

Jules's voice turned to a sarcastic purr. "That sweet li'l

young things like us might not know how to manage in the big bad world?"

He frowned at her. "I wondered why you'd trust him in a heartbeat and be so suspicious of me."

"Experience and good judgment," she said.

"That's not fair."

"I told you before, Caleb. You're a Watford. There isn't a reason in the world for me to be fair to you."

"He really is hot," Melissa said two days later.

Jules looked up from where she was stripping varnish from the wooden bar, expecting to see Caleb walk through the door. But he wasn't there. At least, she couldn't see him.

Melissa was pulling down the window trim, while Noah was outside setting up a survey level on a tripod.

Jules was momentarily confused and, she hated to admit, a little disappointed. Caleb might be annoying, but he was also interesting. He energized a room.

"You mean Noah?" she asked her sister.

"Who else would I mean? Look at those shoulders and those biceps."

"He does seem to be in good shape," Jules agreed.

She hadn't thought of Noah as particularly hot, although she supposed he was fairly good-looking in a rugged, earthy kind of way. He was dressed in a khaki green T-shirt and a pair of tan cargo pants. A tool belt was slung low on his hips, and his steel-toed boots were scuffed and worn. He had sandy-blond hair, thick and a little shaggy.

"I can't stop staring at him," Melissa said.

"I wouldn't have pegged him as your type."

The men Melissa had dated in college had been mostly preppy intellectuals, sometimes even poets. Occasionally, she'd talked about seeing an athlete. There was one basketball player she'd stayed with for a couple of months.

"Hot and sexy? Whose type is that not?"

Jules smiled, taking another look at Noah through her safety glasses. "So you mean as eye candy."

Personally, she found him a bit dusty for eye candy. But if Melissa found him entertaining while she took on the drudge work of renovating, Jules was happy for her.

"Don't let him slow you down," Jules said.

"I can look and rip trim at the same time."

"Make sure you don't stab yourself with a nail."

"They're finishing nails, teeny-tiny finishing nails. Do you think if it gets hot enough he'll consider taking off his shirt?"

"I think if you ask him we get sued. Sexual harassment goes both ways, you know."

"I won't ask him, at least, not flat out."

"You can't ask him at all. You can't even hint."

"I can hope."

"I suppose there's no such thing as the mind police," Jules said.

Melissa grinned. "That's a good thing. Because what I'm imagining is probably illegal in most states."

"Please don't tell me."

"You're such a prude."

Jules scrunched her eyes shut, not allowing any untoward mental pictures to form. "Pink fuzzy bunnies. Pink fuzzy bunnies," she chanted out loud, bringing the harmless image into her mind.

Melissa laughed at her antics.

"I obviously missed something." This time it *was* Caleb.

Jules popped open her eyes to find him standing in the doorway again.

Talk about hot and sexy. He wore blue jeans, an open-collar white shirt and a midnight blue blazer. He looked casual and classy all at the same time, putting the rest of the male world to shame.

"Pink fuzzy bunnies?" he asked with a raised brow.

"Inside joke," Melissa said. "It's our mantra to keep nasty images at bay."

Caleb glanced around. "Is there something nasty?"

"Not *at all*," Melissa said, her blue eyes flashing mischief before she looked out the window again.

Jules told herself to stop ogling Caleb. "Can we help you with something?"

"I've been doing some research on your project," he said as he stepped inside.

She adjusted her gloves and went determinedly back to working on the varnish removal with a paint scraper. "You're just the Energizer Bunny, aren't you?"

He kept moving toward her. "You've obviously got a rabbit theme going here."

"Stay back," she warned. "This stuff is dangerous."

He stopped but frowned. "Do you know what you're doing?"

"Yes." She dug the blade into the tacky solution and scraped it off in a layer.

"Have you done this before?"

"I watched a YouTube video." She wiped away the goo with a rag and started on another strip.

"So, your answer is no."

"My answer is 'it's none of your business.'"

He seemed to find her response amusing. "You're very prickly."

"And you're a cocklebur."

"A what?"

"A prickly plant. Something that digs in and sticks to you and won't let go."

"Oh. Okay, my mind went to a completely different place with that."

Jules struggled not to smile. She didn't want to encourage him. Or maybe she did. She didn't like that he felt so free to interfere in her life, but she'd admit he was at least as entertaining for her as Noah was for Melissa.

A low clatter sounded from the window where Melissa was working. She swore.

Jules quickly glanced up. "You okay?"

Caleb was there before Melissa could answer, removing an L-shaped piece of window trim from her hands and untangling another piece from around her feet. "Are you hurt?"

"I'm fine," Melissa said. "I just got distracted for a minute."

"Where are you putting all this?" Caleb asked.

"There's a disposal bin in the parking lot."

Caleb spotted a pair of work gloves in a box by the door. He helped himself and gathered up a full armload of discarded trim.

"You're not dressed for work," Jules felt the need to point out to him.

"Not exactly," he agreed. "But I might as well help a bit while we talk."

"We're not done talking?"

He didn't answer, just shook his head as he left through the door.

"You're as bad as me," Melissa said.

Jules realized she was watching Caleb's backside as he walked away. "Is it that obvious?"

"It is when you start drooling."

"You're *such* a comedian. I'm trying to figure out what he's doing here."

"That's not what your expression says. But, okay, let's go with that. What do you suppose he's doing here?"

"He said he'd done some research on our project."

"What does that mean?" Melissa asked.

"I'm assuming more on why we should remove the non-compete clause."

"That seems likely. He's coming back."

"I see that."

Caleb gave Noah a curt nod of acknowledgment as he approached the restaurant doorway.

Jules found the view of him equally pleasant from the front. She didn't have to like him to admire the breadth of his shoulders, the swing of his stride, and the square chin and neatly trimmed dark hair that made him look capable of taking on...well, anything, including her.

A wave of heat passed through her body and sweat tickled her forehead. She swiped awkwardly at her hairline with her bare forearm as he walked back inside.

He looked around the open space. "What else needs doing?"

"Your work is done," Jules said.

He might be pleasant to watch, but she was coming to the conclusion that it might be dangerous for her to spend much time around him.

He removed his jacket and set it aside, rolling up his sleeves.

"You have got to be kidding me," she said. "You're going to ruin that shirt."

He shrugged. "I have other shirts."

"It's *white*."

He glanced down at himself. "So it is."

"Say whatever it is you came to say, and get out of here. Go back to your regularly scheduled life."

He put a mock expression of hurt on his face. "I don't know how to take that."

"Yes, you do. You've got your own construction project to worry about."

"That's the thing."

"Here we go..." She lined up to scrape off another strip of varnish.

"I want to show you some of the numbers from my other Neo locations."

Out of the corner of her eye, she watched him look into their small toolbox. "Showing off your profits?" she asked.

He ignored her gibe. "And the plans for the new location." He selected a claw hammer. "What's your seating going to be here?"

"None of your business."

"Jules." There was exaggerated patience in his tone. "We're not going to be able to work this out if you're going to be hostile."

Melissa spoke up. "Thirty-four at the tables, twelve at the bar and another eighteen on the deck."

Jules glared at her.

"What?" Melissa asked. "It's not exactly a state secret. All he has to do is pull a copy of the business license."

"Neo will have one-seventy-two on two floors, plus fifty seasonally on the patio. We're not your competition." He approached the window opposite Melissa and wedged the hammer under the trim.

"I agree with that," Jules said. "It would be no contest at all."

"Why would anyone choose the Crab Shack?" Melissa asked.

"They wouldn't," Jules said.

"Because they love seafood. And because nobody wants to eat at the same place all the time. And because if they came to Neo, they'd see the Crab Shack and maybe become curious."

"Or maybe they'd come to the Crab Shack and learn about Neo." Jules didn't know why she tossed that out. It sounded ridiculous even to her.

"Sure," Caleb said.

"Don't patronize me. We both know that's not going to happen. What you're offering us is your leftovers."

"Neo is a nationally recognized chain with international awards and a substantial marketing program. I'm not going to apologize for that."

"Fancy it up all you want, but the result will be the same. Neo wins, the Crab Shack loses. We're far better off being the only option at Whiskey Bay."

"Can I at least show you my floor plans?"

"Sure," Melissa said.

"Melissa."

"What's the harm in looking, Jules? Aren't you even a little bit curious?"

Jules was, but there was no way she'd admit it. "Go ahead and look if you want. I'm not interested."

"I'll bring them by later on," Caleb said as he ripped down a long strip of window trim.

"He is *not* changing our minds." Jules put complete conviction into her tone, even as she struggled to drag her gaze from Caleb.

Due to the curve of the shoreline, Caleb could see the Neo construction site through the window of his great room. He could also see the Crab Shack, where lights were on tonight. And he could see the Parkers' house—all dark there.

"Jules wouldn't even look at the plans," he said turning back to his lawyer, Bernard Stackhouse.

"What did you expect?" Bernard asked in an even tone.

"I thought she might look. I hoped she'd look. I hoped she'd see reason and stop being so stubborn."

"And then do things your way?"

Bernard was sitting in one of Caleb's leather armchairs. His suit was impeccable as always, and he looked distinguished with a touch of gray at his temples. He could flare into passion in a courtroom when the need arose, but Caleb knew it was an act. He wasn't sure Bernard even felt emotions. But the man wasn't shy about using sarcasm.

"I absolutely want her to do things my way."

His way was the closest they could get to a win-win. But Jules wouldn't take that. She wouldn't even consider it. She insisted on going for a win-lose.

"Her sister, Melissa, seems a whole lot more reasonable," he said.

"Can she change Jules's mind?"

"I'm not sure she's trying. But she did like my restaurant plans." Caleb's gaze was drawn back to the still, silent darkness of his construction site.

He could picture the finished building in his mind, the exterior, the interior, all the people they'd employ and the happy diners enjoying the picturesque waterfront. He was growing more and more impatient to get there. Every day he had to wait he couldn't help calculating the cost: the leased equipment, the crew on standby, the delay in opening that was going to cost him money. If this had to end in a win-lose, he wanted to make sure it wasn't him on the crappy end of the deal.

"I did find an interesting new option," Bernard said.

Caleb turned. "And you're just speaking up now?"

"I thought you wanted to vent."

"I did want to vent. But I want a solution a whole lot more."

"Why don't you sit down?" Bernard asked.

"Exactly what kind of an option is it?" Was it so shocking that Caleb couldn't be trusted to keep his feet?

"My neck's getting sore from looking up at you. Sit down."

Caleb thought better on his feet. But he was curious enough to go along. He perched on the arm of the sofa.

"You look like a coiled spring," Bernard said.

"You drawing this out won't make me less coiled."

"This isn't a five-second explanation."

"I hope not, because you've already used up two minutes in the preamble."

Bernard smiled. "You're a lot like your father."

"You're just going to pile it on, aren't you?"

"There's an easement," Bernard said.

Caleb heard the side door to his house swing open. He knew it would either be Matt or TJ.

"In here," he called out.

"Do you want me to wait until we're alone?" Bernard asked.

"Why would I want that? Is it a secret option? Is it illegal?"

"Is what illegal?" Matt asked as he strolled into the room.

"Yes," Bernard drawled. "As your lawyer, I feel it's my duty to advise you to break the law."

"That's a first," Matt said, taking another armchair. "What are we drinking?"

"I'm considering tequila," Caleb said.

Matt rose again and headed for the bar.

"Keep talking," Caleb prompted Bernard.

Bernard exhaled an exaggerated sigh of impatience, like he was the one who'd been kept waiting.

"There's an easement," he repeated, producing a map from his briefcase and unfolding it on the coffee table between them. "The access road for the Crab Shack crosses your land." He pointed. "Right here."

"You mean TJ's land."

"No. All four residential lots were originally a single parcel. TJ's, Matt's and the Parkers' lots were carved out at minimum size, and the remainder stayed with the parcel your grandfather purchased. The effect is a peninsula of land owned by you that runs in front of each of the other properties. Nobody pays attention to it, because it's mostly the sheer face of a cliff. That is, except for the access road."

Caleb leaned forward to study the map lines.

Matt returned with three glasses of tequila.

"I thought you'd know I was joking," Caleb said to Matt. He'd expected Matt to open a few beers.

"Too late now."

Caleb wasn't a big tequila fan, but he accepted the glass anyway.

If he was reading the map correctly, where the Crab Shack driveway branched off the access road, it crossed his land for about two hundred yards.

"On one side of the driveway is a cliff," Bernard said.

Matt crouched on one knee. "And the other is too close to the high water mark. It's vulnerable to tidal surges if there's a storm."

"Is it possible for her to reroute along the shore?" Caleb asked.

"I talked to an engineer," Bernard said. "In effect, she'd have to build a bridge."

"They're on a budget."

"Then, there's your answer."

Matt gave a whistle. "That's playin' hardball."

"I'm losing ten thousand a day in idle equipment rental."

"So, you'd bankrupt her?"

"I'd use it for leverage." Caleb straightened to contemplate.

He'd already tried the carrot. Maybe it was time for the stick. He'd show Jules that if they didn't work together, it would mean mutual assured annihilation. Surely she couldn't be so stubborn as to choose that option.

Caleb's front door opened again, and TJ strode in from the hall. "We ready to go?" There was an eagerness in his tone.

The three men had agreed to hit a club in Olympia tonight. It had seemed like a good idea at the time. But now Caleb was regretting the commitment. He'd rather stay home. He didn't plan to confront Jules with the threat of canceling her easement tonight, but he wasn't in the mood for dancing and inconsequential conversation with random women either.

"Is that an ambulance?" TJ asked, gazing out the window.

Caleb turned as he stood, immediately seeing the flashing lights closing in on the Crab Shack.

"That's not good," Matt said, rising to his feet.

Caleb was already heading for the door, with Matt and TJ at his heels.

The fastest way to the Crab Shack was along the footpath. Caleb broke into a run. He knew every inch of the pathway, and it took him less than five minutes to get to the peninsula, his mind going over all the possible scenarios where Jules might have been hurt. Had she fallen off the ladder? Had she burned herself with the paint stripper?

Matt stuck with him, with TJ falling a bit behind. Caleb had no idea whether or not Bernard had even bothered to come along. As he ran up the gravel driveway, he could see the paramedics moving a stretcher. He put on a burst of speed.

Then he saw Jules under the lights. She wasn't the one on the stretcher. He felt an immense surge of relief. But then his fear was back. If it wasn't Jules, it must be Melissa.

He finally got close enough to call out.

"What happened?" he asked.

Jules looked over at him in surprise. "What are you doing here?"

"We saw the ambulance lights," he said through the gasps of his breath. "What happened?"

"Nail gun," Melissa said from the stretcher, her voice sounding strained.

Caleb was relieved to hear her speak. But then her words registered.

"You were using a nail gun?" He moved his attention to Jules. "You have a *nail gun*?"

"*I* don't have a nail gun. Noah has a nail gun."

"Where's Noah?" Caleb wanted to have a word with the man. What was he thinking letting Jules and Melissa use a nail gun? Was he crazy?

"It was my fault," Melissa called from inside the ambulance.

"Are you coming with us?" the paramedic asked Jules.

"Yes." She moved for the door.

"I'll meet you there," Caleb said.

"Why?" she asked as she stepped up to climb inside.

"Just go."

"Melissa seemed pretty good," Matt said.

TJ arrived, panting.

"You need to hit the gym," Matt told him.

"No kidding," TJ said. "Who got hurt?"

"Melissa," Caleb said. "Something about a nail gun."

TJ gave him an incredulous look. "Is it bad?"

"She was talking from the stretcher. But I'm going to head down to Memorial and find out what happened."

"You are?" TJ seemed surprised.

Caleb thought it was a perfectly reasonable course of action. The women were their neighbors, and Jules might need something. At the very least, she'd need a ride back home.

"White knight syndrome," Matt said.

"Who's he rescuing?" TJ asked.

"Good question." TJ raised a brow at Caleb. "The rational one or the difficult one?"

The difficult one. "Neither."

Caleb was simply being neighborly...and practical. He was being neighborly and practical. There was nothing remotely unusual about that.

Three

Jules couldn't decide whether to sit down and wait patiently for news or to pace the hospital waiting room floor and worry. Melissa had seemed okay in the ambulance, in surprisingly good spirits considering she had a large nail protruding through the middle of her left hand. Jules had assumed her sister couldn't have been too badly hurt if she was awake and joking. But she might have been in shock. She could quite easily have been in shock.

Opting for pacing, Jules walked the hall then turned at the narrow, vinyl sofa and walked back toward the vending machines. If Melissa was in shock, then the pain might not have been registering. She could be really hurt. The hospital staff had certainly taken the injury seriously, whisking her off to a trauma room. Jules had tried to follow, but the nurse had urged her to stay out of the way and let the medical staff do their work.

When Jules turned again, she saw Caleb at the end of the hallway walking swiftly toward her. He looked tall, broad-shouldered and capable, and she felt an inexplicable sense of relief at the sight of him. As soon as the feeling registered, she banished it. It was embarrassing to react that way. He wasn't a medical professional. He wasn't a friend. He wasn't a significant person in either her or Melissa's life. There was no reason his presence should be comforting, none at all.

"Is Melissa all right?" he asked as he approached, concern clear in his tone.

She felt an inexcusable urge to walk straight into his arms. She wouldn't do it, of course, but a little part of her couldn't help wondering how he'd react if she did.

"They've taken her into surgery."

He frowned as he came to a halt. "That sounds concerning."

"They told me it was a precaution."

His intense look of interest prompted her to continue.

"There's a hand specialist in the hospital tonight, and he wants to be sure they don't damage any nerves or tendons taking out the nail. At least that's what they said." She had to fight the urge to lean on him again. "You don't think they'd downplay it, do you?"

"Are you worried?" he asked, moving slightly closer.

She wished he'd keep his distance. It was easier to resist him that way.

"No. I can't decide. Should I be worried? The truth is I'm worried that I'm not worried. Does that make sense?"

"Yes."

"She was still talking when we arrived. I thought that was a good sign. But now I'm thinking she might have been in shock."

"I suppose that's possible." He looked thoughtful.

"You could have just said it was a good sign."

He gave a slight smile. "I think it was a good sign."

"Too late."

"I suppose." He paused. "But it was probably a good sign."

"Noble effort."

"I don't see why they'd downplay it for you. They'd want you to be prepared for any bad news."

"Okay. I'll give you that one." Jules relaxed a little. She moved and sat down on a padded chair.

Caleb followed, taking a chair across from her. They were both silent for a few moments.

It was Caleb who broke it. "Do you know what was she doing with the nail gun?"

"She was showing me how it worked. Noah had shown her earlier. And, well, it went off. We didn't expect that."

An expression of annoyance crossed Caleb's face. "Noah showed her how to use a nail gun?"

"It's not Noah's fault."

"What was he thinking?"

"That she asked a question and he answered it."

"I don't mean to sound sexist—"

Jules felt her spine stiffen. "But you're about to."

"I guess I am. Are you sure that the two of you should be undertaking a construction project?"

"We're not undertaking a construction project. We're helping with a construction project. Noah has been great about showing us what to do and how to do it."

Caleb frowned again. "He didn't do so well with the nail gun."

"Ms. Parker?" A nurse interrupted.

Jules immediately switched her attention. "You have news?" She came to her feet.

Caleb rose with her.

The smile on the nurse's face was encouraging, but it seemed to take forever for her to speak. "Your sister is out of surgery. It went very well."

"Thank you," Jules whispered, relief rushing through her. She realized then just how frightened she'd been.

"She's in recovery for the next hour or so, and then she'll likely sleep through the night. There's no need for you to stay."

"So her hand will be fine?"

"The surgeon is anticipating a complete recovery. She'll need to rest it for a couple of weeks. She can follow up with her family doctor."

"We're new in town. We don't have—"

"She can see my doctor," Caleb put in. His hand went to the small of Jules's back and rested lightly there.

She looked skeptically up at him. Good doctors had been difficult to find in Portland. Most had closed practices and weren't taking new patients.

"He'll see her." Caleb spoke with authority, seeming to guess Jules's hesitation.

She was reminded of his wealth, and the power it likely brought him. She realized his doctor would probably grant any favor Caleb asked. Her first reaction was to refuse on principle. But Melissa's health was at stake, and Jules knew she couldn't let pride stand in the way of the best care for her.

"Thank you," she said instead.

Caleb smiled, and his hand firmed against her back. Warmth and pleasure flowed through her before she remembered to shut it down.

"Can I see Melissa?" Jules asked the nurse.

"Not for at least an hour. She's in recovery." The nurse's gaze went to the clock on the wall, which showed that it was well past midnight.

"You might as well come back in the morning," Caleb said. "You need some sleep, too."

Again, Jules wanted to argue with him on principle. But she was tired, and he wasn't wrong, especially if Melissa was only going to sleep anyway.

"I'll drive you home," he said, seeming to take her silence for agreement.

It was, but that didn't mean she wanted him to make the assumption. But now wasn't the time to make an issue of it.

She directed her attention to the nurse instead, reaching out to squeeze the woman's hands in gratitude. "Thank you so much. Will you thank the surgeon for me?"

"I will."

The nurse departed, and Jules stepped away from Caleb's touch as they walked down the corridor.

"I can get a cab," she said as they approached the double doors of the foyer.

"Sure you could," he said. "And that makes perfect sense. Especially since I'm driving past your house on my way home."

"We're not your responsibility," she felt compelled to point out.

He pushed open the door. "Nobody said you were."

"What are you doing here anyway?" The night wind was brisk against her thin T-shirt, and she wrapped her arms around herself.

"I wanted to make sure Melissa was okay. And I knew you'd need a ride home."

"You barely know us."

He indicated a black Lexus parked near the door. "I've known you for twenty-four years."

"You've disliked me for twenty-four years. It's not the same thing."

"I never disliked you." Something softened in his tone. "I barely knew you."

"You dislike me now."

"I'm annoyed with you right now. That's not the same thing either."

"Close enough."

He cracked a smile as he opened the passenger door. "You do make it difficult to like you, Jules."

"Because I won't give in and give you what you want."

"That's part of it." He closed the door and crossed to the driver's side.

"What's the other part?" she asked as he took his seat and pressed the starter button.

To her relief, warm air immediately blew through the dashboard vents.

"You disagree with virtually everything I say."

She thought about that. "Not with everything you say."

He gave an ironic shake of his head, but he smiled again, too.

She liked his smile. She had to stop liking his smile. And his touch, she really had to stop liking his touch.

He pulled out of the parking spot and headed for the

winding coastal road back to their houses. "Name one thing where you've agreed with me."

"I'm letting you drive me home."

"I had to talk you into that."

"Proving I can change my mind," she said with triumph. "I'm a reasonable person who can change her mind when presented with evidence."

"In that case, let me explain about how…"

Her heart sank a bit. "Not tonight, Caleb."

"I was joking."

She suddenly felt drained of energy and realized she'd been running on adrenaline since the accident, and the relief that had buoyed her at learning Melissa would recover had already worn off. Now she was just exhausted.

"Are you hungry?" he surprised her by asking.

She was, but she didn't want to admit it. It felt like she'd be showing him another weakness.

"I'm starving," he said. "Do you mind if we stop?"

"You're driving. It's your car. You can do whatever you like."

He glanced her way. "Have I done something to annoy you just now?"

She instantly felt guilty. "No." That was a lie. "Yes." That wasn't quite right either. "I wish you'd quit being nice. It makes me nervous."

He laughed, and the rich sound was somehow soothing to her nerves.

He took an abrupt left, entering the parking lot of a fast-food place. "Burger okay with you?"

"Whatever you're having," she said. She was hungry, not fussy.

He pulled up to the drive-through window, and a young woman slid back the glass.

Considering the late hour, the girl's smile was positively perky. "What can I get for you?"

"Two cheeseburgers, two fries and two chocolate shakes," Caleb said.

She rang up the order, and Caleb handed her some bills.

"Coming right up." She pulled back, the smile still in place.

"Comfort food," Jules said, thinking it fit the circumstances.

"I forgot you were a chef."

"I wasn't being critical."

"You weren't?"

She gave him an eye roll. "If you're going to jump to conclusions, you should learn to interpret my intonation."

"I thought that was sarcasm."

"It wasn't. I've got nothing against burgers and fries. They get a bad rap. They're tasty. Okay, maybe not so nutritious as to be a daily recommendation. But I'm not really in the mood for nutrition right now."

He smiled and seemed to relax. They both fell silent.

"Thanks for this," she said a few minutes later.

"Not a problem."

The window opened and the girl handed Caleb his change and the food.

He set the milk shakes in the console between them and passed the warm, fragrant paper bag to Jules. Then he pulled across the shoreline road into a parking lot overlooking the ocean. He shut off the engine and released his seat belt.

"This okay?" he asked her.

"Perfect." She released her own seat belt and sat back in the comfy leather seat, letting the tension of the past few hours drain from her.

Melissa was going to be okay. Everything else would work itself out around that.

Caleb relieved her of the bag and handed back a burger wrapped in waxed paper, and then a small carton of fries. She popped one of the fries in her mouth. It was crisp and flavorful, salty and satisfying.

"Mmm," she said.

He smiled and gave a small shake of his head. "You're awfully easy to please."

"My needs are simple." She took the closest milk shake and drew the cold, creamy liquid through the straw.

"You surprise me, Juliet Parker."

"You should be the one surprising me by appreciating burgers."

"Why is that?"

"I'm an ordinary Portland girl. You're a successful millionaire who lives in a mansion on the hill."

"I suppose that's true," he agreed, a trace of laughter in his voice.

She unfolded the wrapper, pulling it away from the sticky cheese. "If anyone should be snobby about fast food, it's you."

"I normally add a garnish of caviar."

"Now, *that's* more what I expected."

"Then I'm likely to keep surprising you."

"Is this your pitch for being an ordinary guy?"

"I am an ordinary guy."

"You own seventeen restaurants."

"You did some research."

"I did," she admitted. "I've concluded you don't need an eighteenth."

He paused. "You really want to have that argument now?"

She didn't. She wasn't sure why she'd brought it up. Or maybe she was. They were getting along, and that made her nervous. She'd wanted to remind herself of what stood between them. She didn't want to like Caleb. She didn't dare.

The burgers finished and the drive complete, Caleb stepped out of his car at the top of the stairs that led down to the Parker house.

"What are you doing?" Suspicion was clear in Jules's tone as she closed the passenger door behind her.

"I'm walking you to your door." He came around to meet up with her at the edge of the gravel driveway where the long staircase took off for the house below.

"Don't be silly."

"I'm never silly."

"I'm perfectly capable of walking down my own front steps. I've done it a thousand times."

"Maybe so." He gestured for her to go first. "But I'm incapable of leaving a woman on her dark doorstep and hoping for the best."

"Caleb." Her exasperation was clear.

"Give it up, Jules. I'm walking you to your door. My old man might not have done much right, but he did raise me to be a gentleman."

"This is senseless." But she started to move.

"Maybe. But it's not going to hurt anything either. You really do need to learn to pick your battles."

"And you need to learn how to deploy your energy."

He smiled to himself as he followed her down. He was perfectly happy with his deployment of energy. He had a feeling he'd walk miles just to keep arguing with her.

The wooden steps felt punky beneath his feet, springing slightly with his weight. Squinting, he could make out what looked like moss growing at the edges.

"How old is this staircase?" he asked.

"I have no idea."

He gave the rail a pointed wiggle. "It needs to be replaced."

"I'll get right on it."

"I'm serious, Jules. This could be dangerous."

Forget the possibility of it giving way, the aging wood was slimy and slippery. Somebody was going to fall, and it was a long, long way down. He peered at the dim, distant porchlight.

"It's none of your concern, Caleb. And there are a lot of pressing issues in my life right now, including an injured sister."

He immediately felt like a heel. "I'm sorry."

He wished he'd gone first. That way, if she slipped in the dark, she'd have him to break her fall. He should have thought of that. Why hadn't he thought of that?

As a stopgap measure, he reached for her hand, enveloping it in his, thinking he could at least brace her if she slipped.

She tried to tug her hand away.

He was having none of it. "Pick your battles," he reminded her.

"This isn't a date," she tossed over her shoulder.

"I sure hope not." The idea was downright alarming. "Fast food and a trip to the emergency room? That would be the worst date in the world."

"To be clear, this little walk to the door, holding my hand, cozying up. You're not getting a kiss good-night."

"I'm holding your hand to keep you from falling."

"Of course you are." The sarcasm was back.

"You're a very suspicious woman."

"You're a very calculating man."

"I'm not angling for a kiss." Though he'd be lying if he pretended he didn't want one. "But, just for the sake of argument, what would it take? Exactly how good would the date have to be for a guy to get a kiss from you?"

"It has nothing to do with the quality of the date. I mean, of course, it would have to be a good date. By that I mean an enjoyable date. But it wouldn't have to be an expensive date. I'm not about to be bowled over by opulent surroundings and fine wine."

"Cheap wine it is."

They'd reached her porch, and she turned. "It's the caliber of the company that counts."

She was beautiful in the starlight.

"I've been told I'm a good conversationalist," he noted.

"I bet you have. And I bet it was by women who were enjoying fine wine and opulent surroundings?"

"You have a low opinion of your own gender, Juliet."

His response seemed to throw her, and her brow furrowed.

"I didn't mean it that way," she said.

"I know how you meant it. You think I date women who like me for my money."

"Not exactly…"

He had her off balance, and he took advantage of it, easing forward. "I don't believe this. You've actually talked yourself into a corner."

"No, I haven't. Just give me a second."

"Sure." He waited, enjoying the view of her blue eyes, pupils overlarge in the dim light, shining like windows to her soul.

"This isn't fair," she finally said in a husky voice.

"Why not?"

"I'm tired. I'm not at my best."

"You need me to give you a head start?"

It was clear she had to fight a grin.

"You know what your problem is?" he asked, brushing the back of his hand softly against her cheek.

He expected her to pull back, but she didn't.

"What is my problem?" Her voice was suddenly breathy.

"You don't know what to do about me."

She paused, and her white teeth scraped across her bottom lip. "I wish I could argue with that—"

"But you're tired," he finished the sentence for her. "And you're not at your best."

His gaze and his mind fixated on her lips. He wanted very badly to kiss them.

"I'm tired," she agreed and seemed to sway toward him. "And I'm not at my best."

He cupped his other palm over her shoulder. "Jules."

Her blue eyes clouded, and her lips parted. She seemed unfocused as she gazed up at him. "Yes."

His voice was husky to his own ears. "Do you want me to kiss you?"

"Yes." Then she seemed to realize what she'd revealed. "I mean—"

If she was about to change her answer, she was too late. She'd said yes. He'd heard it loud and clear.

Their kiss was better than he remembered, even better than his imagination. Her lips were tender and hot. She tasted sweet. And when he probed with his tongue, she answered in kind, tipping her head and leaning against him.

Her body was soft and warm, her curves smooth against his angles. He wrapped his arms around her, enveloping her while the kiss went on. Arousal throbbed deep and hard within him, and his mind galloped ahead to an image of a soft bed, with her naked body entwined around his.

Why couldn't it always be like this? Why did they have to fight? She was smart and sassy, and probably the most interesting woman he'd ever met. She was certainly the most exciting.

And then reality slammed into him.

They did have to fight. And no amount of wishing would change that.

His interests were diametrically opposed to hers. He probably had to hurt her. He had no choice. And if he was going to hurt her, he shouldn't be kissing her. He absolutely couldn't sleep with her—not with the secret he was keeping right now.

He pulled back, breaking the kiss.

She all but staggered in shock. "What—"

"I'm sorry," he said, reluctantly letting his arms drop away from her. "That was out of line."

She still seemed to be getting her bearings. "Uh, okay."

"It's late. You're tired," he repeated the words, forcing

himself to keep talking. "This wasn't a date, and I shouldn't be so presumptuous."

"You did ask permission," she pointed out.

He couldn't believe she was arguing his side. "And you were about to change your answer. I knew that. I could tell."

"I was weighing the pros and cons."

"There are a lot of cons." That at least was the truth.

Her gaze was opaque and welcoming. "There are a lot of pros."

"Don't do that, Jules."

"Don't do what?"

"Don't give me permission."

"But—"

"Tomorrow we'll be fighting again. I can guarantee it."

She offered a small smile. "We're not fighting now."

Caleb gritted his teeth. If he didn't walk away right now, he wouldn't walk away at all.

"Good night, Jules." He told his feet to move.

She took a staggering step back. "Wow. Talk about hot and cold."

His brain echoed her tone of incredulity. He couldn't explain it to her, but he felt like he'd been doused with ice water. "I'll set it up with the doctor. Let me know if there's anything else Melissa needs."

Jules didn't respond. She just blinked in obvious confusion.

He finally forced his feet to move, turning away from temptation before he did something they'd both massively regret.

The next day, Jules struggled to keep Caleb's kiss from her mind. She'd picked Melissa up from the hospital and tried to convince her to rest at home. But Melissa insisted on coming with Jules to the Crab Shack.

As they walked in the door, Noah took in her bandaged hand. His gaze went immediately to where they had discarded the nail gun before swinging back to zero in on Melissa's face.

"*What* did I tell you?" he asked her pointedly.

"Not to touch—"

"*What* did you do?" He advanced on her.

"I was only—"

"Only what? Only *what*?" Noah's shoulders were squared, his voice harsher than normal.

"She was showing me how it worked," Jules put in, surprised by Noah's strong reaction. He was normally easygoing and totally restrained.

Noah turned his head to give Jules a look of disbelief. "Can I speak with your sister alone?"

"Not if you're going to yell at her."

"I'm not yelling."

"He's not yelling," Melissa said, resignation in her tone.

"She was at the hospital last night," Jules told Noah. "They had to do surgery."

Noah's expression immediately turned to concern. He flipped his attention back to Melissa. "Are you all right? No permanent damage, right?"

"I'm fine," Melissa said. "They only kept me overnight—"

"They kept you *overnight*?"

"Just because of the anesthetic. I was sleeping."

He gently took hold of her forearm and lifted her injured hand to look at it from a few angles. "You're not allowed to touch anything."

"I get it. I won't."

"Ever again," he added. "None of my tools. None of any tools. I don't want you hammering or sawing."

"Noah," Jules interrupted, realizing he was going overboard.

"Painting?" Melissa asked with a little tease in her tone.

"Fumes," Noah said.

"I'll wear a mask."

"You need a helmet and body armor."

"Oh, come on. I'm not that bad."

He gazed pointedly at her bandaged hand. "Yes, you are."

Jules realized the tone of the argument had changed. He wasn't angry. They seemed to be having fun.

"Well, I'm not doing all the work myself," she put in lightly. "I don't mind keeping Melissa away from sharp objects."

"And heavy and hard objects, too," Noah said with a glance Jules's way.

"But she has to be able to help. We need her contribution."

He returned his attention to Melissa. "Painting is okay."

"I'm not sure who put you in charge of the project."

"I'm a skilled professional with industrial safety training. Have you had industrial safety training? When you can produce a certificate that says you have, you can be in charge of the jobsite."

Caleb's voice interrupted from the doorway, tight and demanding. "You let her use your nail gun?"

The memories of last night flooded back to Jules. Her skin heated up, and she swore she could smell Caleb's woodsy scent.

Noah clamped his jaw shut, and his gaze darkened on Caleb. "She wanted to see how it worked."

"And you showed her?" Caleb asked Noah.

"I told her not to touch it without me."

"That didn't work out so well, did it?"

Melissa spoke up, "It was my fault, Caleb, not Noah's."

"But you're the one who got hurt," Caleb said to her. "How are you? Should you even be here today?"

"She insisted," Jules said, finally finding her voice.

Whatever had happened, or not happened, between her and Caleb last night, it was over. She needed to forget about it and move on. Though she'd spent most of the night restless and disappointed, he'd been right. They were on opposite sides of a fight, and that fact wasn't about to change.

"Melissa is going to sit down," Noah said.

He still had hold of her forearm, and he led her across the restaurant.

Caleb moved closer to Jules, and her reaction to him intensified. She didn't want to be attracted to him, but she couldn't seem to turn it off. *Logic*, she told herself. If she used logic and reason, and remembered who he was and what he wanted from her, she'd be fine.

She braced herself.

"Can we talk?" he asked.

"About what?"

The last thing she needed was an intimate little rehash of last night. He'd had his chance. He didn't take it. And she was glad of that. At least she would be glad of that, once her logic and reason kicked in.

"Business," he said, surprising her.

"Oh."

His expression tightened, and his nostrils flared ever so slightly.

"Sure," she said, making to follow Melissa across the room.

"Just you," Caleb said, keeping his voice low.

"What's going on, Caleb?"

"I don't want to upset her."

"But you're willing to upset me?"

A beat went by before he answered. "There's something you need to know."

She gave up trying to guess what he was getting at. "Sure. Fine. Out on the deck?"

"That'll work." He turned for the door.

She followed, out into the sunny June afternoon. Seagulls swooped through the salt-tang that hung in the air. The tide was high, waves battering the rocky shore, sending spray into the air and roaring softly in rhythm.

"Talk," Jules said, widening her stance and tipping up her chin.

Caleb halted at the rail and turned. "I've been talking to my lawyer."

"You can't sue us."

"I'm not going to sue you. Sue you for what? Why would I sue you?"

"I don't know. What else do lawyers do?"

Her comeback seemed to stump him for a moment.

"Defend criminals," he suggested.

"Have you committed a crime?"

"Of *course* not."

"Then why do you need a lawyer?"

He reached behind himself and braced a hand on the wooden rail. "He's a corporate lawyer."

"So you're dissolving the Whiskey Bay Neo location." She knew it was a long shot, but she figured she might as well go for the brass ring.

Caleb gave her a crooked frown. It was kind of endearing. No, no, no. She didn't want him to be endearing.

"My lawyer was looking at the land survey of your property."

"You can't have my land, Caleb."

"I don't want your land. Okay, I'd take your land if you didn't want it. Would you sell it to me?"

"And then I couldn't build the Crab Shack."

"Brilliant deduction."

"Don't get all superior on me."

"I'm not superior. I'm trying to tell you something."

"Then spit it out. Put some nouns and verbs together that make sense."

"I would if you'd be quiet for a minute."

Jules might not like his hostility. But her keeping quiet was the only way he could tell her what was on his mind. She made a show of zipping her lips shut. Then she folded her arms across her chest and waited.

Caleb's chest rose and fell with a deep breath. "There's no easy way to say this."

"I'm getting that impression," she muttered.

"I thought your lips were zipped."

She rezipped them.

"You have an easement. It's for your access road, and it goes across my land." He looked toward the shore, and she followed the direction of his gaze. "If I revoke the easement, nobody can get to the Crab Shack."

It took a minute for his words to penetrate.

When they did, she couldn't accept them. What he was saying didn't make sense.

"No," she said simply.

He had to be lying.

"It would take me a while to give you all the details," he said. "But it is the truth."

"I want the details."

He reached for his inside pocket and handed her an envelope. "This isn't a bluff."

"It can't possibly be true."

"Stroke of a pen, Jules. It's my land, and I can revoke your rights. Even if you build the Crab Shack, nobody will be able to come."

She felt the world shift beneath her. "You wouldn't."

"I don't want to."

"It can't be legal. I'm getting my own lawyer."

"That's your choice."

"You bet it's my choice." Like he could stop her.

"But I'd rather we worked together and made both places a success." He looked completely unfazed by her threat.

"You think you can scare me into removing the non-compete clause." She tilted forward, trying to look tough.

"I'm not trying to scare you. I'm attempting to appeal to your sense of reason and logic."

"By threatening me?"

"It's not a threat." But then he paused, obviously framing his answer, obviously knowing, as she did, that it *was* a threat. "Remove the noncompete, and I'll give you the easement. It's a mutual win."

"You call that mutual?"

He might win, but she sure wouldn't.

"I want to help you," he finally said.

"No, you don't." Of that she was certain.

"I like you, Jules."

She scoffed in disbelief.

"Last night—" he began.

"We are *not* talking about last night." She sure wasn't going to let him use her colossal lack of judgment against her.

"I knew last night. I knew about the easement last night. I couldn't..." He raked a hand through his short hair. "I couldn't let things go any further between us before I was honest."

"You want points for that?"

"I want you to know why I stopped."

Even through her anger, she had to admit it was the honorable thing to do.

But she couldn't give him credit for a single honorable thing. She wouldn't give him credit for that. He was still trying to destroy her dream by any means possible. And that was far, far below the bar anyone would set for honorable.

Four

Caleb forced himself to keep his distance for a few days in order to let Jules think things through. Though he was anxious to hear her answer—which he had to believe would be an agreement to work together—he didn't want to press too hard. She might be stubborn, but she was smart enough to know that any other approach would be just plain foolish.

He made it to Thursday evening before he cracked. Then he sought her out, knocking unannounced on the door of her house. The lights were blazing, and he could hear a Blake Shelton tune through the open windows.

He knocked again and waited, half bracing himself, half humming with the anticipation. Despite their animosity, he'd missed her. He'd missed her a lot, and he couldn't wait to see her.

But it was Melissa who opened the door. She seemed startled to see him standing there. Her hair was in a high ponytail. She was dressed in a gauzy purple blouse and tight blue jeans. Her makeup looked fresh, and she was wearing a pair of jazzy copper earrings.

"Am I interrupting?" he asked. "Did you have a date?"

"No." She gave a quick shake of her head. "No date." But her gaze strayed to the staircase behind him.

"How's the hand?" he asked, attempting to gauge her mood.

If Jules had told her about the easement, he'd expect her to be angry. She didn't seem angry, exactly. But she did seem unsettled.

She raised her hand to show him. "Getting better fast. It really doesn't bother me much." She gave a little laugh.

"The doctor said I have good aim. A quarter inch in either direction and I'd have done some real damage."

"I'm glad to hear that." Caleb realized how it sounded. "I mean, I'm glad it wasn't worse."

"Me, too." She let her hand fall to her side again.

He glanced past her into the house. "Can I speak to Jules?"

"She's not here."

The answer took him by surprise, putting the brakes on his plans.

But then he wondered if Jules was dressed up, too. Did she have a date? He hated the idea that she might.

"Can I help you with something?" Melissa asked.

The question gave him an idea.

He hadn't considered the merits of explaining the situation directly to Melissa, bypassing Jules. It was obvious to him she was the more reasonable of the two. There were even a couple of moments when he thought she would have supported some of his ideas, had it not been for Jules's staunch refusals.

Maybe he'd been talking to the wrong sister.

"You might be able to help me," he answered. "Do you have a few minutes to talk?"

She hesitated for just a second, glancing behind him again. "Sure."

He knew he should ask if it was a bad time, offer her an out if she hadn't been sincere. But it wasn't often he saw her alone. And co-opting her could turn out to be a good idea. He didn't know why he hadn't thought of it before.

She opened the door wider and moved out of his way.

Although the Parkers had been neighbors his entire life, due to the family feud he'd never been inside their house. As he moved from the small foyer, he saw that it was compact. It was mostly kitchen with aging fir cupboards and light green walls. The ceiling was off-white, and a row of three windows looked over the bay. It was a clear night, and the moon reflected off the black water.

A faded sofa and armchair took up the corner beside a stone fireplace. Nothing was new, not the brocade furniture, nor faded linoleum nor powder blue countertops. But nothing was shoddy either, and everything was clean.

"Can I offer you some iced tea?" Melissa asked, walking farther around the corner, turning down the music and moving into the kitchen.

"Thank you," Caleb answered following her.

He stopped partway, bracing his hands against one of six kitchen chairs. They were painted white, made of wood, with curved backs with dowels spaced at four-inch intervals and cotton-print cushions tied onto the seats.

She filled two glasses with ice and retrieved a pitcher of tea from the refrigerator.

He tried to guess at the refrigerator's age. It had to have been around for several decades. All he could think was that they didn't make them that sturdy anymore.

"I guess Jules didn't mention the easement," he opened.

Standing silent while she poured drinks and letting her wonder about his purpose didn't seem productive.

"She told me about it," Melissa said.

It wasn't the answer he was expecting. "She did?"

"You expect me to be hostile."

"Yes. No. On the surface, it's a setback for you."

"On the surface?" Melissa crossed to the table and handed him a glass.

She pulled out a chair, and he followed suit, sitting down cornerwise. "I would say all the way through."

She still didn't seem angry, and he had to wonder if they had a counter-strategy.

Rather than argue, he came to his point. "She didn't get back to me on it."

"She said she gave you an answer."

"In the heat of the moment, maybe. I didn't assume it was final."

"You expected her to change her mind?" Melissa's tone wasn't accusatory, more curious, and perfectly pleasant.

Again, he had to wonder if they were up to something. "I thought she'd think about it, at least consider the implications."

Melissa gave a light laugh. "I can assure you, she's fully considered the implications."

"And?" He was growing more curious by the minute.

"And she called our father. And then she called a lawyer."

"What did they say?" Caleb asked, braced and ready.

She gave a smirk. "I don't think I'll repeat what my father said."

Caleb could only imagine. "He never did like me." Caleb took a sip of the iced tea while he digested the information.

"You have a particular gift for understatement."

"Can you tell me what the lawyer said?"

"In a nutshell. That you have a case. That we also have a case. And that it'll take a long time and a lot of money to resolve it."

He rotated his glass, the ice cubes clinking against the sides. "There's no benefit in that."

"Not for you," Melissa said.

"Or for you."

She took a drink and set her glass carefully back on the wooden tabletop. "That's where you're wrong. There's a benefit to us if we win."

"You won't win."

She looked him square in the eyes. "What do you want, Caleb?"

"To be friends." He realized he meant that. "I truly don't want to annihilate the Crab Shack."

She smiled indulgently but gave an eye roll at the same time. "Forgive me if I have a hard time believing either of those things."

"I want us to work together. I meant what I said about cross-promotion."

"My father warned us about you."

Caleb had no good comeback for that, since Roland Parker had every reason to distrust the Watfords. He bought himself some time by taking another drink.

He set down his glass. "All I can say is that I'm not my father. And I get the feeling you're not your sister."

Her gaze narrowed in obvious suspicion.

He kept on talking. "I think you can see the benefits of working together. My guess is that you're very rational, and you can clearly see the downsides of a fight. It hurts us both. It'll cost a whole lot of money. And no matter who wins, we'll both be weaker and poorer for the effort."

Melissa didn't answer. She traced her fingertip down the condensation on her glass.

Caleb sat still while Blake Shelton crooned. He didn't want to make a wrong move.

She finally looked up. "You can't divide and conquer. It won't work."

He wasn't about to admit that was his strategy. "I don't want to conquer anyone. But I'm a million dollars into this project."

She seemed to think about that. "So you have a lot to lose."

"I have a lot to lose."

"Yet another reason why we shouldn't trust you."

"I understand." He did. "Tell me what I can do to—"

There was a sharp rap on the door.

Melissa jumped in her chair and her head turned sharply toward the sound.

"Expecting someone?" Caleb asked.

"No." A flush had come up on her cheeks, and her hand went to her hair. "Maybe."

The knock came again.

"You want me to get it?" he asked, seeing she was anxious.

"Melissa?" called a voice that Caleb recognized. It was Noah.

"What's *he* doing here?" Caleb had learned some worrying things about Noah today. Things he'd planned to share with Jules and Melissa.

Melissa started to rise, but Caleb jumped up.

"There's something I need to say to him."

Before she could respond, he rounded the corner to the foyer and opened the door.

Noah was clearly taken aback by the sight of him.

"Yeah," Caleb responded to the man's unspoken question. "I'm here. What are you doing here?"

"Business," Noah said, his tone even.

"I mean what are you doing in Whiskey Bay?"

Noah's eyes became guarded.

"Been in town long?" Caleb pressed.

"It's obvious you know I haven't."

"It wasn't hard to find out."

"I wasn't hiding it."

"Caleb?" Melissa called out.

"Give me a second." Caleb had learned today that Noah was recently released from jail. "What did you do?" he asked Noah.

"About what?" Noah came back without flinching, clearly ignoring the unspoken implication.

"To get thrown in jail."

Noah paused for less than a heartbeat. "I killed a guy."

Caleb's jaw went lax.

Noah didn't elaborate.

"On purpose?" It was the first question that popped into Caleb's mind.

"Not really."

"And you expect me to let you anywhere near Jules and Melissa?"

"I don't think it has anything to do with you." Noah's gaze was level, his manner straightforward. He didn't seem to have the slightest inclination to cover up or apologize.

The attitude gave Caleb pause. He supposed there were a lot of ways to accidentally kill someone—from a car accident to a hunting accident to a fistfight gone bad.

Noah had gotten off with two years less a day in the county jail. And he'd been paroled for good behavior after only nine months. Upon reflection, the sentence strongly suggested mitigating circumstances.

"Are we going to have a problem?" Noah asked Caleb in an undertone.

"Was it a car accident?"

"No."

"Was there a weapon involved?"

Noah curled his fists. "No."

Seeing the unconscious gesture, Caleb was going with a fistfight gone bad.

"What did he do?" Caleb asked Noah.

A muscle twitched next to Noah's left eye. "Something unforgivable."

Caleb found he was inclined to accept the vague explanation. He had no cause to throw Noah out of the house. And that meant his time alone with Melissa was up, and he hadn't made any meaningful progress.

It was late. But Jules wasn't letting this one slide.

She pressed hard on the doorbell next to Caleb's tall cedar door. The Watford mansion was made of stone and reclaimed wood, with huge panes of glass soaring two stories high. The roof was a peak on the ocean side, and a four-car garage stretched out the back. Soft orange light shone through the windows.

Caleb opened the door.

"I can't believe you would sink that low." She didn't wait for an invitation, but marched passed him into the interior.

"How low did I sink?"

"Melissa is barely out of surgery."

"That was five days ago." He closed the door behind him.

"*That's* your excuse?"

"My excuse for *what*?"

"To badger her." Jules struggled to ignore the magnificence around her.

Caleb's house was something out of a magazine. The entry room was open and soaring. The finishing was finely polished redwood. The sconce lights gleamed as if they were plated in real gold. And she didn't dare speculate on the price of the abstract oil paintings along the stairway or the jade sculptures on the console table.

Caleb folded his arms over his chest, looking completely at home in the opulence. "That wasn't badgering. There was no badgering."

"You tried to get her to change her mind."

"No."

She couldn't believe he'd said it. "You're going to lie to me?"

"I tried to get her to change *your* mind."

His answer momentarily threw her.

He moved closer to her. "I haven't made any secret of intending to convince you we should work together."

"She's in pain." Her initial anger wearing off, Jules noticed the inlaid maple floor.

Crown molding accented a swooping ceiling, and the hallway led to a great room furnished with smooth leather and more fine wood. She didn't know what she'd expected, but it wasn't this.

"She told me she was fine," he said.

"She's not fine." Jules returned her attention to Caleb. "You took advantage of an injured woman for your own selfish desires."

"When you say it like that, it sounds creepy."

"It was creepy. Don't go to her. You want a fight? Pick me."

"I tried. You weren't home. She was. Did she talk to you about Noah?"

"Don't change the subject."

"I'm serious. Did she tell you he stopped by earlier?"

"Yes," Jules lied. This was the first she was hearing about Noah. But she didn't want Caleb to get the impression she and Melissa kept things from each other.

"You want a drink?"

"No, I don't want a drink. This is not a social call."

"Well, do you want to come in?" He gestured down the hallway to the living room. "Or would you rather stand here and fight in the foyer?"

Jules hated it, but her curiosity was piqued. She was curious about the rest of the house. She was curious about the view, and about the kitchen. His kitchen had to be so much better than hers.

She was also inappropriately curious about the rooms upstairs and, for a split second, she glanced that way.

"I can give you a tour of the house," he said.

"Not necessary."

His gestured down the hall again. "I'm guessing you have more to say?"

"I always have more to say."

He cracked a smile. "I've definitely noticed that."

"This isn't funny."

"You don't get to dictate my emotions. Shall we at least sit down?"

She agreed and started down the hall, trying hard not to be bowled over by the surroundings. It got better and better. The furnishings were gorgeous, but looked comfortable. The artistic touches were understated and classy, while the great room's high-peaked ceiling was breathtaking.

"Hi, Jules," came a man's voice.

She nearly stumbled into the sofa.

"I'm Matt," he said, rolling to his feet from an armchair. "I was with Caleb when your sister got hurt."

Jules was momentarily speechless. This man had overheard her tirade? What had she said? She scrambled to remember.

Caleb entered the room behind her. "You sure you don't want a drink? We're having beer, but I can open a bottle of wine."

She turned to glare at him, transmitting her irritation. "You have *company*?"

"Matt's a neighbor. He owns the house above the marina."

"You could have *said* something."

"It was hard to get a word in."

"Don't mind me," Matt said, a trace of laughter in his tone.

Jules turned back, embarrassed and annoyed. She wasn't here for their entertainment. "I obviously didn't know you were here."

"You didn't say anything embarrassing," Matt said. "In fact, I'm on your side. Caleb shouldn't have taken advantage of your sister in her moment of weakness."

"I didn't," Caleb protested. "And she's not in a moment of weakness. She said it herself that she was feeling fine."

"She's probably high on painkillers," Matt said. "She only thinks she feels fine."

"Shut up," Caleb said.

Jules couldn't help but appreciate Matt's support. "See? Even Matt agrees with me. It's very nice to meet you, Matt."

"Care for a beer?" Matt asked her.

"Sounds good," she said.

"Seriously?" Caleb grumbled. "To him you say yes?"

"I'm a lot more appealing than you." Matt started across the room. "Women like me."

"You've been divorced a single month, and you're already a gift to women?"

Matt held his arms wide. "What can I say?"

"He does seem very nice," Jules said in a clear tone.

"Not to mention handsome." Matt had reached a wet bar tucked in the corner of the room and bent over to open a hidden fridge.

"He is rather handsome," Jules said, content to keep the conversation two against one. "And, I bet he's not trying to undermine or destroy any of the women in his life."

Caleb's expression tightened for a second.

"She's got you there," Matt said.

"I'm not trying to destroy anyone," Caleb said.

"Glad to hear it." Jules made a show of reaching into her handbag. "If you could just sign these papers to guarantee my easement."

"Melissa said you saw a lawyer."

"I did see a lawyer."

Caleb took a couple of steps and lifted a manila envelope from a side table. "So did I. If you could just sign these papers removing the noncompete clause."

Jules paused. "Do you actually have those papers at the ready?"

He didn't respond, and she couldn't tell anything from his expression.

"Because I was bluffing," she said. She didn't have papers of any kind in her handbag.

He held up the envelope. "This is a charitable donation to the new health clinic."

She opened her bag and made a show of peering inside. "I can't even come that close. All I have are text messages on my phone."

Matt chuckled as he twisted open a bottle of beer and pushed the fridge shut with his thigh.

"You can't win," Caleb said to her.

"Neither can you."

"So, we should compromise."

"You don't want to compromise. You want me gone."

"I don't want you gone." He tossed down the envelope and moved to stand next to an armchair. "Why don't you sit down?"

Matt arrived and handed her the beer.

She glanced from one man to the other and decided she might as well sit down. If she hoped to reason with Caleb, they'd have to have a conversation. She lowered herself onto the sofa.

Caleb sat, as well.

"He's not a bad guy," Matt said.

"Sure he is. He comes from a long line of bad guys who can't stand the Parker family."

"I've got nothing against the Parker family," Caleb said.

"Then give me my easement."

"You're like a broken record."

"I only want one thing."

"I agree." Caleb lifted a half-full beer that was sitting on a coaster on the table next to him. "But it's not an easement."

"It's not?"

"What you want is for the Crab Shack to succeed."

Jules couldn't disagree with the statement, so she elaborated instead. "And for the Crab Shack to succeed, customers need to get to the parking lot."

"I'll give you the easement," he said.

"Thank you."

"As soon as you remove the noncompete clause."

"Thereby guaranteeing the annihilation of the Crab Shack. Do you think I turned stupid over the past three days?"

"I hoped you'd turned reasonable. You have no other move."

"I can fight you in court," she said.

"I can out-lawyer you a hundred times over."

"Whoa," Matt said from the sidelines.

"Care to reassess your opinion of him?" she asked Matt. Caleb frowned at his friend.

"This is where I tap out," Matt said, finishing his beer and making to leave.

"So much for being on my side," Jules muttered.

"You should listen to him," Matt said.

"Exactly as I thought." She shouldn't be disappointed. There was absolutely no chance that Matt was going to back her against Caleb. But she'd liked Matt. She wanted him to turn out to be a good guy.

"See you later," Caleb said to Matt.

Matt gave him a nod as he exited the room.

"I guess it's just you and me," Jules said.

"Just you and me," Caleb agreed.

The door shut behind Matt.

Caleb knew it was time to change the conversation with Jules. They'd been going round and round for days now, and it had become obvious they were going to end up in court.

He hated that it would come to that. Going to court would hurt Jules the most. It would slow him down, and he'd lose money, but she'd lose everything.

She seemed to realize it, too, a dispirited expression taking over her face as she sipped the beer.

Even looking so sad, she was extraordinarily beautiful. And despite the circumstances, he liked having her in his house. She did something to it, seemed to bring it alive. He realized it was likely the last time she'd be here, and it made him feel almost as despondent as she looked.

"Did Melissa tell you what Noah said?" he asked.

If these were their final moments before the court battle began, he felt a duty to let her know about Noah's past.

"Not exactly." She hesitated. "I do know he has an idea for—" She seemed to change her mind and pressed her lips together.

"I'm not going to steal your restaurant plans, Jules."

"You want them to die on the page."

Restless, Caleb came to his feet. "It doesn't have to be this way."

"Yes it does."

"Even Melissa understands my position."

"Did she say that?" Jules asked sharply. "What did she say? What exactly happened between the two of you?"

"Nothing happened between us."

Could she be asking what Caleb thought she was asking?

"Noah showed up," he finished.

"And that stopped *what*?" She *was* asking that.

"Me trying to reason with her." He waited to see how far Jules would take her wild accusations. Caleb had no romantic interest in Melissa. He was nuts about Jules.

"Reason with her?" Jules voice went up. "Is that a euphemism for romance her?"

Before he could answer, she abandoned her beer and came to her feet.

"Is that your master plan, Caleb? Cozy up to my sister and turn her against me?"

He started to deny it, but then he stopped himself, seeing a whole new angle of attack. He guessed Jules would do almost anything to protect her sister.

"What if I am?" he asked.

"Then you're a complete and reprehensible jerk."

"I think you've already decided that."

"I'll just tell her what you're up to. That'll shut you down."

"Will it?" he asked softly. "We both know she wants to trust me." He watched the uncertainty cross Jules's face and pressed his advantage. "She wants to find a solution. She's a very beautiful woman."

"I can't believe you'd sink that low."

"I'd sink very low," he bluffed. "There's a whole lot of money at stake here."

"You stay *away* from my sister." Jules cheeks were glowing pink. Her blue eyes flashed with anger.

He held himself steady against the guilt he was feeling. This bluff was for her own good.

"If it's that important, I'll make you a deal," he said.

"I am *not* removing the noncompete."

He took a couple of steps forward, craving intimacy with her. "That's not my deal."

"What other deal is there?" She tipped her chin as he grew closer.

He wished he could take the last couple of steps, draw her into his arms and apologize for upsetting her. Of course he wasn't interested in her sister. And he'd never use Melissa's trusting nature against her. It was all Jules. Everything was Jules.

He could still taste her last kiss, and he desperately wanted another. He was acutely aware of the fact that they were alone in the house. All of their cards were now on the table and there was nothing stopping them from doing anything they wanted.

"Caleb?" she interrupted his wandering thoughts.

"Hmm?"

"The deal?"

He couldn't help a small smile. "You date me instead."

She went speechless for a moment. "That gets you where?"

He gave a shrug. "Not your concern. One date. Let me take you on one date, and I'll back off on Melissa."

Jules tilted her head to one side.

It made it even harder to keep from kissing her.

"What on earth are you up to?"

"I'm attempting to make you see things my way."

"You don't need to date me to argue with me."

"Take the deal, or leave it and I try something else."

"You try to cozy up to Melissa."

Caleb countered with an ambiguous shrug.

He'd come up with an ad hoc plan for using the date to help Jules see reason. But if he was honest with himself, right now, he mostly just wanted the date.

"One date?" she said.

"One date."

She considered the offer, looking like she was making a very painful decision. It was hard on a guy's ego, but it was what it was.

"Okay," she finally said in a small voice and with a whole lot of uncertainty.

"Your enthusiasm is gratifying."

"We both know you're practically blackmailing me."

He gave in to the urge to move closer. "And we both know what happens when I kiss you."

She put the flat of her hand against his chest.

The warmth of it seeped through his shirt, and he couldn't stop himself from closing his eyes to savor the touch.

"Stop it," she said huskily.

"I like it when you touch me."

"I'm holding you off."

"I know."

"That's not the same as touching you."

He opened his eyes. Big mistake, because she was right there, so close.

"Do you have any idea how beautiful you are?" he asked.

"When?" she asked.

"All the time."

"When is the date?"

"Are you not feeling anything?" He didn't want to believe the physical attraction was all on his side.

She swallowed. "No."

She was lying. He'd bet the new Neo location that she was lying. And that meant there was in fact hope. Their date could turn out to be very interesting.

"Friday night," he said.

"Fine." She dropped her hand and took a backward step.

He missed her already.

Five

Melissa abruptly stopped sanding the old barstool with her good hand, straightening to stare across the Crab Shack at Jules. The morning sun streamed through the window behind her, highlighting the fine sawdust and making her blond hair glow like a halo.

"There's something I'm not getting," she said.

"What's not to get?" Jules sized up one of the dining tables.

"The part where Caleb asks *you* on a date."

"What's wrong with me?" Jules's plan had been to off-handedly mention tomorrow night's date with Caleb and blow past it on to more important subjects. The blowing past it wasn't working as well as she'd hoped.

"He can date anyone. I've Googled the guy and you should see some of the women who go out with him."

"Thanks, tons." Jules pretended to be offended.

Melissa waved a hand through the air. "Don't be ridiculous. That wasn't an insult. Why you?"

"That sounds like an insult." Jules pushed the table toward the center of the room, making space along the walls where Noah planned to work on the electrical system later in the day. "Were you thinking paint or stain for the barstools?"

Melissa wouldn't let it go. "There's something you're not telling me."

Her sister was too astute, but Jules had no intention of letting on that Caleb had initially targeted Melissa to romance. It would sound like Jules didn't trust her. She did.

It was Caleb she didn't trust. He was underhanded, and Melissa's instinct was to search for an amicable solution.

That made her vulnerable to his bogus claims of both restaurants succeeding.

"All right," Jules said, frowning. "Maybe it's because I kissed him."

"You *what*?"

"Well, he kissed me. I suppose that's more accurate. He was the one doing the kissing. I simply..." Jules wasn't exactly sure how to finish that sentence.

Luckily, she didn't have to. Melissa jumped back in.

"Where? When? Why didn't you say something?"

"It was a nonevent. That day we were moving the pictures, while you were talking to Noah. Caleb kissed me. I kind of kissed him back. It's embarrassing, but he is pretty hot. And, well, I'm guessing he might be under the impression that I'm attracted to him. And, maybe, well, maybe he thinks if he dates me and, I don't know, sweeps me off my feet, he can change my mind about the noncompete clause. You know that's all he really wants."

Melissa stared wide-eyed through the entire explanation, which Jules realized had gone on way too long.

"You kissed him back."

"A little bit."

"Okay." Melissa rubbed the sandpaper a few strokes. "I get that you might kiss him. He's a handsome, charming guy. But why did you agree to a date? What's in it for you?" She paused. "Unless, ooh, are you genuinely interested in—"

"No!" Jules barked too quickly. "I'm not interested in him, genuinely or otherwise."

"You just admitted he was hot."

"He isn't—" Jules stopped herself. She wanted to lie as little as possible. "Okay, fine, in an objective sort of way. I'd have to be dead not to notice that Caleb is hot. And Noah's hot."

Melissa's brows went up, and she opened her mouth.

Jules bowled forward, talking louder. She wanted to get

this over with. "There are a lot of hot guys in the world. That doesn't mean I'm automatically attracted to them. I have a mission when it comes to Caleb, and I'm executing part of that mission through a fake date. I think I can use it to our advantage. Period."

"Jules," Melissa said.

"What?" Jules hoped she'd put it to rest.

"He's behind you."

"Who?"

"Caleb."

Perfect. Now he had her on record admitting he was handsome. This was going to be a pain.

She felt her cheeks warm as she turned. "Hello, Caleb."

"Hello, Jules."

Silence fell.

She couldn't stand it, so she leaped in. "I was telling Melissa about our date."

"So I heard."

She walked to the next table and started to push it out of the way. "Was there something you needed?"

He immediately joined her to help move the table. "Yes. There's something I meant to tell you."

Jules realized that Melissa had to wonder why Caleb wasn't reacting to her outburst. She couldn't for the life of her come up with a reason, so she decided on the blow-past-it strategy again. Hopefully, it would work better this time.

"What was it?" she asked Caleb.

"Do you want me to leave you two alone?" Melissa asked, obviously assuming, quite reasonably, that they had things to discuss.

"You need to hear this, too," Caleb said. "What are we doing?" he asked Jules, nodding to the table now held between them.

"Stacking them all in the center of the room. Noah wants to work on the electrical today."

"Is Noah here?" Caleb asked.

"He's at the hardware store," Melissa answered.

"Good."

"Jules isn't interested in him," Melissa said.

Both Jules and Caleb turned to look at her.

"She might think he's hot, but she doesn't want to date him."

Jules realized her protestations about the date hadn't worked. Melissa thought she was genuinely attracted to Caleb.

"Don't worry about explaining," Jules told her.

"He's really not her type," Melissa said.

"It's *fine*, Melissa."

Caleb could barely hide the amusement in his tone. "Jules and I have an understanding."

"An understanding?" Melissa asked in obvious confusion.

Caleb wrapped an arm around Jules's shoulders. "She's not convinced we're a good idea, but she's agreed to give me a shot."

Jules fought not to shrug him off. Then she fought not to enjoy his touch.

"So, all that…" Melissa drew a little circle in the air. "All that song and dance about only using the date to change your mind?"

"She's in denial," he said.

"You know, I thought that had to be it," Melissa said.

Jules shot Caleb a look of frustration. He was unnecessarily complicating things.

"But I'm an optimist," he said.

She did shrug her way from his arms.

"About Noah," Caleb said, moving on. "I learned something about him that I think you two have a right to know."

"You mean his criminal record?" Melissa asked.

Jules couldn't contain her surprise. "Noah has a criminal record?"

"It's nothing serious," Melissa answered.

"What did he tell you?" Caleb asked.

"That he got into a fight."

"What happened?" Jules asked them both, trying to wrap her head around the revelation. "Was someone hurt?"

Caleb's attention was on Melissa. "You knew but you didn't tell Jules?"

"It wasn't serious," Melissa said, dusting her hands together and contemplating the barstool. "He told me about it when he applied for the contract."

Jules wasn't sure what it took to have a criminal record. "Did he assault someone? Was there a trial? Did he actually go to jail?"

"Not serious?" Caleb challenged Melissa. Then he turned to Jules. "Yes, he went to jail. The other guy died, and Noah went to jail."

Jules's stomach clenched with anxiety. "Noah is a killer?"

"It was self-defense," Melissa said staunchly. "It was self-defense, and it was an accident. I looked up the newspaper articles."

Jules didn't know how to react. She was confident Melissa had done her research, and she was sure Melissa thought Noah was harmless. But Melissa always saw the best in people. No matter how it had happened, Noah had killed someone.

Jules moved toward her sister. "You should have told me."

Melissa looked contrite. "I know. I know I should have. But, well, you know what you're like."

Jules didn't follow. "What am I like?"

Melissa's gaze flicked to Caleb. "You don't trust anyone."

"And you trust everyone. Not trusting killers is just common sense."

"He's *not* a killer," Melissa repeated. "He's a decent guy who was in a bad situation, and he deserves a second chance. Besides, his prices are half of anyone else's."

"Because he's a convicted killer," Jules felt the need to

point out. "I would imagine they all charge less than their competition."

Noah's flat tone echoed across the room. "Don't worry. I'll clear out."

Jules turned, and her stomach sank. She instantly realized how judgmental her words had sounded. Seeing him in front of her, she found it impossible to believe he was dangerous. She'd been working with him for days on end, and he'd been nothing but respectful and kind.

"I'm sorry," she began.

"I'm the one who's sorry," he said. "I didn't realize Melissa had kept it to herself."

"Because it doesn't matter," Melissa said.

"It does matter," Noah said.

"You can't blame her for asking questions," Caleb said.

Noah glared at Caleb. "Who said I blamed her? I just said I'd clear out."

"We need you." Melissa rushed to Noah and grasped his arm, as if she could hold him there with her one good hand.

When Noah looked at her, his emotion was stark. It was obvious he liked Melissa. He clearly liked her very much.

"Stay," Jules said. "If it was an accident. If you were in a bad position. If it's behind you, well, Melissa is right. You deserve a second chance."

Noah seemed to hesitate.

"We do need you," Jules added. "We don't have much money, and—" She couldn't help glancing at Caleb.

His expression was taut and unreadable.

She finished her thought. "And we've run into some unexpected complications."

"Please stay," Melissa implored.

Noah stared at her as if he was mentally weighing his options. But then his expression softened and his shoulder dropped with what looked like relief. "Okay," he finally uttered.

Melissa emitted a heartfelt sigh. "Thank you."

"Thank *you*." His hand moved slowly to cover hers.

"You're sure about this?" Caleb asked Jules in an undertone.

"You're not?"

"I don't want you taking any chances."

"Funny. It seems like my biggest risk is you, not him."

Caleb didn't seem to have an answer for that, and he obviously didn't care that it was true. Jules reminded herself that it was true. He was her biggest risk because he cared only about his own interests. She had to remember that.

Jules stood in front of the mirror in the loft bedroom she was sharing with her sister.

"It seems silly not to tell me where we're going," she said to Melissa who was sprawled across the plaid bedspread on one of the two twin beds.

"I'd call it romantic, but I still think this whole date thing is strange."

Jules didn't want to rehash her decision. "Strange or not, I have to wear something."

"Go middle of the road," Melissa said, sitting up cross-legged. "That's way too fancy."

"You think?" Jules turned one way and then the other in her high heels.

The little black dress was her favorite. Held up by spaghetti straps, it was sparkly, short and sassy, with just enough swish in the skirt to make dancing fun.

"Do you want to change his mind about the easement or get him naked?"

Jules made a face at her sister. "Change his mind about the easement." But then she had to shake away an image of Caleb naked. That wasn't where she was going tonight, not at all.

"Then, unless you're heading for a high-end club... Do you think he'll take you clubbing?"

Jules couldn't begin to guess. "Last time he took me to

a drive-through. Not that it was a date. I mean, there obviously wasn't a 'last time' to compare this to. But he did seem to think the drive-through would be a terrible date."

"And you jumped from that to glitz and glam?"

"You think pants? I've got skinny jeans and that leather-trimmed sweater."

"Too far the other way." Melissa unfolded her legs and came to her feet.

She headed for their shared dresser and pulled open a middle drawer.

Jules kicked off the shoes, stripped off the dress and hung it in the makeshift closet. Years ago, their grandfather had attached a piece of doweling across one corner of the room. Their grandmother had sewed a cotton floral curtain to cover it, and it had been the room's closet ever since.

"What about these?" Melissa produced a pair of snug-fitting black slacks. "Your black ankle boots with my silky pink tank. You can layer on some gold necklaces, big earrings, and you're good to go."

"You have better clothes than me," Jules couldn't help commenting as she stepped into the pants.

"I spent forever in your hand-me-downs. I deserve a few nice things."

"I think you might just have better taste." Jules didn't go out very often. That, combined with their years'-long focus on building up their savings account, meant she didn't have a particularly extensive wardrobe.

She slipped into the bright pink tank top. It was supple and soft against her skin.

"That looks great on you," Melissa said.

Jules turned to the mirror. "I think this'll work. The boots are comfortable in case we walk anywhere. But I look good from the waist up if the place is fancy."

"You look good from the waist down, too. Are you sure this is a smart idea?"

"It's the best idea I've got."

No matter how confusing the tactic might seem, Jules needed to humor Caleb to keep him away from turning his attention to Melissa.

"Your emotions are muddled," Melissa said quietly. "On some level, you want the date. Because this really isn't the best way to change his mind."

"Quit worrying, and let me try. You know he has the upper hand right now. We can bluff and bluster all we want, but we can't afford much in the way of lawyers. We have to appeal to his sense of decency."

"You think he's decent?"

"I don't know. But I'm going to find out."

Melissa put a hand on Jules's shoulder, and their gazes met in the mirror. "You're my big sister, and I respect your judgment. But you really don't have to do this."

"You're my little sister, and I respect your opinion, but I know exactly what I'm doing." Jules mustered up a carefree smile. "It's a date. It's not like I'm going bull-riding or base jumping. What's the worst that can happen?"

Melissa mimicked their father's voice. "You, young lady, could come home pregnant."

Jules couldn't help but crack a smile. "You know, I honestly think Dad would prefer me getting pregnant to us re-opening the Crab Shack."

"What if Caleb Watford was the dad?"

"Whoa," Jules intoned, letting her mind wrap itself around that. Her father hated the Watfords with a single-mindedness that had only grown over time.

"Good thing you changed out of that sexy dress." Melissa patted Jules's shoulder before letting go. "Big earrings and a chunky necklace, that's what this outfit needs."

There was a knock on the door downstairs.

"He's on time," Melissa said.

Jules felt a flutter in her stomach. It wasn't excitement, she told herself. It was anxiety.

"I'll tell him you'll be a few minutes."

As Melissa left the room, Jules focused on her jewelry box, coming up with a pair of dangling earrings with multiple gold bead drops. She found a complementary necklace, six strands with scattered gold beads of increasing size.

She made a last-minute decision to put her hair up, and swooped it into a loose topknot. She shook her head back and forth, liking the way the earrings swayed. Caleb's voice sounded downstairs, its deep timbre reverberating through her chest as she sat down on the bedside to pull on her boots.

Then she was ready. She put her hand against her stomach in an effort to quell the butterflies, took a final look in the mirror and headed for the narrow staircase.

Caleb abruptly stopped talking and watched her as she descended, a worried expression taking over his face.

"Did I get it wrong?" she asked, gesturing to the outfit. "Are we going hiking or something?"

He shook his head. "You got it right."

She relaxed a little bit. "Good. You had me worried there for a minute."

"So, where are you taking her?" Melissa asked.

"Do you really want me to spoil the surprise?"

"It's not like it's her birthday, or you're proposing or something. Why the big secret?"

"She'll see." Caleb kept his attention on Jules. "Do you want to take a jacket?"

"I don't know. Do I?"

He was wearing designer jeans, an open-collar blue striped shirt and a steel-gray blazer. Like her, he'd gone middle of the road. His outfit didn't give away a thing.

"You shouldn't be cold," he said.

She picked up her purse. "Okay, then let's do this."

"Good luck," Melissa said as they moved toward the door.

"Luck?" Caleb asked Jules.

Jules kept her tone bright, as they stepped onto the porch. "She means in trying to change your mind."

"Oh. I wasn't thinking about that at all."

"Good. It gives me an advantage."

"I was thinking about showing you a really great time."

They made it to the top of the stairs, and he opened the passenger door to his SUV.

"You can drop the act," she told him as she stepped inside.

"What act?"

"You know this isn't a real date."

"This is absolutely a real date." He shut the door behind her.

Confused by the statement, she waited until he was settled in the driver's seat. "Listen, Caleb. I don't know what your expectations are for tonight."

He pressed the start button. "My expectations are for dinner and some interesting conversation."

She told herself to take him at his word. It seemed counterproductive to belabor the point.

"What if I'm boring?" she asked.

He backed out of the short, gravel driveway. "You couldn't be boring if you tried."

Now, there was a challenge. "Sure, I could."

"How?"

She mentally ran through a couple of ideas. "I could talk about the stock market."

"Do you know anything about the stock market?"

She didn't. "That's Melissa's area of expertise. I know. I could talk you through the process of making a turducken. It takes eight hours, and it's painstaking."

He swung the SUV onto the coastal highway. "What's a turducken?"

"A chicken inside a duck inside a turkey. It's all boneless and layered with savory stuffing. It has Cajun roots, and it's absolutely delicious."

"Sounds fascinating. Where did you go to school?"

"Oregon Culinary Institute."

"Did you like it?"

"Quit trying to make this conversation interesting. First, you have to purchase a chicken, a duck and a turkey. Personally, I like to go both fresh and organic. There's a poultry farm outside Portland that will—"

Caleb chuckled. "You're hilarious."

"You think I'm joking. I'm dead serious."

"You're going to last about five minutes."

"Hey, I could write a thesis on this stuff."

"You have to write a thesis to become a chef?" he asked.

"Papers, yes. But not a thesis. The exams involve creating and cooking dishes. I once did a spiced, seared ahi tuna that made the testers cry."

"With joy, or did you overdo the spicing?"

"I got a perfect mark. Where are we going?"

They'd turned off the main highway, taking a road that led inland.

"It's a surprise."

"We're not going into Olympia?"

"What part of the surprise concept is foreign to you?"

"I thought we'd at least be in Olympia." She looked for a road sign, trying to remember where this road led. One came into view, getting closer and closer. "The airport?" she asked. "What's on the other side of the airport?"

"Not much."

"Then where are we going?"

He gave her an odd look. "The airport."

"It's the community airport. They don't even have flights from there." She was setting aside for the moment the outlandish concept that there might be a plane ride involved in this date.

"They don't have commercial flights," he corrected.

"Are we going sightseeing?"

He smiled at that.

"We're taking a jet," he said as the airport building loomed up.

"You have a jet?" The evening was starting to feel completely surreal.

"No, I don't have a jet. Exactly how rich do you think I am?"

"Pretty darn rich from what I've seen so far."

"I don't own a private jet. I merely booked it from a service."

"Oh, well that makes a big difference," she drawled.

"It does to me. I'm not about to tie up capital in a jet I barely use."

"How very frugal of you."

He turned the vehicle into the small airport parking lot. "I like to think so."

"That was sarcasm."

"No kidding." He chose a parking spot in front of the low building and brought the SUV to a halt.

As he shut off the engine and killed the headlights, she realized she was nervous and tried to figure out why. The airport was quiet, but not deserted. She could see an agent sitting inside what looked like a plush boarding lounge. There were several planes parked beyond the chain-link fence.

But the uneasy feeling refused to leave.

Caleb came around to her side and opened the door.

She didn't move.

He held out his hand.

She turned her head. "I don't trust you."

"You don't trust me to what?"

"Am I going to end up stranded in Ecuador or Brazil?"

He looked amused. "Ecuador?"

"It occurs to me that you could dump me in some foreign country and come back and coerce Melissa."

"You have an active imagination."

"You have a conniving mind."

He crossed his arms over his chest. "Exactly how would I explain your absence?"

"You'd come up with something. Maybe you already have a plot in the works." But as she spoke, she realized he made a good point.

Her suspicions were starting to feel silly.

"We're going to San Francisco," he said.

"That's your story." But she was joking now. She was starting to relax. "Once we're in the air, how will I know the difference?"

"You'll recognize the Golden Gate Bridge." He reached out again, offering her his hand. "When we board, the pilot can show you the flight plan."

She was willing to admit that sounded reasonable—surreal, but reasonable. "I've never flown on a private jet." She took his hand and stepped out.

"You'll like it."

"So, what's in San Francisco?"

"The original Neo restaurant."

As they crossed the nautical-themed wooden walkway that led to Neo's front entrance, Caleb tried to see the restaurant through Jules's eyes. The two-story building sat oceanfront on a peninsula that provided views of both the marina and the ocean. The salty scent of the air and gentle hum of the waves gave the restaurant its signature ambiance.

The structure was West Coast-style, as were all of the Neo locations, with soaring beams and plenty of windows. The polished wood reflected the interior light and gave a warm, welcoming glow.

They walked inside to find several other couples in the foyer. The maître d' immediately recognized Caleb, and gave him a nod of acknowledgment. But Caleb knew the maître d' would seat the customers in order. He didn't ask for preferential service. In fact, he insisted the customers were more important.

The foyer was dramatic, two full stories in height, with a river stone feature wall that camouflaged the short hallway to the restrooms. The reception desk was carved from drift-wood, another feature duplicated at each of the other res-taurants. The hanging lights had burnished copper shades, and occasional tables were decorated with large, earth-toned pottery vases filled with fresh flowers.

Beyond the foyer, muted saltwater fish tanks were in-terspersed with privacy screens that dampened sound and broke up the tables in the main dining room. Caleb planned to take Jules to the second floor where they would overlook dining tables and the open kitchen, and be parallel to one of the features—a carved redwood chandelier inset with nautical glass floats.

Jules leaned close to him, speaking beneath the murmur of conversations. "This place is stunning."

"We renovated two years ago."

"You should be taking someone else on this date."

Her words made him grin with amusement.

"You know," she elaborated. "Someone who's impressed by you, who'd be bowled over by your power and prestige, where you'd at least have a chance..."

"I got your meaning," he said.

Regular date or not, he didn't want to be with anyone but Jules right now. Their relationship was beyond compli-cated, but for now she was here, and that was his initial goal.

Having assisted the other customers, the maître d' ap-proached. "Good evening, Mr. Watford."

"Hello, Fred. It's nice to see you." Caleb shook the man's hand.

"I didn't realize you were joining us tonight." Fred's gaze moved to Jules.

"It was a last-minute decision. This is Jules Parker."

"Nice to meet you, Ms. Parker. Welcome to Neo."

Jules tipped her head back to gaze at the soaring space. "This place is spectacular."

"I'm so pleased you think so," Fred responded. "Did you have a seating preference this evening?" he asked Caleb.

"Something on the second floor? On the rail?"

"Absolutely." Fred motioned to one of the hosts, who immediately came forward.

"Table seventy," Fred said.

"This way, please," the crisply dressed man offered, gesturing with his arm.

Caleb put his hand lightly on the small of Jules's back, guiding her forward.

"Be careful on the stairs, ma'am," the host cautioned over his shoulder.

The polished stair rail was subtly illuminated, and there were mini lights in the seams of the stairs, making it as safe as possible for patrons.

Caleb followed her up and waited while the host pulled out her chair and placed her napkin.

"Very nice view," she noted gazing across the room and down to the dining area below. "Is that a real ship's bell? Is everything antique?"

"It is. Most of the decor is from the twentieth century, but it's all authentic."

"I'm stealing some of these ideas."

"Good."

She turned her teasing attention to him. "You don't care?"

"It'll make it easier for us to coordinate efforts."

"You don't miss an opportunity, do you?"

"Never."

She seemed to reconsider her approach. "The Crab Shack is not going to be Neo's poor cousin."

"I never suggested that."

"Everything you've said and done is suggesting that."

"Poor cousin is a negative term."

There was a sudden rattle of dishes, and the floor beneath them vibrated.

Jules eyes widened, and she gripped the edge of the table.

"It's a small earthquake," he assured her. It wasn't the

first he'd experienced in San Francisco. "This building is designed to withstand—"

But the rumbling beneath them increased. The lights swayed, and some glassware fell over, shattering. A couple of people screamed.

"Caleb?"

Caleb jumped to his feet. "Shelter under your tables!" he called to the patrons around him, projecting his voice over the rail and to the people below. "The building is earthquake-proof. Get down, but stay put. You're safer in place than trying to exit."

The shaking increased. "Everybody under the tables," he called louder. "Staff, help anyone who needs it."

He quickly moved to Jules, assisting her as she crawled under their table. "You'll be fine," he told her.

Then he looked around, seeing an older couple struggling. He quickly gave them a hand.

The shaking increased alarmingly, becoming more violent. Decorations began falling from the walls, and the dishes were cascading from their tables.

"Caleb!" Jules cried.

With a fast look around to ensure people were sheltering, Caleb rushed back to her, all but diving under his own table.

The noise grew deafening, as more items fell and people cried out in fear. He grasped Jules, pulling her close. "It'll be all right."

"I know."

"The building won't fall down."

Just then, out of the corner of his eye, he saw the redwood chandelier shift. One of the anchor bolts popped and the whole contraption dangled precariously, the glass floats raining down. "Look out!" he cried.

Then the chandelier crashed two stories to the floor.

Caleb craned his neck, immensely relieved to see it had hit the open kitchen instead of a table.

"Anybody hurt?" he called down.

"I don't think so." It was Fred's voice, and Caleb saw that a group of staff members had clustered with him around the rock wall. That was a good decision. The wall was anchored in concrete set deep in the earth.

As the shaking started to subside, Caleb could see flames licking up from the gas grill, through the redwood chandelier.

He clasped Jules's hand and looked her straight in the eyes. "Everybody needs to get out of here."

"What can I do?"

"Help that older couple." He pointed. "I have to make sure the gas is turned off."

She nodded.

"You okay?" he asked.

"I'm fine." She looked calm and capable.

He was grateful for that.

The shaking had all but stopped, and he stood again. The lights flickered but stayed on.

"There are five exits," he called out. "One in each corner on the first floor, plus the main entrance where you all came in. There's no need to panic, no need to run, but you should leave the building and gather at the back, away from the beach. Staff will help anyone who needs it. I repeat, slowly leave the building and gather at the back away from the beach."

He leaned down to Jules who was crawling out from under the table. "You're good?"

"I'm good. Go. Put out the fire."

Caleb left her to help the older couple and made his way downstairs. Fred was there to meet him, along with the manager and the head chef.

"The gas needs to be shut off," he said.

"We're working on the back kitchen connections," said Kiefer, the head chef. "But I'm worried there might be leaks in the lines."

A couple of staff members arrived with fire extinguishers and doused the flames in the central kitchen.

"Is there a main valve outside?" Caleb asked.

"Behind the kitchen, but you need a wrench," one of the staff replied.

"Where can I find a wrench?"

Fred answered, "There should be one in the basement, on the bench in the utility area."

"Make sure everyone evacuates," Caleb told Fred.

"Yes, sir."

Then Caleb spoke to the manager, Violet. "You've called the fire department?"

"The lines are jammed, but we'll keep trying."

"Shut off everything you can," he directed Kiefer. "Absolutely no open flames."

The lights went off, sending up a collective gasp from the people who were still shuffling their way out the doors. The battery lights came on immediately. It was dim, but people would be able to find their way.

"We have to assume we're on our own for a while," Caleb said. He could only imagine emergency resources were stretched thin. And there could be damage to roadways. "Who knows first aid?"

"Three of the kitchen staff are certified," Violet said, "along with me."

"Grab whatever we have for first aid kits, and check out as many people as you can. Get someone to distribute bottles of water." Caleb caught a small movement and saw that it was Jules.

"What can I do?" she asked.

"I need to find a wrench in the basement."

"I'll help."

His first instinct was to say no, to tell her to go outside to safety, but he wanted to keep her with him. He told himself a second set of eyes would help find the tools quickly. And the priority was to shut off the main gas valve.

"This way," he said, wending his way through the up-turned tables toward the basement stairs. "There's glass all over the floor," he warned her.

"I'm wearing boots."

"Good choice."

"We have Melissa to thank for that."

Caleb opened the basement door. He thought he caught another whiff of gas, and he knew they had no time to waste.

Six

Three hours later, with the gas shut off and the customers safely on their way home, a firefighter approached Jules and Caleb at the front of the building.

"Are you okay, ma'am?" he asked her.

She was tired and a little cold, but otherwise she was fine.

"I'm good," she told the man in the heavy jacket and helmet.

He turned his attention to Caleb, removing his glove to offer a handshake. "Zeke Rollins, Station 55."

Caleb shook the man's hand. "Thanks for your help."

"You'll need the building cleared by an engineer before anybody goes inside or you start repairs."

"Already set up for tomorrow," Caleb replied. "Except for the smashed grill area, we're hopeful it's superficial."

"I hope you're right. You're definitely at the epicenter of the damage. We lost a couple of historic buildings down the block. Luckily they were empty."

"Anyone seriously hurt?" Jules asked. She'd been immensely relieved to learn the customers at Neo had gotten away with minor cuts and bruises.

"A few broken bones, and one patient is in surgery. But it could have been a lot worse."

Jules nodded her agreement. She'd never been in an earthquake before. It had been terrifying.

"We're hearing it was a 6.0," Zeke said. "Good thing it was offshore. You won't reenter the building tonight?"

"We won't," Caleb said. "I've got security posted on the doors. I'm meeting the engineering firm in the morning, and we'll take it from there."

"Glad to hear it. And I'm glad you're both all right."

"Thanks, again," Caleb said.

Zeke gave him a clap on the shoulder before taking his leave.

"You were really great in all this," Jules felt compelled to tell Caleb.

He'd taken charge, made sure people didn't get hurt, ensured the building didn't burn down.

He gave a shrug. He'd long since discarded his blazer, and the sleeves of his shirt were rolled up. He had a scrape on one cheek, and there was dirt on his arms. He looked confident, capable and strong, if a little tired around the eyes.

"What now?" she asked him, following his gaze to the building. It looked perfectly normal from outside, but she knew the interior was a mess.

"You must be hungry," he said.

She hadn't really thought about it. "I meant for Neo."

"We'll do the repairs." He didn't sound particularly worried.

"Just like that?"

"We have good insurance. We'll have to close for a few days, but I'm confident we'll be back in business soon."

"You are an optimist." She found herself admiring his attitude.

"Let's go." He surprised her by looping an arm around her waist. Then she surprised herself by leaning in.

"Where?"

"Somewhere they'll feed us. Do you mind heading home tomorrow instead of tonight?"

"No problem."

Transportation home seemed like the least of their worries. She'd have to call Melissa. Then it occurred to her that Melissa didn't even know she was in San Francisco. Wow. That was going to be an interesting phone call.

"I'm sure you'll want a shower," Caleb said as they made their way toward the parking lot.

She frowned as she looked down at her dirt-stained clothes. She'd torn a hole in the knee of her pants. "These are Melissa's."

"Clothes can be replaced."

"I know. I didn't mean that the way it sounded. I was just thinking that she doesn't even know I left Olympia."

"I didn't mean to sound critical."

"You didn't. Buying new clothes is nothing. I guess I'm a little rattled."

He gave her a squeeze around the waist. "We're all a little rattled. You were fantastic back there. Why don't you call Melissa while we drive?"

They'd picked up a rental car at the San Francisco airport, and he unlocked the doors.

Jules realized she didn't have her phone. It was the first time she'd even thought of it. "I left my purse inside the restaurant. My phone, my keys, my credit cards."

Caleb slid his phone from the pocket of his pants and held it out to her. "My wallet is in my pants. But I haven't a clue where I left my jacket." He paused, leaning on the door as she got in. "This didn't go exactly the way I'd planned."

She knew she shouldn't smile, but she did. She accepted his phone. "I don't think tonight went the way anybody planned."

"It seemed like such a good idea."

"I did like your restaurant," she admitted. "Though I guess it'll look different after tonight."

"We'll make it better." He pushed the door shut.

When he entered on the other side, she handed back his phone. "Password."

He punched it in. But before handing the phone back to her, he scrolled through some messages.

"Matt's worried," he said out loud. "He knew we were coming down here."

"Do you need to call him?"

Caleb typed in a couple of words. "It can wait." He handed her back the phone.

She dialed while he navigated their way from the near-empty parking lot.

It took Melissa a couple of rings to answer.

"Did I wake you?" Jules asked.

"Not really. Why? What's going on? Did you lose your phone?"

"I'm using Caleb's."

"Really?" There was clear speculation in her voice.

"It's nothing like that." Jules couldn't help glancing at Caleb.

He seemed focused on driving.

"We're in San Francisco," she said.

"What are you doing in San Francisco? Wait a minute. They had an earthquake in San Francisco."

"I know. I felt it."

"What happened? Are you okay?"

"I am. The Neo restaurant was pretty badly damaged." Jules gave her sister an abbreviated version of the evening, assuring Melissa that she was unharmed and that they were staying the night.

"I guess that explains it," Melissa said.

"Explains what?" Jules couldn't imagine what tonight's event could possibly explain.

"Dad called. He was trying to get hold of you and wanted to know where you were."

Again, Jules glanced over at Caleb. "You didn't tell him who I was with, did you?"

This time Caleb looked back.

"Of course I didn't," Melissa said. "It's my hand that's injured, not my brain."

"Thank goodness."

Caleb smirked. "You are hard on a man's ego, you know that?"

"Your ego's just fine."

"What?" Melissa asked.

"Nothing. Don't tell him."

"I won't tell him. Why would I tell him? You get some sleep. I'll see you tomorrow."

"I will," Jules said. "Thanks."

Jules ended the call, looking up to see they were pulling into Blue Earth Waterfront Hotel.

"You don't think this is overkill?" she asked him. "All I need is a burger and some hot water."

"Their beds are very comfortable," Caleb said as he brought the car to a halt at the valet. "And they'll have twenty-four-hour everything. It's nearly midnight, and I don't want to take a chance."

"A chance on your every whim not being satisfied?"

"On having to eat a cardboard something from a vending machine."

The valet appeared and Caleb unrolled his window. "Checking in?" the valet asked.

"We'd like two rooms."

"Certainly, sir." The man stood back, keyed his mic and asked about availability as he turned away.

He was back in a moment. "We can offer you two superior view rooms on the thirty-second floor, with upgraded soaker tubs and king-size beds."

"That'll be fine," Caleb said, releasing his seat belt.

Jules followed suit, deciding she was through arguing. An upgraded soaker tub sounded like a slice of heaven.

A waiter set up the room service order at a table in the corner of Caleb's hotel room. The man added a rose in a narrow crystal vase and lit two candles on the white tablecloth, making the setup very romantic.

After he left, Caleb blew out the candles and set them aside along with the rose.

He considered the table for a moment then decided it

looked naked, and he put everything back. He relit the candles and dimmed the overhead lights.

He was about to knock on the connecting door, when he changed his mind. Cursing himself for his indecision, he strode across the room, blew out the candles and removed the romantic touches.

Then he went back to the connecting door and gave a knock.

Jules opened it from the other side. She'd showered and changed into the exercise pants and T-shirt the hotel had sent up. Caleb was dressed in a similar outfit.

She leaned on the half-opened door, her half-dried hair wispy around her freshly scrubbed face. "You did this on purpose, didn't you?"

"Connecting rooms?"

She nodded, arranging her expression in comical suspicion.

"You heard the entire conversation."

The connecting rooms were happenstance. Though Caleb supposed the valet could have taken one look at Jules and decided to do Caleb a big favor. He thought back to the man's nametag. It was Perry something. He should give Perry a big tip.

Not that he had any expectations. He was more than certain that dinner would be the end of their date. Still, Perry's effort was appreciated.

"Well, they're really great rooms," she said, sauntering into his room.

"I'm glad you like them."

"What did you order?"

"You said you wanted burgers."

"You ordered burgers at a five-star hotel?"

"I did."

She turned to face him and put on a mock pout. "That's all you *ever* buy for me."

"You want me to send them back?"

She pulled out one of the chairs. "I know you know I'm joking."

He joined her, taking the other chair. "You're in a very relaxed mood."

"I'm too tired to do anything else."

"I got us wine instead of milk shakes."

"Good call." She lifted the silver warmer from her plate. It took her a second to react. "That's not a hamburger."

"Did they get the order wrong?"

"You're such a comedian."

He removed his own warmer. "Lobster chanterelle agnolotti. I hope that's okay."

She leaned in. "It smells fantastic."

"Chardonnay?" He lifted the bottle.

"Yes, please."

He poured. "I think I should get a do-over."

She watched the golden liquid cascade into the crystal glass. "A do-over of this dinner? So far it seems pretty great."

"A do-over of the date. I take back what I said to you about the drive-through that night. Nearly being killed in an earthquake is the worst date ever."

"We survived," she noted, raising her glass.

He touched his to hers. "I still want to try again."

"Why?"

"What do you mean why? Because everything that could possibly go wrong did. Look at us." He gestured to their workout clothes, bare feet and damp hair.

"I think I look terrific."

He agreed.

"And I'm seriously comfortable." She took a bite of the agnolotti and chewed. "Oh, man. This is delicious. You don't need a do-over, Caleb."

He knew what she meant was that she didn't want another date. He shouldn't be disappointed. He had no right to be disappointed. She only agreed to this date under duress.

He wasn't even sure what he'd hoped to achieve. Whatever it was, he hadn't come close to achieving it.

At least he'd kept her alive. He had that going for him.

He gave up and began eating.

"It's funny," she said between bites. "Years ago, when I had that crush on you, and when I was a typical rebellious teenager, I spun a silly fantasy about thumbing my nose at my father and riding off into the sunset with you."

"Tell me more." Caleb would ride off into the sunset with her any old time she wanted.

She didn't react to his question. "But when it happened for real, all I could do was hope my father never found out. I can't even imagine how he'd react to this."

"Will you tell him?"

"I'm never going to tell him."

"You keep a lot of secrets from your father?"

"Don't you?"

"My life doesn't have much to do with my father anymore." Caleb's parents had moved to Arizona years ago.

Jules had stopped eating and was watching him more closely. "When you were younger?"

"Kedrick and I didn't always see eye to eye." That was an understatement. There wasn't much about his father he admired.

"My dad hated sending Melissa and me to Whiskey Bay. He wanted to leave the bad memories behind. But we loved going, and our grandparents loved having us there."

"I know your dad fought with mine."

"There was bad blood between them from the day they were born."

"So you know about our grandfathers' feud."

"I know the basics," she said. "Your grandfather stole the woman my grandfather loved."

"Then your father stole my father's girlfriend," Caleb returned. "That should have made things even."

"Except that your father bullied my father his entire

childhood, then had him arrested the minute he fought back."

"I don't think that's quite the way it went."

Kedrick had told Caleb the story years ago.

"That's exactly the way it went," she said.

"It's always a risk going after another guy's girlfriend," he countered.

"Are you saying my father was at fault?"

He shook his head. "I'm saying your father threw the first punch. No, that's not what I'm saying. I'm just sharing information. I'm telling you the story the way I heard it. Your father knocked out my father's front teeth."

"He was strongly provoked."

"Okay." Caleb was more than sorry they'd gotten into this argument. "Let's leave it at that."

"And he was arrested," she continued.

"He only ended up with probation." It was on the tip of Caleb's tongue to remind her that his own father had required dental surgery.

But he stopped himself. He didn't know who had said what, and how the incident had escalated, but it seemed like both of the teenage boys had lost out.

"By the time the case was settled, it was too late." Jules's voice rose with emotion. "My dad had lost his scholarship. While your family could afford Stanford or any other college your father wanted, because your grandfather had, years earlier, swindled my grandfather and stole the woman he loved."

Caleb was through defending his father, especially because there was every chance Jules's version of the story was true. But his grandfather was another story.

"She freely chose Bert over Felix." Of that, Caleb was certain.

"Yeah, well I'm not so sure she was a prize."

"That is my grandmother you're talking about." It didn't take a genius to feel the conversation going way off the rails, but Caleb felt honor-bound to defend his grandmother, Nadine.

"Your grandmother agreed to marry the first who made his fortune." The disdain in Jules's tone was clear.

"Maybe she couldn't decide between them," he offered.

"A woman can always decide."

"You're an expert?"

"I'm a woman."

"Yes, you are definitely that."

She took a swallow of her wine. "I'm saying, if she let money make the choice for her, then she wasn't in love with either of them."

"Maybe she was in love with both of them."

"That's not possible. You can love two men, but you can't be *in love* with two men."

"I saw my grandparents together. They seemed very happy."

Jules's smile was cynical. "I'm sure they were very comfortable together what with the mansion and the Rolls-Royce they bought after your grandfather swindled my grandfather."

"I'm sure that's the way you heard it."

"That's the way it happened."

Caleb knew it had been emotionally complicated, but the business deal was straightforward. "Your grandfather bought my grandfather's half of the Crab Shack."

"For twice what it was worth."

"They had it appraised."

"They'd made a gentleman's agreement a year before the appraisal, when the property value was lower, after your grandfather stopped putting in any effort to build the business."

Caleb took a drink of the wine. It was crisp and tart. A shot of alcohol was exactly what he needed right now. It was easy to see how the difference in perspective had caused so much bad blood. But he didn't want to fight about it.

"We're not all bad guys, Jules." He hated that her low opinion of his family included him.

"The facts seem to show otherwise."

"How can I change your mind?"

"Easiest thing in the world for you to do." She let the statement hang.

She didn't have to finish it. If he capitulated, she'd believe he was a nice guy.

"You saw Neo," he said instead. "You saw what I can do, what I can build. I can help you with the Crab Shack."

"But you won't, Caleb. You won't help me. You'll only help you. Of all the chances I might take in this life, trusting a Watford is *not* one of them."

"I know my father's not a nice guy, but I've never done anything to hurt you."

She gave a sad smile and set her napkin on the table, rising. "I should go."

"Don't." The last thing in the world he wanted her to do was go.

"I'm not sure what you expected out of this, Caleb. But this date thing is not going to work. No amount of fine food and fancy wine is going to change my mind."

Caleb rose with her. "I wish we could go back."

"Back to what? When were we ever in a good place?"

He closed in. "Back to the part where you wanted to run away with me."

Her expression turned calculating. "Are you saying you'd walk away from Neo?"

He laughed softly at himself. "You're too quick for me, Juliet Parker. I can't even hope to keep up."

"You know that's not true."

"It's entirely true."

She pushed back her damp hair. "The truth is, you're more cunning than I could ever hope to be."

"I'm not cunning." He completely lost his edge around her.

Her tone softened on a sigh. "You're dangerous, Caleb."

"The last thing I want to do is hurt you."

She started to say something, but seemed to stop herself.

He touched his index finger to the bottom of her chin, tipping her head ever so slightly. "Can this date at least end with a kiss?"

"Caleb." She sounded sad.

"I really want to kiss you, Jules."

The silence stretched.

Her blue eyes blinked once. "You know what's going to happen if you kiss me."

"I'm going to want you so bad it might kill me?"

The defensiveness slipped away from her expression. "We step over that line, we can't control ourselves."

He didn't have a counter to that. He knew she was right. Still, he didn't care. This was too powerful to let slip away. "And what does that tell you?"

Her shoulders relaxed an inch. "We have chemistry."

"We have chemistry. That's not a crime. It's not going to hurt anybody. It's just you and me, Jules, maybe for the one and only time."

The silence stretched again.

"If we do this," she said.

Anticipation nearly burst through his chest.

"What happens in this hotel room has to stay in this hotel room. We can't talk about it. We can't think about it. We can't ever, *ever* do anything like this again."

He didn't hesitate. "Deal."

Her head tilted to the side. "Did we just agree on something?"

"We did."

"You don't have a counter, a caveat, a condition?"

"None."

She moved her hand, and their fingertips brushed together. A small smile curved her lips. "Then what are you waiting for?"

He stopped waiting.

* * *

Caleb's kiss nearly buckled Jules's knees. A rational part of her brain told her this was a bad idea. But there was a more powerful part loving the feel of Caleb's strong arms around her. She leaned into his body, leaned into his kiss, let the fear and uncertainty of the night, of their circumstances, of her world slip completely away.

She pressed her palms on his arms, sliding them up over his muscled shoulders, along his back until she'd wrapped herself around him. She opened to his kiss, tasting the sharp wine, inhaling his musky scent, feeling the power of his heartbeat thud right through her skin.

His kisses grew deeper. His hands slipped down her back, finding the seam between her pants and her T-shirt. When his fingertips feathered along her skin, she shivered. He wrapped his hands around her shirt, drew back and slowly peeled it over her head.

Coming out of the shower, she hadn't bothered with her bra, so her breasts were bare to his gaze.

"Beautiful," he whispered under his breath.

She pulled off his T-shirt, smiling as she gazed at his broad chest, his perfect pecs, the strength in his arms and shoulders.

"Beautiful," she told him in return.

He smiled at that. "I like the way we're agreeing on things."

She trailed her fingers along his washboard stomach. "It's better when we get along."

"Much better."

"Let's see what else we can agree on."

"We're overdressed," he said.

She found herself grinning. She playfully hooked her thumbs under the waistband of her pants.

He did the same, and they both stripped off the last of their clothes.

"Better," he said, his gaze feasting on her.

"Better," she agreed, doing a visual tour of his magnificence.

"You're too far away," he said, taking her hand and drawing her to him.

"I can agree to that."

"You're talking too much."

"I don't think that's a—"

His lips descended on hers again.

Okay, she'd give him that one. The kiss bloomed between them, and she sank deeper into his embrace. His skin was hot against hers. She reveled in the feel of his contours, the dips and hollows, the bulges fitting so neatly against her own.

"You're so soft," he muttered.

"You're so hard."

He coughed out a surprised laugh.

"I didn't mean it that way." She paused, desire ramping up inside her at the feel of him. "Okay, maybe I did."

"We're still agreeing," he said. "I am hard, very hard, and I want you very much."

"I want you, too." She drew back to look into his eyes. "Very much."

He kissed her forehead, the tip of her nose, her cheek, then her temple, then he moved his way down her neck. "You smell amazing. You taste amazing."

She let her hands roam freely, covering him from his shoulders to his thighs, touching everything in between, while her heart rate sped up, her breathing accelerated and her skin heated in the breeze from an open window.

The traffic below was a steady hum. Caleb's breathing rushed past her ear. His phone pinged, but they both ignored it. The outside world meant nothing right now.

He took her hand, led her the few steps to the bed and swept back the covers.

She sat down on the crisp sheet, and he gently eased her back.

"Oh, this is going to be good," she said.

"I so agree."

His hot, heavy body covered hers. His hand closed over her breast, and the most intense, exquisite sensation zipped from her nipple to her abdomen.

She gasped.

"Good?" he asked, and he did it again before waiting for her answer.

She gave a small moan, and her hand clenched his shoulder, holding on to him as an anchor while the world began to spin around her.

Her hips arched, and she pulled him to her, watching his expression as their intimacy increased.

"Oh, Jules." His gray eyes darkened to pewter, and his free hand moved to the small of her back, tipping her to him.

Her entire world shifted to the touch of his body. He was hard and hot, and tantalizingly close. Nothing mattered. Nothing existed. Her primal brain clamored for the release he could bring.

She flexed, and he groaned, and their bodies melded together in perfect unison. He didn't pause in his motion, sliding in and out, gaining speed, then slowing down, then speeding up again.

She clung tight, letting him take her higher. Her legs wrapped around him. Her mouth sought his. And when they finally had to breathe, she kissed his neck, licking, tasting, drinking in the complex flavors that were Caleb.

Her hands gripped his back. He covered her breast. He kissed her mouth, probing deeply with his tongue while his thrusts grew harder and faster.

She felt herself float, go disembodied, beyond controlling her actions and reactions. She let it go, curled against him, felt the rush of desire hit a crescendo. Then she cried out his name, and his body stiffened. His guttural rasp echoed in the room as convulsions of pleasure overtook them both.

It took long minutes for Jules to spiral down. Caleb's

weight felt good. The warmth of his body was comforting. His breathing was raspy. She liked it. She also liked the solid beat of his heart that seemed to sync with her own.

"Should I move?" he asked, twirling his fingers through her hair.

"Not yet."

There was a smile in his voice. "I have to say, we're batting a thousand here."

"Maybe we should hold really still and stay quiet."

He chuckled. "Before we can mess anything up?"

"That's what I was thinking."

"There's absolutely nothing I want to fight with you about."

"Good."

He cradled her face and gave her a tender kiss.

She couldn't help but think that this was perfect. They were perfect in this moment, and all was right with the world.

"Can we just stay here forever?" she asked.

"It's worth a shot."

Holding Jules in his arms, Caleb had lain awake for a long time. For a while, he'd actually hoped she'd have a change of heart, and this could be the start of something between them.

But eventually, he'd fallen asleep, and in the morning she was gone. The door between the two rooms was closed tight.

On the drive back to Neo, he'd tried to broach the subject of their night together, but she'd cut him off, citing the terms of their deal. It was obvious, even now, three hours later, that she intended to stick to her guns.

He'd managed to retrieve her purse and cell phone. That, at least, earned him a smile.

She scrolled through her messages. "Six calls from my dad."

She pressed a button and put the phone to her ear.

Caleb knew he should walk away and give her some privacy. But his curiosity won out. While the engineers combed through the building, and the electricians and gas fitters readied their gear to get to work, he stayed put.

"Hi, Dad," she opened.

There was a pause.

"She did? She didn't need to call you." Jules glanced Caleb's way. "Everything turned out fine."

Caleb could easily guess the other side of that conversation.

"On business. I came here on business."

The voice on the other end was indistinct, and Caleb couldn't hear any words, but the tone was obviously impatient. Part of him wanted to take the phone and tell Roland Parker to back off already. Roland might be bitter about his upbringing and want to forget all about Whiskey Bay, but Jules didn't. She hadn't done anything wrong. She was an adult, and she didn't have to explain herself to him.

"Checking out the competition." She looked at Caleb again, her expression appearing decidedly guilty this time.

"It doesn't matter. The important thing is I'm fine."

She paused again.

"I am. There was some damage to a few businesses, but it's all repairable."

Caleb's gaze moved to the front of Neo. He sure hoped it was repairable. Although he supposed anything was repairable. It only depended on time and money.

"I'm going home today," she said.

Roland started talking again, or maybe it was shouting from the expression on Jules's face.

"Did she tell you that? Then she is. No, we're not coming home."

Jules pressed her lips tightly together as she listened. "Dad. Dad, stop. It's *our* money."

Caleb was itching to grab the phone again.

"We've been through all that." Jules turned her back on

Caleb, but she didn't walk away. "We both know how you feel about it, but nothing has changed. We're doing this. Goodbye, Dad."

A pause.

"Yes."

Another pause.

"No."

She turned back, shaking her head and gritting her teeth. "Maybe soon. Goodbye." She ended the call.

"Everything okay?" Caleb asked.

"It's fine."

"It didn't sound fine."

"That's just the way he is. Sometimes he frets. He's convinced I was hurt worse in the earthquake than Melissa admitted, and that I'm glossing over it."

"You want to send him a quick photo to show you're healthy?"

"Of me in front of Neo? Yeah, that'll throw gasoline on the fire."

"You should stop in and see him."

"When?"

"Now."

She frowned. "He's in Portland, Caleb."

"You're about to fly home."

"That's Olympia. I don't have a spare day to drive down to Portland. Are you trying to delay construction at the Crab Shack even more? Is that what last night was about?"

He gave her a hard look. "Last night had nothing to do with the Crab Shack or Neo or anything else related to business. And I sure didn't plan the earthquake. Hell, if I could do that, I wouldn't need Neo or anything else to make money."

She had the grace to look embarrassed. "Sorry."

He moved closer. "Don't be sorry. Last night was complicated."

"Which is why we agreed not to talk about it. I was wrong to bring it up."

"But now that you have…" He fought an urge to reach for her hands. He wanted to touch her. He felt like he had a right to touch her.

"No," she said sharply. "I didn't. I shouldn't. I won't do it again."

He regrouped, knowing this wasn't the time or place. "Obviously, I'm going to be here awhile, maybe a couple of days. You can take a cab to the airport and get the plane. I'll tell them to expect you. The jet will stop in Portland, and you can see your dad for an hour."

Her expression was incredulous. "The jet will stop in Portland?"

"It's on the way."

"So, what, we'll just pop down and land."

He fought a smile. "That's exactly how it works."

"And how do I explain it to my father?"

"Tell him you had a stopover. You don't have to go into detail." He fought an urge to ruffle her hair. "You know, you'd be the worst covert operative ever."

"And you'd be the best. That's one of the things that scares me about you. I can never tell what you're up to."

He softened his tone. "I like it that way."

"Don't." She meant don't get intimate.

"I won't. I'm sorry. I'll call you a cab. You don't have to wait around here any longer."

Much as he hated for her to go, she had to get back. And he had to get started assessing the damage.

Seven

Jules had practiced her lie over and over on the short taxi ride from the Portland airport to her father's town house. He was obviously baffled when he opened the door to find her on the porch.

"I had a stopover," she said, taking Caleb's advice and keeping the explanation short. "I thought I'd come by and say hi."

"What's wrong?"

"Nothing's wrong."

"You sounded funny on the phone."

"It was an unsettling night." She silently acknowledged to herself that it had been unsettling in far more ways than one. "Can I come in?"

"What kind of question is that?" He frowned as he stepped out of the way.

She realized it had been too much to expect that he'd be in a good mood. "I have an hour or so, and I thought we could talk."

"About what?"

"I've got some pictures of the construction." She opened her purse to retrieve her phone.

He waved her away as he closed the door behind them. "I don't want to see them."

"We've got a carpenter helping us. He's really good, and his prices are reasonable."

"You should come home. You should both come home, find real jobs, give up that run-down, ramshackle restaurant. There are a lot of nice men in Portland."

Jules mind went involuntarily to Caleb, and she quickly banished the picture.

"You know we want to do this, Dad. We think we can make it work, and we promised Grandpa."

"You should never have made that promise to your grandfather. And he should never have asked you. I should contest the will."

"You're not going to contest the will."

Although her father would have loved nothing better than to sell the land under the Crab Shack as well as her grandfather's house, no court in the country would overturn the will, and he knew it.

"You're going to lose all your money."

Jules took a seat in the compact living room. "We told you, we're willing to take that chance."

"You dragged your little sister along on this misadventure."

Jules clenched her purse on her lap. "Melissa is perfectly capable of making up her own mind."

"She follows you. She always has."

"But she argues with me when she doesn't agree."

Roland scoffed. "Don't give me that. You know you're the one in charge."

"I'm not—" Jules stopped herself, realizing the futility of going around and around on the issue.

"I wanted you to know I was fine, that we're doing fine. I thought you might be worried."

"When I think of the two of you next door to *that family*," he spat.

"It's only Caleb now. Kedrick moved to Arizona."

Her father pounced. "How do you know that?"

She realized she'd made a mistake. "It's a small neighborhood."

Roland's eyes narrowed. "That's a lot of detail."

"It's not."

"How did you hear so much about that family?"

"We've run into Caleb and a few of the other neighbors." She tried to move the conversation past the Watfords. "Matt

Emerson owns the marina now and lives in the house above. It's really grown. And TJ Bauer bought the O'Hara's place and rebuilt. Ours is the only original house left."

"The land is worth a fortune by now. Selling is the only logical choice."

Something in his tone gave Jules pause.

"Do you need money?" She hadn't thought of it from that angle before.

Her father had never made a lot as a hardware store manager. They'd never talked much about money, in general. She and her sister had grown up in a very modest household without any extras.

He glared at her. "I can take care of myself."

"It was your family home."

Her grandfather might have willed it to Jules and Melissa, but her father had an equal moral call on the money tied up in the property—which was the only family legacy the Parkers had.

"This is about you and your foolish idea, and my father's irresponsible decision to have his pipe dream cross generations. As your father, it's my responsibility to save you from yourself."

Jules felt her spine stiffen. She loved her father, but he was irrational when it came to Whiskey Bay, and he was just plain wrong on this. It was a dream worth pursuing.

She realized she shouldn't have come here. She'd thought she might be able to make it a bit better. But she was only making it worse. She made a show of looking at her watch, and she came to her feet.

"As an adult, it's my responsibility to make my own decisions."

"You don't know these people."

She knew them better than he could ever imagine. She didn't trust Caleb, but she did know him, intimately. Last night tried to rush back into her brain, but she fought it off.

"I know me, and I know Melissa, and I know what

Grandpa wanted. I'm doing the right thing, Dad. I hope you'll see that someday."

"I hope I'm not around long enough to see you ruined."

"Can you at least have a little faith?"

He didn't answer.

She gave a sad smile, crossed to his chair and bent down for a quick hug. "I hope you're around for a long, long time."

He gave a grunt.

She left the town house and headed for the corner where she could hail a cab. Her father's harsh words fought with an image of Caleb.

Last night might turn out to be one of her biggest regrets in life, but it was also one of her most fantastic experiences. And right now it was a balm to everything else.

She stopped fighting and let the memories of Caleb crowd in.

Caleb had spent nearly a week in San Francisco. Jules invaded his thoughts at every turn, while he ensured the building was safe and the repairs got underway. His marketing staff was busy planning an exciting reopening event, and the community support had been enormous. As soon as things were under control, he left the manager in charge and flew back to Whiskey Bay.

Back home, his first interest was definitely Jules, so he made his way down to the Crab Shack.

Coming up on the building, he couldn't believe what he was seeing.

It was Jules. She was on the roof. Noah was up there with her, tools hanging from his belt as he set up the first row of cedar shingles.

"Hi, Caleb," Melissa greeted him, coming out onto the patio.

Noah turned and looked down.

"That's not happening," Caleb said to Noah, nodding his head in Jules direction.

"She's not using the nail gun," Melissa said.

"She's coming down *right now*," Caleb said in a booming voice that caught Jules's attention.

"It's not hard," she told him, walking down a plank on the steep pitch toward the edge of the roof.

"Stay back from the edge," he warned her.

She seemed completely unconcerned. "I'm not going to fall off the roof."

"Get her down from there," he told Noah.

"I work for her," Noah said.

"Noah wanted to hire an assistant to do the roof," Melissa said to Caleb.

"We don't need to pay for an assistant," Jules said.

"This is ridiculous." Caleb marched to the ladder and began climbing.

"Go away," Jules told him. "This is none of your concern."

He wanted to argue that it was most definitely his concern. Since last weekend, everything about her felt like it was his concern. He wasn't about to stand back and watch her get hurt or worse.

"Come down, Jules."

Her expression turned mulish as she crossed her arms over her chest. She looked adorable in dusty blue jeans, a red plaid shirt and leather work boots. Her braid stuck out of a red baseball cap, and she had a measuring tape clipped onto her waistband.

He wanted to take a picture. More than that, he wanted to throw her over his shoulder and carry her like a fireman down the ladder. Then maybe he'd keep going, all the way to his house, all the way to his bed, where he'd strip off those work clothes and join her in his tile shower.

He stepped onto the roof. "I'll be the assistant."

He didn't have a ton of time to spare, but there was no way he was risking her.

"We don't want your help," she said. "And we don't trust your help. You'll probably put holes in my roof."

"I'm not going to put holes in your roof." Grateful that he'd worn treaded hikers, he walked up the pitch of the roof.

Noah watched from the sidelines, apparently content to let them work it out between themselves.

"You are going to listen to reason," Caleb told her.

"You're not being reasonable."

"You're a complete novice and roofing is dangerous. How is that not reasonable?"

"This isn't your restaurant, it's mine. I'll be careful, and Noah's doing most of the work."

"You're just as high off the ground as he is. You don't have to be operating a nail gun to fall twenty-five feet."

"I'll stay away from..." Her expression shifted, turning resolute. "Hang on. I don't need to justify this to you. It's my decision."

"Get down off the roof, Jules." There was no way he was leaving her up here.

"Or what?"

"Or I'll carry you off."

"Yeah, right."

"Look at my face. Do you think I'm bluffing?"

"I think you're trespassing."

"You want to go that route?" Once again, he was confronted by her intellect. She was way too smart. Why did she always have to make things so hard for him?

"Yes, I do," she said.

"You can."

"I know I can."

"But what about this?" He was fully aware that brute force wasn't going to succeed. "I help Noah up here, and you help Melissa down there. You get my free labor and the irony that goes with that."

It was obvious his offer gave her pause.

"You'll get more done," he said.

"Stop making sense."

He fought a smirk. "I'm only forced to do that because you're so stubborn."

"I'm not stubborn. I'm independent."

"Noah?" Caleb called over his shoulder. "Would you rather have Jules help you or me help you?"

"You have any idea what you're doing?" Noah asked.

"Yes."

"Then you."

"I've got Noah's vote," Caleb said to Jules.

"Since when is this a democracy?"

"He's right," Melissa called from the patio. "We'll get more done if Caleb helps us."

Jules kept her gaze on Caleb while she answered. "He's up to something. Watfords don't help you. They stab you in the back."

Caleb blew out a breath of frustration. "You honestly think I had time in the past five minutes to come up with a master plot to do you some kind of harm by roofing?"

"You've got the cunning gene."

He pulled out his phone. "Tell you what. I'll sweeten the deal." He pressed Matt's speed dial. "I'll get us another guy and speed things up even more."

"Who are you calling?" she asked, but Caleb was already speaking to Matt.

He quickly sketched out the problem and ended the call. "Matt's heading over," he told Noah.

Jules's face had gone a shade darker with her anger. She was even prettier if that was possible.

"You are an unbelievable bully," she told him.

He leaned in close, lowering his voice. "Now that I've seen that beautiful body, I can't bear the thought of anything happening to it."

She sucked in a breath of obvious shock.

He pulled back and put a hand on her shoulder. "Please get down off the roof, Jules. It's more dangerous than you know. And I truly don't want you to get hurt."

"He's right," Noah said. "Facts are facts. We've got two capable volunteers, it makes sense they should do the work up here."

"Okay," Jules said tightly, clearly reluctant to give in to logic and reason. Then she leaned close to Caleb's ear. "Don't you *dare* bring that up again."

She was right to be annoyed. He truly wanted to keep his promise to leave San Francisco in San Francisco. But he wasn't sure if he could. They'd made love. He couldn't undo it, and he sure couldn't forget it.

She was in his head and under his skin. He liked her, and he desired her. In his weaker moments, he found himself contemplating a relationship with her. But that wasn't about to happen. They were locked in a battle only one of them could win.

She climbed down the ladder and disappeared inside with Melissa.

"I wasn't sure which way that would go," Noah said to Caleb.

"Neither was I."

"She definitely doesn't trust you."

"Yet, she trusts you." Caleb glanced around to see shingle bundles and strips of flashing.

"I'm not trying to destroy her business."

"I've never killed anybody." As soon as the taunt was out, Caleb regretted it.

But Noah seemed to take it in stride. "Put that on your résumé, do you?"

"That was out of line."

Noah gave a shrug. "Nothing I haven't heard before."

Caleb hesitated over his next words. But because it was all wrapped up in Jules, he dived in. "I'll understand if you don't want to tell me what happened."

Noah extracted a blade from his tool belt and headed for a bundle of shingles. "It was my stepfather. He attacked my sixteen-year-old sister. I stepped in and stopped him, and he grabbed a knife." Noah raised his bare forearm. "I got a scar, and he hit his head on the way down."

"So, totally self-defense." Caleb couldn't understand why Noah had gone to jail at all.

"My sister mentally blocked the attack, so I didn't have a witness."

"Did she ever remember?" Caleb was thinking Noah might be able to get his record expunged.

"I hope she never does."

"Okay, now I trust you, too."

Noah gave a wry smile. "Not my priority, but I'll take it."

"I'm trying to find a way through this, you know." For some reason Caleb wanted to explain himself to Noah.

"Nothing to do with me," Noah said, shifting the bundle of shingles.

"She's better off with Neo down the street than being out here all on her own."

"You mean they're better off?"

"Yes, them. I meant both of them." Caleb hoped Noah wasn't too perceptive. But just in case, he gave himself some cover. "Melissa's been the reasonable one all along. I think part of her is on my side."

Noah scoffed a bit at that.

Caleb found himself curious. "You don't agree?"

Had Melissa said something to Noah? Was she only humoring Caleb by seeming agreeable?

"She knows her own mind," Noah said, cutting the black straps that held the shingles in a bundle.

"Has she said something? About me, my offer, Neo?"

"She admires your success with Neo."

Caleb guessed there was more to that statement. "But?"

"She's excited about the Crab Shack, and she's loyal to her sister."

"But she *can* see there's a path forward with me?"

If Melissa could understand what was in everyone's best interest, there was still a chance she'd help convince Jules.

"I don't know what you think she's told me," Noah said. "We're not exactly best pals. I work, she... Well, she does as much as she can. But she's here every day, and she never complains."

"And, Jules?" Despite himself, Caleb had to ask.

"Jules is a force of nature."

Caleb couldn't help but chuckle at that. He didn't disagree.

"If I was you, I'd give her whatever she wants."

"If I give her what she wants, it'll cost me a million dollars and my dream."

Noah paused at that, a considering expression on his face. "Might be worth it in the end."

Caleb narrowed his gaze, trying to penetrate Noah's poker face. Had he somehow guessed at Caleb's feelings for Jules?

That was impossible, because Caleb didn't have feelings for Jules. Okay, he had *feelings* for her. But a million dollars and his life's dream? After only one night? Not a chance.

While the sun was setting over the ocean, TJ Bauer had arrived at the Crab Shack carrying boxes of pizza and a bag of soft drinks. Jules found it hard not to like Caleb's friends. She didn't know why Matt had dropped everything at the marina today to help out, and TJ acted like it was the most natural thing in the world to spring for dinner for a group of people, half of whom he barely knew.

They were all good-humored about the situation, concerned about Melissa's healing hand and even joking with Noah.

TJ had set the food on the drop cloth–covered bar and invited everyone to dig in. Jules would admit to being starving. She'd scooped a slice of Hawaiian and plunked into a chair near one of the picture windows, setting a cold can of cola on the wide sill.

Caleb approached, using his foot to push a second chair close to her.

"I feel like I need to thank you," she said as she took a first bite.

The three men had finished over half the roof today.

"But you're not feeling grateful?" he asked as he sat down.

"What I'm feeling is confused." She'd been mulling the possible reasons for his help all day, but had come up with nothing. "This seems out of character for you."

"What makes you think you know anything about my character?"

She bought herself some time by taking a bite of the pizza. It was heavenly. She didn't want to insult him. He'd been a huge help today, as had Matt. But she didn't trust him either. Nothing he did would come without strings attached.

She composed an answer in her head. "I know you're willing to put me out of business."

He shook his head. "I'm trying very hard not to do that."

"Pretend all you want, Caleb, but you're threatening to close my road."

"I haven't done it yet. And I don't want to. I've told you that."

"I don't believe you."

"What part don't you believe?"

"That you care anything about me. You want what you want, and you don't care how you get it."

He stretched out his legs, leaning back in his chair. "Think that statement through, Jules."

"Don't patronize me." There was nothing wrong with her thought processes.

He took a bite of his pizza and followed it up with a swallow of his soda.

She hesitated for a minute, but then did the same. She was tired and she was hungry, and arguing with Caleb wasn't going to get her anywhere. She let her gaze wander the room.

Noah was talking with Matt, while Melissa seemed to be engrossed in something TJ was saying. Noah was playing it cool, but his attention kept flicking to Melissa. It was obvious he was attracted to her, but so far he hadn't made any kind of a move. He was polite, but he didn't flirt, and he didn't seek her out.

"Did you tell Melissa?" Caleb asked.

"Tell her what?"

He didn't answer, and she turned to look at him. His expression made it clear where his thoughts had gone.

Jules fought annoyance. Then she fought arousal.

She bit down hard on the pizza. She wasn't going to do this. *They* weren't going to do this. Her tone was tart when she spoke. "Why would I tell her about something that never happened?"

"I thought sisters shared things."

"Irrelevant information? No, we don't share that."

"You can't seriously pretend it never happened."

"Yes, I can."

That had been their deal. It had been crystal clear, and he'd agreed to it.

"Okay," he said, amusement in his voice.

"This is what I mean about your character," she said, feeling the need to fight. "You say one thing, and then you do the opposite."

"I've had a week to think about it."

"You're exactly like your grandfather. A gentleman's agreement, a handshake deal means nothing to you."

He lowered his voice. "You and I are not a couple of gentlemen, and we did a heck of a lot more than shake hands."

"*You're* certainly not a gentleman."

"At least I'm honest."

She huffed out an exclamation of incredulity.

"I can't stop thinking about you, Jules."

"Can we just eat our pizza?" She hadn't stopped thinking about him either. But she had to stop. She had to find a way to get back on an even keel. Too much depended on her keeping her distance from him.

"Are you going to tell me it meant nothing to you?" he asked.

She desperately wished she could. "It meant what it meant. It was a thing at a time and a place, and that's that."

"I have no idea what you just said."

"I just told you to back off. A deal is a deal, and we made one, and I expect you to honor it."

"Circumstances change," he said.

She got to her feet. She couldn't do this anymore.

"Matt," she said in a bright voice, walking toward him. "Thank you so much for helping today. I can't believe how much work you guys got done."

"My pleasure," he said.

"It can't have been a pleasure. It was eighty-five degrees out there."

"I'm happy to help out. I'll be back tomorrow to finish."

"You don't need to do that. You must have a lot of work at the marina."

Matt's glance went past her shoulder, obviously looking for a signal from Caleb.

"I insist," Matt said smoothly. "We're neighbors, after all."

Feeling suddenly uneasy, Jules glanced to TJ to find he was closely watching the exchange. She turned sideways to catch Caleb in her peripheral vision. There was an undercurrent in the room.

She felt like she was missing something. She probably was. Nobody was this neighborly without an ulterior motive. Stopping by with a Bundt cake, sure, but reroofing a building?

They all looked innocent, maybe too innocent.

"It'll save you a whole lot of money," Noah said.

"You're such a huge help," Melissa put in cheerfully.

If there was an undercurrent, it was clear Melissa wasn't picking up on it.

"We can't impose on you," Jules said.

Melissa moved to take her by the arm. "Why are you being so difficult?"

"I'm not being difficult." The real question was why Melissa was accepting their help so easily.

"They're going to finish our roof."

"They're going to want something in return." Jules moved her gaze to Caleb. "I don't trust any of them."

Melissa frowned in reproach. "Now, that's just rude."

"You're looking for something that isn't there," Caleb said.

"No strings attached," Matt said.

"All I did was bring pizza," TJ said.

"I should pay you for that." Jules moved from Melissa, glancing around the room for her bag. She'd tossed it somewhere this morning.

She felt Caleb's arm slip under hers. "Stop," he whispered in her ear.

She paused. She took in the four other faces in the room. TJ looked affronted. Matt looked amused. Melissa seemed embarrassed, and even Noah looked surprised.

She realized none of them knew about her and Caleb. None of them knew how precarious her hold on independence had become. None of them knew that with every second that passed he entwined himself more tightly into hers and Melissa's lives.

He might have promised not to cozy up to her sister, but he was still being extraordinarily nice to her. He seemed to think that if he did it in front of everyone, he wasn't breaking his promise.

Jules tried to remember their exact words when she'd agreed to the date. But she couldn't. And she couldn't hold him to something she didn't remember for certain.

She centered herself and decided it was best to let things slide. She'd regroup later.

"Fine," she told them all. "Thank you all very much. Your help is making a big difference."

Everybody smiled, and Jules forced herself to smile in return. But something terrible was going to happen. She could feel it in her bones.

"Are you saying you're ready to pull the pin?" Matt asked Caleb.

It was morning nearly two weeks later, and the two men were on the Whiskey Bay Marina pier where Matt had just finished a pre-charter inspection of one of his largest yachts, *Orca's Run*.

"Bernard has the paperwork ready for me to sign."

"But?" Matt seemed to spot something on the dock in front of him.

He crouched down and pulled his multitool from the case on his belt.

"Would you do it?" Caleb asked.

He'd lain awake last night mapping the likely outcomes of his rescinding the Crab Shack's easement. The lawyers, a protracted court case, Jules's anger, her disappointment, her eventual bankruptcy because she'd spend all her money fighting him.

Why on earth did she have to be so stubborn?

"I'd have done it already." Matt tightened the bolts on a piece of stainless steel mooring hardware.

"You would?" The answer surprised Caleb.

Matt wasn't a hard-nosed man. He was normally more compassionate than Caleb. TJ, now, TJ saw the world in dollar signs alone.

"If all I cared about was my business." Matt rose. "And I *know* how much you care about the Whiskey Bay Neo location."

Caleb gazed over the sparkling waves, wondering if he was being a fool. "I can't bring myself to destroy her."

"You've given her options A, B and C."

"More than once."

"She knows the risks."

"I keep thinking there has to be an option D or an option E. There must be something I haven't thought of that'll break the impasse."

Matt's mechanic Tasha Lowell approached along the dock. "I've signed off on *Orca's Run*," she said to Matt.

"Tip-top shape?" Matt asked her. "It's for a beachhead client from the Berlin show."

"I'm aware of that."

"The guy has contacts all over Europe. He has influence, and can send us dozens of new clients. We need this cruise to go off without a hitch."

She gazed at the sky, as if praying for strength. "I know that. That captain knows that. *Everybody* knows that."

"Is that sass?"

"It's an update," she said.

"It sounded like sass."

"Well, you're stressing everybody out. Chef Morin was just yelling at the steward, something about Alaskan king crab. Poor kid nearly wet his pants."

Matt's gaze went to the office building. "Do I need to—"

"Gads, *no*," Tasha said. "Stay out of the way."

Caleb couldn't help enjoying the exchange. Tasha might be rough around the edges, but she was also smart and fearless. Caleb liked that.

"I am the boss," Matt said.

Caleb couldn't resist. "If you have to point that fact out, something's not working for you."

He caught Tasha's smirk. Her green eyes lit up, and he suddenly realized that under that baseball cap she was quite pretty.

"You're a girl," he began, thinking this might be an opportunity to get some advice.

She immediately seemed to take offense. "Excuse me?"

He wasn't quite sure where he'd gone wrong with the simple statement. "You're female."

She widened her stance in her canvas, multipocketed work pants. "Your point?"

Caleb didn't know what he'd been thinking. Tasha wasn't going to have any insight into how to handle Jules. The fact that he'd even thought of asking her showed how desperate he'd become.

"Caleb is having woman trouble," Matt said.

Caleb shot his friend a glare. "You're not helping."

Tasha pressed her lips together, as if she was holding back a retort.

"It's a business deal," Caleb told Tasha, deciding since he'd come this far, he might as well give it a shot. "I've offered a reasonable compromise, but she's set on mutual annihilation."

"My best guess? It's not a good compromise. It favors you. You're deluding yourself that it doesn't, but she knows that it does."

Caleb took offense to the assessment. "It's the *only* solution."

"Are you looking for my advice, or asking me the secret to changing a stubborn woman's mind?"

Matt laughed, and they both glared at him. He quickly turned the sound into a cough. "She's got you pegged."

"We women aren't stubborn," Tasha said. "We're smart. It just rattles you guys when we're also self-interested. My guess is she's right, but you don't want to admit it."

Apparently having said her piece, Tasha turned her attention back to Matt. "*Orca's Run* is mechanically sound. You should back off now and let everybody do their jobs."

She gave both men a nod.

Caleb watched her walk away. "Well, that was…"

"Emasculating? It happens to me all the time."

"I was thinking illuminating."

"You agreed with her?" Matt sounded surprised.

"I agreed with what she said to you. You do tend to meddle sometimes."

"Ha. I agreed with what she said to you. It's making you nuts that Jules is standing up to you."

Matt was wrong there. Caleb had no problem with someone standing up for their own business interests. What was frustrating him was his hesitation to stand up for his own because he had feelings for Jules.

"I slept with her," he said.

Matt did a double take. *"What?"*

Matt was a brilliant man and a good friend. Caleb knew he wasn't going to be able to give Caleb decent advice unless Caleb was honest.

"In San Francisco," Caleb continued. "She made me promise to forget it happened, and I can't get her out of my mind."

"Wow."

"That's an understatement."

"She slept with you? Was it because of the earthquake?"

"Are you asking if I took advantage of her vulnerability after she was terrified for her life?"

Matt seemed to reconsider. "No. Of course not. You wouldn't do something like that."

"She likes me. I mean, on some level, I know she must like me. She's definitely attracted to me. And she hates that. She fights it tooth and nail. She's really funny. And she's really smart. And sassy. Unlike you, I like sassy. Sassy is sexy."

"I like sassy, too."

That caught Caleb's attention. "Tasha?"

Matt looked surprised. "No. Tasha's...different. And we're not talking about me. Are you falling for Jules?"

Caleb reached out to brace his hand against a pillar. "I don't know what I'm doing. If she was anybody else, I'd revoke the easement, meet her in court, drain her resources until she was willing to make a deal."

"But she's not someone else."

"That's" my problem. I don't want her to hate me. And I

don't want to destroy her. Deep down, I'm hoping for the Crab Shack to succeed. Beyond Jules, there would be a certain justice in that for her grandfather."

"Your family really did pull a number on the Parkers."

"According to Jules, it might be even worse than I thought."

"Yeah?"

"My father." Caleb hesitated to share too much of what Jules had told him. He didn't care about his father's reputation, but it wasn't really his story to tell. "Let's just say Roland Parker might have had a really good reason to throw the first punch."

"Why doesn't that surprise me?"

"Because you've met my father?"

The wind blustered across the dock, and the line of gleaming white yachts bobbed against the bumpers, making hollow clunks on the incoming tide.

"What are you going to do?" Matt asked.

"I truly don't know. I'd considered reasoning with Melissa."

"Melissa seems great."

"She's the more reasonable of the two. But Jules warned me off, and I promised I wouldn't try to co-opt Melissa."

"Why would you promise that?"

"It was the only way to get Jules to come to San Francisco."

There was amusement in Matt's tone. "You bargained away your best play to spend time with Jules?"

"I did." It was as simple as that.

He'd wanted to be alone with Jules, but it sure hadn't worked out the way he'd expected.

It had been better, so much better. It had been amazing. But the aftermath was killing him.

Eight

It wasn't the first time Jules appreciated the pot lights along the trail from the Crab Shack to the house. It was nearly nine o'clock and full-on dark as she and Melissa made their way home. The sky was black, and the wind was coming up, a storm moving in from the Pacific.

The distinctive sound of Noah's pickup truck faded to nothing behind them as he turned off their access road and headed up to the highway. They'd been refinishing the wood floor today, and the work was heavy. Jules was tired, focusing on putting one foot in front of the other and wishing they had a proper bathtub at home. She'd give a lot for an hour-long soak before she fell into bed.

Her mind went on a tangent to the giant tub at the hotel in San Francisco. But she quickly banished the memory. The last thing she wanted to think about was Caleb.

"Did something happen when you visited Dad?" Melissa asked her.

The question seemed to come out of the blue.

"What do you mean?"

"You've been off. And I realize it's since you got back. You're a little blue and unhappy. Did he get inside your head?"

"Nothing more than usual." Jules didn't want to consider the lingering memories of sleeping with Caleb might be affecting her. "Dad blames me for leading you astray."

"You know that's not true."

Jules linked her arm with Melissa's. "Sometimes I wonder. If it wasn't for me, would you be here?"

Melissa could use her business degree in any number of industries. Jules was the one who'd become a chef. She was the one who'd spent hours as a teenager sitting inside the closed-down Crab Shack, musing on its possibilities. And she was the one who'd promised her grandfather they'd reopen.

"I suppose you are the more passionate of the two of us."

The answer gave Jules pause. "Are you having second thoughts?"

"No. Not second thoughts. But you have to admit, we're in pretty deep financially. And lately you seem so tired."

"I'm not tired. Okay, I'm tired right now. But that's from working on the floor all day long."

The trail became steeper as they approached their house.

"Are you sure that's all it is?" Melissa asked.

"I'm positive." If Jules was coming across as blue, she was simply going to readjust her attitude. She wasn't truly blue, and there was nothing messing with her enthusiasm for the Crab Shack, not Caleb or anything else.

"Because we have options, you know."

Unease rose in Jules. She slowed to a stop, turning to face Melissa. "What do you mean we have options?"

Had Caleb somehow gotten to Melissa? If he had, there was going to be trouble, Jules vowed.

Melissa kept walking as if they were having a perfectly ordinary conversation, and Jules had no choice but to move with her.

"Noah said something interesting today. I was talking to him. Okay, I was flirting with him. But I think I'm losing my touch. I'm acting like a schoolgirl, and it's like he's completely oblivious."

"You really have a thing for him, don't you?" Jules's heart went out to her sister, and she relaxed a bit, far more comfortable with the topic of Noah than with any talk of options for the Crab Shack.

"Who wouldn't? He's so, I don't know, solid, laid-back. Nothing rattles that guy. You've seen that, right?"

Noah was always there, lifting, carrying, power tools

reverberating through the building. He'd become background noise.

"I can't say that I've paid all that much attention." Jules was usually focused on what she was doing herself.

"He's so efficient," Melissa continued. "He makes it look easy, but he gets a ton of work done."

Jules agreed with that. "We're lucky we hired him."

"And his hands. I have a thing for his hands. They're so capable. You know, scarred, callused, big, über-sexy."

Jules couldn't help but smile at her sister's confession.

"But he won't notice me." Melissa sounded both earnest and sorry for herself. "Why won't he notice me?"

"Maybe you're trying too hard. Guys usually want what they can't have." Jules shrugged. "Maybe don't be so obvious. Let him chase you for a while."

"And if he doesn't?"

"You're no further behind."

"Hmm. I could try that. I have to say, he did come up with a good idea."

"Tell me." Jules felt like a better big sister than she had a few minutes ago.

"Noah thinks we should consider selling to Caleb."

Jules stopped dead on the pathway. "Sell Caleb the Crab Shack? Why would we do that? Why would he even want it? We're not in the market to sell. We're in the market to succeed. What's Noah even talking about?"

"He figures Caleb would easily give us jobs at Neo. You could be a chef. I could go into management. We could make it part of the deal that he had to give us careers."

Jules couldn't believe what she was hearing. "We'd bribe Caleb to employ us? We'd help *the Watfords* make Neo even more successful and give up the Crab Shack?" She tried to imagine her grandfather's reaction. "You know Caleb would bulldoze the place."

Had Melissa lost her mind?

"We need to be realistic." Melissa's voice was small.

"We are being realistic."

"Are we? We didn't count on court costs."

Jules swallowed. "We'll manage."

"Noah says—"

"What's with Noah? He's a carpenter. What does he know about running a restaurant? I know you're attracted to him, but you're the one with the business degree."

The hurt expression on Melissa's face was clear. "This has nothing to do with me being attracted to him."

Jules immediately felt terrible. "I'm sorry. I'm just trying to figure out why Noah would…" And then it hit her. This wasn't Noah's idea.

This idea had Caleb written all over it. It played right into his hand. Caleb had to be using Noah as an unwitting conduit to Melissa, and Melissa as a conduit to Jules.

Jules closed her eyes and gave her head a shake.

"I'm sorry," she told Melissa, re-centering herself and opening her eyes. There was no point in addressing this with anyone but Caleb. Everyone else was perfectly innocent. "It's an interesting suggestion," she continued. "And I shouldn't have gotten upset like that. But I don't think we need to give up. Not yet. The easement case may go more smoothly than we're anticipating. Caleb could even be bluffing."

Melissa looked decidedly hesitant. "You think?"

"It's a possibility. Let's not make any rash decisions." They were in front of their house, but Jules was too restless to go inside. "You know, I'm going to walk awhile longer."

"You're mad at me."

Jules shook her head. "I'm not mad. I'm sorry if I sounded mad. This is your decision as much as it is mine."

"It was only an idea."

"And I only need to clear my head. I'll just walk."

"If you're sure."

"I'm sure. I'll see you in a while."

Jules wasn't angry with Melissa. She wasn't even angry

with Noah. There was only one person to blame for this, and he had a lot of explaining to do.

Caleb didn't often drink brandy. Beer was his bar beverage of choice. Wine was nice with an elegant dinner, and he enjoyed the occasional single malt.

Brandy was soothing. He supposed it wasn't often that he needed to be soothed.

He'd signed the paperwork tonight. Tomorrow Bernard would take the documents to the land office and rescind the easement for the Crab Shack. Then, it would be up to Jules to take him to court. She'd need a lawyer. And it would cost her money she didn't have. And she would probably never forgive him.

Slumped on the sofa in his living room, he stared out at the ocean. Rather, he stared in the direction of the ocean. The clouds were thick tonight, rain splattering on his windows, splashing on the dimly lit deck. Jazz floated from his speakers. The volume was low. Again, it was soothing.

He took another drink of the brandy, hoping it wouldn't turn to acid in his stomach.

Someone banged on his door. The sound was jarring and annoying.

He glanced at his watch, wondering who would stop by. Matt and TJ wouldn't knock, and other people would phone or text first.

The sharp, rapid knock came again.

He set down the snifter and rolled to his feet. He supposed an interruption wasn't the worst thing in the world. Whatever it was might take his mind off his guilt for a moment.

He followed the hall to the foyer and swung open the door.

It was Jules.

She was wet from the rain that was now streaming down

hard, and she looked angry. Her glare was punctuated by a rumble of thunder behind her.

"What's wrong?" he asked.

He knew she couldn't possibly know about the easement. Only he and Bernard were aware that he'd signed the documents.

"I need you to be honest with me."

"Honest about what?" He wouldn't let himself believe it was the easement.

"About using Noah to push your agenda."

Caleb was baffled by the statement. "Come in," he said instead of responding.

She walked stiffly through the doorway, her hair wet, her T-shirt clinging to her body.

"We had a deal," she said. "You promised."

"Jules, you're soaking wet. Come in and dry off."

"Who cares if I'm wet? Being wet is nothing."

He ducked into the guest bathroom and retrieved a towel, holding it out to her.

She didn't take it. "How could you?"

"What do you think I did?" He resisted an urge to dry her hair.

"Don't play dumb, Caleb."

"I'm not playing anything." He looped the towel around her shoulders.

She grasped the ends and backed away from him. "I'm talking about Noah, about how you manipulated him. He's now told Melissa that selling you the Crab Shack is our best move."

Caleb rolled the idea around in his head. It was quite brilliant, but it wasn't his idea. Why hadn't he thought of it? He could buy the place outright, and solve every one of his problems. Jules and Melissa would have the money to start any business they liked.

"I didn't suggest that to Noah," he said.

"Come on, Caleb. I knew you offering free labor to fix

the roof was too good to be true. You had two full days up there, you and Matt, to co-opt Noah to your cause."

"I *didn't*. We didn't." Caleb wouldn't have done it covertly. "If I wanted to buy your property, I'd have come out and asked you."

The words seemed to give her pause. "I wish I could believe that."

"You can."

She looked miserable.

"Are you okay?" he asked.

"No." She stiffened. "I'm *not* okay. You're trying to destroy my dream."

He couldn't argue with that. He was trying to destroy her business, and along with it her dream. But Noah had nothing to do with it.

"I've been up-front with you," he said. "All along, I've been honest about my desires and my intentions. Why would I go behind your back now? Why would I use Noah—who I barely know, by the way. Why?"

"Because you thought it would work."

"Rescinding the easement will work."

"It won't get you out of the noncompete."

"But it'll trap you in a corner." He gave in to his impulse, removed the towel from her shoulders and pressed it to her wet hair. "You'll give in. You'll have no choice."

Surprisingly, she didn't seem to notice what he was doing. "I could win in court."

"You're not going to win, Jules. You'll be bankrupt before the first hearing. I have a simple path forward—why would I use Noah?"

She seemed to hesitate again. "Speed?"

"I hadn't thought of that. It might be faster. But I didn't do it. Whatever your sister said, whatever Noah told her, it had nothing to do with me. I worked on your roof to keep you from potentially killing yourself. Period. That's it. That's all I did."

Her shoulders drooped. "So Noah's against me, too?"

Caleb stopped rubbing her hair, and draped the towel around her shoulders again.

"Noah's trying to help you. He sees the impossibility of your situation."

"It's not impossible." She pressed her lips together. "It can't be impossible."

Caleb told himself to take his gaze off her lips.

She raised her blue eyes to look at him. They were glimmering. "And Melissa?" she asked. "How does she feel? She brought me the idea."

Caleb wasn't sure how to answer that. He tried to be gentle. "It sounds like she wants to sell. She may not be as committed as you."

He couldn't help but hope they would take Noah's suggestion and consider selling. Then he wouldn't have to be the bad guy. He wouldn't have to cancel the easement. He could call Bernard and tell him to stand down. His heart lifted at the possibility. He couldn't help it.

"How do I fight?" Jules asked, her voice breaking. "I'm fighting you. I'm fighting my dad. How do I fight Melissa, too?"

Caleb gave in and pulled her into his arms.

To his surprise, she came willingly, burrowing her head against his shoulder.

Jules couldn't believe she was crying. But stubborn tears seeped silently out of the corners of her eyes, soaking into Caleb's shirtfront. She accepted that he wasn't lying. She was under siege by everyone around her. For the first time, she considered that she might be wrong, she might completely fail. Her heart hurt for her grandfather.

She desperately tried to control her emotions, to slow the deluge of tears. Falling apart in front of Caleb was the worst thing she could do. But she couldn't seem to stop, and she couldn't seem to give up the comfort of his embrace.

It was as if he was two different men. When she was close to him, he seemed rock solid and compassionate. All she wanted to do was lean on him. She couldn't even picture the alter ego that was undermining everything she did. Then when she walked away, she couldn't see his kindness. From a distance he was nothing but an enemy.

She needed to walk away now. She needed some distance. But he was hugging her tight, and she needed another minute, just another few minutes while she gathered her strength.

"It's okay," he whispered, kissing her hair.

"It's not." She hated the quaver in her voice. "It's not okay."

"You can take a break from fighting."

"I can't."

"Just for a minute. Relax." His hands rubbed over her back.

She felt her body soften. Her limbs grew suddenly heavy, and the flutter in her stomach turned to a dull ache.

He must have sensed her weakness because he scooped her into his arms.

She didn't have the strength to protest. She kept her eyes shut and focused on the security of his arms. There would be plenty of time to fight with him later.

He moved to the sofa and sat down, settling her on his lap.

The storm was full-blown now, rain clattering against the big windows, nearly drowning out the soft music in the background.

She sat still, feeling the beat of his heart, letting the thunder and the rhythm of the rain roll over her. He didn't say a word. His chest rose and fell, and the heat of him seeped into her damp clothes.

After a long time, she tipped her head back to look at him. He gazed directly into her eyes. His expression was compassionate, and his gray eyes were opaque.

He brushed his thumb across her cheek.

Then he smoothed back her hair.

He dipped his lips forward, slowly and steadily moving toward hers.

Her heart rate increased, deepening, steadying. She could taste his lips before they even touched hers. They were amazing, fantastic, breathtaking.

Then he kissed her, and the world seemed to convulse around her heart. Her body strained against him. Her arms went around him. And she opened to his kiss as sound roared in her ears.

He eased slightly back. "Is this okay?"

"No. It's not. It can't be." She felt his arm tighten around her. "But don't stop," she whispered.

"We'll work it out."

"We won't. But that's someplace else. It's something else. This is just this."

He kissed her again.

It suddenly felt as if her damp clothes were cloying. She impatiently clawed at the laces of her work boots, until he took over and stripped them off. He broke their kiss to peel off her T-shirt. Then he stripped off his own shirt and drew her close, skin to skin, heat to heat.

Now that she'd made up her mind, she simply let it happen. The last time had been hurried, but this was to be savored. She kissed Caleb deeply, letting her hands and lips wander over his body.

He seemed to sense her mood, and he worked his way slowly from her neck to her navel, bringing gasps from her lips, and ramping up the passion that heated her to her very core. He slowly removed her clothes, and he removed his own, laying her gently back on the sofa, where he made leisurely love to her.

The rain pounded harder, the room heated up, her damp hair all but steamed in reaction to his lovemaking. The leather was smooth against her skin, and his hands were firm then gentle then firm again.

Their bodies joined, and his scent surrounded her. The taste and feel of him filled her senses. His breathing was a rasp in her ear, deeper, louder, faster. Her body kept up with the pace, until she was floating from the earth, hovering in pure bliss for thrust after thrust before imploding in a cascade of pleasure that had her crying his name.

The room slowly righted itself, and she could tell which way was up.

Neither of them spoke. He turned, balanced her gently on top of him, covering her with his shirt. She wasn't cold. But she liked the cocoon. For the first time in days, she felt at peace.

Caleb would have happily held Jules sleeping on top of him forever. But sooner or later, somebody would come looking. Even as the thought crossed his mind, her phone buzzed. The ring was soft, and it didn't disturb her sleep.

He smiled, smoothing her hair and giving her a kiss on the temple. When he eased out from under her, she simply settled into the heat of the soft cushions. His smile widened. She was serenely beautiful, and his shoulders felt lighter.

He retrieved a blanket from the linen closet and tucked it over her, feathering her mussed hair off her face. Then he took a few more sips from his brandy snifter. Brandy had never tasted so good.

He guessed it was probably Melissa trying to call Jules. He took his own phone and scrolled through the history to find the call Jules had made from it in San Francisco. He put Melissa's saved number in his contacts and called her.

"Hello?" Melissa answered.

"Hi, Melissa. It's Caleb."

"Caleb?" Melissa sounded surprised and a little distracted.

"I wanted to let you know that Jules is here."

There was a pause. "Where's here?"

"My place. She came by."

There was another moment of silence on the line before Melissa spoke. "I don't understand. She said she was going to walk. Caleb, what's going on?"

"She was angry."

Distress came into Melissa's tone. "At me?"

The response surprised Caleb. With a last look at Jules, he moved down the hall to the kitchen to continue the conversation. "Me," he said as he walked. "She was mad at me."

"What did you do? Wait, why is she still there? Why didn't she call me herself? Caleb, what did you do?"

He sure wasn't about to give a complete answer to that question. "We argued." He chose his words. "She eventually calmed down. She must have been exhausted because she fell asleep on my sofa."

There was complete silence at that. He wasn't even sure Melissa was breathing.

"Melissa?"

"Are you *sure* she wasn't mad at me?"

"It was definitely me." He took a chair at the table and set down the brandy.

"What did you do to her?"

"She thought I coerced Noah into lobbying you to sell the Crab Shack to me."

"No, that was his…" She paused. "It *was* his idea, wasn't it? You didn't. You wouldn't."

"No. I wouldn't use Noah to get to you. I know I'm on the opposite side of this, Melissa. But I play fair."

"I don't know why," she said softly. "But I believe you."

"Thank you." For some reason, it meant a lot to him that she did.

"Would you consider it?" Her question was hesitant. "Would you buy the Crab Shack if Jules was willing to sell?"

He paused, remembering his promise to Jules about not

using Melissa, and wondering how far he could ethically go in this conversation.

Before he could answer, she spoke again.

"Do you think it's a good idea?"

"From my perspective," he said, "it's a fantastic idea. I'd buy the property in a heartbeat. But Jules feels very strongly on the subject."

"I know she does. Sometimes… I sometimes think she's blinded by her love for our grandfather."

"What is it you want?" Caleb found himself asking Melissa.

"Mostly, I want Jules to be happy."

Caleb swirled the brandy in his glass. "You have no reason to believe this, but I want her to be happy, too."

"What should we do?"

Although he would have loved to use the opportunity, Caleb's conscience kicked in. "I'm not the best person for you to talk to about that. It's a definite conflict of interest. But I will tell you I'm not bluffing about rescinding the easement."

"That's what Noah said. He said you were too far into the project, and you couldn't afford to back down."

"Noah seems very logical."

"I've never met anyone like him."

Caleb thought he could peg the tone in her voice. Noah was a lucky guy.

"What do you want for yourself?" Caleb repeated.

"I want to help run a business. I want to put my degree to work. I want to make a meaningful contribution to something successful."

He read between the lines. "But it doesn't necessarily have to be the Crab Shack."

"I'm not as invested as Jules."

"We could—" He stopped himself.

It took Melissa a moment to speak. "You don't want to feel like we're ganging up on her."

He vividly remembered what Jules had said about not being able to fight him, her father and Melissa all at the same time.

"I don't," he said. "Even if it's for her own good."

"Do you think forcing her to give up is for her own good?"

"I think…" He hesitated on how to frame it. "I know she can't win this fight."

"Unless you give up."

"Why would I give up?"

There was a smile in Melissa's voice. "I'm beginning to figure out the answer to that."

Melissa had ended the call then, and Caleb found himself coming to his feet, moving back down the hall just far enough that he could see Jules. She was unbelievably beautiful. He couldn't believe they'd made love a second time. He couldn't believe she was here.

He stood and gazed at her for a long time.

There had to be a path forward for them. More than ever now, he needed a path forward that kept her in his future.

Nine

It took Jules a moment to realize she was still in Caleb's living room. She was warm and comfortable. She was also still naked.

Last night came flooding back, and she knew she'd made a terrible mistake in confronting him. It might have turned into wonderful lovemaking, but she was now more conflicted than ever.

She sat up in the morning light, spotting her clothes neatly folded on the chair beside her. She couldn't help but be grateful for the small gesture, and she quickly got dressed.

Half of her wanted to slip out the door and go home. But that would be cowardly. She'd done what she'd done, and pretending it hadn't happened wasn't going to change that.

She heard sounds down the hallway and guessed they were coming from the kitchen. Running her fingers through her hair and gathering her courage, she determinedly walked toward the noise.

Caleb was in a bright, spacious kitchen, pouring coffee.

He looked up to stare at her.

Her stomach lurched with nervous energy. "I have absolutely no idea what to say."

"How about 'morning'?"

"Morning," she said, relieved by his relaxed posture and demeanor.

"Coffee?"

"Please."

He retrieved another cup and poured. "Do you take anything in it?"

"Black is fine." Any form of caffeine was fine with her at the moment.

He came around the breakfast bar, a cup in each hand. "Did you sleep okay?"

"Soundly."

He smiled. "I'm glad to hear it."

The polite chitchat was stringing her nerves tighter and tighter. "Caleb… I don't know what happened last night."

"You mean you don't remember it, or you don't know what caused it."

"I remember it fine."

Their gazes locked as he handed her a cup.

"Good," he said.

"No, bad."

"That's sure not how I remember it."

"You know what I mean." She took a drink, hoping to jump-start her brain. She needed to be fully functional right now.

He gestured toward a round wooden table, with four padded chairs. It was set in a bay window facing southwest. The storm was over, and the sun was coming up, lighting the calm ocean.

"What do you want to do?" he asked as they sat down.

"Nothing."

"Nothing?"

"Go home, go back to—" Her thoughts went to her sister. "Melissa must be worried."

Come to think of it, why hadn't Melissa called? Had Jules's phone battery died?

"I talked to her last night," he said, then immediately put the cup to his lips.

Jules felt her embarrassment and anxiety rise. Her voice came out raspy. "What did you tell her?"

"That you were angry. We'd fought. You were exhausted and fell asleep on my sofa."

"That's it?"

"That's it."

The morning light softened his expression, and he looked more like a friend than a foe. This was the up close Caleb. This was the Caleb she had to avoid if she wanted to stay sane.

"I did tell her you thought I'd put Noah up to it. And I also told her that wasn't true."

Jules found herself nodding. She believed Caleb when he said that. Which meant Noah thought she was going to fail. And Melissa must still have her doubts.

The aspen trees outside fluttered in the breeze, and the waves pushed against the rocks below. The only sound in the kitchen was the faintest hum of the refrigerator.

"If we're going to keep doing this," he said.

She sat up straight. "We are *not* going to keep doing this."

"We keep saying that, yet…" He spread his hands.

"This time it's true."

"I should have used some protection." He seemed to hesitate. "But you must be using birth control, right?"

She worked her jaw for a moment. She wanted to tell him it was none of his business, but she didn't believe that was true.

"Hormone shots," she said. "Not specifically for birth control," she felt compelled to explain. She didn't want him to get the wrong idea about her sex life—which for the most part didn't exist. At least, until he'd come along. "But that's one of the effects."

He gave a nod. "Good."

"Caleb." She put a warning note into her voice. "We're not going to—"

"I heard you." He spun his empty cup on the polished surface of the table. "I like you, Jules."

She didn't want to hear this. She didn't want the good Caleb to make her do something stupid. Truth was, if she operated on emotion alone, she'd drag him straight back into bed.

He caught her gaze again and held it. "I'm ridiculously attracted to you, and—"

A sound caught their attention. The front door opening and closing.

"Caleb?" It was Matt.

Panic hit Jules straight in the solar plexus, and she lost her breath.

"He knows," Caleb said.

The panic grew. "He *what*?" She rose to her feet.

Caleb looked like he regretted the admission. "He's a close friend."

Her tone was a harsh whisper. "I haven't even told my sister."

"I didn't tell anyone else," Caleb whispered back as Matt's footfalls grew closer.

"*That's* supposed to make me feel better?"

"Morning, Caleb," Matt said as he entered the room. "Oh, morning, Jules."

"I…" she started, but came up blank and ended up blinking.

"This isn't what it looks like," Caleb said.

Matt held up his palms. "None of my business."

She took another stab at it. "We have a…"

"Love-hate relationship," Caleb finished for her.

"Lust-hate relationship." She couldn't see any point in pretending.

"I really don't need to know," Matt said, pouring himself a cup of coffee.

"You're the only one who does," Jules said. "Not Melissa, not *anyone*."

"I'm not going to tell anyone," Matt said, stopping the pour to look affronted.

"Matt's not going to tell anyone," Caleb said.

Jules realized that who Matt did or didn't tell wasn't the problem. The problem was her conflicted feelings for Caleb and how she was going to get them under control.

The other, bigger problem was how she was going to get the Crab Shack up and running.

"Do I need a lawyer?" she asked Caleb.

It was clear from his expression that he'd followed her change of topic. "My lawyer is rescinding the easement this morning."

"Seriously?" Matt asked from the other side of the kitchen.

Caleb shot him a look of annoyance.

"I thought it was just a threat," Matt said.

"I never thought it was just a threat," Jules said. The words felt heavy as she uttered them. "I've known all along he was serious."

"You left me no choice," Caleb said.

"You always had a choice. You could live with seventeen Neo locations and however many tens of millions that pulls in."

"It's not about money."

"If it wasn't, you wouldn't be doing this."

"What about you?" he asked. "You had a choice, too. Neo and the Crab Shack could live amicably side by side."

"That's not a choice. That's a Watford trying to con a Parker. That's history repeating itself. It's the very thing I came here to fix."

"You are so misguided."

"You just hate it when we don't roll over and play dead."

Caleb's eyes darkened. "You couldn't be more wrong."

"I'm wrong a lot." She rose to her feet, reminding herself all over again how stupidly wrong she'd been to come here last night. "But not about this."

She took two steps back, trying desperately to see the distant Caleb, the one she despised, the one out to harm her. She backed into the wall, but she quickly recovered. She concentrated with all her might, but it didn't work.

She couldn't separate him into halves anymore. She couldn't see her enemy. She saw only Caleb.

* * *

"Thanks for doing this," Caleb said to Matt a week later as they watched Noah climb the stairs to the marina deck.

It was nearly ten o'clock, and things had been dark at the Crab Shack for over an hour.

"Are you sure he's an ally?" asked Matt.

"I think so. I hope so. I'm running pretty short on moves, so I better be able to make this happen."

"Jules still not talking to you?"

"I can't get anywhere near her." And Caleb had certainly tried.

Since his lawyer had filed the papers, she was refusing to have anything to do with Caleb. He'd tried three different carrots, and none of them had worked. Now the stick had been an even more colossal failure. If he didn't come up with something new, Jules was going to lose all her money, and he was never going to have a chance at exploring their feelings for each other.

"Hey, Noah," he greeted the man, stepping forward to shake his hand. "Thanks for coming."

"You said it was about work?" Noah asked.

Matt gestured to the cluster of deck chairs.

"Melissa told me what you suggested," Caleb opened as the three of them sat down.

It was a clear night, but breezy waves crested higher than usual as the tide rolled out. The yachts creaked against their mooring ropes, while the flag over the dock snapped in the wind.

"What did I suggest?" Noah asked, his expression becoming guarded.

"That they sell to me. It's a good idea. And she listened."

"It had nothing to do with what's best for you," Noah told Caleb.

"I get that." Caleb guessed Noah had Melissa's best interests at heart when he made the suggestion. "But Jules won't go for it."

"No kidding."

"Melissa explained what happened?"

"That Jules thought I was your pawn? She told me. You do know that's never going to happen. So, if that's what this is about..." Noah started to rise.

"No," Caleb quickly assured him. "It's not."

Noah hesitated for a second, but then settled back down.

"You want a beer?" Matt asked Noah.

"Are you going to ask Melissa out?" Caleb asked Noah.

"No."

Caleb was curious. "Why not?"

"I'm getting the beer." Matt rose and crossed to the wet bar.

"Because she's a university graduate, and I'm an ex-con with a GED."

The answer took Caleb by surprise. "You're also a licensed carpenter."

"Can you imagine her bringing me home to Daddy?"

Matt handed around the beers and sat back down. The wind gusted, and he settled his cap more firmly on his head.

"You're selling yourself short," Matt said.

"This can't be why you asked me here," Noah said.

It wasn't.

Caleb had a different motive. "If I can get Jules on board, would you consider working for Neo?"

He knew Jules and Melissa respected Noah. Caleb liked him, too, and he admired Noah's work. What he wanted was a solution that worked for everyone.

"Or for me," Matt said. "If it turns out the Crab Shack job ends, I've got plenty of work here at the marina for a good finish carpenter."

Noah looked from one man to the other. "Even if I think you're right, that the sisters should sell, they're never going to agree."

"I can't give up," Caleb said. "Melissa admitted she'd like to work at Neo."

"Melissa's not Jules," Noah said.

"I'm not through trying."

"Then I wish you luck." Noah came to his feet.

"Ask Melissa out," Matt said to Noah. "I hate that you're hesitating over your past."

"He's divorced, so probably not the best advisor on women. But I agree with him." Caleb had seen the way Melissa and Noah looked at each other. They deserved a chance.

"Divorced or not—" Noah cracked a half smile "—I'd rather take his advice than yours. I've never seen a guy get himself into such a mess over a woman."

Caleb wished he could disagree. "If I can't change her mind—"

"It's going to cost you a million dollars," Matt finished the sentence.

"That's not what I was going to say."

Noah polished off his beer. "You're not going to change her mind. And, Matt's right, you're the one who's going to cave."

Matt laughed at that.

Before Caleb could work up a counter-argument for the both of them, Noah was gone.

"Noah asked me out." Melissa was beaming as they laid out copper light fixtures and polish on the drop cloth-covered bar. She lowered her voice, glancing surreptitiously at Noah where he was working outside on the deck. "Your plan worked. I've been staying aloof and playing hard to get for nearly a week."

Jules forced out a smile for her sister. She was genuinely happy for her. "Congratulations. Where are you going?"

Jules wouldn't use this moment to feel sorry for herself. She'd been avoiding Caleb all week. She missed him, but that was too bad. She might as well start getting over it.

"Dinner and a club. Saturday night. We're going to drive into Olympia."

"What are you going to wear?"

"Your black dress." Melissa peeled a soft cloth from a stack and opened a can of polish. Her hand was finally back to normal.

"I suppose that's only fair," Jules said.

"I'll try not to ruin it."

"It's not like I have a right to complain if you do."

Melissa didn't laugh, and Jules looked up.

Her sister's eyes were round.

"Dad," Melissa said.

Jules didn't blame Melissa for being concerned. "Dad's reaction is a whole other—"

"Hi, Dad," Melissa said more loudly in a brittle, bright tone.

Jules realized Melissa was looking past her.

A prickle zigzagged its way up her spine.

She turned to see her father, Roland, frowning in the doorway. He was unshaven, which wasn't unusual. His plaid shirt was open at the collar, tucked into a pair of work pants, and he wore his usual scuffed leather boots.

"Is something wrong?" Jules quickly asked. She couldn't imagine why he would have shown up unannounced.

He glanced contemptuously around the restaurant.

"Do you like it?" Melissa asked, her tone still unnaturally bright.

"It's worse than I thought," he said.

Jules fought a rush of indignation. "It's going to be terrific. We've expanded the windows, refinished the bar." She gestured, but the bar was completely covered with the drop cloth. "We've redone the floor, not to mention all the structural fixes, like the electrical."

"And you've spent all your money."

"Not all of it. Not yet."

"We have a budget," Melissa put in, sounding more confident. "It's all laid out. And we've had fantastic help from…" She gazed through the windows, obviously looking for Noah. "Where's Noah?" she asked Jules. "He was just out there."

"Why are you here, Dad?" Jules asked, dropping her polishing cloth and moving away from the bar.

"Your mail was piling up." He lifted a large manila envelope held in his hand.

Jules didn't believe for a second that was his purpose. "You drove up from Portland to deliver our mail?"

"And to talk some sense into you girls." He gazed around the room again. "But I can see that I'm too late. The damage is done."

"Damage?" Jules raised her voice. "Is that what you call our work?"

"I call it folly," he said.

"If that's the only reason you're here—" Jules began, prepared to send him packing.

"Please don't," Melissa broke in. "I hate it when we argue."

Roland took a few paces and tossed the package of mail on the nearest table. "Then listen to reason."

Jules crossed her arms over her chest. As always, when it came to her father's temper, she felt protective of Melissa. "We've been through every bit of this before."

"Is there a problem?" Caleb appeared in the doorway.

Roland turned and it seemed Caleb recognized him instantly. His brow went up, and his nostrils flared.

"You're a Watford," Roland snapped.

"Caleb Watford, Mr. Parker." Caleb seemed to hesitate, but then stepped forward to offer his hand.

Roland didn't shake. "What the *hell* are you doing here?" He shot an accusatory stare at Jules. "What the hell is he doing here?"

"Mr. Parker," Caleb said.

Roland pointed a finger in Caleb's direction. "I'm talking to my daughter, not to *you*."

"He's our neighbor," Melissa said in a conciliatory tone.

"He and Matt—Matt owns the marina—have helped us with the—"

Roland's complexion turned ruddy. "You accepted *help from a Watford*?"

"I'm not my father," Caleb said in a deep, level voice.

"Get out!" Roland shouted. "This is Parker land, and you're not welcome here."

"I'd like to apologize to you," Caleb said to Roland. "On behalf of my family."

Roland's hands clenched into fists. "Did you not hear me? Do I need to repeat myself?"

Caleb didn't move. "We're never going to resolve this if we don't talk to each other."

"We're not resolving anything. There's nothing to resolve." Roland took a step toward Caleb. "Get out of this building and away from my family."

"Dad!" Melissa sounded horrified.

Jules felt like she might throw up.

Caleb raised his palms and took a step back. "I can see this is not the time."

"There's never going to be a time," Roland spat.

Caleb turned and walked away.

Jules shook herself out of her stupor. She realized Caleb must have had a good reason for coming. He'd agreed to stay away, and he'd been respecting her wishes.

"Caleb, wait," she called, rushing after him.

Her father reached for her on the way past, but she avoided him, bursting through the open door.

"Caleb," she called again.

He stopped in the parking lot next to the SUV.

"Why did you come?" she asked, halting a few feet back from him.

Heaven help her, she wanted to barrel forward into his arms. The decision to keep her distance had been the right one. But she missed him, never more acutely than while he was standing so close.

"They've set a court date," he told her, his tone remote. "It's Monday. I came to give it one last shot, to see if we could find a compromise." He nodded past her. "When did he show up?"

"Just now. He's here to tell us we're fools, that we should give up this nonsense and come home with him."

Caleb gave a dry chuckle. "Ironic. He and I agree on something."

"I'm sorry." She gestured behind herself. "He can be…"

"Pig-headed?"

"Stubborn. He's always been that way. He loves us, but he can't see past… Well, you know what he can't see past."

Caleb's gaze unexpectedly softened. "Can you see past it, Jules?"

She'd already seen past it. She'd already seen way past it. But she could never admit that to him. "Not while you're stomping on my dreams."

He gave a sharp nod. "That's what I thought." He opened the driver's door. "I'll see you in court."

He drove away, and she felt pummeled from all sides. For the first time in years, she wondered if she could do it. Maybe her father had been right all along. Maybe she was a fool to get anywhere near the Crab Shack, never mind the Watfords.

And maybe Caleb was right. Maybe she should cancel the noncompete and at least get out of the court case without wasting all their money. There was also the possibility that Noah was right. Selling out to Caleb would at least cut their losses. She and Melissa could take the money and find something else to do. Somewhere not here. Somewhere where she wouldn't see Caleb anymore.

And what about her sister?

How could Jules know what was right? How could she choose?

* * *

Noah's pickup was parked at the end of the Crab Shack access road, and he sat in the driver's seat. Caleb pulled over, exiting his own vehicle. He walked up to the window.

Noah unrolled it.

"What are you doing?" Caleb asked.

Noah stared straight ahead, jaw tight, lips narrowed. "Feeling like a coward."

The answer shocked Caleb. "Why? What happened?"

"Her dad showed up."

Caleb leaned his elbow on the open window, feeling sympathy for Noah. "He just kicked me out of the Crab Shack."

"I wasn't waiting around for that to happen to me."

"At least you would have had company."

Noah's jaw tightened even further. "I won't put Melissa in that position. She's not going to have to explain me to her father."

"So, you asked her out?" Caleb guessed.

"I did."

"She said yes?"

The question brought a ghost of a smile to Noah's face. "She was pretty excited. I was excited, too."

"So what's the plan now? Are you going to break her heart?"

"Her heart's not involved yet, and I'm going to keep it that way."

"You can't really be afraid of her old man." Caleb would be sorely disappointed if he'd misjudged Noah so badly.

The look Noah gave him told him he hadn't. "I'd take on a hundred guys like him. It's Melissa I'm protecting, not myself."

"Then you're making a mistake."

If Noah stood up to Roland, he just might win. He had a good explanation for his criminal record. And at least he wasn't a Watford. If Caleb had thought fighting Roland would get him anywhere near Jules, he never would have left the restaurant.

Noah sat silent, his hands clenched around the steering wheel.

Caleb stood between the idle heavy equipment costing him a fortune on the Neo site and the half-finished Crab Shack that meant so much to Jules. He wished he was only an ex-con who was self-conscious about his profession.

"You want to fight for her," he said to Noah. "And you want it pretty bad."'

"I want to fight for her," Noah agreed.

"She's waiting. It might be ugly at first, but what guy didn't have some kind of battle with a woman's father?"

"Not like this," Noah said.

"Not like this," Caleb agreed. "But it could be a whole lot worse. Look at me."

"You've got it bad for Jules?"

"I've got it bad for Jules." And it was getting worse. Day by day by day, it was getting worse.

"At least you're a rich, successful guy."

"At least your families aren't mortal enemies. I don't know what you've heard…"

"A little," Noah said. "I get the gist."

"Well, Roland Parker just finished meeting me. I have to think you're going to look pretty good in comparison."

Noah shook his head in obvious self-deprecation. "I really am being a coward."

"You're protecting Melissa. You're just doing it wrong. Get back out there."

Noah reached for the ignition key. "I will."

He started the engine and drove away in a cloud of dust.

Caleb watched the loud, battered truck until it came to a stop in the parking lot. The engine went silent, the waves and the wind taking over. Caleb felt a rush of envy. He'd give a lot to be walking back into that room to fight for Jules.

Ten

Numb, Jules was back inside when Noah's truck slid to a halt outside the restaurant.

"Well, *there* he is," Melissa said, all but rushing for the door.

"Not that Watford again," her father growled.

"It's Noah," Melissa answered over her shoulder.

"Our contractor," Jules clarified, ordering herself to get her emotions under control.

Noah jumped out of the truck and took Melissa into his arms, kissing her soundly.

"Contractor?" her father asked.

"They're also dating." Jules had never seen such a display of affection from Noah.

"Melissa has a boyfriend?"

"He's not exactly—"

Before Jules could finish her sentence, Roland left the building.

Jules's first instinct was to follow. But she was tired. And this was Melissa and Noah's situation. They didn't need her inserting herself into the middle.

She moved to the nearest chair, sitting down to take a minute for herself. When she let her mind go blank, an image of Caleb danced in front of her eyes, looking handsome as ever.

She dismissed the idea, telling herself to change focus. As she did, her father's stuffed manila envelope came into view.

She reached for it and flipped open the flap, grateful for the distraction.

It was mostly junk mail. She couldn't imagine why her

father had saved credit card company solicitations and letters from local politicians. There was a letter to Melissa from her college, which she set aside. And there was a notice for Jules from her medical clinic.

She opened it, finding a standard reminder to book an appointment. She needed a routine physical and her hormone shot was due. She scanned over the date then did a double take.

It couldn't be right. There had to be a typo.

She reread it. Then she reread it again. Dread slowly built up, elevating her temperature, making her skin prickle with anxiety. She searched her memory, desperately trying to pinpoint the last shot.

She couldn't remember. There was nothing in her memory that could dispute the date on the clinic's letter. If she couldn't dispute it, then she had to allow for the possibility that it was right. And if it was right, her shot was late. It was late by over a month.

She told herself not to panic, even as her hand went reflexively to her stomach.

No way. It couldn't happen. Even with a late shot, the mathematical odds were in her favor. They were far and away in her favor.

They had to be.

The alternative was beyond unthinkable.

Her gaze went to the trio outside.

Melissa was smiling. Noah looked relaxed, and her father was nodding at whatever Noah was saying.

Jules didn't have time to puzzle at her father's uncharacteristic calm. She had to find out. She had to know for sure. And it couldn't wait until morning.

She gripped the letter in her fist and rose from the chair, grabbing her purse on the way out the door.

"I'm heading to town. Need anything?" She didn't look at them as she breezed past. She wouldn't have heard if they'd answered.

She wrenched open the door of the minitruck, panic pulsing through her brain cells.

She couldn't be pregnant. It would be a disaster of epic proportions.

As she headed for the Whiskey Bay plaza drugstore, she forced herself to think positively. She wasn't pregnant. She didn't feel pregnant. She felt like a perfectly ordinary twenty-four-year-old woman.

Okay, maybe a panicky twenty-four-year-old woman. But that would be short-lived. She'd take a pregnancy test. She'd reassure herself. She'd breathe a huge sigh of relief. Maybe she'd laugh at herself. Then she'd get back to worrying about the easement.

The easement seemed like a smaller problem now. It was surmountable. With a sympathetic judge, their lawyer thought they had a good chance of winning.

Perhaps this scare would turn out to be a blessing in disguise. It would put her world in perspective. She'd defeat Caleb in court. He'd be forced to leave the easement in place. And the Crab Shack would proceed as planned.

No competition. No baby. No tie to Caleb whatsoever. It was exactly what she wanted, exactly what she needed, even if the thought of never touching him again did leave her hollow.

She was in and out of the drugstore without a fuss. She checked the pregnancy test instructions, confirmed the timetable, then stopped at the public restroom in the lookout park. It was the place Caleb had brought her for that first burger, the night Melissa had been hurt.

She didn't have time to ponder the irony as she walked past the parked cars. Couples and families and groups of teenagers played and picnicked on the grass. Groups walked along the cliff path, chatting and laughing, their hair blowing in the breeze.

To them, it was a perfectly ordinary day.

Jules was shaking slightly as she entered a stall. Sunlight

streamed through the high windows. Disinfectant invaded her nose. A woman and her young daughter chatted as they washed their hands. And down the row a toilet flushed.

Jules tore into the test, discarding the box in the waste bin. She reread the instructions then gritted her teeth, her heart pounding and her lungs rapidly inhaling and exhaling the warm, close air as she urinated on the stick.

She checked her watch, closing her eyes and regulating her breathing as she waited for the minutes to tick past. She concentrated on what she'd do after. She'd have to pick something up at a local store, something that was plausibly important enough for her to have rushed out of the restaurant.

Maybe something for dinner. Her father's favorite was lasagna. She'd go back to the plaza and pick up the fixings for lasagna. That way she'd look like a good daughter rather than an irrational one.

Dangling the test by her side, out of her sight, she opened her eyes and checked her watch. There were just a few seconds to go. She counted down.

Then she took a very deep breath and lifted the test, half turning away and squinting her eyes like she did in a horror movie.

It didn't help. She could see the result. It was positive.

She was pregnant.

Another toilet flushed. Someone's keys clanked as they set them down on the metal shelf and a tap turned on, roaring into the sink. Voices shouted outside, while a seagull screamed.

Jules stared at the two lines in the test window. How could she have been so stupid? Why had she made love with Caleb? She'd never, ever, not even once mixed up her shot dates before now.

How could the universe have played such a cruel trick?

Her phone rang inside her purse.

It would be Melissa, but Jules couldn't answer. There was

no way she could talk right now. She knew if she didn't answer, Melissa would worry.

Melissa was going to have to worry.

She'd probably be happy in the end. Because the Crab Shack would fail, her father would definitely be happy in the end. And Caleb, Caleb would be the happiest of them all. He was about to get everything he wanted.

Caleb was certain he couldn't have heard Noah right. "She'll sell?"

"I just finished talking to her," Noah said as he followed Caleb into his living room.

Matt and TJ were already visiting. They were out on the deck with the barbecue warming up. Caleb had sought them out as a distraction. He hadn't wanted to be alone with his thoughts.

"Why?" he asked Noah, blown away by the statement. "What could have changed her mind?"

He was thrilled, of course. But the turn of events was completely unexpected. They had a court date in the morning.

"Reality, I think," Noah said.

Could it be as simple as that? Had the impending court date made her see reason? Finally? Caleb wanted to believe it, but something didn't quite fit.

"What did she say?" he asked. "How did she phrase it?"

"Just that she thought I was right."

"I have you to thank?" Caleb asked.

"Melissa agreed with me. So did her father, and it made me points with him, big-time."

Caleb had to smile at that. He was genuinely pleased for Noah. At least Noah was having success on the romance front.

Caleb was having success on the business front. He should be thrilled. He really ought to be thrilled. He dragged open the glass door.

"Hey, Noah," Matt said as the two men stepped outside.

"Hi," TJ echoed.

"Jules agreed to sell," Caleb told them both.

Matt grinned at the news. "Fantastic. Should I break out the single malt?"

Caleb wasn't ready to celebrate yet. "I can't figure out why she did it."

"Because of her dad?" Noah speculated.

"Her dad?" Matt asked.

"He showed up today," Caleb said, checking the temperature gauge on the barbecue then turning the knob.

"Seriously?" TJ asked.

"Did you see him?" Matt asked.

"For a minute," Caleb said.

"What happened?"

"We had words."

Matt gave a cold laugh. "I can only imagine. He hates you with a passion."

"He hates my father and grandfather," Caleb said. "It's not the same thing." He paused. "It shouldn't be the same thing."

"Close enough," TJ said. "Beer's in the fridge," he said to Noah.

"How much?" Matt asked.

"Who cares?" TJ said.

Caleb was inclined to agree. He'd pay any price she asked. He'd give her anything she asked. He wondered if there was any hope he could use his generosity to make peace with her. He was sure going to try.

He opened the lid to the barbecue and began brushing the grills.

"What are their plans?" Matt asked Noah as Noah returned to the deck.

"Move back to Portland."

Caleb stopped brushing. "What?" He turned to look at Noah. "I offered them jobs."

Noah gave a shrug. "Jules was adamant."

"What about Melissa?" Caleb had been certain Melissa would want an opportunity at Neo.

"She's staying with Jules."

"What about you?" Matt asked Noah.

"About the job offer…" Noah began.

Matt gave a knowing grin and lifted his beer in a toast. "You're going to Portland."

Noah gave a sheepish smile. "There are construction jobs in Portland. And her father doesn't hate me."

"I'll hire them both," Caleb said.

"You can offer," Noah said, taking a seat. "But I wouldn't put money on it happening."

"It's the perfect solution." Caleb looked to his friends, expecting their concurrence. "Their money problems are solved. They can stay in Whiskey Bay. They love Whiskey Bay." Caleb was itching to go talk to Jules.

Noah seemed to consider. "I'm not sure it's about the money. I think the Crab Shack was Jules's dream for an awfully long time."

"But…" Caleb tried to come up with a counter-argument. But unfortunately, he understood.

The Whiskey Bay Neo location had never been about money for him, either. If it had only been about money, he'd have found another location in Olympia. For years, he'd pictured the exact restaurant in that exact location. It was the thing he'd built toward from the very beginning.

He dropped into the fourth chair.

Jules was abandoning her dream. A month ago, he'd have been celebrating. But now that was unacceptable. Sure, it was important to save Neo. But it was equally important to support Jules.

"Caleb?" Matt prompted.

Caleb looked up. "This can't happen."

TJ cocked his head. "Since you just got everything you wanted on the business front, I'm assuming you mean Jules."

"I mean Jules." Caleb saw no point in denying it.

"You mean because you're in love with her?" Noah asked. "Complicates things, doesn't it."

"I'm not... Yes," Caleb said to Noah, giving in to what could be the only truth to the situation. He loved Jules. "It does complicate things."

"What are you going to do?" Matt asked.

Funny, when it came down to it, the question wasn't even hard for Caleb. "I guess I'm going to lose a million dollars."

"Ouch," TJ said.

Matt laughed.

"It's about time," Noah said.

"What do you know about love?" Matt asked Noah.

"Nothing yet," Noah said. "But I'm trying hard to find out."

"I can still get you some new investors," TJ said.

"I don't need them," Caleb replied.

For now, seventeen Neo locations were enough. His immediate plans had a whole lot more to do with his personal life than with his business.

He realized he could lose the Whiskey Bay Neo and still not win Jules. She might not love him back. She might already hate him, and his eleventh-hour gesture might mean nothing to her. But he was still going to do it. If nothing else, she'd have her dream. She'd be here, and she'd be happy, and that would have to be enough for him.

Jules was beyond numb. It had been three days, and her mind still couldn't comprehend the truth. The ocean roared in her ears as she made her way down the stairs from the driveway to her grandfather's house. Or maybe it was panic roaring in her ears.

She'd wanted medical confirmation. And a tiny part of her had still held out hope the test had been wrong. It wasn't wrong. In fact, her hormone levels were so high the doctor had done an ultrasound.

Jules was pregnant all right. She was very pregnant. She was twins pregnant, and she had no idea how she was going to explain it to her family. She could never tell her father this was Caleb's baby. *Babies.* The knowledge would kill him.

She should have listened to Melissa a long time ago and given up on the Crab Shack. She'd put her sister through so much unnecessary work, so many wasted expenses. Now Jules was going away forever, and Caleb was sure to bulldoze the place.

"You got what you wanted." Melissa's voice carried from the porch up the stairs. "You won. You don't need to rub it in her face."

"I'm *not* rubbing it in her face." The sound of Caleb's voice stopped Jules cold.

"Our lawyer sent you our price," Melissa said. "It's non-negotiable."

"I'm not here to negotiate, Melissa. I'm here to give you what *you* want."

Jules knew she should leave, but she couldn't make herself move. She stared at Caleb's handsome profile, unable to look away.

"What we *wanted*," Melissa said, her voice going louder, "What Jules' wanted was the Crab Shack."

"I know," he answered. "And I'm here to give *Jules* what she wants. You can have the easement. You can build the Crab Shack. I'll give up on Neo."

Jules let out a gasp.

Caleb turned.

He saw her, and his dark gaze pinned her down.

"Jules?" Melissa peeked around the corner.

"Jules." There was a sigh of relief in Caleb's voice, and he started up the stairs.

Jules struggled to keep her voice even. She had to hold it together. "No."

His brow furrowed, clearly confused.

"No," she repeated, calling on her strength. "We don't want the easement. The decision's been made."

He drew closer. "Change the decision. You won. You win. I'm giving you everything you asked for."

He was clearly baffled, and he was annoyed. And she was in love with him. And she was never going to see him again.

Melissa started up the staircase. "Jules?"

"It's not just about you," Jules told Caleb. "It's about my dad, and Melissa and me."

"But—"

"Go away," she told him as she leaned against the railing, trying to make herself as narrow as possible on the staircase. The last thing she wanted was for him to touch her on the way past. "Just leave me alone. I don't ever want to see you again."

He stopped beside her. "Listen, Jules. I know I've been unreasonable."

"Didn't you hear me?" Her heart was breaking, and she needed this to be over with.

He stared at her in silence.

Melissa's voice was hesitant. "Jules? Are you okay?"

"I'm fine. Completely fine. And I want to be alone."

She moved past Caleb, and she moved past Melissa.

Caleb stayed put, but Melissa followed her down the stairs and into the house.

"Jules?" Melissa closed the door behind them and touched Jules's shoulder.

Jules flinched.

"What on earth?" Melissa asked. "Dad will get over it. This is our chance."

Jules knew she had to come clean.

Tears threatened, and she sniffed.

"Jules?" There was worry in Melissa's voice as she came around to face Jules.

"I'm pregnant," Jules whispered.

Melissa froze.

Jules nodded, oddly relieved to speak the truth. "I'm pregnant with Caleb's baby."

"That makes no sense."

"It happened in San Francisco."

"You made love with Caleb?"

"He can't know," Jules said. "And Dad can never know. I'll come up with a story, say it was a one-night stand with some other guy. He'll be disappointed, of course."

"*What?*" Melissa was obviously astonished.

"But he'll believe me. He'll have no reason not to believe me."

"Forget Dad. What about Caleb?"

"He thought I was on birth control. I was. The hormone shots. But, I got mixed up." She put a hand to her forehead. "I can't believe I got mixed up."

"You're going to lie to Caleb." Melissa's gaze went to Jules's stomach. "You're going to lie to him about his own child?"

Children. It was children. Caleb's children.

Jules's chest swelled with emotion that she couldn't seem to make go away.

"I'm not going to lie to him," she managed. "I'm simply going to stay silent."

"You have to tell him, Jules."

"No." Jules shook her head. She knew she was making the right decision. "I won't. I can't." The only way this worked was if she disappeared from Caleb's life and kept the secret forever.

Melissa took Jules's hand. She walked backward, leading her into the living room. Her voice went softer. "You're not thinking straight, Jules. You're in a panic. How long have you known? When did you find out?"

"Three days. The day Dad got here."

"Sit down."

"You won't change my mind."

"I won't try to change your mind. For now, I'm just try-ing to calm you down. Being this upset can't be good for the baby. Sit." Melissa sat on the sofa and waited for Jules to follow suit.

The baby. The babies. Melissa was right. Being this upset couldn't be good for them.

Jules's legs were shaking. She sat down.

It took Caleb less than an hour to figure out his next move.

It took him three more to make it to Portland and Roland Parker's front door.

When Roland recognized Caleb, he looked fully capa-ble of murder.

"Hear me out," Caleb called as Roland started to slam the door in his face. "Please, just hear me out. For Jules's sake, for Melissa's and for yours."

"I'm not interested in a thing you have to say." But Ro-land didn't immediately shut the door.

"I'm sorry," Caleb said, speaking swiftly, knowing he had only one chance at this. "What my father did to you was unforgivable. My grandfather, too, for all I know. But that's behind us. My grandfather's dead, and my father is far away. I'm not them, and I want to make things right."

"There's no way to make things right."

"Will you let me try? Will you give me ten minutes of your time? Ten minutes for me to make up for six decades?"

Roland hesitated.

"If you don't like what I have to say, you can throw me out."

"I can throw you out anytime I want."

"That's true, but I'm asking anyway."

Roland glared a moment longer.

Caleb waited, edgy as the seconds ticked off. But then, to his relief, Roland's expression softened the slightest de-gree and he stepped back.

Caleb took the silent invitation and entered the town house. It was small, modest, with a slightly close musty scent. The furnishings were aged, and the carpets were dated. He couldn't help thinking that Jules had grown up here. She'd grown up just shy of poverty, while Caleb had grown up with every advantage. A whole new kind of guilt weighed down on him.

Roland didn't ask him to sit down, so Caleb remained standing in the small foyer. He was relieved enough just to be inside.

"I know there's no way to make up for the past," he opened.

Roland grunted his agreement.

"But I have a proposal for you." Caleb found himself nervous.

He'd negotiated dozens of high-cost business deals, managed countless crises, but this situation had him second-guessing every syllable that came out of his mouth.

"It's a partnership," he told Roland. "A business partnership involving the Crab Shack."

Roland's gaze narrowed and his lips pursed.

"I know the restaurant belongs to Jules and Melissa. But I'm looking for your blessing."

"You won't be getting anything from—"

"Please." Caleb held up a hand. "Fifty-fifty. Like it was before. Like it should be again. I'll work hard. I promise you. I'll work hard, and I'll be fair to your daughters. I'll be respectful and honest in everything I do."

"There's no way I will ever trust you," Roland spat out. "There's no amount of money in the world that will put me back into bed with snakes like the Watfords. Is your father behind this?"

Caleb could feel the plan slipping away from him. "My father has no idea that I'm here. He has nothing to do with my business. And he no longer has anything to do with

Whiskey Bay. This is me and only me. May I finish my offer?"

Roland compressed his lips even tighter together.

"I'm not proposing cash. I'm proposing a trade. Fifty percent of the Crab Shack for fifty percent of the Whiskey Bay Neo location. Both restaurants can thrive. Jules doesn't believe me. She thinks Neo will take customers from the Crab Shack. I disagree, and I'm willing to back my belief." Caleb stopped talking.

Roland didn't respond.

Caleb was tempted to keep selling. But he'd made his pitch. More wouldn't help. More might simply annoy Roland further. Caleb forced himself to let the silence stretch.

Roland finally broke it. "What's the catch?"

"There's no catch."

"You're a Watford. There's always a catch."

The catch was that Caleb was in love with Jules, and he intended to use their business partnership to romance her for as long as it took. But that was the future. That was his business. And he didn't think Roland was anywhere near ready to hear news like that.

"I brought the building plans for Neo," he said instead. "If you'll let me, I'd like to show them to you. And, if you'll let me, I'd like to write you a check to hire a lawyer, any lawyer you want, to review the deal and make sure it's fair to you and your family."

Roland's expression went from suspicious to perplexed, and he braced a hand against the wall. "Why would you do all that?"

"Because it's right, and it's fair, and it takes a lose-lose situation and turns it into a win-win. And because Jules told me a few things, about the past, about the Watfords." Caleb paused, framing his next words. "As you might imagine, my father wasn't completely honest with me about what happened. And though I have no proof either way, I believe Jules's version, your version." He paused again, giving his briefcase a little lift. "My father destroyed your dream. Let me give your daughter hers."

Roland's gaze locked on the briefcase.

Caleb took a chance, moving to the nearby kitchen table and opening the case.

Roland didn't stop him, so Caleb pulled out the plans, unfolding them over the woven place mats.

"We've already done some work preparing the ground," he said. "It's bedrock under the building, but we'll need to sink piles for the deck."

Roland came up beside him to look.

"It's two stories," Caleb continued. "I don't know if you've ever seen a Neo location, but the front windows are the signature feature. Well, along with the seafood."

Roland's aged hand reached out to smooth the plans. "This has to be worth ten times the Crab Shack."

"Like I said," Caleb answered, meaning every word. "This is long overdue."

Eleven

Jules's heart was breaking. Melissa looked just as miserable, while Noah looked grimly determined. He was packing his tools, loading everything into his truck in preparation to shut down the construction job.

Jules couldn't help but wonder what Caleb would do with the place. Would he bulldoze it right away? Unfinished, she guessed it would turn into an eyesore and impact the views from Neo.

Yes, she decided. That was exactly what he'd do. It made sense.

It was also emblematic of the entire history of the Parkers and the Watfords. The Parkers lost. The Watfords won, and their empire grew larger and larger.

She ran her fingertips over the smooth surface of the bar, recalling the hours of sanding and polishing. It had all been a waste of time. Everything they'd done here had been a waste of time. She wanted to be angry, but she knew she had no one to blame but herself.

Melissa should be angry. Melissa deserved to be very angry with Jules.

Jules gazed across the room to where Noah and Melissa were talking softly, standing close together. Her sister looked sad as Noah smoothed his fingers over her cheek. Jules knew their romance had bloomed. This moment aside, she'd never seen Melissa so happy.

She didn't know what was next for them. But she hoped it was something. She'd bet it was something. Noah didn't strike her as the type to go quietly into the night.

Neither was Caleb. But Caleb had what he needed from her. There was no reason for him to fight for anything anymore, not a single reason in the world for him to even seek her out. Their lawyers would take care of the paperwork.

At least the Parkers would get something out of this deal. Her father would be pleased. Her father would be thrilled. She hadn't called him yet. She didn't have it in her to deal with his happiness.

"Jules?" The sound of Caleb's voice sent a trill along her spine.

At first she thought she'd imagined it. But she turned to the door, and there he was, big as life, looking just as he had that first day he'd walked in. He'd been scowling then. He looked joyful now. She supposed he was, since he'd won.

"We're almost finished here," she told him, imagining he was already warming up the bulldozers.

The truth was, they were completely finished. There were no more excuses to linger. Moments from now, she'd walk away from the Crab Shack forever. She'd failed her grandfather. She'd failed everyone. She fought the urge to touch her stomach.

Caleb strode inside. "I'm here to offer you a new deal."

Her heart sank another notch. "Less money?"

He had her over a barrel, and he knew it. It would be just like a Watford to turn the screws.

"No." His tone was unexpectedly gentle as he moved toward her.

"What kind of a deal?" Melissa asked, joining the conversation.

Both she and Noah moved in, as well.

"A partnership," Caleb said, his attention focused squarely on Jules. "Half the Crab Shack for half of the Whiskey Bay Neo."

Jules parsed his words inside her head, certain she was misunderstanding.

"Why would you do that?" Melissa asked.

"Because I think they're both going to succeed. I wasn't snowing you earlier. We should coordinate efforts. I'm putting my money where my mouth is. We thrive together or we sink together."

Melissa found her voice first, and spoke haltingly. "That's ridiculously generous."

"No," Jules said.

Melissa shot her a look of disbelief.

Jules answered her sister with a hard look. They couldn't stay here. She was pregnant, and Caleb was the father. There was no way she could stay in Whiskey Bay and let him find out.

Caleb gaped at Jules in clear astonishment. "What do you mean no? It's everything you wanted. You can finish re-building. You can run the place. I'm not going to interfere."

"We can't," Jules said.

"Jules," Melissa pleaded.

"It's perfect," Caleb said with what looked like mount-ing confusion. "You get your dream. We all make money. Noah doesn't have to follow Melissa to Portland."

Melissa looked up at Noah. "What? What does he mean by that?"

Noah gave her a sheepish smile. "I can't be without you, Melissa. You're amazing."

She gave her head a swift little shake. "You're coming to Portland?"

He put an arm around her. "You don't think I can get work in Portland?"

In return, she leaned into him and smiled. Jules was forced to quell a surge of jealousy. Caleb standing just a few feet away made it all the worse. She wanted to go to him. She wanted to lean into him. She wanted to wake up from what had become a nightmare of errors and secrets.

"So you see," she managed to say without her voice cracking with emotion. "We're all good. We're looking forward to Portland."

"What are you talking about?" Caleb demanded.

Her stomach was churning with guilt and nervousness. "I'm saying thanks, but no thanks. Our minds are made up."

"You should at least hear what he has to say," Noah put in.

Jules looked to Melissa for support.

"It's almost too good to be true," Melissa said.

"It *is* too good to be true." Jules couldn't believe she was losing her sister's backing. Melissa knew the stakes. She knew why Jules couldn't accept Caleb's offer.

"It's not too good to be true. It's just flat-out true." Caleb directed his attention to Melissa, too. "We'll draw up a contract. You get half of Neo. I get half of the Crab Shack. It's as simple as that."

"It's not as simple as that." Jules's hand did go to her stomach. There was nothing remotely simple about the situation.

"What is *wrong* with you?" Caleb moved even closer to her.

"With *me*? There's nothing wrong with me."

He reached for her. "Jules, you know—"

"No, I don't know. I don't know why you're doing this." She looked at Melissa, trying hard not to feel abandoned. "And you, you know this won't work."

"Jules, just listen. Let's consider—"

"I can't." Jules was mortified. Tears threatened and she swiped them away. She'd made a mess of her life. Melissa's, too. And now...now, she... "I'm sorry," she mumbled, rushing from the restaurant.

"Jules!" Caleb called as she passed through the doorway.

She started running. She reached the mini pickup truck, wrenched open the door, turned the key and peeled down the driveway. In the rearview mirror, Caleb was standing in the middle of the driveway watching her roll away.

"What was that?" Caleb asked to no one in particular as Melissa and Noah arrived behind him on the driveway. Jules was disappearing in a cloud of dust.

What had gotten into her?

"She's afraid," Melissa said, coming up beside him.

That didn't make sense. Jules wasn't fearful. She was tough and she was brave.

"Of *what*?" he asked, trying to wrap his head around the strange turn of events. Jules should be thanking him, not running away.

"Of you," Melissa said.

"Jules isn't afraid of me. She's anything but afraid of me."

Melissa sent him a look of disbelief.

"What?" Caleb repeated. "What am I missing? I gave her exactly what she wanted. I made an impossible situation work. It was a solid plan. It was a brilliant plan."

"She's afraid of her feelings for you," Melissa said.

His brain instantly switched gears. Jules had feelings? Scary feelings? For him?

"What feelings?" he asked Melissa.

Melissa gave her head a shake of disbelief. "Well, it's not that she doesn't like you."

He worked his way through the oblique sentence.

Jules liked him. That was good. She was behaving strangely. But at least she liked him. Maybe there was hope.

"What should I do?" he asked Melissa.

She took a beat. "Be honest with her."

The advice made no sense to him. "I have been honest. I am honest. What do you mean be honest?"

"How do you feel about her?" Noah asked.

Caleb hesitated. "Oh, that kind of honest."

Noah gave him a sympathetic smile. "That kind of honest."

"Get her to be honest with you," Melissa said thoughtfully.

Caleb knew they were right.

They were more right than they realized. Jules couldn't read his mind. She still thought they were adversaries. He'd turned the tables too quickly, and she needed a chance to catch up.

"She's headed up to the house," he said out loud. "She's going to pack up and leave."

"That would be my guess," Melissa said.

Caleb realized he was wasting time standing there talking. He started to walk. Then he broke into a run.

His pace increased as he made the end of the driveway. The path angled up, and he ran harder. It would take Jules ten minutes to drive around on the road. He could make it up the pathway in seven if he pushed. And he was pushing. He was pushing very, very hard.

He took the stairs to her deck two at a time. Then he vaulted over the rail at the side of the house, scrambling up the steep grade to the side porch and the staircase that led up to her driveway.

The parking spot was empty. He dragged in huge gulps of air. He'd won the race. At least, he hoped he'd won the race. She'd better be on her way here. If she'd gone somewhere else, he didn't know what he'd do.

Other than track her down, he acknowledged. He'd track her to Portland. He'd track her to the ends of the earth if that was what it took.

He thought he heard the little pickup.

He cocked his head, holding his breath until the sound grew louder and the blue truck appeared.

She parked, set the brake, opened the door and stepped out.

At the top of the stairs, she spotted him. She froze, staring down in disbelief, her hair lifting in the wind, her dark T-shirt snug against her body, those faded blue jeans clinging to her hips. She was so intensely beautiful.

It looked like she was going to turn and leave. If she did, he'd have to run up the stairs to catch her. He hoped he'd make it. He was in pretty good shape, but he was winded from running the trail.

To his relief, she started down.

"This has to be the end of it," she said as she came to the step above him, seeming more in control. She stared at him in defiance.

"This will be the end of it." At the end of this conversation, she'd have no doubt about how he felt.

"Fine." She gave a jerk of a nod as she passed him to open the door.

He followed her inside, part of him wondering what to say, another part of him itching to get it said.

The house had seemed tattered the first time he'd seen it. But now it looked cozy. He associated it with Jules. And he loved everything about Jules.

"You're afraid," he said, following her into the living area.

"I'm not afraid of you," she denied, opening a closet door and retrieving a suitcase.

"You're afraid of us." He was a little bit afraid of them, as well.

He wanted her so badly it scared him. He wanted her as his business partner and his lover. He wanted her today and tomorrow. He wanted to wake up with her every morning and go to sleep with her every night.

She dumped the suitcase on the aging sofa and opened it up. "There is no us." She marched back to the closet and pulled clothes off the hangers.

"There's definitely an us," he said to her back.

She returned and stuffed the clothes into the suitcase. "Well, there won't be after today."

She was wrong about that. She couldn't be more wrong about that.

"Jules?"

She didn't look up. Her voice was full of snark. "What?"

"I'm in love with you."

"Well, that's just—" She looked up sharply. "What did you say?"

"I said, I love you."

She looked completely baffled, more frightened than ever, and ready to bolt.

"No," she said, her face going pale. She shook her head in denial and took a few steps backward. "You don't. You can't."

"I can, and I do."

She reached behind herself and gripped the windowsill. Her voice was little more than a rasp. "You don't know what you're saying."

"I know exactly what I'm saying. What I don't know is why you're fighting it."

"I'm not fighting anything."

"Jules, what we have together… It's exciting. It's energizing. It's amazing. And I want it forever. I want to marry you." He couldn't believe that had popped out. Then he was glad it had.

He wished he had a ring. He'd rather do this properly. But he wasn't taking it back. He wanted to marry her. He desperately wanted to marry her.

Her jaw worked, but nothing happened.

He gave her an encouraging smile. He was through fighting. It was a complicated situation, but it was as clear as day to him that the next step was a wedding.

"I can't," she finally croaked out.

He wasn't accepting that answer. "Why not?"

"I just can't."

He moved closer, keeping his voice gentle. Whatever had her spooked, they were going to work through it. "Do you love me?"

"I… I…"

"Jules, honey, *what* is going on?"

"Nothing."

It was the biggest lie he'd ever heard. "You can tell me anything."

She shrank away. "No, I can't. Not this."

"So, there *is* a this." He'd known it had to be something. "What's the this?"

Her gaze darted around the room, as if she was looking for an escape.

"Jules, get it over with."

"I can't."

"You can."

She finally met his eyes. "I've done something terrible."

He didn't care. Nothing she'd done would change his mind.

"Most people have," he said easily.

"Caleb," she pleaded.

"Do you love me?"

"It doesn't matter."

"It matters a lot."

Her hand went to her forehead. "All this time." She stopped for a moment. "All these years. I've accused your family of lying, cheating and betrayal."

He reached out and took her hands. "Most of it was true."

She stared down at their joined hands.

"Did you steal something?" he asked, impatient. "Kill somebody? Because Noah did that, and it doesn't make him a bad person."

"This isn't funny, Caleb."

"I know. No, I don't know. Maybe it's funny. Maybe it's not. But I don't know because you won't tell me." He stopped talking. He had to shut up. She couldn't tell him anything if he didn't let her speak because—

"I'm pregnant."

The breath whooshed out of him. "You're *what*?" he choked out.

Did she have a boyfriend? What had he missed?

She kept talking, her voice going faster. "I wasn't going to tell you. I was going to keep it a secret. I know that wasn't fair, and I knew all along it wasn't right. And, I don't know, maybe I would have cracked and told you eventually. I mean you deserve to know. It wouldn't be fair to keep it from you. I'd like to think I would have told you before…you know… you were a father."

Everything inside him went completely still. "Wait a minute? The baby is mine?"

She drew back. "What kind of a question is that?"

"I don't know. The way you were talking… I mean… It was only a few weeks ago."

There was defiance in her tone. "Well, I'm only a few weeks pregnant."

Caleb's brain was racing. Jules was pregnant with his child. She was pregnant. They were having a baby. Joy obliterated everything else in his brain.

"How is this a bad thing?" he asked, his hands tightening on hers. "I love you. You love me. You need to admit it. Now more than ever, you need to admit that."

"I'm so sorry," she said, her eyes starting to shimmer.

He drew her into his arms. "I'm not sorry. I'm thrilled."

"Thrilled?" she asked.

"Over-the-moon thrilled."

"But I was going to keep it from you. I lied by not telling you. I'm a terrible person."

"You didn't not tell me. You just told me now."

"Only because you said you loved me." She looked down at the suitcase. "I was leaving."

He cradled her face in his palms. "Are you still leaving?"

"I guess not."

"Say it," he told her.

Her entire body seemed to relax. "I love you, Caleb."

"It's about time." He leaned in to kiss her.

"It's only been five minutes since you told me."

"That's five minutes too long."

He leaned in to kiss her, but she put her hand to his lips and stopped him.

"What?" There couldn't be anything else. He wasn't going to let there be anything else.

"Uh…"

"Stop doing this to me, Jules."

"It's twins."

His world stopped again. "Say what?"

"Twins. Not one baby. It's two."

His grin grew a mile wide. "Twice the reason for you to marry me. Right away. As soon as we can arrange it."

"Okay," she said.

"We have a deal? No negotiation? No caveat?"

"We have a deal," she said.

He kissed her then. Finally, it was the kiss he'd been waiting for. The complete and utterly honest kiss that told him she'd be in his life forever.

Jules gazed around the Crab Shack three weeks later, loving every single thing she saw.

Noah had added a crew of three to help him finish, and he was getting ready to move to the Neo site and start work there. The decorators had also finished their work, and new dishes, tablecloths and accessories were being delivered every day.

She leaned into Caleb who was standing next to her.

"It's perfect," she said.

"You're perfect," he responded, his hand coming to rest on her stomach. "Have you decided?"

"On names?" They didn't even know if they were boys or girls.

Caleb gave a low chuckle. "On a wedding date. I don't want to wait any longer."

"I know." She didn't want to wait any longer either. She wanted to be married to Caleb.

"We need to tell him."

Jules knew that Caleb's offer to partner on the Whiskey Bay Neo location and the Crab Shack had gone a long way toward mollifying her father. But becoming business partners with Caleb was a whole lot different than having him as a son-in-law. Not to mention the idea of Caleb as the father of his grandchildren.

"Could we do it here?" she asked.

"Tell your dad about us?"

"No. I mean the wedding. I know the court house makes sense. But it would be nice to do it here before we open."

His hold on her tightened. "That's a great idea. We can fly to Portland and tell Roland in person."

"Okay," she said with a nod. "I'm ready to tell him."

Caleb gave her a tender kiss, and she turned into his arms.

Roland unexpectedly spoke from the doorway. "I *thought* that's what had to be going on."

Jules sprang guiltily back from Caleb.

Roland kept talking. "No guy makes a deal that bad without a woman involved."

"Dad," Jules said, her heart racing. "We were going to tell you."

"I imagine you'd have to at some point," Roland said strolling inside.

"I'm in love with your daughter," Caleb said.

Jules elbowed him. Could they not take this one step at a time?

"What?" Caleb asked. "It's better that he knows that, instead of thinking that I'm randomly kissing you."

To her surprise, her father smiled. "I guessed that when you came to Portland."

"You're not upset?" she asked.

"Do you love him?" Roland asked.

"I do."

He seemed to take Caleb's measure. "He showed me what he was made of when he came to see me." He spoke directly to Caleb. "You're not like your father."

"I'm not."

"There's some irony in this," Roland said. "I suppose some kind of justice, too. What with the Watfords sharing their wealth with the Parkers. Your grandfather would roll over in his grave."

"I've proposed to her," Caleb said. "She said yes. We're getting married."

"That's even better."

Jules was astonished by the conversation. "You're truly not upset?" she asked her father.

"I want you to be happy," he told her. "I thought Whiskey Bay would make you miserable, like it made me. I thought Caleb would hurt you, probably cheat you. I thought he was cut from the same cloth as his father and grandfather. I'm happy to be proven wrong."

Jules found herself moving to her father.

She gave him a hug.

She couldn't remember the last time she'd hugged him. It felt slightly stiff and awkward, but it still felt good. "I'm pregnant," she told him.

The words seemed to take him completely by surprise.

"You're going to be a grandfather." She couldn't hold back the smile.

Melissa spoke from the doorway. "Hello? You told him?" She looked worried.

"A Parker-Watford baby?" Roland seemed to test the idea inside his head.

Jules tensed, waiting for his reaction.

"Dad?" Melissa asked, concern in her tone.

"That's astonishing news." Then Roland smiled again. "Congratulations. To both of you."

"You don't mind?" Melissa asked, moving into the restaurant, followed by Noah.

"They are getting married," Roland said.

Caleb moved to put an arm around Jules. "We are definitely getting married. We thought we'd do it here," he told the group. "Before the grand opening."

"Grandpa would like that," Melissa said.

"Caleb's grandfather would have hated it," Roland put

in, though he laughed as he spoke. "But that's justice. And I think we can declare an end to the feud."

"I would love that," Jules said.

"We'll start a whole new era," Melissa said.

"We'll start a whole new family," Caleb whispered in Jules's ear.

* * * * *

If you loved this story, pick up these other
sexy and emotional reads from
New York Times *bestselling author Barbara Dunlop!*

ONE BABY, TWO SECRETS
THE MISSING HEIR
SEX, LIES AND THE CEO
SEDUCED BY THE CEO
A BARGAIN WITH THE BOSS

Available now from Mills & Boon Desire!

All she could think about was that big bed and Derek pleasing her.

She flushed and cleared her throat, which was suddenly very dry.

She tried to push the images out of her mind—of his naked body moving over hers. But she couldn't. She had seen him at the pool and knew his chest was solid and muscled. Now she wondered what it would feel like under her fingers.

He arched one eyebrow at her.

"What?"

"I think you just realized the most thrilling thing in this room is me."

She shook her head. "That's a lot of talk, Caruthers."

"Again with you thinking it's all ego. I promise you, it's fact," he said.

"Another promise?" she asked.

"This one I'm happy to demonstrate," he said. Derek stood up and drew her to her feet next to him. "Don't think. No more second-guessing. Let's just see where it leads."

* * *

The Tycoon's Fiancée Deal
is part of the Wild Caruthers Bachelors series:
These Lone Star heartbreakers'
single days are numbered…

THE TYCOON'S
FIANCÉE DEAL

BY
KATHERINE GARBERA

MILLS
BOON

First Published in Great Britain 2017
By Mills & Boon, an imprint of HarperCollins*Publishers*
1 London Bridge Street, London, SE1 9GF

© 2017 Katherine Garbera

ISBN: 978-0-263-92832-7

51-0817

Our policy is to use papers that are natural, renewable and recyclable products and made from wood grown in sustainable forests. The logging and manufacturing processes conform to the legal environmental regulations of the country of origin.

Printed and bound in Spain
by CPI, Barcelona

USA TODAY bestselling author **Katherine Garbera** writes heartwarming and sensual novels that deal with romance, family and friendship. She's written more than seventy-five novels and is a featured speaker at events all over the world.

She lives in the UK with her husband and Godiva (a very spoiled miniature dachshund), and she's frequently visited by her university-age children, who need home-cooked meals and laundry service. Visit her online at www.katherinegarbera.com.

Sometimes we get lucky enough to meet
people who will be more than acquaintances,
more than friends… I've always thought of these
people as kindred spirits, soul sisters. I've been
very blessed to have these women in my life and
on my journey, so this book is dedicated to them.
Charlotte Smith, Courtney Garbera, Linda Harris,
Donna Scamehorn, Eve Gaddy, Nancy Thompson,
Mary Louise Wells and Tina Crosby.

One

Derek Caruthers was a badass. He knew it and so did everyone else he passed in the halls of Cole's Hill Regional Medical Center. He was one of the youngest surgeons in the country to have his stellar record and, aside from a few bumps along the way, he deserved his reputation as the best. Today he felt especially pleased with himself as he had been invited to meet with the overall hospital board. He was pretty sure he was going to be named the chief of cardiology as the hospital prepared to open its new cardiac surgery wing.

Mentally high-fiving himself, he entered the boardroom. Most of the members were already there but the new board member wasn't. The first item of business in today's meeting was to reveal who had been chosen to oversee the new cardiac wing. Derek had no idea who it would be, but given that Cole's Hill was a small town, and he'd heard that the new board member had a local connection to Cole's Hill, Derek was confident it would be someone he knew.

"Derek, good to see you," Dr. Adam Brickell said, coming over to shake his hand. Dr. Brickell had been Derek's mentor when he first started and the two men still enjoyed a close bond. The older doctor had retired two years ago and now sat on the board at the medical center. He had been the one to put Derek's name forward for chief.

"Dr. Brickell, always a pleasure," Derek said. "I'm really looking forward to this meeting. Something I usually don't say."

"Keep that enthusiasm, but there might be a wrinkle. What if the new board member has her own ideas about the cardiology department?" Dr. Brickell said.

"Her? I've yet to meet a woman I couldn't bring around to my way of thinking," Derek said. He didn't want Dr. Brickell to see any signs of nerves or doubt in Derek. Whoever this new board member was, Derek would win them over.

Dr. Brickell laughed and clapped him on the back. "Glad to hear it."

Derek's phone rang and Dr. Brickell stepped away to allow him to check his call. Given that he was a surgeon he never ignored his calls.

He noticed that it was from his friend Bianca. She and he had been besties for most of their lives. It had gotten a bit awkward on his side when he'd developed the hots for her in high school but all of that had ended when she'd moved to Paris to model, fallen in love with a champion racecar driver and married him.

But for Bianca, the fairy-tale romance and marriage had been short-lived; after only three years together, her husband had been killed in a plane crash, leaving her to raise a two-year-old son alone.

Well, because of that, Derek had once again made being Bianca's friend a top priority.

She'd been sort of fragile since she'd moved back to Cole's Hill. He knew it was the pressure her mom was putting on her to find a husband so that Bianca and her son wouldn't be "on their own."

He glanced around the room and caught Dr. Brickell's eye, gesturing that he needed to take the call. Dr. Brickell nodded and Derek stepped out into the hallway for privacy.

"Bi, what's up?"

"I'm so glad you're here. Did I catch you before the hospital meeting?" she asked.

"Yes. What's up?" he asked again.

"Mom has another man lined up for me to go out with tonight. Is there the slightest possibility you're free?" she asked.

No, and even if he were, he wasn't going to go there. They were friends by her design and probably for his sanity, he wasn't about to rock the boat by dating her. He would cancel for her but this was Wednesday and everyone in the Five Families area where they both lived knew that the Caruthers brothers had dinner at the club and then played pool on Wednesday nights. "It's pool night with my brothers and your mom will know that."

"Damn. Okay, it was worth a shot."

"It definitely was. I'm sorry. Who is it tonight?"

"A coworker from the network. He's a producer or something," Bianca said.

Bianca's mom was a morning news anchor for their local TV station. She'd been busily setting Bianca up on dates since she'd moved back to Cole's Hill.

"Sounds…interesting," Derek said.

"As if. Mom has no idea what I want in a man," Bianca said.

And that was a can of worms Derek had no intention of opening right now. "I've got to go. The board is almost all here."

"No problem. Good luck today. They'd be foolish not to pick you."

"They would be," Derek agreed. "Later, Bi."

"Later."

He disconnected the call and put his phone back in his pocket. He adjusted his tie as he looked down the hall for a mirror to check it and heard the staccato sound of high heels. He glanced over his shoulder, a smile ready, and his jaw dropped.

The woman walking toward him was Marnie Masters. Damn. She gave him a very calculated look from under her perfect eyebrows. Her blond hair was artfully styled around her somewhat angular face and teased to just the right height. She moved the way he imagined a lioness would when she sighted her prey and he didn't kid himself that he was anything other than the prey.

"Marnie, always a pleasure to see you," he said, though he'd been dodging her calls, texts and party invitations for the last eighteen months. So calling it a pleasure was a bit of a stretch.

"I would believe that if I didn't have to resort to taking this role on the board and leaving my practice in Houston in order to 'run into' you," she retorted.

"You're back in Cole's Hill?" he said, shaken. He knew he needed to get his groove back and put on the charm.

"Well, it's the new me. Daddy donated the money for this new cardiac surgery wing—at my suggestion—and the board agreed to his suggestion that I be hired to oversee the new wing. I just finished doing something similar in Houston and Daddy really wanted me to come home… So it seems as if you and I will be working together for the foreseeable future," Marnie said.

"I'm glad to hear the board has hired someone with your qualifications," he said.

"I imagine we will get to know each other much better now that I'm working here. It will give us a chance to spend more time together and get caught up."

Derek knew he couldn't just say hell no. But there was no way he was getting involved with her again. "I'm afraid that's out of the question."

"Why? There are no rules against it," she said, with a wink. "I checked."

"Of course there aren't any rules. It's just that I'm engaged," Derek said. "I wouldn't want my fiancée to get the wrong idea."

"Engaged?" Ethan Caruthers asked as he and Derek ordered another round of drinks at the Five Families

Country Club later that night. "Why would you say something like that?"

"You know Marnie. She wasn't going to accept a no. So I panicked and…"

"Said something over-the-top. Derek, that's crazy. I think when it becomes clear you don't have a fiancée, this could backfire," his brother said.

Ethan had a point. Already, his lie had added a wrinkle to his prospects for becoming chief of cardiology. Marnie hadn't been happy to hear about the engagement and had told the board that she was considering a few other applicants. Dr. Brickell had firmly been in Derek's corner, saying that the decision needed to be made sooner rather than later, but Marnie had stood firm. She'd insisted it would be two months before the final decision would be made and had enough support from other members to win the argument and temporarily table the decision.

The board had adjourned and Derek had gone back to work, doing two surgeries that had wiped the fiancée problem from his mind until he'd shown up here. Ethan was the only one of his brothers waiting when Derek had arrived.

"Tell me about it," Derek said. "If I could just find a woman…someone who needed a guy for a few months."

"Would Marnie believe one of your casual friends was your fiancée?" Ethan asked.

"No. I told her it was someone special and that's why it was under wraps."

Ethan took another swallow of his scotch and shook

his head. "Damn, boy, you always did have a gift for telling whoppers."

"I know. What am I going to do?"

"About what?" Hunter asked, joining their group. Hunter had recently moved back to Cole's Hill after spending the better part of ten years playing in the NFL and traveling the country promoting fitness while dodging the scandal of being accused of killing his college girlfriend. Recently the real murderer had been arrested and charged with the crime, which had enabled Hunter to finally break free of the dark cloud of suspicion. He was now engaged and planning the wedding of the century according to their mother and Ferrin, Hunter's fiancée. Everyone was in wedding fever in Cole's Hill.

"He needs a fiancée," Ethan said with a bit of a smirk.

Derek reached over and punched his brother. Of course Ethan would think it was funny. With only eleven months separating the two of them they were "almost twins," and as Ethan was the older of the two, he had always been a little smug.

"Do I want to know why?" Hunter asked, signaling the waitress for a drink as he sprawled back in his chair.

"Marnie Masters."

Hunter threw his head back and started laughing. "I thought you broke up with her years ago."

"It's been eighteen months," he said. He had broken up with her two years ago but had given in one night six months later when he'd been in Houston and slept with her again. It had just renewed Marnie's belief that he wasn't over her and that they should get back together. He'd been avoiding her ever since.

"So why do you need a fiancée?" Hunter asked.

"Marnie's the new board member brought in to oversee development of the surgical wing at the hospital. I panicked when I saw her and announced that I was engaged when she suggested we'd have a chance to spend time together."

"Ah," Hunter said. "Do you have someone in mind?"

"Not really," he said, but he knew that wasn't true. His mind kept pushing one face forward. She had nicely tanned olive skin, thick long black hair and the deepest, darkest brown eyes he'd ever gazed into. She was also not looking for marriage and needed a break from her matchmaking mother. He could provide her cover. But she'd have to be crazy to go along with his idea.

And she wasn't.

She was a single mom who needed her best friend to be there for her. Not come up with some scheme that would enable him to act out his long-held fantasies of calling Bianca Velasquez his.

Even if it was only for two months, three tops.

Damn.

Just then, Derek noticed her walk into the room with a guy who was a couple of years older than they were. She was smiling politely but he knew her routine. She'd brought him to the club for dinner so that when it was over she could politely bid him adieu and then walk the few blocks back to her parents' house in a nearby subdivision.

She was elegant. Graceful. The kind of woman whom

dashing A-listers fell for. Not the kind of woman who'd agree to a fake engagement.

"Uh-oh," Ethan said.

"What-o?" Hunter said.

"That has never been funny," Derek said.

"It's a little funny," Ethan pointed out.

"Not tonight," Derek said.

"I'm still not caught up. Where is Nate?" Hunter asked. Nate was their eldest brother and the last of three of them to arrive. He had recently married the mother of his three-year-old daughter, Penny. Derek liked seeing his eldest brother take on the role of husband and father.

"He's running late. Something to do with taking Penny on a ride before he could drive into town," Ethan said. "Being a daddy has changed him."

"It settled him down," Hunter said. "You two should try it."

"I am, sort of," Derek said. The idea of really settling down and getting married wasn't appealing. He was married to his job. It took a lot of focus and concentration to be a top surgeon and most women—even Marnie—didn't really get that. They wanted a man who paid at least as much attention to them as the job.

"What you're doing doesn't count," Hunter said. "Bianca deserves better than a fake proposal."

"It's probably as close as I'm going to get," Derek admitted. He knew that Ethan was hung up on a woman who was married to one of his friends. So that was probably not going to happen, either. "You know we're the ones who aren't letting the gossips of Cole's Hill down.

They like to think of us as the Wild Carutherses, which we can't be if we are all married up."

"I'll drink to that," Ethan said.

Derek toasted his brother and when Nate joined them a few minutes later the conversation thankfully changed from his fake engagement. Derek ate and drank with his brothers and kept one eye on the bar area where Bianca and her date were. He was ready to help her out. Like a friend would. That was all. Hunter had been right: there was no decent woman who wanted a fake fiancé.

Bianca Velasquez wasn't having the best year. She'd rung in New Year's by herself on the balcony of a royal mansion in Seville while Jose was en route to meet her. His plane had crashed and that had been…well, devastating. She'd never had the opportunity to finish her business with Jose. She'd been mad at him and had said to herself she'd hated him but the truth was he'd been her first love. They had a child together and no matter how many women he slept with while traveling the world on the F1 racing circuit, she…well, she hadn't been ready for him to leave her so abruptly.

She rubbed the back of her neck as what's-his-name droned on about a hobby he'd recently taken up. To be honest she had no idea what he was talking about. She'd zoned out a long time ago. And the thing was, he seemed like a nice man. The kind of man who deserved a woman who would engage in conversation with him instead of marking time and eating her dinner and dessert so quickly she gave herself indigestion. But Bianca couldn't be that woman.

"And I've lost you," he said.

She smiled over at him. He was good-looking and charming, everything she'd normally like in a man. "I'm sorry. This is a case of it really not being you, but me. I'm just…"

He shook his head. "I get it. Your mom mentioned this was a long shot but I couldn't resist seeing if you were as beautiful in person as you were in your photographs."

She blushed. She'd been a full-time model by the time she was eighteen and had gotten a contract that had taken her to Paris and launched her career as a supermodel. It had been in Paris where she'd met Jose and fallen for him. But she was older now and no longer felt like that carefree girl. "Those photos were a long time ago."

"Which photos? I'm talking about the one on your mom's desk," he said.

"Oh. This is embarrassing. I am totally not myself tonight," she said. "I'm sorry to have wasted your time."

"It wasn't a waste and if you ever feel like trying this again," he said, "give me a call."

He got up and left and she sat there at the table, staring out the windows that led to the golf course. The sun had long since set. She should head home but her son was already in bed and her mom would probably want to grill her about the date. And that wasn't going to go well.

So instead she signaled her waiter to clear away the dessert dishes and ordered herself a French martini.

"Want some company?"

She glanced up to see Derek Caruthers standing next to her table. He wore his hair short in the back and longer on top; it fell smoothly and neatly over his forehead. When they'd been kids his brownish blond hair had been unruly and wild, much like Derek himself. These days he was a surgeon renowned for his skills in the operating theater.

"I have it on good authority that I am not that charming tonight."

He pulled out the chair that her date had recently vacated and sat down. "Surely not."

"It's true. I was the most awful date. I felt like the worst sort of mean girl."

He signaled the waiter for a drink, and a moment later he had a highball glass filled with scotch and she had her martini.

"To old friends," he said.

"To old friends," she returned the toast, tapping the rim of her glass against his.

"How'd the meeting go today?" she asked. She envied Derek. He had his life together. He knew what he wanted, he always got it and unlike her he seemed happy with his single life.

"Not as I'd planned," he said.

She took a sip of her drink and then frowned over at him. "That's not like you. What happened?"

"An old frenemy showed up, making problems as is her habit and I had to shut her down," Derek said, downing his drink in one long swallow.

"How?" Bianca asked. "Tell me your troubles and I'll help you solve them."

It was nice to be discussing a problem with Derek. A problem that didn't involve her. The thirty-something who'd moved back in with her parents. She knew the gossips in Cole's Hill had a lot to say about that. From jet-setter to loser in a few short months. She pushed her martini aside realizing she was getting melancholy.

"Actually you can help me out," Derek said, leaning forward and taking one of her hands in his.

"Name it. You're one of my closest friends and you know I would do anything for you."

"I was hoping you'd say that," he said.

She smiled. Of course she'd help Derek out. He'd always been her stalwart friend. When she'd dreamed of leaving Texas and going to Paris to model, he'd listened to her dreams and helped her make a plan to achieve them. When she'd been lonely that first year, he'd emailed and texted with her every day.

"What do you need from me?"

"I need you to be my fiancée."

Two

Fiancée.

Was he out of his mind?

She shook her head and started laughing. Once she started she couldn't stop and she felt that tinge of panic rise up that she thought she'd been successfully shoving way deep down in her gut.

"Thanks, I needed that," she said. "You have no idea what kind of week it's been."

Derek leaned back in his chair, crossing his arms over his chest, which drew the fabric of his dress shirt tight against his muscles. Distracted, she couldn't help but notice the way his biceps bulged against the fabric. One thing that had been hard for her in the years of their friendship was to ignore how hot Derek was. He worked out. He had said one time that a surgeon had to be a precise machine. And that everything—every part of his body and mind—had to be in top shape.

"I'm not joking."

"Uh, what?" she asked. She was tired. Life hadn't worked out according to her plans and if she'd thought that once she reached this age she'd have everything all figured out, she was wrong. Really wrong.

She pushed her martini glass away, feeling a bit as if she'd followed Alice down the rabbit hole. But she knew she hadn't.

"I need a fiancée," Derek said. "The new board member who holds the fate of my career in my hands? It turns out she's a borderline obsessive I dated a while ago. The only way to keep her off my back is to make sure she knows I'm off the market."

"And how do I fit into this?"

Derek tipped his head to the side and studied her. "You could use a fake fiancé as well."

She still wasn't following. She was tired and her heart hurt a little bit if she were completely honest. Derek was one of her best friends and this sounded fishy to her.

"Why?"

"So your mom will quit setting you up on blind dates. You're too kind to tell her you aren't ready to date. If we are engaged then everyone will back off and leave us alone. I can focus on wowing everyone on the board at the hospital so that they have no choice but to name me chief. You can figure out what you want to do next without the pressure your parents are putting on you."

She put her elbows on the table and leaned forward.

When he put it like that she'd be a fool to refuse. "Are you sure about this?"

"I am," he said.

When wasn't Derek sure? She should have already known that would be his answer.

"If we're engaged, why would we have kept it quiet?" she asked.

He leaned in closer to her. "To give Hunter and Nate time in the spotlight. Hunter's wedding is really taking up everyone's energy."

"It is. And Kinley is busy planning it. She's going to wonder why I never even mentioned we were dating."

Bianca and Kinley were good friends. They both had been single mothers with toddlers the same age. Of course, Kinley wasn't single anymore and had found happiness with Derek's brother Nate.

Derek took her hand in his and a tingle went up her arm. "Tell her I asked you to keep it quiet."

"Hmm…it might work. Could I have until the morning to think about it?" she asked.

He nodded.

She pulled her hand away and then sat back, linking her hands together in her lap. Her palm was still tingling. She knew that saying yes would be the easy choice. But what about her son? Benito wouldn't understand that they were just pretending. Though given that he was only two years old he might not understand much of anything that was going on. He was good friends with Kinley's daughter…so he had been asking about his papa lately. He really didn't remember Jose at all.

"That sounds like it would be ideal but we live in the real world."

"Really? I hadn't realized that when I was operating on two different patients today," Derek said.

She recognized the sarcasm as one of his defense mechanisms and she didn't blame him. She was scared. The last time she trusted a man it had been Jose and his word hadn't been worth much.

"I'm not bringing this up to be difficult. I have a son. He's not going to understand why you are in our lives for a short time and then gone," she said. "We aren't twenty anymore, Derek, it's not like when you came to Monaco and we were wild. I'm a mom. You're in line to be chief of cardiology. We're…we are adults."

"Dammit. We can be adults and still be ourselves. You know me, Bi. You always have. I'm not going to disappear from your life when this is over. We're still going to be friends and I'd never cut Benito out. He's your son and just as important to me as you are."

Derek stood up. "Come on. Let's go for a walk where we can talk without worrying who might hear us."

She looked around and noticed they were gathering attention. She should have realized it sooner. "What about the pool game?"

"The boys can make do without me," Derek said. "This is more important."

There was a sincerity in his eyes; she wanted to believe in him. Well, that stunk, she thought. She'd thought she'd somehow become immune to the charm of handsome men. Of course, this was Derek and not some playboy whose parents she didn't know.

But still she'd like to think that her heart beat a little faster when he said she was important. She'd always liked Derek. He'd been one of her closest friends in middle school. He'd had the classic Caruthers good looks, but he'd been supersmart and once he'd graduated high school early and gone off to college and then medical school, they'd kept in touch first on AOL messenger, then on the different social media apps.

Years had passed before she'd seen him as an adult and she'd been blown away by how attractive her old friend had become. Of course, she had a different life by then, but there were times when it still surprised her. She never grew tired of the strong, hard line of jaw, his piercing eyes and the way his hair curled over this forehead. There was something about him that made her want to keep looking at him.

Dangerous.

As dangerous as listening to his idea for this fake engagement. Was there ever an idea that sounded dumber?

Maybe her mom setting her up with young men she knew in the South Texas area.

"What would this entail?" she asked.

Derek didn't allow himself to relax. This was Bianca. Bianca Velasquez. She'd been the prettiest girl at the Five Families Middle School. Though he'd taken an accelerated course in Houston so he'd be able to leave Cole's Hill and go to college early, they'd always kept in touch. At first he'd thought it was because of their families. Growing up there had been a lot of cotillion dances and Junior League events where their moms had thrown them together. But then as they'd both become adults, he'd thought the crush would fade.

It hadn't.

He knew that she wasn't the girl he'd dreamed about in middle school and high school anymore, but there was another part of him that wanted to claim her. That wanted to know that he had won over the prettiest girl from the Five Families neighborhood. That she was his.

Even just temporarily.

She was watching him cautiously. Almost as if she were afraid to trust him. That hurt.

More than it should have.

Granted, he was coming to her with a harebrained scheme, the kind that make his dad laugh his ass off at him. But she did need a break from the blind dates. And he did need a fiancée. He wasn't about to get involved with Marnie again and she would be relentless if he didn't provide a distraction.

"The hospital board has promised to make a decision in two months' time. So I'd need you to be my fiancée for about three months just so that you can attend the gala after I'm announced chief and the wing is opened," he said. Three months. That should be enough to convince him that any crush he'd had on her was well and truly dead. He could go back to being her friend and stop having hot dreams about her.

"Three months? Would we live together?" she asked. "I've been looking for a job and have some modeling gigs set up so I won't be in town continuously during that time. Would that be a problem?"

Derek leaned back in his chair trying to stay cautiously optimistic, but it seemed to him that she was almost on board with the idea. "I don't think so. In fact, I might be able to swing some time off and go with you. It would probably enhance the entire engagement story."

"Fair enough. What about the bachelor auction? I see you're already on the list. Would an engaged guy be on there?" she asked.

"Yes, because we were hiding our engagement. You can bid on me and win me now," he said with a wink.

"If we're engaged why do I have to bid on you?" she asked with a wink back. "My brother is already into me for a month of babysitting if I win him."

Derek had to laugh. The bachelor auction might have been one of the Five Families Women's League's largest fund-raisers but the men were always trying to get out of it. He just didn't like the idea of being at the mercy of someone who'd "won" him.

"I'm offering you three months of no blind dates," he said.

"That's something that Diego can't match."

"Yeah, I'm pretty sure people would not believe you were dating your brother."

"Thank God," she said, laughing. This time there wasn't the manic edge to her tone that had been there earlier when he'd first mentioned the whole engagement scheme.

"Yes. So what do you say? Are we going to do this?" he asked.

"Where would I live?" she asked.

"With me or not. Your choice," he said. "What do you want to do?"

He hadn't thought of anything beyond finding a woman who'd agree and then telling Marnie about her. But now that Bianca had mentioned living with him he knew he wanted her in his house.

Then he immediately had a vision of her in his bed. That thick ebony hair of hers spread out on his pillow, her chocolaty brown eyes looking up at him with sensual demand. Her limbs bare...

"Derek?"

"Huh?" His mind was fully engaged in the fantasy that had taken hold.

"I said, would you mind if I lived with you? I've been staying with my folks but we really need our own space."

He nodded. Living with him worked. "That sounds perfect. What do I need to do to get the place ready for you? Are we doing this?"

She leaned forward and he saw that same concern and uncertainty in her eyes and he realized that fantasies aside, he never wanted to put Bianca in a position where she was anything but a friend to him. He wanted her to be able to count on him. Even if that meant ignoring his own need for her.

"I want to say yes. Can I have the evening to think it over?" she asked, tucking a strand of her hair behind her ear. "I want to make sure I haven't missed any details and I want to run it by Benito. Make sure he's okay with another man in my life."

"He's two, right?"

"Yes, but he and I are very close and I just...after

losing his father, I want to make sure he's going to be okay," Bianca said.

Derek nodded. He wasn't going to force her. He was surprised she'd considered his offer and was willing to go along with it as far as she had this evening.

"That sounds fair," he said, pulling his phone from his pocket and checking his calendar. "I don't have any surgeries scheduled for tomorrow morning so I'm free. Would you and Benito like to come over to my place for breakfast? You can check it out and he can meet me."

"Sounds like a plan."

Too bad she didn't seem so convinced of that. He wasn't too sure how to convince her. This wasn't like the operating room where he knew all the variables and could make sure nothing went wrong. This was life where he tended to make mistakes, and he really hoped this didn't turn out to be a big one.

As she sat there with Derek, Bianca knew that one night wasn't going to be enough time to ensure she made the right choice. But then a two-year-long engagement to Jose hadn't really been beneficial in hindsight. This would work. She needed it to.

She had been struggling since she'd returned to Cole's Hill. She'd stayed in Spain for nine months after Jose's death and then just after Benito had turned twenty-two months old had decided to come back to Texas but she was no closer to figuring out what was next. She was the first to admit that her knee-jerk reaction of divorcing Jose when she'd found out about his mistress had been just her way of getting out of a bad marriage. She'd never thought beyond hurting him the way he'd hurt her. Now that he was dead, she'd hoped the anger would be gone, but she knew it was still there.

And not working, living with her parents where they had a cleaning staff and wanted to hire a nanny for her, just gave her too much time to think about—dwell on—the past. It was humiliating and not productive.

This idea of Derek's was a little bit on the crazy side, she knew that, but there was a part of her that really liked it. From certain angles, she saw it as the solution to all of her problems. She wanted to be out of her parents' house and out from under their overprotectiveness. She could research some career options besides modeling and give her a chance to be the kind of mom to Beni that she wanted to be.

"Yes. That sounds good to me," Bianca repeated. She realized she might have been staring at Derek. As their eyes met something passed between them that never had before.

A zing.

An awareness.

Oh, no. Had he figured out that she'd been secretly crushing on him for the last few months? How embarrassing. She gave him her cotillion smile—the one she always used to put boys in their place back in the day—and then pushed her chair back. "I think I should be getting home."

"I'll walk you back," he said. "Or we can steal one of the golf carts."

She shook her head. "I thought we both agreed to never speak of golf carts."

"No one will suspect a thing," he said.

"That's what you thought the last time. And I'm pretty sure that the groundskeeper knew it was us, even though he could never prove it."

"I'm pretty sure you're right. So, walking might be the safer option," Derek said in that easy way of his.

She felt silly thinking that there might have been something between them. It was probably all on her side. It had been a very long time without sex—since before Beni was born—and she wasn't dead. She had been hoping she'd at least feel okay hooking up with one of her mom's blind dates. But so far it hadn't worked out.

"You okay?" he asked, coming around to hold her chair while she stood.

"Yes. Sorry. Just tired. Being 'on' with a stranger is draining," she said.

Derek put his hand on the small of her back and she felt that zing again. This time a shiver spread up her spine and she stepped aside, fumbling for her handbag.

He followed her out of the dining room. She had an account at the club like all of the families who were members, so they didn't have to settle any bill.

"I need to let my brothers know I'm leaving," Derek said.

She nodded, still more in her head thinking about what he'd asked of her. His family was large, like hers, and she understood the dynamics of having siblings around.

The evening was warm; the unseasonable heat of the day hadn't dissipated yet. The parking lot was full of cars and though it was the middle of the week it felt like the weekend. The night was busy and full of life and she realized that was what she'd been missing.

She hadn't felt busy in a long time. She wasn't saying she had the whole mothering thing licked but she and Beni had fallen into a routine where she knew what to expect. And life had become routine instead of fun. She knew that was why she was thinking of taking Derek up on this idea. It was the first unexpected thing to happen to her since...well, for a really long time.

"I'm glad you're back in Cole's Hill," he said.

"Me, too. Remember how badly we wanted to get out of here?" she asked. "I really thought modeling was going to be the life for me. I mean I figured I'd be like Kate Moss and spend the rest of my life living in the jet set...but now, I'm sort of glad that I'm right here."

"Was Benito planned?" he asked.

"That's kind of personal," she said, but only because he'd stumbled onto an argument she and Jose had had many times.

"We're going to be 'engaged' and we're friends," he said. "Just asking because your dream life didn't sound like it included motherhood."

"It didn't. With all my brothers, I never thought about having a family of my own. I figured I'd be the cool auntie to my nieces and nephews," she said.

"So what happened?" he asked.

"Well..." She paused as they turned off the sidewalk onto the path that led to the manmade lake adjacent to her parents' house. She stopped on the bridge over the lake.

"Well?"

She put one hand on the railing and looked over at Derek. He was her good friend but there were so many things about her he didn't know. The embarrassing stuff that she shared with no one. And this was something that she never needed to tell him. This bit of humiliation had died with Jose.

She looked into Derek's eyes and started to tell him what she always did when she was asked about the baby. But in her heart, she remembered Jose saying that a baby and a family would stop him from looking outside of their marriage bed for company. That a family would ground him in a way nothing else could.

Three

Derek thought she'd have some sort of easy answer. Her modeling career hadn't been conducive to children, but she came from a big family as he did. It might be a bit old-fashioned but he had assumed she would end up wanting kids after she married. But her hesitance told him there was something more to it. He'd struck a nerve that he hadn't meant to and he should have just let it go.

But this was Bianca, and there was that look of sadness in her eyes that he didn't glimpse very often. He put his hand on her shoulder, felt that spark of awareness and shoved it down. She needed a friend not a guy who was turned on by her. That damned perfume of hers wasn't helping. It was subtle and floral and when the wind blew, he couldn't help inhaling a little more deeply.

"Bia?" he asked. "It's okay if you don't want to answer me."

She just glanced over at him with those big brown eyes of hers and he was lost. He realized this was exactly how he'd let himself get friend-zoned by her. She had very emotive eyes and he had always been suckered into wanting to comfort her, to be there for. To slay dragons for her. But Jose was dead so if he was the dragon there wasn't anyone to slay.

Besides she'd had the fairy tale: first-love marriage with Jose. That wasn't the problem.

"Hey, forget I asked. I was just making small talk," Derek said even though that was the farthest thing from the truth.

He heard his old man's voice in his head: *start out as you mean to go on*. Well, lying didn't seem like a really good place to start. But he'd asked her to be his pretend fiancée, not his real one. So maybe that meant they both were entitled to their secrets.

"It's okay. It's just that once I got married my life changed… I mean my priorities changed and then I got pregnant and once I held Beni in my arms, everything just sort of…" She paused, glancing over at him and arching one eyebrow. "Don't make fun of me."

"Why would I?"

"Well, when I had my son it was like a veil was lifted from my life and I realized how shallow I had been. When I considered that little face I wanted to be more. To be better. To give him the world—not material things—but experiences. It changed me."

He could see that. She pretty much glowed whenever she talked about her son. And Derek had seen her in town with the little boy and she seemed to be in her element when she was with him. He couldn't reconcile it but she almost seemed prettier when she talked about her son.

He remembered something his brother Hunter had said once…that women in love were more beautiful. And he finally saw that. He saw it on Bianca's face when she talked about her son. He had to be very sure that he was careful when she moved in with him. She might be his secret crush from adolescence but she was a woman now, a mother, and he couldn't afford to explore a "crush" unless she was looking for the same thing.

He took a deep breath, put his hands on the wooden railing and looked out over the lake. He'd grown up on the Rockin' C but he'd spent a lot of time with his dad on the golf course and hanging out at the club after school.

And as he looked at the moonlight reflecting on the water he thought about how much his town had changed. There was now a NASA training facility on the Bar T. Bianca was a famous supermodel, his brother a former NFL wide receiver. It was crazy.

"I don't think anything has lifted a veil from my life," Derek said out loud. He was still the same inside as he'd always been: determined to do whatever he had to in order to keep on track with his medical career. He'd left the ranch at fifteen and Cole's Hill to go to college, finished undergrad in three years and then gone on to medical school. There had been no stopping him.

"Maybe that's why this setback with being named cardiology chief has been such a shock. I just have always been focused on becoming a surgeon and then on making sure I was the best."

"You are the best," Bianca said. "You're lucky, Derek. You've always known exactly what your purpose is. Some of us stumble around until we find it."

"You? You never seemed to be stumbling."

She threw her head back and laughed, and he listened to the sound of it, smiling. She had a great laugh.

"That's just because I only let people see what I want them to."

"Like the Wizard of Oz?" he asked. They'd both been in the play in middle school. He'd been the Tin Man and she'd been Dorothy.

"Just like that. 'Pay no attention to the woman behind the curtain' should be the motto for my life."

"But not now, right? You have Beni," Derek said.

She shrugged. "I'm still faking it sometimes. I mean, he has given me purpose, but being a mom is tough. Every day as I reflect on what has gone on, I wonder if I've screwed him up…that's why I want to think this engagement over. I don't want to say yes and then realize that this decision is the one that ruined him."

Derek nodded. He was pretty confident in his personal life and in the operating theater but there were times when something went wrong and he had to keep going over the surgery to see what had happened. Had he missed something? Had the error been his? How could he keep it from happening again? He'd never thought that Bianca would be like that.

She seemed confident and able to conquer anything. Seeing that she wasn't perfect made him want her even more. It made her real. Not the image of the girl he'd had a crush on, but the real woman.

This night had taken a turn and she wasn't sure she was that upset by it. She had been saying that she wanted something different to happen. That she was tired of the Wednesday night blind dates set up by her mom that coincided with her dad taking Beni and her brothers out to dinner at the Western Two Step. Her father had missed out on bonding with Beni after his birth as they had been living in Spain. So her father was determined to make up for lost time. And the Wednesday nights with the boys were a long-established tradition in their family. It was a sports bar of sorts that had a huge gaming area in the back; they served what her father called "man food." Pretty much just burgers, steaks and fried everything. It was a tradition in their family for as long as Bianca could remember.

When she'd been in her teens every Wednesday she and her mom would have a spa night and go and get pedicures and manicures or facials or massages. And have a "girl's night out." Somehow her mom's desire to see her with a new man had taken over girl's night. Bianca knew that saying she was engaged to Derek would probably make her mom happier than just about anything else right now. The top of her bucket list was seeing her daughter happy again.

She'd said that to her.

And now she was standing next to the lake with the

cicadas singing their song in the background and Derek was watching her with that too intent look of his. It was something she associated mostly with him when he was in surgeon mode. But tonight, he was concentrating on her.

She knew how important being named chief of the cardiology department was to him. He'd laid out his life plans when they were fifteen; at the time, he'd been getting ready to leave for college and she'd just gotten her first modeling job in Paris. They had been sort of thrown together as the two outsiders. The two who were leaving. And here they were again.

There was a bubble of excitement in her stomach, something that she hadn't felt since Beni had started walking and talking. She shook her head and cursed under her breath.

"What? Are you okay?" Derek asked.

She nodded wryly at him. "I just hate it when my mom is right. I mean, it would be nice if she started screwing up sometime. But every time I rail against her interfering in my life, something happens to show me she's onto something again."

"What are you talking about?" he asked.

She realized she couldn't tell him how she felt. He wanted a friend. Not a woman who was feeling all tingly and very aware of the shape of his mouth. He had a great-looking mouth. Why was she noticing it now? And now that she'd noticed it why couldn't she stop wondering how it would feel pressed against hers?

"Nothing... I think I can make it safely home from here if you want to get back to your brothers," she said.

The sooner she got away from the temptation that Derek offered the better she'd be. Maybe it was just her reaction to being with a guy who—what? The nice man her mom had set her up with had been good-looking, too. So why was she attracted to Derek and not to him?

And shouldn't that be a mark in the con column for going through with the pretend engagement?

But she knew she wasn't going to say no. Not now. Not since she'd noticed his mouth and couldn't get out of her mind if he was a good kisser or not.

It was shallow, but for once the weight that had been on her since Jose's death seemed to be long gone. She didn't feel like the hot mess she'd been. She felt almost…well, almost like her old self and there was nothing that would make her walk away from this.

She'd forgotten how fun it was to not know what was coming next. How much she enjoyed the first flush of attraction. And this was safe. Right? Derek wanted a fake fiancée. She could do that. Be close to him, have her little infatuation but protect her heart. She wasn't going to fall for Derek Caruthers. The man was married to his job.

Everyone knew that.

There was no sense in pretending that he'd ever be interested in any woman for longer than a few months. It was precisely why he'd suggested a temporary pretend engagement.

"You have the funniest look on your face," he said. "I'm not going to abandon you before I see you home. My dad would whup me if word got back to him."

She smiled because she knew he meant for her to.

"You can see me to the sidewalk outside the house. If you come to the door my mom is going to grill us both and we haven't made a decision yet. You promised me time to think."

As if thinking was going to do her any good now that lust had entered the picture. She closed her eyes, desperately tried to remember what fifteen-year-old Derek had looked like. Tall, gangly, still wearing braces and with a little bit of acne, but it didn't matter because as soon as she opened her eyes she found herself staring at his mouth.

Adult Derek's mouth was lush; his lips just looked kissable. She'd kissed her fair share of men and some of the kisses had been disappointing but his mouth... he looked like he wouldn't disappoint.

"Bianca, I'm trying not to notice but you are staring at my mouth," he said.

"Mmm-hmm," she said.

"It's making me stare at your mouth and that is putting some decidedly different thoughts into my head."

"Like what?" she asked, throwing caution to the winds. Maybe he'd suck at kissing and she'd be able to walk away from him.

Or maybe not.

Derek knew he was treading very close to the edge of someplace that there would be no turning back from. He might be able to make the whole platonic-friends-helping-each-other thing work if he was able to keep his mind off the curve of her hips and the way she nibbled her lower lip when she was mulling over something.

But when she looked at his mouth, chewed her lower lip…it didn't take a mind reader to figure out what she was contemplating.

And for the first time since his ill-fated affair with Marnie he was on the cusp of doing something that might derail his career goals. Because he was afraid one kiss wouldn't be enough. He wasn't ready to settle down until he'd been established as head of cardiology. He wanted to keep his focus on medicine. He needed someone like Bianca because she was respectable, well-liked and not the kind of woman Marnie would ever believe he'd coerced into being his fiancée. A smart man would remember that instead of reaching out and touching a strand of Bianca's hair as it blew in the summer breeze—and possibly blow his chance of her going along with the fake engagement.

A smart man would be taking two steps away from her instead of one half step closer and letting his hand brush the side of her cheek. Her skin was soft, but really that wasn't a surprise. She looked like she'd have prefect skin. The scent of her perfume once again drifted on the breeze and he couldn't help himself when she tipped her head to the side and her eyes slowly drifted closed.

She wanted his kiss.

He wanted to kiss her.

He leaned in and felt the soft exhalation of her breath over his jaw just before he touched her lips with his. Just a quick brush. That was all he intended but her lips were soft and parted slightly under his and he found himself coming back and kissing her again. He angled his head slightly to the right and she shifted as well and the kiss deepened. His tongue slipped into her mouth. She tasted of Indian summer and promises.

He shifted his hand on her head, cupping the back of her neck as he took all that she offered in the kiss. She was like the sweetest addiction he'd ever encountered and he knew that walking away, just forgetting this, wasn't going to happen. He wanted her.

He felt the stirring in his groin and his skin felt too tight for his body. He started to draw her closer to him but stopped. He didn't want to rush any second of this. He wanted this embrace to last forever.

Because this was Bianca. The girl who'd always been too pretty, too smart and some would say too good for him. He didn't want the kiss to end and her to come to her senses.

Maybe it was the moon or the night or the warm breeze making her forget that they were friends. That she'd friend-zoned him a long time ago but he knew he wasn't going to want to let her go. Not tonight.

But he had to.

He pulled his head back, looking down at her. Her lips were parted, moist and slightly swollen from his kiss. Her eyes slowly blinked open.

"Derek…that was…"

He put his finger over her lips. He didn't want to discuss it. "Just a kiss between friends. We're doing each other a favor and tonight, seeing you here in the moonlight, I just couldn't resist."

She chewed her lower lip for a second and then nodded. "Do you think it was an aberration? That maybe it won't happen again?"

Lying to himself was one thing, but lying to her was something else. "Honestly, I think we'd be kidding ourselves—or at least I'd be kidding myself—if I said I wasn't going to be tempted to kiss you again."

"Me, too," she admitted. "I was sort of afraid that you didn't feel the same."

"That kiss was…"

"Magic," she said. "Like you intimated earlier it was probably the pale moon and the balmy night that are making us a little crazy. We're friends. We are doing each other a favor. Complicating things by kissing each other and thinking about each other in a non-friend way—"

"Non-friend way?" he interrupted. "I didn't realize friends couldn't kiss each other."

"You know what I mean," she said, crossing her arms under her breasts in a defensive pose.

"I do. But I wanted you to know that your friendship comes first. I have to admit I've thought about kissing you since you came home this summer. I hadn't realized how much you'd changed. You're prettier than I remembered, which is saying a lot, since you were so beautiful when we were teenagers."

"Thank you. That is one of the sweetest things I've ever heard. I should be getting home," she said.

He took her hand in his and led her up off the footbridge to the sidewalk in front of her house. She didn't say anything else and neither did he. He felt like there had been too much between them for this one night. He needed her.

For his career.

And he wanted her.

For himself.

And never had he been so conflicted about what he wanted.

"I guess this is good-night."

"Good night," he said. "I'll see you and Benito in the morning?"

"Yes. Probably around eight unless that's too early."

Normally eight on a day off would be too early but this was Bianca. And he had a feeling he was going to spend a restless night remembering that kiss. And trying to figure out how he was going to keep from repeating it once she moved in with him. Unless he could sleep with her and then let her walk away. But since he'd promised to stay friends with her and her son, Derek thought it would be wiser to try to keep them from becoming lovers.

And his gut seemed to say that her answer would be yes. That they were going to be living together.

He needed a plan to keep himself together when that happened.

"That's perfect," he said.

He stood there until she entered her house and then headed back to the club.

Four

Her mom was waiting for her in the formal living room when she walked in the door. Bianca took her shoes off and then walked into the room and sat down on the settee next to her mother.

"Another dud?" her mom asked.

"*Si,*" Bianca answered her in Spanish. "But I did have something interesting happen."

"Good. Tell me all about it," she said.

"Not yet. Probably tomorrow. I'm tired and need to process it."

Her mom reached over and pushed her hair back from her forehead. "Are you okay?"

She shrugged. She'd kept the gory details of Jose's cheating from her parents but her mom had somehow figured it out. Somehow talking about it out loud had always made her feel like it would be more real. Bianca had almost been able to fool herself into believing that no one else knew if she kept it silent.

"I'm getting there," she said. And she was. "I think you might be right that dating is a good idea."

"Of course I'm right," her mother said with a smile. "Want something to drink?"

"Not tea. Maybe sparkling water with lime."

"I have to work early tomorrow," her mom said as they approached the kitchen. Their housekeeper always kept the bar cart stocked with sliced citrus, maraschino cherries and olives.

Her mom drove to Houston very early in the morning for work at the TV station. She could have requested that the family move to Houston to make her commute easier but she never had. The Velasquez family was rooted in Cole's Hill. Bianca's father's family had settled here with a land grant from the Spanish king generations ago. The fact that they now made their money from a world-class breeding and insemination program for thoroughbred horses instead of from actual ranching didn't make a difference.

"Beni will have me up very early, too. And I have an appointment in the morning."

"That little scamp does like sunrise," her mom said. "Sit down. I'll get our drinks. I gave Caz the night off. No sense having her in the house with just me."

"Makes sense. Do you and Dad think you'll downsize any time soon?" Bianca asked. She wondered how long her parents would keep the big house now that it was just the two of them. Having her and Beni here really hadn't made a difference in the huge house. Growing up with four brothers she'd never felt crowded.

"I don't know. Your poppa doesn't want to consider moving. Instead he wants to be here for our grandkids. Are you thinking of moving somewhere else?" her mom asked.

"I don't know. I am really happy being back here and am trying to find something I can do so that Beni can grow up here, too," she said.

Her mind drifted to Derek. His idea was a sort of solution. This was what she needed to mull over. Was the risk of the attraction she felt for him worth the chance she'd have to really figure out what she wanted? The fake engagement would give her space to think. She was afraid if she kept living with her parents she'd start to want what they wanted for her and Beni. Not what she wanted for herself.

Her mom talked about the housekeeper and her father's new idea to trade his pickup in for a Harley and Bianca listened with half an ear. She missed her son. It was only a little after eight o'clock but he had a late nap on Wednesdays so he could stay out until nine with his uncles and his grandfather. She wished he were home so she could stare into his little face and try to decide if going along with Derek's idea was the right thing or not.

It was hard to believe that she was considering it. Why wouldn't she agree to it?

After that kiss she had another reason to think twice about his proposition. This wasn't as straightforward as it had been when Derek had first sat down at her table in the club and made his offer.

But she didn't regret the kiss.

How could she?

"Don't you think?" her mom asked.

"What?"

"You aren't listening to a thing I've said. Are you okay, sweetie?"

She shrugged. "Yes. But I have a decision to make and I'm not sure what to do."

"Can I help?"

"No!"

"Well, I was just offering."

"Sorry, Mom, I didn't mean it like that. This is just something I need to decide for myself. And it's weighing on my mind. I didn't mean to ignore you. What were you saying? Something about Dad and a motorcycle?"

Her mom took a sip of her sparkling water and then reached across the table, putting her hand on Bianca's and squeezing it. "When I was trying to figure out if I should give up my job and be a stay-at-home mom like everyone expected me too, I spent a lot of time mulling things over. And in the end, well, you know I chose the morning news job."

"I know. That must have been hard, Mom," Bianca said.

"It wasn't as hard as living with the decisions afterward. The first three or four months I second-guessed everything. Should I have been home when Diego fell off his skateboard and broke his arm? Was my job the reason it happened? All of these were making me crazy and I was very unhappy. But your poppa pulled me aside one night and sat me down and said no matter what decision I had made, not picking the other choice was going to haunt me. He told me to commit to the decision I had made. And enjoy my life."

Bianca hadn't thought she needed to hear anything from her mom tonight but as always, her mom had found the exact right thing to say.

"Thanks, Mom. Every time I think I'm all grown up and know what you are going to say you surprise me."

"Good. Keeps you on your toes," she said with a wink. "Want to talk or watch a reality show?"

"Reality TV, please. I need some fake drama in my life," Bianca said.

They spent the rest of the evening watching TV until her dad and Beni got back home. Beni was dozing in her dad's arms and her father carried the little boy up to his bedroom. After her parents left, Bianca changed him into his pj's and then lay down on the bed next to her son, watching him sleep.

She wanted to say yes to Derek's proposition. And if she was very careful maybe he could be the transition between this and the next phase of her life. He wanted temporary and she had the feeling temporary was all she could really handle right now.

Plus, it was Derek. He was one of the few men she could count on always having her back and usually not expecting anything in return. And he had never asked her for anything before. She was intrigued and knew that she wanted to do it.

Why was she hesitating?

The last time she'd followed her gut, it hadn't worked out so well, she admitted.

* * *

Derek had taken the long way back to the clubhouse and now was headed to the billiards room—which was just what the club called one of the fancy private rooms that had a pool table.

"What'd she say?" Nate asked as Derek walked into the room.

What had she said? He hadn't thought of anything but that kiss and how complicated she really was. So much more than he'd anticipated when he'd first thought of asking her to help him out. But he realized now that even though they were friends there was a lot about Bianca he didn't know. He was intrigued— he'd be lying if he said he wasn't. And a part of him was worried that if she said yes she'd be a constant distraction. The other part of him was concerned if she said no that he wouldn't be able to stop thinking about the kiss and he'd go after her.

And his track record with long-term wasn't the best. So that would mean losing her completely from his life when they were done with their arrangement. He wasn't sure exactly what it was he did wrong with women but generally speaking he wasn't friends with any of the women he'd slept with.

"D? Something wrong with your hearing?" Hunter asked.

Derek gave him the finger while he opened a bottle of Lone Star beer and took a deep swallow.

"She's thinking it over," Derek said, turning to face the room and his brothers. Ethan and Nate stood near the table, while Hunter was racking the balls.

"That's not really much better than a flat-out no. Are you sure about this?" Hunter asked.

Hell, yes. If he'd had any doubts they had been amplified the minute her lips had melted under his. He rubbed the back of his neck, glanced at his watch and realized only forty-five minutes had passed since he'd left her. How was he going to make it until eight the next morning when time seemed to be moving so incredibly slowly?

But telling his brother that wasn't something Derek wanted to do.

"Yes. I've never been as sure of anything other than that I am the best surgeon in the world."

Hunter clapped him on the back. "Okay. But you know we are going to tease the hell out of you about this."

"How would that be any different than what you always do?" Derek asked. "You're forgetting that you have a honeymoon and a wedding night coming up. I think you're in for your share of teasing."

"But you also have the bachelor auction," Hunter added. "You and Ethan are going to be representing the Caruthers. Don't let us down. Or are you going to use your engagement to get out of it? I wouldn't blame you one bit."

"That's a good idea. I should line someone up. We need to bring in the big bucks like we always do," Ethan said. The auction raised money for the women and children's shelter.

"We don't always beat everyone else. The Velasquez boys beat us last year. And the Callahans think they are going to have a better shot this year because of Nate and Hunter being taken," Ethan said. "Liam was bragging about it over at the Bull Pit last night."

"How'd that go for him?" Derek asked. Ethan might be a lawyer and a damned fine one but he was also a Caruthers and they were all fighters.

"He left with a black eye and I'm wishing I'd listened to Dad and learned to lead with my left."

Derek laughed. Ethan was too much. He sensed there was something going on with his brother but right now he needed to concentrate on his own problems.

"Good," Nate said. "We only were behind the Velasquez brothers last year because Hunter wasn't here. Even if he's off the market now, he's good luck. He always brings the women with deep pockets. Remember that year you had that socialite from New York bid on you?" Nate asked.

Hunter grimaced. "Yes. She was interesting, to say the least. I'm glad I'm out of the running this year."

"Don't breathe a deep sigh of relief yet. Mom is talking about having an auction next year where wives bid on husbands to raise funds for the women's shelter."

"Ugh. Let's play pool and drink so we don't have to think about this," Hunter said. "Besides, we are supposed to be making fun of Derek and his fake engagement."

"Is it on?" Nate asked. "I thought she was thinking it over."

"I wouldn't have figured Bianca would stoop so low."

"Just proves you're not as smart as you think you

are, Ethan. She's considering it. We're friends, so it's not like it's that far of a stretch."

"Whatever you say," Ethan said. "Better you than me."

They played pool and ribbed each other until two in the morning. Ethan had too much to drink and decided to bunk at Nate's apartment in town. Nate dropped him off on his way home to the family ranch and Derek walked to his house on the other side of the country club from where Bianca's family lived.

He'd bought the house once he'd decided to come back to Cole's Hill and practice medicine. He could have had a bigger career in a bigger city but it wasn't about bigger for him. It was about doing what he loved and helping the people of his community.

He let himself into his house and his dog, Poncho, came running to meet him. The pug had been a gift from his parents last Christmas. The house was empty though and he thought about how nice it would be to come home and have Bianca waiting for him.

And maybe taking her to his bed and finishing what they'd started with that kiss.

Beni woke Bianca up at five with his little hand on her face and she opened her eyes and stared into his wide-eyed gaze and smiled. She hadn't meant to fall asleep in her son's room last night. "Good morning, *changuito*."

She called him her little monkey just as her father had called her when she was little. Beni had a stuffed monkey—whom he called Gaucho—they'd gotten at the Rainforest Café in London the last time they'd been in the city.

"Morning, Mama. Didya miss me?" he asked.

"I did. That's why I slept in here with you," she said, kissing the top of his head and then ruffling his hair. "Is that okay?"

He nodded. "I missed you, too."

She hugged him close for a minute and then shifted back. "This morning we are going to have breakfast with a friend."

"Yay!" Beni said, moving with lightning speed from under the covers to sit up. "Who is it? Penny?"

"Not Penny. But we are going to see her on Friday night for a movie in the square. This is a friend of Mommy's. He's..." She trailed off. How was she going to explain to her son that Derek had asked them to live with him for a little while? "He's asked us if we want to stay with him while we are waiting to live in our own place."

"What about *Abuelo* and *Abuela*?" Beni asked.

"They'd live here. It's not far from here. We are going to take the golf cart over to his house."

"What about my car? And Gaucho?"

Bianca let her gaze drift over to the motorized miniature F1 car that Moretti Motors had sent him for his last birthday. The car was an exact replica of the one that Jose used to drive for them. She ruffled her son's hair. "All of your stuff will be there, too. Even the stuff we have in storage."

"Yay!" he said, jumping to his feet and then bouncing around on his bed. It would be nice to have her own space. Her parents had had to make one of the guest rooms into a playroom/nursery for Beni. She hadn't wanted to impose on them especially since she hadn't intended to stay her that long.

Moving in with Derek would be the impetus she needed to really get moving on finding her own place. He wasn't going to want her to stay after he received his promotion. And overnight she'd realized that one kiss wasn't really that scary. She could handle the attraction she felt for him.

She'd reminded herself they were friends first. And she wasn't all that sexual. That was one of the reasons Jose had used for having a mistress. The kiss was a fluke. One that she was determined wouldn't happen again.

Beni bounced close to the edge and Bianca grabbed him around his middle, catching him midair. She turned and pulled him down on the bed next to her.

"Tickle time," she said.

He started laughing and she felt his little fingers moving over her ribs. She laughed along with him, tickling him until her heart felt too full. She hugged her son close and thought more about this move and realized that she really was going to say yes.

She couldn't stay here in her parents' house forever. Though they'd never ask her to leave outright, Bianca realized all the matchmaking might have been her mom's way of telling her it was time to start thinking about what she was going to do with the rest of her life.

Even though she and Jose had been headed for divorce when he'd died, Bianca realized that she'd never had a chance to deal with her anger toward him. They'd fought, of course, but she'd always thought she'd see him again. She'd been so mad at him for dying that she hadn't really wanted to move on. She had unfinished business and she guessed that was why she'd been hiding out.

But Derek had given her something new to focus on. So she'd do this. She'd be his fiancée for three months. And she'd keep her lust for the surgeon under wraps so that they could both get what they wanted. A promotion for Derek and some breathing room for herself.

Beni's tummy grumbled and she sat up. "Hungry?"

"Yes," he said.

"Why don't you use the potty and then meet me on the patio for breakfast," she suggested. The sun was just starting to come up.

"Can we swim after?"

"Yes," she said. "We have to be over at my friend's at eight so we have a little bit of time."

"Yay!" he said. He'd used to say *fantástico* whenever he was excited but his new friend Penny said yay. So he'd been using that a lot more. She noticed that his language was changing from mostly Spanish to English since they'd been back in Texas. Her family spoke some Spanish but mainly English at home, which was different from how it had been when Bianca and Beni had lived in Seville near Jose's family.

"I'll leave your bathing suit on the bed," she said to him in Spanish. Though it was early autumn it wasn't cold in Texas and her parents kept their pool heated.

"*Gracias*, Mama. I love you," he replied in Spanish. She watched him run toward the bathroom and then got out of bed. She found his racing bathing suit, a tiny Speedo that he liked to wear, and his water shoes and placed them on the end of the bed after she made it. Even though her family had always had a housekeeper her mom had insisted they make their own beds.

Bianca went into her room and donned her bikini and a cover-up. She pulled her hair up into a ponytail and then headed downstairs to get breakfast together for her and Beni. Even though it wasn't even six her mom had already headed out for work and her father had left a note saying he had gone to Austin to pick up something he'd ordered.

She and Beni had a light breakfast of fruit and then swam for an hour before she took him upstairs for his bath. She realized she was nervous and excited as she blow-dried her hair and put on her makeup. She took care using all the tips and tricks she'd learned from stylists during her years as a model to ensure she looked her best.

And only then did she feel like she was ready to go and see Derek.

She knew this was a fake engagement but the rest of the world wouldn't. Or at least that was what she told herself. Deep inside she knew that she wanted Derek to want her. Not to pity her. To see her as a woman he wanted by his side, not one he needed in order to keep his she-wolf at bay.

Five

Derek had never been around kids much. He had a new niece who was Benito's age—Penny. She was Nate's daughter but Nate had only found out about her a few months ago. So Derek and the rest of the Caruthers family were just getting to know her. Penny talked a lot. And now, as the morning progressed, Derek soon realized that Benito was a bit of a chatterbox as well.

He was adorable. He spoke English with a slight accent and he was very polite. It was also clear to Derek that Benito and Bianca had a close bond. The little boy never did anything without checking with his mom first.

While Derek had been awake most of the night waiting for Bianca to come over, this morning he'd thought a lot about her marriage to Jose and how this temporary thing he'd suggested could ever only be something between friends. Everyone—and he meant everyone in the world—knew that Bianca and Jose had been a fairy-tale love match. Her marriage had even been covered by E! and *InStyle* magazine. Not that Derek watched or read either of those things but his office manager did and she'd kept him up to date on the details.

How could she ever move on from the love of her life? And if she did, Derek suspected it wouldn't be with him. He was the rebound guy. The one who would make it easy for her transition to whoever was next in her life. And that was fine with him, he thought. He wasn't looking for more than that and neither was she.

He had brought them to the courtyard of his house. Built back in the 1980s, it was a large Spanish mission-style place with a central courtyard. There were two bedrooms on the ground floor that both opened onto the courtyard; the living room, kitchen and dining room did, too. He had a pool in the backyard and a large fire pit and outdoor kitchen. But the courtyard had a big fountain in the middle that had to be turned on. Benito had brought a stuffed monkey with him and Derek led him to the small stash of boats that Penny had played with the one time that Nate had brought her to his house.

He had asked his…well, butler sounded silly and housekeeper always made everyone think of a woman. Anyway, he'd asked Cobie, the guy who took care of the house and grounds and lived in the pool house, to make sure the fountain was on this morning and that breakfast was waiting for them on the table. It was just scrambled egg whites with spinach and turkey bacon, but Derek wanted to be able to offer Bianca and her son something to eat.

"Have you had breakfast?" he asked.

"Yes, but that was hours ago and we've had a swim, so we are hungry, aren't we?" Bianca asked her son.

"Si. Muy hambriento."

Benito ate the turkey bacon and a small portion of the eggs before asking if he could get down. Derek had noticed his eyes drifting to the fountain.

"There are some boats over by the fountain if you want to play with them while your mom and I finish eating," Derek said.

"Can I?" he asked Bianca.

"Si, be careful."

"Yay! I will be," Benito said. "Mama, will you watch Gaucho?"

"I will."

Bianca helped her son out of his chair. They placed the stuffed monkey in the center of the cushion on the chair and Bianca took her son over to the fountain. Derek listened as she gave the boy a few instructions, but he was distracted by watching Bianca. She was breathtakingly beautiful this morning. She wore a slim-fitting sundress, and when she knelt next to her son to talk to him, the skirt pooled around her legs. Her arms were lean and tanned. As she stood up and turned to walk back to the table, she noticed him staring at her.

He simply shrugged. She had to be used to men staring at her.

She arched one eyebrow at him but smiled.

He stood and held her chair for her so she could sit

down. Once he was seated again he took a sip of his orange juice and then folded up his napkin and placed it next to his plate. He wasn't hungry and pretending he was seemed foolish to him.

"Have you made your decision?" he asked as she carefully broke a piece of the bacon in half.

She put the bacon down on the plate and then wiped her fingers on her napkin. "I have."

He waited, expecting her to expand, but she didn't reply. Instead she pushed her sunglasses up on the top of her head, glancing over at her son, who was happily splashing the boat around in the water.

"And?"

She turned back to face Derek and nodded. "I'll do it. I think… I think we can make this work for both of us."

Something shifted deep inside his soul and he felt a surge of excitement. "Good. Very good. I will figure out how to ask you in public so we can announce it to our families. We can say the meeting at the hospital forced us to go public before Hunter's wedding."

"Okay. I don't want to leave it too long. I've already mentioned to Benito that we might come and live with you," Bianca said. "And he's a toddler so keeping secrets is pretty foreign to him."

"That works for me. How about a dinner here on Friday night? That's tomorrow so it only gives us a little time for me to plan it and see if I can get my brothers and parents here. Can your parents attend?"

Now that she'd said yes, he wanted to get things rolling and get her moved in and his ring on her finger.

Then he wanted to announce their engagement at work and at the hospital.

"I will have to change our plans. We were meant to go the movie in the square on Friday night, but I think this should take precedence. My brothers might want to come," Bianca said.

"Fair enough. My dining room seats twenty. Or I could rent a room at the club," he suggested.

"That might be more public," Bianca said. "Do you need it to be public?"

Having Bianca's agreement made him want to get everything moving. He wanted everyone in Cole's Hill to know she was his fiancée. He knew it was temporary, but that didn't mean they had to act that way in public.

And the more people who knew about the engagement the more likely Marnie would hear about them together and then he wouldn't have to do anything other than be awesome at his job.

Being in public made her uneasy when she thought about what would be her second engagement. Everything about her marriage to Jose had been fodder for the gossip websites and part of that had been her fault. Her manager had suggested that if they publicized the wedding then she might be able to transition her career from cover model into lifestyle trendsetter—writing blogs, doing videos talking about products that her followers would then buy and showing people a slice of her life. She'd gone along with it. She had thought that it would be the next logical step in her career.

And Jose had loved the spotlight so his first instinct

was to say yes. And they'd done it all. Cameras had followed them around as they made selections for the wedding ceremony. Nothing had been private and a part of Bianca had always wondered if that had been the beginning of the end for her and Jose.

"I don't need it to be public. I'm happy to have it here. In fact we could set up some tables here in the courtyard and have dinner out here," he said. His brow was furrowed and she wondered what he was thinking.

She felt that shiver of fear down the back of her spine and realized that she'd forgotten this part of relationships. Second-guessing and never really being sure she was doing the right thing. She didn't want to start this again. What had she been thinking?

Before Jose had died but after she'd made the decision to divorce him, she'd thought she'd never get involved with another man again. It had been unrealistic but she realized now why she'd made that decision. She reached for her glass of juice, missed it and spilled it on the table.

She stood up to avoid getting any on her legs and reached for her napkin to dab it.

"Sorry about that," she said.

Derek put his hand over hers and stood up as well. "It's okay. What have I done?"

"What?" she asked.

"Something I said triggered a look of panic on your face and I don't want that. Listen, we're partners in this. We're helping each other out," he said, his voice calm and assertive.

In fact, it was so reassuring that she remembered

this was her friend. Derek. She didn't have to worry that he was going to fall out of love with her and start cheating on her because they weren't in love. But they were in this temporary thing together. And a man who was trying to convince the town and his ex-girlfriend and potential new boss that he was engaged wouldn't be tomcatting around.

She took a deep breath.

"Sorry. I just remembered the craziness of my last wedding and engagement and I didn't want to repeat that."

"No problem. I prefer to keep it private. That's more our style anyway."

"We have a style?" she asked, slightly amused now that her panic had subsided.

"We do. And it's kid-friendly and family-focused," he said. "I'd like to invite my best friend and my brothers and their significant others and of course my parents but otherwise that's it."

"Same. Kinley's my best friend so she's already on the invite list. We don't have to invite her twice," Bianca said, smiling. "Let me clean this up and then we can start making a list."

"A list?" he asked, reaching around her and scooping up the plates after sopping up the juice with both of their napkins. "I got the cleanup. You stay here with Benito."

"Thank you," she said, realizing how different Derek was from Jose, who never would have touched a dirty dish. To be fair to him he had employed a fairly large staff for the three of them. But still.

"No problem. It's not the 1950s. I think I can handle

cleaning up. Would you be okay if I bring Cobie back to help out with the planning? He's probably going to do the bulk of getting the courtyard ready since I've got surgery tomorrow morning."

Every word out of Derek's mouth just was further confirmation of how different he was from Jose. And she felt the last of her tension melt away.

She nodded. "That would be great."

He turned toward the French doors that led back into the kitchen and she followed him, putting her hand on his shoulder to stop him. "Thank you, Derek. I hadn't realized how much baggage I was carrying around from Jose and the way things ended with him. And this... I think this fake engagement is going to be very good for me."

He tipped his head to the side and gave her one of those smiles of his that was sweet and true and re-minded her of the boy he'd been before life had shaped him into the arrogant surgeon he was today. "That's exactly what I was hoping."

He continued into the house and she turned to see Benito splashing in the fountain. He was maneuver-ing the boat and making huge waves with his hands. She smiled and started laughing. The sun was shining, her little boy was happy and for once she didn't feel the shadow of her past, of her doubts and of her ennui, hanging over her the way it had been for too long now.

She went over to Beni, scooped him up and kissed him on the top of his head.

"Mama! I'm playing," he said, squirming to get down.

"I know, *changuito*, I just needed a hug."

He stopped squirming and wrapped his little arms around her neck and held her tightly. "It's okay. I like your hugs."

She set him down and watched him go back to his play before realizing that it had been a while since she'd seen Derek. She glanced over her shoulder and noticed he was watching her. And the look on his face made a shiver of awareness go down her spine.

Derek knew he had to keep things cool. But seeing the expression on Bianca's face at breakfast had given him the first clue that things maybe hadn't been perfect in her marriage to that F1 racecar driver. He knew it was none of his business. They had an arrangement, but this was Bianca and he had never been able to be cool around her.

Well, he'd been able to maintain appearances on the outside, of course, but inside she'd always had the ability to stir up his base instincts and make it impossible for him to think.

Again he had that fleeting thought that this might be a mistake but there was no way he wasn't going through with it. Bianca Velasquez was going to live with him. She was going to be his fiancée.

And even if that was temporary, he was okay with it.

He struggled to keep his eyes and his mind on the planning of the party where they'd announce their engagement to their friends and family. Instead all he could think of was how long her legs were and how hot that kiss had been the night before.

He wanted another kiss. In fact his libido was hinting

that they should probably practice kissing again before they had to do it in front of everyone tomorrow night. It made sense. It was logical. They had to convince the people who knew them best that this was a love match and his brothers…well, they knew the truth. He had to warn them not to say anything to anyone else.

Not that they would but he wanted to chat with them before the dinner. He didn't want to have any problems on the night of the announcement.

"You have a very serious look on your face," Bianca said. "If you don't want lights strung over the garden, it's okay to say no. Remember what you said, we're partners in this."

"It wouldn't be that hard to rig it up," Cobie said, who had now joined them in the living room. "We already have the anchors from the Christmas lights in the beams. I'm not sure if I can get all the lights we'd need in town but I could drive to Houston for more if I need them."

"I think Mom has some. I'll call and ask her if I can borrow them," Derek said. "I don't mind the lights. I was thinking about something else."

"The food? I am a pretty fair cook," Bianca said.

"No. You're not cooking the food for the party," Derek said. "Cobie, call that catering company we used for Christmas and see if they can do it."

"Cobie, would you mind giving us a minute?" Bianca said.

Cobie raised both eyebrows at her and then shrugged and turned away. "Hey, little dude, want to see the pool?"

"Mama, is that okay?" Beni asked her.

"*Si,*" she said.

Cobie held his hand out to Beni, who took it. Derek watched them both leave.

"What's up?" he asked.

"I don't mind if you prefer a caterer but I will not have you tell me what I can't do. It sends the wrong message to Beni and personally I don't like it. I'm a grown woman and I can make my own decisions," she said.

Derek hadn't meant it the way she'd obviously taken it. "Sorry. I just meant it was a special night for you and I didn't want you working to prepare food for twenty or more guests."

"Fair enough. I think it was the delivery method. Maybe next time you could phrase it less like you were trying to boss the little woman around," she said.

"I'm happy enough to do that," he said. "Sorry if it came out that way."

"No problem. And now that I know where you're coming from, I believe a caterer would be a good idea. I think Mom has one that she uses and I know the club will cater in your home," Bianca said. "Since Cobie is handling the lights and decoration, would you like me to handle the food?"

Derek hadn't thought about asking her to plan any of this. "Sure. Do you have time?"

"Well, since I didn't get the job of receptionist at your medical group…yes, I have the time," she said. She'd applied for a job at his medical practice thinking that would give her something to do. But his office manager had pointed out that Bianca didn't have any skills to be an office worker.

"You didn't want to be a receptionist. I did you a favor," he said. "And you did a favor to Jess whom we hired because she needs the job and the money. She's going to college and had been working two part-time jobs and making less than what we're paying her now."

"That makes me feel better. But I'm still not working and could use something to occupy my time."

"I thought you had a modeling gig booked," he said. They had never really discussed what she'd be doing once they were engaged.

"I do. But it's not for a couple of weeks. We probably need to sit down and compare our schedules. That gig is in Paris. Normally I stop by Seville when I'm done with my work, to visit with my…with Jose's parents before coming back to Texas. Would you like to meet them?"

No. He most definitely didn't want to meet Jose's parents. But he had a feeling that was jealousy. "That would be fine. I'll have to check my schedule and see if I'm available. I have surgeries scheduled and of course I'm on the ER rotation. Most of my time off isn't until October."

"I had no idea," she said. "I've never really paid attention to a surgeon's schedule. I'll go by myself to Paris. And I'll make it a short trip. Might be better if you didn't meet them after all."

"Why?"

"Because this is temporary," she said. "It felt a little real for a minute and I need to remember it isn't."

He didn't want to dwell on the temporary part of it

or the jealousy he'd felt when she'd mentioned Jose's parents. But the truth was in three months she'd be back out of his life and he'd be right back where he was now, except he'd be chief of cardiology at Cole's Hill Regional Medical Center.

He ignored the part where she'd said it felt real. Because no matter how hollow he felt at the thought of her leaving, he knew she would leave. And that needed to stay in the front of his mind.

Six

Derek came out of emergency surgery and washed up at the sink. The day had been long. Longer than he'd anticipated. But being on call was by its very nature unpredictable and he couldn't complain since it was also invigorating. He knew better than to ever say it out loud but there was something about having a patient come in who no one had thought would make it and then saving the person.

His skills, training and natural ability made it possible. But now that he was out of surgery he was exhausted. He cleaned up and then turned to find Marnie standing in the doorway that led to the waiting area. He had to talk to the patient's family and he really didn't have the time to deal with her.

She looked thinner than when they'd been together

and she'd done something different with her eyebrows that made her look like she was scowling. She seemed so…defensive, and he hadn't even said anything to her yet.

"I have to see the family," he said. "I don't have time to discuss anything with you."

"We can talk when you're done," she said. "I have all night."

"I don't," he said.

"Oh, that's right, you have to get back to your fiancée," she said. "Who is the mystery woman?"

"We're having a dinner tomorrow night to announce it to our families and then I'll be happy to share the news with you," he said, brushing past her to walk to the waiting room and the family of his patient.

"Are you sure there is one? It doesn't seem your style to keep things quiet. I figured you'd have a skywriter do your names in a heart in the sky."

He stopped walking and turned to face her. "Really? Marnie, that sounds like something you'd like. I'm not that kind of guy. Besides, my fiancée's first marriage was very public and she'd like to keep this one quiet."

"Her first marriage? Are you sure you want to take a chance on a divorcée?" Marnie asked.

He sighed heavily. "I don't have time for this. And if I did I'd have to point out that following me around while I'm trying to work isn't exactly giving me space."

She held her hands up at shoulder level. "Sorry. I'm leaving. I look forward to hearing more about your mystery woman."

Marnie turned and headed down the hallway and

Derek went to talk to the family. The patient was a high school student who'd collapsed during football practice so the family was…well, it took Derek a while to explain everything to them. He stayed with them as long as they needed to talk. The mom kept hold of his hand and said thank-you so many times that Derek was starting to feel uncomfortable. Finally, his nurse came and rescued him.

"That took forever," he said to Raine as they walked away from the family.

"Sorry, the new board member stopped by and wanted some details and it took me forever to get rid of her," Raine said.

"Marnie."

"Yes. Didn't you use to date her?"

"Don't remind me. I'm going to shower and change. Is Dr. Pitman here?" Derek asked. Pitman was a partner in Derek's practice and they checked in on each other's patients when they did rounds at the hospital.

"He just arrived. He's ready to debrief with you," Raine said. "His nurse is running late. Her kid had something after school so I'm going to stay until she gets here."

"Okay. I'll see you in the office tomorrow morning," he said. "Oh, by the way, I'm engaged."

"Engaged? I thought you said one woman couldn't tame you," she said with a wink.

Raine might work for him but they'd always had a good relationship and she treated him like a kid brother. She was ten years older and Derek had relied heavily on Raine when he'd first started practicing on his own.

She had experience with people, which he'd lacked. He'd been a wiz in surgery but patients and their families had complained about his bedside manner—a lot. And Raine had been the one to help him figure out how to deal with them.

"Well, one did. Don't be surprised. I wasn't shocked when you finally roped a guy into marrying you."

She punched him in the shoulder. "Show some respect. I didn't even have to hogtie him."

"I'll remind Jer of that the next time I see him," Derek said.

"You do that," she said with a cheeky grin. "Who's the lucky girl?"

"I need you to keep it quiet. We are telling our families tomorrow night," he said.

"It won't be hard. You know I don't gossip," she said.

"I know," he said. "It's Bianca."

"Velasquez. Isn't she a model?" Raine asked. "She's the one whose husband died in the plane crash, right?"

Derek realized that everyone was going to know little pieces of Bianca's story. She was a pretty big deal in Cole's Hill because of the fame she'd found as a supermodel. "Yes. We grew up together and have been friends forever."

"Congratulations, Derek. I'm happy for you," Raine said. "Can't wait to meet her."

"Thanks," he said. Just then Raine got paged and he waved her off as he headed to the locker room to shower and change. He wanted to pretend that it didn't matter to him that everyone knew Bianca had married the love of her life. And that he could never be more than the second choice.

It was fake, for God's sake. He knew that. So why did it hurt?

Why was he upset that everyone was going to assume he was a runner-up for the woman who'd had it all?

He hated losing and he hated even more when people thought he lost. And he was still fuming, even after he'd showered, put on his clothes and got in his Lamborghini, speeding out of the parking lot and out of town toward the Rockin' C.

Bianca had arranged to meet Kinley and Penny at the coffee shop in town. The beverages were really nice and the pastries and bakery items were made here in town. Once the morning commuters were all at their nine-to-five jobs it became the place for young moms and their kids to hang.

Benito and Penny were sitting together in one of the padded armchairs. Penny had gotten a new book in the cowboy picture book series she was reading and together they were making up stories that went along with the pictures in the book.

Kinley had volunteered to go and get the drinks and as soon as her friend returned with the tray of iced tea for them all—the kids' drinks in cups with lids— Bianca glanced over her shoulder to make sure no one was close by.

"Why are you acting like a spy with some top secret info to pass?" Kinley asked.

Kinley was newly married to Nate Caruthers, the father of her child. The fact that Penny was almost three years old and that Nate—Kinley's new husband and Derek's brother—had just found out about Penny a few months ago had given the couple a few bumps but they were happy together now. Bianca noticed how easily Kinley smiled these days; it was like a weight had been lifted from her.

Which of course it had been. Keeping the secret from Penny's father had been a heavy burden for her friend.

"I have something to tell you, but don't want anyone to hear. Where's Pippa?" Bianca asked. Kinley's nanny usually accompanied her and Penny when they were in town.

"She's at home," Kinley said. "She needed some time alone today and since the bride I was supposed to meet canceled I'm free all day. So I told her to take the day. What's up with you?"

Bianca nodded. Kinley was one of the most in-demand wedding planners. She planned the weddings of A-listers and royalty, and was currently planning Hunter's wedding to Ferrin. They would be getting married at the end of the month.

"Lean in," Bianca said, putting her iced tea down and leaning forward.

Kinley did as she was told. "Okay, should we whisper?"

"I'm not being silly. I'm engaged."

"You're what?" Kinley asked, loudly.

"Kin."

"Sorry, it just took me by surprise," she said, leaning

back. She glanced around to see if anyone was paying attention to them and no one was. "Who is the lucky man?"

"Derek."

"What? How is that even possible?" Kinley asked. "I think I would have known you were dating."

"We kept it quiet and everyone was busy with your impromptu wedding and the planning of Hunter's big one," Bianca said. She'd been thinking about how she was going to tell her mom, and Kinley was sort of the test run. Her chance to test out the story she and Derek had come up with and to see if it was believable.

"Wow," Kinley said. "Does Nate know?"

"I'm not sure. So far, Derek and I have just kept it between ourselves," Bianca said.

"I bet he knows. Derek and he talk a lot. That rat. He should have told me," Kinley said.

"It's not his secret to tell," Bianca said.

"Fair enough. So when did it happen?" she asked. "Where's the ring?"

"Well, we are having a party for our families tomorrow night and after that I'll wear the ring in public," she said. Actually, she didn't even have a ring; she was going to need to do something about that. She made a mental note to talk to Derek about the ring thing.

"So that's what the dinner is for," Kinley said. "There is a lot of speculation about what was going on when you invited us all. Ma Caruthers is sure that Derek put you up to the party so he can weasel out of the Women's League bachelor auction."

"I wouldn't put it past him to try something like that. But that's not why we invited everyone to dinner."

Kinley grabbed her hand and squeezed it. "I'm so happy for you, Bianca. I love the idea of being sisters with you. Now I'm not trying to be mercenary but have you thought about a wedding planner."

"You know I want you to plan the wedding," she said because she knew that Kinley would expect her to. And she realized that the lies that she'd thought she'd have to tell by pretending to be engaged were bigger than expected. Each lie was leading to another one and she was going to be buried underneath them all.

In a way it was embarrassing that she'd lied to her best friend. She knew that her reasons were good but how was she going to fake-plan a wedding that she knew she was never going to have? She hadn't even considered this.

"Great. I can't do one for a few months. I'm slammed but I will make room for you," she said.

"That's okay. We want to let Hunter get married and then Derek is up for a promotion at the hospital so he'd have to settle in to a new job before we could marry and have a honeymoon. Just know when it's time to plan it, you're the only one I want to help with it."

Kinley nodded. "Are you sure about this? I remember watching your last wedding on TV."

"Yes. I am very sure. That was all for show and I never got to pick anything I really wanted. I had to use sponsors and what looked best in photos."

"Ugh. I mean from an industry insider I totally get

why they were insistent on stuff like that, but it was meant to be your special day."

In hindsight Bianca thought maybe the chaos of that first wedding was a harbinger of what her marriage had ended up becoming.

"Yes."

"Don't worry. Derek is a great guy and when you are ready to plan it, I know this wedding is going to be spectacular."

Kinley sat back and they chatted about other things, but Bianca was startled to have that out-of-control feeling again. She wondered if it was just because for once she had something going on in her life besides planning playdates for Beni or if it were something else.

Something more to do with Derek. An image of him in a tuxedo danced through her mind. She definitely wasn't going to do any pretend marriage planning because that made everything real.

Derek arrived at the Rockin' C driving through the big fence gates that he and his brothers used to climb on and ride when they swung open. The gates were always open these days since they didn't roam the cattle up this way anymore, and he sped past them.

Suddenly he realized he had no idea what he was going to say to his parents when he got out to the ranch. But as he turned his car toward the main house where Nate lived he decided to talk to his brother first.

He parked the car in the circle drive and hopped out, bounding up the stairs to the front porch in a couple of steps. He started to let himself in then remembered that

Nate and Kinley were married now and they might not want him just bursting in.

He rang the doorbell and listened to it chiming through the house. A few minutes later the house-keeper answered and directed him to the study where his brother was working.

"Why'd you ring the bell?" Nate asked as Derek came into the study and closed the door behind him.

"You're married now. Figured I shouldn't just barge in."

Nate laughed. "Very true. But Kin's in town with Penny so you're safe. What's up?"

Derek opened the little fridge in the credenza at the side of the room and took out a Dr. Pepper and offered one to Nate, who nodded. After he gave his brother his drink, Derek sat down on one of the leather guest chairs that were a new addition to the study since Nate had taken over running the ranch from their dad.

"I wanted to talk to you about tomorrow night. I need you and the boys to keep quiet about the fake engagement thing. I didn't tell Bianca that you guys know and I don't think she's going to mention it to anyone else."

"Not a problem. I'll make sure Ethan and Hunter keep quiet, too."

Derek knew his brothers would be okay. He wasn't really worried about any of them spilling the secret once they knew he wanted it kept hidden. They had always been good about having each other's backs.

"What else?"

"I need a ring for Bianca. I know it's not real but no

one else will know and if I were getting engaged…"
He trailed off.

"You'd give her one of the family rings," he said.
"Hunter didn't use one. But he wanted something new
for Ferrin after his past troubles."

"I know, it made sense, but I've always thought when
I did find the right woman I'd give her Grandma Jean's
ring," Derek said. He realized that part of the reason
he wanted that ring now was that it was for Bianca. If
he'd asked another woman, someone whom he didn't
care about the way he did Bianca, he would have gone
into town to the jeweler's and picked out a ring. But
this was Bianca.

"It's your ring to give to whomever you want," Nate
said.

"What do you think? Is it stupid to give her that
ring?" Derek asked his older brother.

Nate stood up and walked around the desk, leaning back against it. "I don't think so. You're going to
need one of us to go with you to the bank to get it,"
Nate said. "I've got a breeder coming by in an hour
so I can't go today. I might be able to do it first thing
tomorrow."

"I have surgery at ten so I was going to call Pitt-
man and see if he'd come in and open early for me,"
Derek said.

"That'll work for me. I don't have anything tomorrow morning except Penny. I'm taking her to school but
I can bring her with me to the bank if you need to be
there early so you can get to the hospital."

Derek loved that his brother had a daughter and that

being a father had made huge impact on Nate's life. He wondered if a real marriage would have the same effect on him. Nate wasn't really different, he just seemed... well, happier for one thing, and more mellow. He had taken the news of his daughter well and he'd changed completely the way he used to be.

They wrapped up their plans for tomorrow morning and Derek drove back to town at a more sedate pace. Thinking about Grandma Jean's ring had made him realize that even though his career had always come first, in the back of his mind there'd been the realization that one day he'd marry.

And the thought of putting that ring on Bianca's finger seemed right. Dangerous thinking, he reminded himself. He was just getting caught up in the same fever that was infecting everyone else in his family.

Hunter was getting married, Nate had settled into married life and fatherhood... Derek needed a night out with Ethan to remind himself that he was still one of the Wild Carutherses. And this thing with Bianca was temporary.

Temporary.

But it didn't feel temporary and when she called to ask if he wanted to join her and Benito on the tennis courts, he said yes. It was only a little after six in the evening.

It wasn't what he'd planned for the evening but he didn't dwell on it. He needed to be thinking like a fiancé if he had any chance of convincing the people who knew him best and the town gossips that this was real. Marnie was going to be looking for chinks in the story and only by playing it like it was real was he going to convince her and get that job he craved.

Though when he got to the tennis court thirty minutes later and saw Bianca in her cute tennis skirt with hair pulled up in a ponytail he realized he craved her even more than the job he'd been pursuing his entire life.

Seven

Bianca had been teaching Beni to play tennis, and she used the term loosely. He had a small plastic racket and he swung it in a clunky manner at the balls. Since they'd moved back to Cole's Hill, he needed something to do outside. They already swam most of the day at her parents' house, at least when it was warm enough. So she'd thought that tennis would be fun. Mostly she imagined she'd hit the ball and he'd chase it. Which he did. But he wanted to hit the ball, too.

And it wasn't her measly athletic skills Beni had inherited but Jose's abilities for sports. He was actually pretty good with the racket. She'd gotten him a child-sized one. And she was pretty confident that once he was older he'd be able to bat the ball over the net.

Inviting Derek to join them had seemed like a good

idea when she'd called him but then as she'd waited for him to show up she realized she'd done it so they could talk.

After her coffee with Kinley she realized how silly she was going to look when the engagement was over. While she didn't want to change the parameters of their arrangement, she did need to make sure that neither of them ended up being alienated from their families.

"Mama, your friend," Benito said.

She glanced at the entrance to the court they were playing on and saw Derek standing there. Benito waved at him as Derek walked toward them. The club didn't have a lot members using the courts at night and Bianca and Beni were the only ones out there.

"I'm your friend, too, Benito."

"I'm Beni. What's your name?"

"Derek. I'm Penny's uncle."

"Unca Derek," Benito asked.

Bianca rubbed the back of her neck. Uncle seemed the safest name. Or maybe just Derek. Derek looked over at her and she was at a loss.

She realized there were a couple of things she was going to have to sort out that she hadn't considered.

"Let's all go sit on the bench for a few minutes," she said.

"Okay, Mama," Beni said, skipping toward the bench in the shade at the side of the court.

Derek stopped her with his hand on her wrist.

"Is Uncle Derek a good idea?" he asked.

"Well you're Penny's uncle and our families are close. It's either that or just Derek or Dr. Derek."

"Dr. Derek sounds weird. And my brothers would make fun of me if they heard it."

"Are you coming?" Beni asked. He was sitting on the bench swinging his legs.

"Yes," Bianca said. "Listen, I'm not trying to make things harder than they have to be but we need to talk about this before tomorrow night. I want to make sure that Beni knows we're moving and when I talked to Kinley today... I just told her we're engaged. I didn't want to say it was fake." She put her head in her hands. "Oh, my God. I sound pathetic. This is a mistake."

The panic she'd felt when she thought he was going to try to manipulate her like Jose always had was nothing compared to what she felt at this moment. What kind of loser needed a fake engagement to jump-start her life? It didn't matter that she knew she wasn't doing it for any bad reasons. All of the things that Derek had said made sense. And he was her good friend.

He pulled her into his arms and just hugged her. Beni ran over. She felt his little arms around her legs and never had she felt more inadequate to be a mom than she did in this moment. She shouldn't be responsible for another person when she couldn't even get her own choices right.

"Mama," Beni said.

She pulled out of Derek's arms and stooped down by her son. Derek followed suit and soon they were a little circle of three on the tennis court. Beni had his hand on her shoulder and Derek put his hand on Beni's.

"Kiddo, your mom and I are really good friends and she and I are thinking about spending more time together. You and she would live with me, if that's okay with you," Derek said.

Beni turned to face Derek, his little face scrunched up as he studied him for a long minute. Then he nodded. "Like Penny's new papa?"

"Yes, just like that. Except I wouldn't be your papa. Your papa is watching over you from heaven so I'd just be…well, a good friend, and if it's okay with your mama, I'd be your daddy down here."

"Forever?" Benito asked, looking over at her for confirmation. She wasn't sure how to answer him.

"Yes. No matter what happens. If you and your mom move out of my house we will still always be friends and I'll always be your daddy down here."

Bianca felt her throat tighten and realized that already Derek was being more of a father to Beni than Jose had ever wanted to be. He only needed his son for photo shoots in the winner's circle. But Derek was making an offer to Beni that Bianca knew was real.

Beni turned to her and leaned in close, whispering in Bianca's ear. "I'd like that, Mama."

She nodded. She didn't feel like a loser anymore. She realized her son needed a male influence and not just his grandfathers and uncles. He needed a man who was his own, a father who was here and not in heaven.

"I'd like that, too," she whispered back to him.

"Now that we've settled that," Derek said, "tomorrow night there is going to be a party where we will talk to everyone in our families and let them know. But for tonight I believe we are supposed to be playing tennis."

"Mama's not very good."

"Well, thanks, *changuito*, who do you think taught you?" she asked, scooping him up in her arms as she stood and shifted him around to dangle upside down while she tickled his belly.

"You did," he said between squeals of laughter and she spun him around to his feet setting him down.

"That's right. But you are better than me."

"I know!"

Derek's attitude toward the promotion and the engagement changed after that moment with Beni. He'd made a commitment to the little boy and he'd honor it. Being friends with Bianca hadn't changed in the twenty years he'd known her; he didn't anticipate that ever changing. What had started as a gut reaction and, if he were being totally honest, anger at Marnie for trying to manipulate him had suddenly gotten real.

Just like the kiss.

He might need to start avoiding these two after twilight, he thought. There was a very real danger that he'd fall for them. Like, really fall for them, and this was supposed to be temporary.

His commitment to his profession was real, too. He had three things vying for his attention right now and he had always been a man of his word. That was one of the things that the Caruthers were known for. Their daddy hadn't raised his sons to be wishy-washy or to go back on their promises or shirk their commitments.

"You okay?" Bianca asked.

"Yeah. Just thinking."

"Well, stop it. You look like you are trying to obliterate the court with your stare."

"Sorry," he said with a shrug. "What do you say we stop playing and head over to the club for a cherry Coke and maybe I teach you how to play pool."

Derek knew actually learning the game wasn't something that Beni would be able to do now but his father had started doing things like playing pool and cards with them when they were toddlers and then as they had grown up it had felt natural to play.

"I know pool. Mama and I swim lots," Benito said.

"This is a different pool with balls and sticks."

He said something to Bianca in Spanish and Derek made a mental note to start listening to the Spanish language tapes when he worked out so he could talk to them both in that language.

"Okay," Benito said. "But not soda. I like juice."

"Juice it is," Derek said. "When your mom was little she only drank pineapple juice."

"That's my favorite," Benito said.

"I'm not surprised. Bia, I walked over to meet you. I don't have my car," Derek added.

"It's okay. We brought the golf cart so we can give you a lift to the club," she said.

"Can we ride in the back?" Benito asked.

Derek wasn't sure what that meant but Benito seemed pretty excited about it. When they got to the cart he realized that Beni wanted to ride in the seat that faced backward.

"Do you mind riding with him? He's too small to

ride back there by himself," Bianca said. "Or you could drive…"

"You drive. I'll ride with Beni," Derek said.

His promise to the little boy had been heartfelt but maybe a little bit impulsive. He realized that he didn't know Bianca's son at all. He was going to need to rectify that and a ride on the golf cart seemed a good place to start.

So he sat next to Beni on the back seat and put his arm around him. And when Bianca started driving the vehicle that couldn't have been going more than fifteen miles per hour he realized that there should be seat belts on the golf cart and lifted Beni off the seat and onto his lap, holding him securely with one arm.

Beni put his hands on Derek's forearm and he looked down at those tiny, chubby little hands. He'd never held a child's hand before, not even Penny's. He hadn't realized how small they were. Hell, that made him sound like an idiot but he'd never realized it.

"You two okay back there?" Bianca asked, not taking her eyes off the road.

"Yes, we're good."

Benito talked to him the entire time. Some of the words were hard to understand because he shifted between English and Spanish as he spoke. But the gist of it was that he liked speed and the wind on his face. And he laughed at lot.

When Bianca stopped in the special parking lot for golf carts in front of the club Derek was disappointed. He liked listening to Benito. But this was only the beginning.

He lifted him in his arms as he stood up, placed the little boy on the sidewalk next to him and turned to face Bianca. She looked cautiously at the two of them and then he felt Benito's hand slip into his and he knew why she was nervous.

He wanted to promise her that he'd never hurt her son. That he was a man who could make the world bend to his will. It was usually the case in life and in the operating theater but when it came to this woman and her child, he knew the stakes were higher.

She'd ceased being a girl he'd had a crush on and become a real flesh-and-blood woman to him when they'd kissed. She'd moved out of the realm of fantasy and into his real world that night. And now as her tiny son held his hand, he felt something, some emotion that was foreign to him.

It was as powerful as his connection to his patients and how he felt when he couldn't save them. There was the fear, disappointment, guilt and even a little bit of anger. He couldn't name but it felt the same in the pit of his stomach. It was something he couldn't control.

But then Bianca came over and touched his shoulder and it abated a little bit. They began walking toward the club together. He didn't allow himself to think of anything except showing Benito around the facility. He had a lot of stories about Bianca that he told to entertain the little boy and when they finally made it to the billiards room, Bianca was looking at him differently.

He thought maybe she finally saw him as a man, too. Not the awkward teenager who'd been her friend so long ago. For the first time he wondered if this might be something like love. Both of his brothers had fallen hard for women and were happy now.

But Derek had always felt like the odd duck in his family. He'd left home to go to college when he was fifteen. And though he could ride, rope and do ranch chores just like his brothers, he'd always been more of a bookworm. He was different.

But with Bianca he never felt different.

He felt...well, home.

Pool. She shouldn't be surprised that Derek wanted to teach her son to play pool. She was still grappling with how easily Beni had warmed to Derek but to be honest, she'd sort of sensed lately that he was a little bit jealous of Penny and her new father. The little girl had something that Beni hadn't been able to have until Derek.

Derek had ordered them a large pitcher of pineapple juice and had a step stool brought into the room. The pool tables at the club were all in private rooms and all themed. This one had been recently redecorated to honor the astronauts of the Cronus mission that would be blasting off to build a space station between Earth and Mars in the next year.

There was a mural of the solar system on one of the walls. Bianca noticed that the artist was clearly old school and had put Pluto into the design despite its demotion from planet status.

She could see Derek was relishing his role as tutor and when he offered to show her how to hold the pool cue, she couldn't resist pretending she needed some help. He was arrogant and his cockiness was showing through as he told Beni that someday he'd be a great player if he paid attention.

Next it was Beni's turn. Derek lifted him onto the step stool and kept one hand on the boy's back as he took the shot. The cue ball was in his hands and he rolled it slowly down the felt, stopping well before the triangle of balls that needed a break.

"Try again. This time push a little bit harder," Derek said, moving around behind Benito and putting his own hand over her son's.

Bianca couldn't resist the image of the two of them together and pulled out her phone to snap a quick picture capturing the twin looks of concentration on their faces as they both watched the cue ball. Derek counted down from three and with his help this time Benito broke the balls. The balls rolled around the table and a solid ball fell into the corner pocket.

"I did it."

"Of course you did. You have a very good teacher," Derek said, winking over at her.

"It's amazing there is room in here for the three of us and your ego," Bianca said.

"That's not ego, that's skill," he said.

"What's next?" Benito asked.

"Because one of the balls went into the pocket, you get to go again. Try to get all of the balls off the table."

She watched her son look over the table and she realized a split second before he moved what he was going to do. But she wasn't fast enough to stop him as reached for the solid ball closest to him and nudged it with his hand toward the pocket.

Derek caught his hand. "That's the trick. But try to do it with the cue—this one. Use this ball to knock them in."

"That's hard. Could we play different?" Benito asked.

She suspected her son was getting a little tired. It had been a long day with lots of time out and about. But Derek just nodded.

"We sure can. Actually when I was little that's how my dad taught my brothers and I to play. I was just showing off for your mom."

"What's showing off?"

Bianca waited to see how Derek would explain it and she wasn't disappointed when he said, "It's something a boy does when he likes a girl and he wants her to notice him."

"That's silly," Beni said. "Mama sees you."

"That's right, I do. He meant that he thinks he's better at playing this than I am. I don't think he was very impressed with my tennis game."

"Was that it?" Beni asked, looking back over at Derek.

"Something like that," Derek said. "It's getting late. Do you have time for ice cream before you head home?" he whispered to Bianca so that Beni wouldn't overhear.

Bianca shook her head. She wasn't sure what she was expecting when she'd invited Derek to join them but she was glad she had. But it was time for them to get home. "Not tonight. Can we give you a ride home?"

"No. A gentleman always sees a lady home. So I'll ride back to your place and then walk home from there."

"Are you sure?" Bianca asked. Her parents lived in the older section of the subdivision a good mile or so from Derek's home.

"Yes," he said. "I insist. I had a long day in surgery and could use the exercise."

"What else does a gennelman do?" Beni asked.

Derek lifted Beni off the stool and onto the floor. "He opens the door for her when he's the first one there like this."

Derek showed him as Bianca picked up her cell phone and the golf cart key and walked over to the open door.

"Thank you," she said.

"You're welcome."

Benito and Derek followed her. As they walked through the club together, she was aware that some of the patrons were watching them and she knew that it wouldn't be long before the gossip got back to her mom and to Derek's mom. It was a good thing they were having the dinner tomorrow night.

When they walked through the foyer toward the outer doors, Beni dashed around in front of her and with Derek's help, opened the heavy wood door.

She smiled down at her son. *"Gracias."*

"You're welcome," the little boy said, smiling up at her.

She wanted this little family to be real. She had to remind herself that it wasn't. That Derek could only ever be their friend. She had to remember that.

But just for tonight she was going to pretend that wasn't the case. That the man riding in the back of the golf cart with her son wasn't just her pretend fiancé but her real one.

Eight

Bianca's mom stood behind her in the bathroom, looking over her shoulder. "I don't know why we all have to go to this dinner at Derek's house. His mother doesn't know, either."

Her mom had been angling for the reason and Bianca had kept her silence. Mainly because after she'd told Kinley she'd started to realize how much confusion it was going to cause their families after they broke things off. She still wasn't sure how she was going to manage that.

She knew that she was going to have to keep her side of the bargain. Derek was proving to be a bit of an enigma. She'd gotten an email from him overnight with an invitation to a benefit at the hospital. It was to support the new cardiac surgery wing and he'd asked if she thought she could find a sitter for Beni.

It was the beginning of building a life together. And her battered heart was cheered by the invite. This was what she'd always thought couple-life would be like. It was what her parents had.

Nothing could have been further from what Jose had wanted with her than this. She realized that she was spending too much time thinking when her mom cleared her throat.

"You're going to have to wait, Mom," she said. "Just like Ma Caruthers. Derek and I will let you know what's going on once we are all together."

"It's just…"

"Ma. I promise you'll be happy about it," she said. "Oh, and I'm probably not going to be able to bid on Diego at the auction so he's going to have to find some other woman who is palatable to him to do his bidding."

"Are you and Derek dating?"

Bianca just shrugged. She suspected she was taking more joy from having this secret from her mom than she should. It was just that Ms. Bossypants was usually so in the know. She had started her career as an investigative reporter before her promotion to the morning news desk and during Bianca's teenage years her mom had shown her investigative prowess many times. It felt good to know something she didn't for once.

"Fine. Keep quiet. I can wait a few more hours to find out what's going on," she said. "Your father wants to take the big Cadillac that he just picked up two days ago."

No one would ever convince her father that anything other than a Chevrolet or a Harley was worth driving.

It had been a source of amusement for Bianca watching Jose try to talk her dad into driving an Italian sports car like the one from Moretti Motors that he'd gifted her dad when they'd first started dating.

She suspected the car was still in the garage under a tarp.

"Fine. That would be nice. We need to move Beni's car seat into it."

"Dad's already on that. And you can tell Diego the bad news about the auction yourself. He's spending the night over here instead of at his place in town. He said that the Caruthers boys were drinkers and he didn't want them to think he couldn't keep up."

She laughed. Her brothers and the Carutherses had always been in competition with each other. Actually it was that way with all of the town's heritage families, the ones who'd been here since the beginning and settled the town. Some of them were big ranching families, and some, like hers, were townies. But they were all constantly trying to one-up each other in a friendly sort of rivalry.

"I will talk to him. What do you think?" she asked her mom. "Do I look okay?"

"You look better than okay. Gorgeous," her mom said. Then she leaned forward in the mirror and did something that Bianca had never seen her do before. She pushed the skin on her temples back and sighed.

There were a few fine lines around her mom's eyes but she still looked younger than her age and beautiful. "Mom, what are you doing?"

"The station suggested I get Botox and…well, what

do you think?" she asked, pulling the skin taut again. "I didn't think I looked that old but with HD and all I guess I look different on air."

Bianca put her arm around her mom's shoulder. Of course, her mom looked fabulous but she worked in a medium that demanded perfection. "How serious was the suggestion? I think you look great but we know that sometimes we have no choice."

"It was truly a suggestion. Howard even said that it would be preventative before these lines started to show on camera. He also suggested I try not to smile so much," her mom said.

Howard was her mom's boss, and Bianca thought he was actually trying to help her mom, with that idea of his. She knew that. She was a model; she knew her days of modeling were numbered. After Beni's birth she'd actually been offered a few plus-sized gigs even though she wasn't truly plus-sized. When image was everything, life could be brutal.

"It's up to you. Actually, I think I might have a friend in Paris who has some products you can try before Botox. Want me to contact her? She's developing a new line."

"That would be great," Elena said. "Thank you."

Bianca squeezed her mom in a hug. "We are the only two Velasquez women. We have to stick together."

"Yes, we do."

Bianca had kept her name after her marriage to Jose because she'd had a career before their marriage. Beni's last name was a compound of hers and Jose's—Ruiz-Velasquez. They had followed the traditional way of naming using the father's surname first and then the mother's.

"So since we are the only two Velasquez women don't you think it would be a good idea to give me a heads-up on what's going to be happening tonight?"

Bianca just shook her head no and led her mom out of the room. She couldn't help feeling a tingle of excitement in the pit of her stomach.

Cobie had worked hard on the courtyard all day and it looked fabulous. As Derek took one last look at it before the guests arrived, he realized he'd wanted this night to be special for Bianca. Even though she meant more to him than he was willing to admit out loud, he had told her this was pretend. But pretend didn't have to mean something that wasn't classy and elegant. He realized that he was hoping it would impress her.

She'd made a few calls and they'd ended up with the catering service from the club. Cobie had even made sure that there was a table just for kids. To be fair there were only two children attending the party, Penny and Benito, but they had their own special area. There was even a buffet table that had been set at their level and food that had been prepared especially for them that only required fingers for eating and serving.

Ethan walked out on to the courtyard and whistled between his teeth. "Very impressive, bro. One might even think—"

"Don't say it. Didn't Nate talk to you?" he asked.

"He did. I was going to say one might even think you cared for her," Ethan said.

"Of course I do. We're friends," Derek said.

Friends. Just friends.

Even though it had been two days since that kiss. Tonight he was hoping for another one, which was probably not the smartest idea, but he'd always been known for being book-smart and not necessarily having the best instincts outside of the operating room.

Bianca was dangerous. He knew that and he liked it.

It was part of the reason why he'd fixated on her from the beginning. Once he said he was engaged, there wasn't another woman who would fit in his mind for a fiancée besides her.

Which was more telling than he wanted to admit, even to himself.

"Just friends."

"Shut up, Ethan," Derek said.

"Okay. But this place looks like something out of a dream. You did a really nice job," Ethan said at last. "I'm glad I came back from LA for this."

"You've been on the West Coast a lot lately. Everything okay?" Derek asked. His brother looked tired, Derek noticed. He reached for Ethan's wrist and then glanced at his watch. Ethan shrugged him off and Derek let him because his brother didn't seem pale. His health was fine. So something else was going on with him.

"Yeah. Just have a client who needs a lot of attention and it can't be dealt with on the phone or via email."

"Is it almost wrapped up?"

"Yeah, I think so. He's got a kid coming and he does a very dangerous job so I'm setting up all kinds of trusts and safeguards so that if something happens to him the kid will be covered," Ethan said.

"Sounds complicated. Just like the kind of puzzle you like to solve," Derek said.

"Yeah, it is. Some days when I'm jetting back and forth to Los Angeles or New York City I can't believe this is my life," Ethan said.

Derek nodded. "You and Hunter were always determined to get out of Cole's Hill."

"Well, Hunter more than me," Ethan said. "I like being home but I need a break sometimes, too."

"I'm feeling you," Derek said. "Last night we were up at the club and it was like the fishbowl effect as everyone watched us. It's the first time I've been aware of it. I mean, sometimes there will be something at the hospital but gossip doesn't really affect my ability to get the job done."

"You've always been a sort of wunderkind and in your own world. Focused on becoming the best surgeon."

He shrugged and nodded at his brother. "That's always been the most important thing to me."

"Still?" Ethan asked. "As I look around the courtyard, it seems like someone else might be in the running for your attention."

Derek didn't want to think about it. He'd flirted with the thought before but he'd been ignoring it. He didn't want to contemplate that Bianca and Beni might be changing his priorities. He had to be laser-focused; that was part of what made him such a good surgeon.

"Nope. This is pretend," he said with more bravado

than he felt. He wasn't about to tell his brother that Bianca had always been right there on the edge of his life and now she was closer to being in it. He wasn't sure what he'd do next.

Luckily the doorbell rang and Ethan went to the bar that Cobie had set up while Derek went to greet his guests. Cobie would have done it but Derek preferred to personally welcome everyone tonight.

He opened the door and his smile froze as he met Bianca's dark chocolate eyes. She wore a slim-fitting sheath in a silvery color that enhanced her tanned arms. A slit on the side showed off the length of her leg. She had on a pair of impossibly high heels, making her almost as tall as Derek.

She had her hair pulled up in one of those fancy ways women wore their hair for events but a tendril had slipped loose and curled against her cheek. He licked his suddenly dry lips and stood there as though he'd never seen a girl before.

And maybe he hadn't. He certainly hadn't seen a woman who took his breath away like Bianca did.

"Won't you come in," he said, stepping back to allow her to enter.

Seeing everyone together tonight made Bianca realize how many men there were in their combined families. She wasn't overwhelmed but she noticed that Kinley seemed...well, out of her element. She wondered if it was simply that she was getting used to being part of this large family.

She knew how much her friend had struggled on her

own after getting pregnant and giving birth to Penny. Kinley had asked if she could bring Pippa to the party and Bianca had agreed. Pippa now sat at the end of the table between Diego and Inigo. Whatever she was saying was keeping her brothers enchanted or maybe it was her British accent or the air of mystery about her.

Nate seemed to notice Kinley's unease and put his arm around her, whispering something in her ear that made her blush and then smile up at him. That was when Bianca, who'd been feeling pretty confident that she was okay with the whole fake fiancée arrangement, suddenly realized she wasn't.

Kinley had something real. Something that Bianca knew she'd always wanted. Something that everyone grew up believing they'd find as adults. Love. Didn't everyone? Didn't everyone want to be held and made to feel like they weren't alone? Bianca did.

She'd thought those dreams and desires had died with Jose but knew they hadn't.

Benito was close to what she wanted. She had poured her love into her little boy but she knew he'd grow up and someday be an adult on his own. She wanted a man to share her life with. She wasn't sure that pretending wasn't the way to get to that. But she wanted someone who was really hers.

Like that party invite that Derek had sent to her earlier. It meant blending their lives so when she attended an event she didn't have to wonder who would be there. If she'd have someone to talk to. A partner could be that. The right partner, she thought. Jose hadn't been that for her.

He definitely hadn't been that after they got married because he'd still been too busy proving he was the hottest guy on the F1 circuit. It was hard because the drivers were arrogant, spoiled and used to women falling all over them. Fair enough. There was something about all the rare masculine power that they exuded.

Derek had it, too. But her view of him was tempered by the fact that she'd known him as a boy. She saw past his arrogance and the cocky charm he wielded effortlessly. But that didn't mean he wouldn't hurt her.

He'd asked for temporary.

She had to remind herself of that fact constantly because of the way he acted at times. Last night in the club's billiards room. Tonight with his enchanting courtyard that looked like something out of a Hollywood romance movie set. Or when he glanced over at her and winked at her.

She felt something clench deep inside of her. She was falling for him. It didn't matter how many times she said "temporary" in her head.

Her heart didn't feel like this was make-believe.

Not at all.

Derek clinked his fork on the side of his wineglass to get everyone's attention and the conversation slowly stopped.

He stood up and then looked over at her, and she felt that nervous excitement again. It felt like there were butterflies in her stomach or more as though she'd swallowed the sun. She felt hot like she was blushing.

"Thank you everyone for coming here tonight on such short notice. I realize that we've kept you in suspense about why we wanted you all here. Bianca and I have a very special announcement."

He held his hand out to her and she took it and stood up. They hadn't rehearsed this and she wasn't sure what she was supposed to say. She tried to remember all of the things that she'd said to Kinley yesterday but her mind was blank. She was simply staring into Derek's blue eyes. She saw that curl that he tried to tame that had fallen forward on his forehead. And when their eyes met her panic stilled.

This was Derek. Her friend. The one man who wasn't a blood relative whom she could count on. She'd always been able to count on him and this was no different.

He lifted her hand and kissed the back of it. And then she felt him slipping something on her finger and she glanced down to see a charming antique engagement ring with a solitaire diamond set in a platinum band.

"I've asked Bianca to marry me and she's said yes. We've been keeping it quiet recently because of Nate's marriage to Kinley and of course Hunter and Ferrin's big day. We didn't want to steal anyone's thunder. But we figured it might be okay to let our families in on the secret," Derek said.

He put his arm around Bianca as everyone clapped for them. Her parents got to their feet as did Derek's and the two of them were surrounded by their folks and their brothers. Her mom hugged her close.

"No wonder all those blind dates didn't work out. You should have mentioned you were seeing someone," her mom said.

"I always thought there was more to the two of you

than just friends," Ma Caruthers said, hugging Bianca after her mom let go.

"Well, friendship is a great way to start a relationship," she said.

"Very true," her mom agreed.

"My sons have good taste in women," Mr. Caruthers said, hugging her close.

"We learned from your example, Dad," Derek said with a wink.

She noticed how her father stood back, though. He had always seemed to know that things weren't perfect in her first marriage and she went to his side. "I'm happy about this, Poppi."

He gave her a long level stare. "That's the important thing."

He kissed her forehead but didn't move toward Derek. Instead Derek came over to her father and held his hand out to the other man.

Her father reluctantly reached for it and shook it.

"I know that I have to prove to you that I'm good enough for your only daughter, Mr. Velasquez, and I promise over time I will make that happen."

Bianca was fooled by the sincerity in his voice. And she wondered at the ease with which Derek was making these promises. First to Beni and now to her dad. She wondered if he thought that this would go beyond temporary or if he had a way out of this for them both that would keep the peace between their families.

For her sake she needed everything between herself and Derek to be the truth. They were lying to their families, to the town, to everyone outside of each other so in order to keep herself in check, she needed to always remember that truth when she looked at him. And his promises were making it a little hard to remember this was temporary.

Nine

Derek pulled her into his arms as the music turned from Pitbull to Ed Sheeran and "Tenerife Sea." He didn't think too much about the lyrics, but just enjoyed holding Bianca in his arms. Beni and Penny had gone home with their grandparents and his brothers, Kinley, Ferrin and Pippa were still here along with Diego, Inigo and Rowdy. Pippa was dancing with Diego, which didn't seem like the best idea since he knew that Diego was a player and that Pippa had secrets she wasn't sharing.

The other guys were in the house either watching basketball on the big screen or playing cards. Since Ethan was at the table and dealing, Derek was very glad he was out here on the courtyard dancing with Bianca. His brother was a card shark and very good at winning.

"So you're making a lot of very convincing promises to Beni, to my father…you thinking something you haven't mentioned to me?" she asked.

He cursed under his breath as he danced her away from the other couples and then rested his forehead against hers and looked down into her eyes. "I think even if this is pretend, we need to make it look real. And any man who is going to try to claim you, Bianca, has to know that your father doesn't give his approval easily. Did he and Jose get on?"

She tightened her mouth and he wondered if he'd asked something he shouldn't, but he'd never been one of those guys to tiptoe around the uncomfortable questions. And tonight more than any other he needed to know what he was up against.

Because Bianca had just echoed the same sentiment that Ethan had expressed earlier. He had been making this real. Too real. And he'd already dismissed the excuse he'd been giving himself that it was okay to do this because she'd been his crush back in the day. He knew that she was so much more to him than that now. But he was supposed to be easing himself into her life.

Not throwing a party like this, he thought. One that left no doubt that he wanted this to last. Which was why she was questioning him and why he'd got his back up and asked her about Jose.

Jose was the one man that Derek would never be able to compete with. The guy was dead. The guy had fathered her son. The guy had been more at ease with romantic gestures than Derek ever would be.

He could only ever be a pale imitation.

Damn.

Screw that.

He imitated no one.

He was the best there was in Cole's Hill and pretty much in the top 1 percent in the country when it came to heart surgeons. He didn't live in the shadows.

And he wasn't prepared to with Bianca, either.

"Jose and my dad didn't get along. At first they seemed to be fine but then…well, about the time I got pregnant something happened and he and Dad stopped being chummy."

"What happened?"

She took a deep breath, looked around the courtyard and then grasped his hand, drawing him toward the glass doors right in front of them. Opening them, she stepped inside with Derek close behind. He knew she hadn't realized the doors led to his bedroom.

She glanced around and flushed.

"I just wanted to be alone."

"It's okay. I'm not planning on sweeping you off your feet and onto my bed…yet," he said with a wink. "I want to hear what happened first."

"It's…embarrassing, really."

"I doubt it," he said.

"No, it is. You know how we had that big wedding with all the cameras and media coverage and how everyone thought we were the romantic fairy-tale couple of the decade?"

He nodded, not really sure he wanted to hear this.

"Well, I thought we were, too. I was deeply in love with him and I couldn't see any faults. Marco Moretti, the head of the Moretti Motors Racing Team, and his wife tried to warn me that Jose was all show."

"Why did they try to warn you?"

"We are good friends. The team travels from country to country and some of the families go along, but I was an outsider and because of the modeling I'd done some of the other wives and girlfriends didn't welcome me. But Virginia, Marco's wife, did. Anyway, one day I was going on about how great Jose was and she said to be careful not to buy into that effortless charm he had with women."

Derek felt a stone in his stomach as he started putting things together. Little things she'd said and the way she'd reacted when Derek had mentioned her late husband. He realized that Jose had been a player.

"It's okay. You don't have to say anything else. I'm not going to cheat on you," he said.

"I know you won't, Derek. This is for three months. That's the part that I'm struggling with. You know? I'm beginning to think it's my fatal flaw. That I fall for guys who are just putting on a show. And this show... it's hard not to fall for it.

"I think Dad is reserving judgment on you until he can be sure you're the guy you claim to be," Bianca said at last.

He was. And he wasn't. He'd thought they would do each other a favor. They'd both get something they wanted and then life would go back to the way it had been. But having kissed her and seen beyond the image of who Bianca was, he knew they never could.

And he didn't want to hurt her the way that Jose

had. He didn't want to put another black cloud over her dreams. He wanted to tell her that maybe this wouldn't be temporary, but he didn't know that himself. Promising to be there for Beni had been easy. But promising her father not to hurt her might have been more than he could deliver. Making a promise to Bianca…he couldn't do that until he knew if he could handle both her and his career.

Nothing had ever competed with surgery for his attention. He'd dated but all of those relationships hadn't drawn him away from medicine the way he feared Bianca could.

She'd said too much; she knew it but it was time to clear the air. Now that their families knew about this engagement there was no changing her mind. Not that she'd really considered it but the time had definitely passed.

"Sorry. I shouldn't have mentioned that," she said, glancing around Derek's room. A lamp on one of the bedside tables was turned on, casting a soft glow around the room. It was large, with a king-size bed against one wall. There was a treadmill facing a flat-screen TV mounted on the wall next to the dresser. A seating area took up most of the opposite side of the room and there was a door that she assumed led to a private bath.

"Your room is interesting," she said.

He walked farther into the room to lean against the dresser. He had his long legs stretched out in front of him and then crossed his arms over his chest. He watched her with that enigmatic Derek stare. The one that she could never read.

"In what way?"

"Just very utilitarian," she said as she walked over to the seating area and noticed the bookshelf behind it. She scanned the titles: not a single work of fiction but a lot of medical journals.

"It's comfortable."

"I can see that," she said.

"You sound like you don't approve," he said, getting up to walk toward her.

She plopped down on one of the overstuffed leather armchairs and reached for the book that was on the side table between the chairs.

"This would put me straight to sleep."

"Are you sure?" he asked, taking the book from her. "It's about an experimental procedure for heart valve stents that has had some limited success. I'm thinking about possibly going to visit with the doctors who did the research to see some of their patients. If it works it would be an improvement on the operation we are using now."

There was that intensity that she'd always noticed in him when he talked about medicine. Any other guy would be trying to bum-rush her into bed and Derek was telling her why the book he was reading was interesting. It made her heart beat a little faster. She liked it when he got all serious and doctorly. "Why can't you just try it here?"

"It's risky. And some of the facts seem off to me. I want to see the actual research."

"Off how?"

"Some of the numbers and ratios don't add up," he said, tossing the book on the table. "But that's boring. I have exciting things in the room, too."

She glanced around it and then pointed to the treadmill. "The exercise equipment?"

He shook his head.

"Do you have sex toys in your dresser?" she asked with a wink. "I've read *Fifty Shades of Grey*."

"Hell, no. I don't need toys to please you," he said.

She flushed and cleared her throat, which was suddenly very dry. And now all she could think about was that big bed and him pleasing her.

She tried to push the images of his naked body moving over hers out of her mind but she couldn't. She had seen him at the pool and knew his chest was solid and muscly but now she wondered what it would feel like under her fingers. Did he have hair on his chest? She couldn't remember.

He arched one eyebrow at her.

"What?"

"I think you just realized the most thrilling thing in my room is me."

She shook her head. "That's a lot of talk, Caruthers."

"Again, with you thinking it's all ego. I promise you it's fact," he said.

"Another promise?" she asked.

"This one I'm happy to demonstrate," he said. "Remember that kiss by the lake?"

"I've thought of little else," she said. "I know that temporary means that we should keep our distance."

Derek stood up and drew her to her feet next to him. "Don't think. No more second-guessing any of this. Let's just see where it leads."

She bit her lip. She couldn't agree to that. They had a deal and she didn't want to shirk her side of it. "Do you mean that you want this to go beyond the three months?"

"I just mean let's take it slow and easy."

"That's not exactly an answer," she said. "I can't 'go with the flow.' I'm a single mom."

"You're an engaged woman who is in her fiancé's arms."

Bianca didn't really think she was, though. She felt those lies of fake and temporary weighing heavily on her and despite the fact that this was Derek and she wanted him more than she had wanted any man in a long time, she wedged her arm between them and stepped back.

"I'm not. This already feels way too damned real and it's not. I see this room and you are a surgeon first, Derek," she said. "There's a reason why you asked me to be your fiancée and it's not because you are waiting for the right woman. It's because no woman can compete with your career. I would love to go with the flow and if I was four years younger then I'd give in. But I'm not. I'm the woman that life has made me. I'm Benito's mom. I have to look beyond what feels good. I have to do what is right."

She hadn't meant to get so real with him but it needed to be said. She couldn't read him. She didn't know if he was faking this or if he thought that lust was enough for them. That an affair would be fine since they knew they'd be going back to their real lives in a few months. But she had already realized that she was in danger of believing every bit of this. And sleeping with Derek wasn't going to help her remember that he wasn't really hers.

The truth in her words cut through the thick lies he'd been telling himself. And it underscored the reasons why he'd been reluctant to make any more promises to Bianca. He had no idea if he could commit to a woman—even her—for more than three months. That was what he'd sort of been implying when he'd asked her to go along with it for now.

But Bianca wasn't that kind of woman.

She wasn't one who could be coaxed into half measures. He knew the reasons for her wariness were well-founded. He'd cut her off earlier because he didn't want her to say it out loud but he suspected she'd been about to tell him that Jose had hooked up with other women when he was married to Bianca bothered Derek. It made him mad as hell and want to find the guy and punch him.

But Jose was dead.

Derek hated him. He was glad that the man was out of Bianca's life but he was angry that he hadn't realized before now that she'd had such a crappy marriage. They'd been friends. Surely, Derek should have noticed.

But what would he have done?

That guy had done a job on Bianca and now he was gone. Maybe she felt relief or sadness… Oh, hell, what if she still loved him? Maybe that was the real reason for the failed blind dates set up by her mother and her agreement to this…idea that was seeming more and more complicated by the minute. He wanted it to be simple again. The way it had been when he'd first conceived it. But he knew that it would never be simple.

What had started out with the best of intentions was now making his gut ache. He wanted her. That was a given. They were young, good-looking and there'd always been a sort of what-could-have-been vibe between them. But now that he was alone with her in his bedroom, he knew he didn't want her to leave.

That even though they'd never discussed it he didn't want their arrangement to be platonic.

"I get that. But there is something more going on between us, Bia. And there always has been," he said. "Do you deny it?"

She shrugged.

"No. You can't get off that easily. I need an answer. If this is just coming from me that's one thing, but when we kissed by the lake the other night something stirred between us. Or was it just me?" he asked.

Three days. It seemed hard to believe that it had only been three days since he'd asked her to be his fiancée because he'd changed in that time. It was inevitable, he thought. They'd always been close and she was one of the few people who'd seen past his nerdy façade to the man beneath. She was special.

But right now he wasn't sure if most of those feelings should have stayed in the past.

"There is something between us. But I don't want to be a fool again. Love and me are adversaries. The last time I thought it was real, it wasn't. This time… I know it's fake. I know we are playing house to get you that chief of cardiology position and give me some breathing room to figure out what's next. But tonight felt real. And this ring...it's not a ring you give a fake fiancée."

He put his hand under her chin and tipped her head back until their eyes met. She'd kicked her heels off earlier when the dancing had started and was back to her normal five-foot, seven-inch height, which meant he towered over her in bare feet.

There were clouds in her eyes and fear as well. And he knew the pain of being hurt. Not of being in love, because he was honest enough to admit he'd been careful about his relationships and never pursued one with a woman who could touch him as deeply as Bianca. But he had been hurt.

He started to open his mouth. To make vows that he had no idea if he could keep or not. He wanted to say he'd never hurt her.

But he wasn't sure whether he was going to hurt himself.

"I... If I said this was a temporary affair, would that make it easier? I think we'd be fooling ourselves if we said we aren't going to sleep together," he finally said.

When he was unsure he always fell back on the bluntness that he'd used in his early residency days. It was just easier to detach when he was blunt. If she said no, it was fine. He'd wanted women before and not slept with them. But of course, they hadn't been living with him.

And she would be.

With her son, who was already starting to make Derek care for him. And with her swarm of brothers, who would probably beat him to a pulp if he hurt their sister. Two of her brothers lived in the Five Families neighborhood and the other two on the family's ranch.

"Maybe. I'm not trying to make this harder than it has to be. It's just that I seem to have the worst instincts when it comes to men. I really thought that since you were such a good friend this wouldn't happen."

"Really?" he asked, a tad disappointed.

She sighed, then shook her head. "No. Since I've been back in Cole's Hill, I have noticed you."

"What can I do to make this work?" he asked. "Drop the fake engagement? Sleep with you? Avoid sleeping with you?"

"I don't know. It would be so much easier if there was a crystal ball we could look into and see the future."

"It would be. Barring that, I think we should return to my suggestion that we sort of just see where this leads. We've been friends for as long as I can remember. I really don't want to think that I've done something that will lead to me losing you."

"I don't want that, either," she said. "Should we get back to our guests?"

"I don't think they'll miss us."

In the distance he heard the music change again. This time to Blake Shelton's "Sangria." He pulled her close and rocked them back and forth to the music. Her arms slipped around his waist and her hands held him tight. She sang under her breath and for now he told himself this was enough.

Ten

Derek moved to the music and she knew that they should leave his bedroom. But being in here all alone made her feel safe. She was in his arms and she felt like she'd found a man she could trust. With her heart and her body. She knew it might be the sangria she'd drunk at dinner or just the fact that he'd given her an heirloom ring. She couldn't put her finger on it but she knew once she left this bedroom she wasn't going to allow herself to be vulnerable around him again.

She had this night.

This chance to be with him.

She opened her eyes and saw he was looking down at her with intent. She tipped her head to the side and ran her fingers through that thick curly hair of his, pushing it to the left the way he liked to. His hair was silky and soft.

He moaned, the sound coming from deep inside of him, and he traced her fingers down over the side of his face and around his ear and then down his neck. She felt his pulse and as she kept touching him it started to speed up a little.

She raised both eyebrows at him, a slight smile playing on her lips. "Like that?"

"Hell, yes," he said, lifting his hand to rub his thumb over the pulse on her neck. He just slowly caressed her, moving his finger back and forth.

Shivers spread from where he was touching her over her collarbone and down her arms. Her breasts felt full and her nipples tingled.

"Like that?" he asked.

"Yes," she said, her voice breathy to her own ears.

He moved his hand to cup her neck and the back of her head. His fingers tangled in her hair and slowly drew her head back as he lowered his. Their lips met and an electric current made her lips buzz.

He parted his and she felt his breath and then the brush of his tongue. He thrust it into her mouth and their tongues tangled. Twisting her fingers into his hair, she held him to her so he didn't change his mind and pull back.

He anchored her body to his with one hand on her waist and the other one in her hair, holding her while he ravaged her mouth. She felt his erection thickening against her lower stomach and she shifted, rubbing herself against him.

He ran one of his hands down her arm, slowly and lightly caressing the outside of her arm, and then drew his hand back up the inside, the backs of his fingers brushing the side of her breast. It had been so long since a man had touched her that she realized that common sense had nothing to do with this.

She had felt empty and so undesirable for too long. And now Derek was holding her. Kissing her like he never wanted to stop as she shifted her hips, gyrating against him. Her eyes were closed, but there was no doubt of who was touching her. His cologne—spicy and masculine—perfumed each breath she took. His touch was precise, his hands sure.

He wrapped one arm around her hips and lifted her off her feet. He carried her across the room and then carefully laid her down on the bed, coming down on top of her. One of his legs bent to fall next to her on the bed while the other stayed between her spread legs.

She let go of him, her arms falling out to the side as she looked up at him and felt the emotion of the moment.

Tears burned the back of her eyes and she felt stupid because this was Derek and he was so sweet and caring and she wanted this to be real.

Oh, damn. Double damn. Just do the physical thing, she told herself. Forget emotions. They couldn't be trusted anyway.

But Derek wasn't Jose and he noticed immediately. He came down on the bed by her side and pulled her into his arms, rubbing one of his hands down her back. The other one wiped away the hot tears that fell on her face.

"What is it?"

She shook her head. She didn't want him to know

how long it had been since she'd had sex. Or that she had felt ugly and unfeminine after she'd given birth and Jose had pushed her away.

All the baggage she'd thought she'd stowed in a locker and buried deep inside of her soul was coming to the surface.

"It's been a long time for me," she said.

He gazed at her, those blue eyes of his full of an emotion that looked a lot like caring. She stopped analyzing and expecting to be hurt and decided to take Derek at face value.

"Sorry. It's just that after I had the baby it took me a while to get into shape and it affected my sex life with Jose. Wow, that's a mood killer, isn't it," she said. "What kind of man wants to hear about this kind of crap?"

"Me. Listen, I'm sorry you had a horrible time with Jose. But I'm not him and I would never hurt you. You are the sexiest woman I've ever seen. I have been crushing on you since I was fourteen."

"Fourteen?"

"Yeah."

"You should know I don't look like that poster of Jessica Simpson in that Daisy Duke getup you used to have in your locker," she said. "I'm real and not airbrushed."

"Good. I like real. I like you, Bianca. I want to make love to you," he said. "But I have no agenda here. If we don't tonight then it will happen when it's meant to."

"I'm afraid if I walk out of here tonight I'll do everything in my power to keep my distance from you."

"I can be pretty damned determined. And we're going to live together," he said. "Trust me—when the time is right it will happen."

Derek hadn't meant for things to heat up. She'd led them into his bedroom and then gotten way too real. But now that he had her in his arms and on his bed the urgency was there, of course, but he had long ago learned to control it. Control was everything to a surgeon and he applied it to every aspect of his life.

He shifted them until they were lying with their heads at the top of the bed. He piled the pillows behind his back and held her close to his side. She wasn't talking and that was okay with him as she kept running her hands over his chest. She slipped her finger between the buttons of his shirt and he had the first inkling that she didn't want this night to end.

But he waited.

She'd cried when he'd laid her on his bed. Any man worth his salt would know that things were going to take time.

"What are you doing?" he asked as he felt her nail scrape over the skin under his shirt.

"Touching you. Do you like it?"

"Yeah," he said. "Want me to take my shirt off?"

She sat up and turned away, only to look over her shoulder at him. She had a tentative expression on her face but she nodded. "Do you mind?"

"Not at all. You know what a big ego I have, so having a woman admire my body just feeds it."

She turned back to him and fake-punched him. "Don't be an ass."

"I'm not. Figured I'd beat you to saying it," he said with a wink. Then he tugged the tails of his shirt out of his pants and slowly undid the buttons. Not because he was trying to be coy but because his hands were shaking.

His surgeon's hands were shaking because Bianca Velasquez had asked him to take his shirt off. He'd pretty much already told himself that he was going to go slow with her. And every instinct in his body wanted to do the exact opposite. But he wasn't about to rush her or make her uncomfortable. It seemed to him as though she'd had enough of that in her marriage.

When he had his shirt unbuttoned she put her hand in the center of his chest. "I couldn't remember if you had a hairy chest or not."

"Just a little bit. Does that bother you?" he asked. One of the women he'd dated had wanted him to wax his chest, which had been the end of that relationship. But if Bianca asked…well, he'd consider it.

"No. I like it. I like the way it feels against my fingers when I do this," she said, rubbing her hand over his pectorals. She spread her fingers wide, the tip of one brushing over his nipple, which felt odd. He didn't really like it and brought his hand over hers to move it off.

She tugged her hand free and traced the hair from his chest along the narrow trail down his stomach. She stopped when she reached his waistband, running her fingernail along the edge. He had to shift his legs to accommodate his burgeoning erection. She noticed and ran her hand over it, stroking him up and down through the fabric of his trousers.

It was the most delicate torture to have her touching him. "I'd like to try this again."

"Now?" he asked.

"Yes," she said.

"Then come over here and kiss me," he said. She kept her hand on his erection and inched upward until she lay curved against his side. He lowered his head and kissed her. He kept the kisses as controlled as he could. He wanted to be ready to stop if she asked him to.

And that was going to be difficult because everything in him wanted to claim her. Wanted to make love to her and really make her his, so that she wasn't just his as far as everyone was concerned but the two of them would know she was his as well.

He skimmed his hands lightly over her side and when he reached the slit of her dress, he groaned. Her skin was soft, smooth and warm. He ran his finger along the edge of the fabric and then slowly inched it underneath around to her back to cup her buttocks in his hand and draw her closer to him. Then he moved her up and over his body.

She sucked his tongue deeper into her mouth and his penis jumped under her hand. She undid his zipper and slipped her hand into his pants, finding the opening in his boxers. Her fingers were long and cool against his erection. He felt his control slowly slipping away but he clung to it.

He reached for the zipper at the back of her dress and lowered it slowly. He was giving her time to say no if she wanted to but she sat up and rolled off the bed, standing up to take her dress off. It fell in a pool on the floor and he sat up to more fully see her.

She wore a balconette bra that pushed her breasts up and created a deep cleavage. He skimmed his gaze down her body, to the nipped-in waist, to her hips. She wore a tiny pair of bikini underwear in a nude color.

She held her arms out to her sides.

"This is me," she said.

He crawled across the bed and sat on the edge of it in front of her. Putting his hands on her waist, he drew her closer to him. He kissed her stomach and then her ribs and slowly worked his way over her entire torso. She was gorgeous. She was Bianca, and he had never seen a woman he wanted more.

"You're lovely."

"I think you're punch-drunk," she said. "But very nice."

"I'm not nice. I'm one big egomaniac, remember?" he said, drawing her down on his lap. She straddled him, wrapping her arms around his shoulders and pushing her fingers into his hair again.

She'd done that a number of times. She must like his hair, he thought. But really he was grasping onto any thought to distract himself from how good she felt in his arms. He told himself he'd take it slow. That he wasn't going to rush or pressure her. She was hard to resist but he did it.

He leaned forward to kiss the top of the globes of her breasts. They were full and creamy-looking in the muted light from his bedside lamp. He used his tongue to trace the lacey pattern of the bra that hugged her breasts and then wrapped his arms behind her back and undid the clasp.

She shifted around on his lap, pulling the fabric free from her body and tossing it on the floor. Her breasts were full and her nipples were pointed little nubs. He rubbed his finger over them as her hands moved lower on his body.

He felt her fingers fumbling for the button at his waistband. He stopped her before she went any further. "Are you sure about this? I think I could stop right now but if you take my pants off…"

"I'm sure. It was just…leftovers from my former life. I hadn't realized how much of myself I'd lost until now. In a way, you helped me, Derek," she said.

"Good. I'm glad to hear it," he replied. "One more thing."

"Yes?"

"Are you on the pill?"

She blushed; the color started at her breasts and went up to her cheeks. "No. I didn't even think… I'm not really that active."

"It's okay, I've got condoms."

"Good. I don't want to stop," she said.

"Me, either. Wrap your arms and legs around me," he said.

She did and he stood up, set her down on the bed and then turned away to take off his pants and boxers. He reached into the nightstand and took out one of the condoms he kept there.

He felt the brush of her fingers along his back and

turned to look at Bianca. She was touching the scarred flesh on his left side.

"Was this from the car-surfing incident?" she asked.

He nodded. During his early teenage years he'd been eager to prove himself as brave as his brothers and had earned a reputation for never turning down a dare. So he'd ended up on his skateboard being towed behind one of his friend's older brother's cars. But he'd slipped off and been dragged along for a few feet.

"Yes. Being dragged along asphalt leaves its mark."

"I'm sorry you were hurt. I remember when I came to visit you at the ranch and your father said that dum-dums shouldn't have pretty visitors."

"Always so eloquent. But he was both pissed and worried. Not a great combination for him."

She ran he fingers lower to Derek's hip bone and then reached around to his front and took his erection in her hand again. She ran her fingers down his length and he turned to face her.

She smiled up at him and scooted back on the bed. He noticed she'd taken her panties off and was completely naked. His breath caught and all of the control he'd always taken for granted deserted him as he came down on the bed on top of her.

He needed to be inside her now. This was Bianca, the one woman he'd wanted above all others for longer than he could remember. He parted her thighs as he rubbed his chest over the tips of her breasts. She wrapped her legs around his waist and he felt the tip of his erection at the entrance of her body.

He cursed.

"What?"

"Condom. I forgot to put it on," he said.

She took it from him and as he shifted to his knees she tore the packet open and put the condom on him. Then she took his length in her hand and drew him forward.

He groaned. Putting his hands on the bed on either side of her body, he fell forward until he could trace her nipple with his tongue.

Now she moaned as she wrapped her legs around his waist again. He found her entrance and lifted his head to look up at her. He wanted to see the moment when he entered her.

Taking her hands in his and stretching them up over her head, he slowly pushed into her body. She was so tight he thought he wasn't going to make it all the way in before he came.

But soon he was buried hilt-deep in her body. Her hands tightened on his, her head rolled back and her eyes slowly shut.

He began to thrust into her, drawing out and then pushing back in. She clutched at his hips as he started, holding him to her, eyes half-closed and head tipped back.

He leaned down and caught one of her nipples in his teeth, scraping very gently. She started to tighten around him. Her hips were moving faster, demanding more, but he kept the pace slow, steady, wanting her to come again before he did.

He suckled her nipple and rotated his hips to catch her pleasure point with each thrust. Then he felt her hands clenching in his hair as she threw her head back and her climax ripped through her.

He started to thrust faster. He tipped her hips up to give him deeper access to her body. She was still clenching around his when he felt that tightening at the base of his spine seconds before his body erupted into hers. He pounded into her two, three more times, then collapsed against her. Careful to keep his weight from crushing her, he rolled to his side, taking her with him.

He kept his head at her breast and smoothed his hands down her back. He finally lifted his head as his breathing slowed and looked up at her to make sure she was all right. She smiled down at him. He held her close in the curve of his body and drew the edge of the comforter over them.

He might have started this as a reason to keep an old girlfriend off his back but as of tonight, he knew that he'd found a woman he wanted to keep. Now and forever.

Something that was underscored when they both got dressed and went back out to the party. She seemed to sparkle as she moved through their guests and occasionally glanced over at him with a secret smile.

He felt more daring than he had when hc'd car surfed and he knew that it was because of her. Bianca.

A woman who held more power over him than he realized he had given to her.

Eleven

Bianca woke up in a strange room wrapped in Derek's arms. She carefully got out of the bed and looked back at him sleeping there. The music had long since stopped and the house was quiet. She glanced at the nightstand clock and saw that it was almost 3:00 a.m.

If she'd had any doubts that Derek was a special man to her, they were all gone now. And the word *temporary* had been shoved so far to the back of her mind that she was trying to figure out how to move forward. She knew there had to be a way.

She just had to figure it out.

Derek stirred on the bed and sat up, the comforter falling to his waist. He scrubbed his hand over his eyes and then looked at her.

"You okay?"

She nodded. "I… I need the bathroom and to wash this makeup off my face."

"Mind if I join you in there?" he asked. "Sorry for conking out on you like that."

"It's okay. I did the same," she said. "Let me pee first and then you can come in."

"Fair enough. I can use one of the bathrooms down the hall," he said.

"Nah. Give me a sec," she said, walking to the adjoining bathroom. Then she paused in the doorway and when she looked back, she noticed his eyes were on her butt.

"Do you have a T-shirt I can borrow?"

"Yeah," he said.

She hurried into the bathroom and did her business, calling out when she was done that he could come and join her. Derek had some decent face soap that was fragrance-free so it didn't irritate her skin. He came in and handed her a T-shirt printed with the San Antonio Spurs logo. She put it on.

It was a master bathroom that had two sinks. She went to the one that was clearly not being used by Derek. His toothbrush and razor were next to the other one.

She braided her hair into two plaits to keep it out of the water and then started to wash her face as Derek washed up as well.

"So…you okay?" he asked, his voice casual.

As she was drying her face on the towel he'd handed her, she remembered how unsure she'd been when she'd first come into his bedroom last night. And how she'd been crying.

The sex was…what needed to happen.

She lowered the towel and looked at him.

"Actually I'm pretty good. Thanks for that. I needed it."

He gave her the biggest, cockiest grin she'd ever seen from him. "Me, too."

She couldn't help it: she started laughing. She felt young and free in this moment, something that she'd lost somewhere in the last few years. There were moments when she held her son that she approached that feeling but it was nothing like this.

He started to walk toward her when his phone buzzed loudly from the next room.

"Crap," he said, brushing past her and stalking into the bedroom.

Her lover was gone and in his place was the surgeon. She'd seen him give a lecture at the hospital a few months ago when she'd attended a charity function and had been impressed by the difference in the personal and professional sides of the man she knew. Derek was by nature a bit of a charming rogue but when he was focused on his career he was intense and there was no time for frivolity.

He had that same intensity and focus speaking on his phone when she walked back into the bedroom. His questions were quick-fire and he had gone to his closet and started pulling out clothes. She realized he was going to have to go work.

It was three…in the morning.

This was something she hadn't considered. Derek tossed her a pair of basketball shorts with a drawstring waist and she drew them on. He was going to have to leave pretty quickly. Staying in his house alone wasn't what she wanted so she started gathering up her dress and clothes. Her purse was in the foyer on a table. By the time he was off the phone she thought she'd gotten everything.

"I have to go to the hospital," he said. "Sorry I don't have time to talk about it. Want me to drop you off at your parents' house?"

"Yes, please. Do you have time? I can walk," she said.

"I'll take you. The patient is en route to the hospital so I have a few moments to spare but we have to leave now."

He led the way through the darkened house. She grabbed her bag as he opened the front door. He had them in the car in a moment. Though he wasn't talking, she had a chance to see him in full-on doctor mode. She saw that he was already thinking about the upcoming surgery. He received an email and called the attachment up on the in-dash screen. It looked like an X-ray.

He pulled up in front her parents' house and she reached for the door handle but he leaned over and kissed her, hard and deep. "Sorry about this."

"It's your job," she said. "We can talk tomorrow."

"Yes," he said.

She let herself into the house and heard Derek speed away. She quietly made her way up to her room, dropping off her clothes before poking her head into Benito's room to check on him. He was sleeping with his mouth open. She stood over him and watched him for a few minutes before going back into her own room.

She took off the shorts that Derek had loaned her but left the tee on. She reached for her cell phone, which she'd left charging on her nightstand, and texted him to say good luck with his surgery.

She was surprised when she noticed the three dancing dots that signaled he was responding.

Thank you. Sorry the night had to end so soon. Looking forward to living with you.

Bianca quickly typed her reply.

Me, too.

She put the phone away and tried to go to sleep but her mind was buzzing. As she drifted off, she remembered the feel of Derek's arms around her, the Ed Sheeran song playing in the background of her mind.

Derek met Raine in the presurgery room where they scrubbed up. She briefed him on the additional information that the EMTs had sent on their way in. They were going straight into the operating room as the patient had shown all the symptoms of a heart attack and had undergone ten minutes of CPR and was failing. They'd finally revived him enough for surgery.

He worked carefully for the next six hours and when they emerged he knew he'd done all he could to save the patient. And it looked like the man was going to survive; Derek was cautiously optimistic. After cleaning up, he looked for Raine but she was with the family. Despite his exhaustion, his mind was buzzing from the surgery. He mentally reviewed every cut he'd made. Which was why he was distracted when he entered the lounge and bumped into someone who was standing there.

Looking up, he was surprised to see Marnie.

"You look tired," she said.

"I am. Surgery does that," he said. He wasn't being curt; his mind just wasn't back to functioning in the real world. He was still going over everything he'd done. He knew he'd done the best he could with a heart that was badly damaged.

"This was one of the things I hated about dating you," she said. "I thought if I worked at the hospital it would help me understand you. But I'm not sure it does."

He looked at Marnie. She'd done something different with her makeup today and she seemed softer. He walked over to the coffeepot and poured himself a cup. He had rounds and then he'd be able to head home and catch some sleep.

"I'm sure it doesn't. It's for the best that we're not together," he said.

"I heard about your fiancée this morning. Bianca Velasquez…very impressive," Marnie said.

"She is. We've been friends for a long time. She knew me before I was a surgeon."

"That might help her. Well, I hope it lasts," Marnie said.

Derek didn't know how to respond to that. "Why wouldn't it?"

"Because you aren't long on commitment," Marnie said. "Remember you started to get itchy about three days after we moved in together."

He wanted to tell her that it was all the junk she'd brought and the schedule she'd put on the fridge. How they both had to check in constantly with each other. But he held his tongue. There was no reason to start an argument with her. She was out of his life and they were both in a better place now.

"It feels different this time," he said.

She looked hurt and he realized that his words might have stung her. "We just weren't a good fit, Marn. You know it and I know it."

"I've changed," she said softly.

"I haven't," he said. "I've got rounds but I'll see you on Wednesday for the board meeting. Have a good Saturday."

He walked out of the room before she said anything else. The board was meeting every week for updates on the progress of the new cardio wing. He would be attending, and there would be no way to avoid her.

His encounter with Marnie made him miss Bianca. It was almost ten in the morning and he did have rounds to make but he pulled out his phone and texted her, and they began a back-and-forth.

Good morning. You awake yet?

I have a toddler. I've been awake since five.

Ouch. I have rounds but maybe this afternoon you and Beni can come over and start planning the move in.

I'd like that. I just got an email asking me to come to Manhattan on Tuesday for a photo shoot. I was thinking of going. Mom and Dad will watch Beni.

Should I wait until I get back to move in?

No. I think you should get settled this weekend.

Derek didn't want her to leave. He wanted them to get settled into living together. And he hated to admit that now part of it was about proving Marnie wrong about his ability to live with a woman. But he knew that he couldn't ask Bianca to not take a job. He'd never have stayed home this morning if she'd asked.

He knew surgery and modeling were different careers but hers was just as important as his.

OK. I'll take you to the airport.

Thanks. Text me when you want us to come over.

:) See ya later.

He pocketed his phone and finished his rounds, including a visit to the patient he'd done emergency surgery on overnight. Derek was pleased to see that he was responding well. He talked to the family and then left the hospital.

He drove home. As soon as he went inside, he headed to his bedroom. He could smell Bianca's perfume and saw the rumpled sheets that reminded him of last night. And there was an emptiness inside him as he looked around the house.

He wanted Bianca here. He needed her here in his house. Marnie had been right when she'd said that he hadn't been able to live with her. But Bianca was different. He took a quick nap, showered and then texted her that he was ready for her and Beni to start moving their stuff in.

He offered to pick her up but she said she was going to bring her own car.

He told himself that this was just a normal afternoon but he felt like a kid getting ready to go to bed on Christmas Eve. He was full of anticipation but when the doorbell rang he forced himself to walk slowly toward the door.

"Hello," he said opening the door.

"Hiya, Derry," Benito said.

He smiled down at her son, but his eyes never left Bianca's. There was something he saw there that made him believe that she had missed him, too.

He stepped back to let them enter, finally feeling like this house was about to become a home. And as much as that thrilled him he had to remember that he hadn't changed the parameters of their agreement.

Benito was pretty excited about having a "new dad." He'd talked of nothing else all morning and since his sentiment matched her mood she didn't say anything.

Derek looked tired but happy to see them. Cobie was in Houston visiting his girlfriend so it was just the three of them in the house.

"Beni, want to pick out your room?" Derek asked.

"Yes, Mama, you can have the room next to mine."

"Do you have any adjoining rooms?" she asked as Derek led the way to the stairs. In Texas, the master suites tended to be on the first floor and the other bedrooms and game rooms on the second floor.

One of the moms in Beni's playgroup had mentioned that not too long ago. Having grown up here it had seemed normal to Bianca but this mom who'd moved from Chicago had said her eight-year-old didn't like it and had been sleeping on the floor of her and her husband's bedroom every night. They were in the process of renovating the upstairs to accommodate the master suite.

She and Derek had slept together last night but she wasn't sure he'd planned on them moving into a room together. Besides they both were still trying to figure this out.

The notion that this was temporary had been put out of her mind but she had no idea if it had been for Derek as well. And it had only been one night. She knew... well, one night could change a lot of things but they hadn't talked so she had no idea where they stood.

Beni took her hand and then started singing a counting song as they went up the stairs. She sang along with him and noticed that Derek just followed behind. When they were all on the second floor, Beni dropped her hand to go explore the rooms.

"What was that?"

"Um…it's kind of embarrassing but I have a tendency to miss steps on the way down and slip on the stairs, so I count them as I walk down so I don't fall and Beni has always heard me because I really didn't want to fall when I was carrying him down the stairs. So when he learned the counting song at his day care he started singing it when we go up and down the stairs."

"I love it. You guys have a pretty close relationship," Derek said.

"We do. It's been mostly just he and I all of his life. He doesn't remember Jose that well. We have a lot of pictures of him and I tell Beni stories about his papa but it's hard." She paused before adding, "I think you should know he told *Abuelo* this morning that he has a new dad now."

Bianca wanted to make sure that Derek wasn't surprised in case Beni said anything to him. "I'll talk to him but he's small and so it's hard for him to understand that you are more like a friend."

"It's okay. We'll do it together."

She nodded. "I hope this isn't more than you intended when you asked me to do this."

"I think it already is," Derek said. "Things are changing but I have no regrets."

Hmm…well that didn't tell her anything. She wanted to pursue this topic further but maybe today wasn't the right time.

"How was surgery last night?" she asked.

"Good. The patient is responding well and I think he'll make a good recovery."

"I'm glad to hear that. I can't imagine what it's like to hold someone's life in your hands," she said. "I couldn't do it."

Derek stared at her for a long moment. "But you do it in a different way with Benito. And you do a wonderful job."

She was touched by his words and reached out to take his hand. "Thanks for saying that. But you haven't seen us in meltdown mode."

"I'm sure it's not as bad as you think."

"I'm going to let you keep believing that," she said.

Toddler-and-mom meltdowns weren't something that could be explained. They had to be seen to be believed. She and Beni were usually pretty good but sometimes he got tired and she got cranky. They weren't perfect.

"I think you should know that my track record with living with someone isn't the greatest," Derek said. "I… I'm not sure what I'll be like."

"I'm sure we'll be fine," she said, but that little dream she'd started to have about maybe making this permanent died a quick death. She didn't need a man, she knew that. Her happiness had never been dependent on one. But she liked Derek. She liked the idea of the two of them together.

She had bought into the advertising once again. She'd seen the party last night, experienced the tender love-making and thought, *This is it. This is real.*

The reason he hadn't expanded on what he'd said earlier was probably that he was still thinking that in three months they'd be out the door.

"Mama, I want this one," Beni said, poking his head out of one of the doorways.

Thank God for her little boy. She smiled at him and started down the hall. She was going to talk to him about Derek and she was going to have to make sure that even though they lived together she kept their lives separate. She already felt…well, like something had been taken from her but that was only an illusion.

She had wanted last night to be all physical and even though it hadn't been for her maybe it was good that it seemed to have been for Derek. She tried to reassure herself that it was much better to find out now before she allowed herself to care even more deeply for the man.

But the words rang hollow to her own ears and felt like a lie.

She smiled as Beni walked her around a room that connected to second one through a Jack-and-Jill bathroom.

She checked the room out and noticed the large walk-in closet. All the while, she tried to focus on the surroundings and not on the man who followed them quietly from room to room.

But that wasn't working.

Bianca had brought all of the stuff she'd been using at her parents' house over, mainly clothes, computers and Beni's favorite toys. Her brothers and Derek's had volunteered to get all of her stuff from storage so they were on their way.

The house was full of noise and men and Bianca wanted to hide out but she had to direct them as to where to put everything. Derek was helpful. She tried not to let it matter but he was so different from Jose. It seemed to her that everything that had been fake with Jose was real with Derek and vice versa.

She hoped she was deluding herself and would snap out of it soon.

Twelve

A month went by in a blur.

Bianca had been to New York and Paris for modeling gigs. Benito had taken over the downstairs area with his books and playthings and Derek was starting to get used to seeing his toy F1 car parked in the courtyard. But sometimes that was all he saw of either of his houseguests.

And they were definitely houseguests. Something had changed the day after he'd made love to Bianca and by the time he'd realized it, it had felt too late to change it back. He was busy at the hospital and she was busy with her son and starting a lifestyle blog and video channel. Some days all he saw of her were the videos she posted.

He watched them and wanted her. But it also made

him miss talking to her. But when he got home from the hospital she'd be at a family event or already in bed. It was hard to figure out how to get through to her and what he'd done to alienate her.

But today was the rehearsal dinner for Hunter's wedding to Ferrin so she couldn't avoid him any longer. They were staying in his old bedroom out at the Rockin' C together. Nate and Kinley had put them together and neither of them had wanted to say no, they couldn't share a room. Beni was having a sleepover in Penny's room. Pippa would be keeping an eye on the kids, including Conner, the son of Hunter's best friend, Kingsley. King and his new wife, Gabi were staying here as well. They were in town from California. The house was full of people and Derek hadn't seen his mom in such a good mood in a long time.

She'd hugged all of them more than once and kept saying how good it was to have all of her boys back on the ranch. It had made Derek realize that he should take more time to come and visit his parents.

He heard the bathroom door open and Bianca walked into the room wearing a jumpsuit with a halter neck that left her shoulders bare. The plunging neckline accentuated her cleavage. She had her hair up and her makeup was flawless as usual.

"I hadn't realized how big this party was going to be. I think there are going to be a few film crews here," Bianca said. "In case they ask about us, I'll try to downplay it. In fact, should I not even mention it?"

No.

"Definitely not. Listen, Bia, I'm not sure what I said

to you that day we were picking out rooms in my house but this isn't going the way I wanted it to. Let's talk."

"Don't we have a party to get to?" she asked, going to the dresser and fiddling with her jewelry bag.

"No. Tonight is the first time we have been truly alone. I want to discuss this," he said.

"Well, I don't," she said. "I have enough on my mind as it is."

"Like what? My brother is the one getting married," he said.

"Like my marriage to Jose. This reminds me of it," she said, but he could tell it didn't. She was trying to come up with a reason not to talk to him.

"I'm sorry but that's not going to fly," Derek said. He went over to her, putting his hand on her shoulder while watching her in the mirror.

She looked up and in her eyes he saw…well, he wasn't sure if he was projecting his own feelings but it looked like sadness. Maybe she was really upset about the high-profile wedding.

He squeezed her shoulder. "We're friends. And we haven't been talking at all. If this is bothering you then tell me about it."

She turned to face him and he stepped back to give her some space because he knew she needed it.

"It's not the filming. It's just me. I've been in a funk lately," she said.

Derek hadn't noticed. He hadn't really seen her so it would be hard to notice her mood.

"What's up?"

She shrugged.

"Well, I've been a real douche at work. Raine told me if I don't come back from this weekend with a better attitude I was going to need to find a new assistant."

Bianca looked up at him then and for the first time in weeks he felt like she really saw him.

"Why?"

"Well, my best friend stopped talking to me and is avoiding me," he said.

"I thought Rowdy was your best friend," she said.

"Don't be coy. You know I mean you," he said. He walked closer to her. "I've missed you. I can't figure out what it was I did that set us on the path we're on."

She chewed her lower lip. "It wasn't really you. I was feeling unsure of how we should proceed and that day... I heard your warning. That you don't really like living with someone else. And I knew I had to be careful to keep our lives separate."

"Why?"

"Beni was already thinking of you as a 'new dad' and that can't be. Not if we are going to be going our own separate ways in a short amount of time. I wanted to make sure I didn't start to believe in something that you never meant for us to have."

Derek rubbed the back of his neck and turned away to keep from cursing out loud. He'd done this. He'd shoved her away to try to make sure that he didn't get hurt.

"That wasn't my intention," he said.

She watched him with those big brown eyes of hers that seemed to see all the way to his soul.

"What did you intend?" she asked.

He took a deep breath. He didn't know. In a way she'd given him exactly what he'd asked for, but it was hollow. Not what he wanted. But he hadn't realized that until he'd spent a month living with a woman he cared for.

"I intended to let you know that I wasn't sure what I was doing," he said. "I just wanted you to know I might screw up," Derek finally replied after a long pause.

"Why?"

"I'd seen Marnie at the hospital before I came home that day and she pointed out how much I hadn't enjoyed living with her. Seriously, after three days I was ready to throw all of her stuff out of the house or move into Nate's condo downtown instead."

Bianca had been dreading getting through this weekend, knowing she'd be so close to Derek and not have an easy way to escape him. This conversation was confirming her worst fears.

Since she'd moved into his house, she'd kept busy and hoped the feelings she had for him would disappear. That was something that happened with Jose once they'd been married.

But she realized the differences between the two men immediately. For one thing no matter how little contact they'd had every morning when she came downstairs she always found Derek's little notes on the counter telling her when he'd be home and wishing her a good day. He'd leave them alongside two glasses of pineapple juice, which he knew she and Beni drank each morning.

It was sweet.

It had been hard to figure out why he didn't like living with a woman, why he was avoiding her, when he did things like that. She'd just figured that maybe he was being polite, that he had wanted them to feel at home in his house. But the gestures didn't stop. One night she had to meet with her attorney in town and Derek had picked Beni up from his day care and brought him home. She'd come home to the two of them making tacos and Beni showing him how to do the salsa. Something his *abuela* in Spain had been teaching him.

It had been sweet but Bianca had faked a headache and gone upstairs to keep from…falling for Derek. He'd said one thing—but his actions had shown her something else.

But she had been afraid to trust her instincts. She'd been so wrong once before and falling for a man had made her…well, not the smartest girl in the world.

And as Bianca mulled over what he'd just said, she realized something she shouldn't have forgotten. They were both coming into this afraid of what the future might hold. Afraid of how they were going to move forward. She wanted to make this work. If the last month had shown her anything it was that even pretending he wasn't important in her life wasn't enough to actually keep her from falling for him.

She wondered how much of his treatment of her was a reaction to what living with Marnie had made him feel. She wasn't sure.

She wrapped her arms around her waist. If there was a scarier thing than falling for another person she had no idea what it was. There was no way to protect herself. She knew that. Because even reminding herself every morning that she had to keep her distance hadn't helped her to stop caring about Derek.

And she didn't just mean caring for him as a friend. She cared about him the way she would a lover. She missed him in her bed.

She missed talking to him at night. And it wasn't as if they'd even had that many conversations, which should give her a clue as to why she was falling for him. It was the quality of those conversations. Derek always listened to her and made her feel like she mattered. Something Jose had never done.

"I'm not Marnie," she said at last.

"Thank God. Listen, you know I'm not the best at saying the right thing. I don't want us to continue on the way we have been. I like you and Beni and I want us to do things together. Can we start over?"

Could they? They only had two months left on their arrangement. Would that be enough to show her what they could really be?

"Yes. But what exactly will we do?" she asked.

"You should stop avoiding me," he said. "I do love watching your videos but I'd rather see you in person."

"You've been watching my videos?" She felt a little thrill despite herself. "Do I look silly? Pippa suggested I try it. She said she's been watching a few of them for years and that they seem to make some good money. So I asked around when I was in Paris and there is money to be made. Plus I have a built-in brand," she said. "I'm rambling. Sorry, it's kind of unnerving to know someone I know has been watching the videos. Especially you."

"I missed you," he said at last. "I like talking to you and you were limiting us to notes on the counter."

"I thought that was what you wanted," she said. "By the way, I love your notes on the counter. Did Marnie hate that?"

She was a little jealous of the woman he'd lived with. For one thing, he hadn't been with Marnie because he needed a fake fiancée. But Bianca also wanted to know what was different about the two situations.

"I didn't do that with her. She used to wake me up in the morning so I could exercise with her. You know I use the treadmill and review cases and read up on experimental stuff, but when I said that to her, she took it to mean that I wanted more space…which made her immediately give me less."

Bianca had a feeling his relationship with the other woman wasn't as good as Marnie might have believed. "I am never going to wake you up to exercise. I'm fine with a dip in the pool in the morning and chasing Benito around in his little F1 car."

"Great. I don't want you to do anything different. I think we should just stop avoiding each other and be ourselves," he said.

Someone knocked on the door.

"Yes?"

"Mom wants a picture of all of us boys and our women," Ethan said.

"Do you have a woman?" Derek asked, going to open the door.

Bianca followed him, trying not to let the fact that she was Derek's woman get to her too much. But it was exactly what she wanted to be. She was glad to know he'd been as dissatisfied with their arrangement as she had been. And that dream that she'd been trying to quash since she'd moved into his house suddenly seemed viable.

Her heart beat a little faster as she listened to Derek and his brother Ethan banter as they went downstairs.

Hunter and King were the life of the party. The best friends had lived for ten years under the cloud of suspicion of murdering Hunter's college girlfriend. Even though Hunter had been arrested and released without being charged, they'd been tried in the media and the damage was done. The scandal had followed them into the NFL and had even continued after their pro careers. It had only been last year when the murderer had been caught—an assistant coach on their college team who'd had a thing for drugging co-eds—and they both had been exonerated in the court of public opinion.

Derek, who'd watched his brother try to ignore the gossip for years, was glad to see him so happy. King had somehow gotten the microphone from the deejay at the party that had been set up in the backyard and was now telling stories about when he and Hunter had crashed a Superbowl party for their rivals. And Manu Barrett, the former NFL defensive lineman who was now a special teams coach on the West Coast, was joining in. Manu's brother was the astronaut Hemi Barrett who'd been chosen as part of the Cronus mission and trained outside of Cole's Hill on the Bar T land.

There were some TV cameras and a few video bloggers at the party. The crowd was a strange mix of college professors—Ferrin was an English professor at UT Austin—professional football players, astronauts, media folks, models, cardiologists, you name it. If Derek had one thought it was about how crazy his family was.

Ethan had been hanging back most of the night talking to Manu but once the defensive-lineman-turned-coach got up on the stage and started sharing football tales about Hunter's wild days, Ethan sought out Ferrin and whisked her away. Derek realized that his brother was trying to protect her from hearing any more stories about Hunter. All of them knew how hard Hunter had fallen for her and didn't want her to have second thoughts on marrying him.

"We need to get everyone dancing again," Derek said to Bianca.

"Agreed. Some of these stories should never have left the locker room. You go get the deejay to play something and I'll rally the guests. Have them play a song we can all dance to."

Derek left her and found the deejay but he had no idea what to request. He hadn't been to a "dance" that wasn't a charity event for the hospital or the Women's League in years. In fact the only song that came to mind was one he'd line-danced to back in middle school. But as soon as the music came on and he heard the laughter, he wasn't sure he'd made the right choice.

"'Macarena'? That's what you thought of?" Bianca asked as she took his hand and led him to the dance floor.

"I think the last time I was in charge of music was middle school."

She shook her head. "Well, it's working."

And it was. Everyone was laughing and dancing now and even all of Hunter's old teammates were on the floor. After the song was over they ended up dancing to "Gangnam Style." Watching a big former defensive lineman do that dance was one of the funniest things that Derek had ever seen. By the time they were doing the Electric Slide, everyone had forgotten about the stories that had been told about Hunter. Then the deejay slowed things down with a classic from Ella Fitzgerald that Ferrin had requested.

Derek pulled Bianca into his arms and slow-danced with her, noticing how all of his brothers were doing the same except for Ethan. Derek was glad he had Bianca. He was happy that he'd talked to her, too, because as the night progressed and the songs got slower and more sensual he realized he didn't want to be the only Caruthers besides Ethan on the outside watching this.

He wanted to be right where he was. In Bianca's arms. The last month had made him realize how much he wanted her in his life. Not temporarily, as he'd initially proposed, but for a long time.

He knew that he had one month, maybe two, to convince her that she wanted the same thing. And he didn't want to go overboard on her the way Marnie had with him. He didn't want to scare her off.

He held her close and his heart melted when she wrapped her arms around his waist and rested her head right over his heart. He was a heart surgeon; he knew that the organ didn't skip a beat or melt. But there was a part of him that would have sworn his heart did both of those things.

Soon they moved from dancing to drinking with his brothers and their friends. Bianca was sitting on his lap and she drifted to sleep while everyone was laughing and partying around them. It was time to call it a night.

Derek carried her up to his old bedroom and stood there watching her sleep. A part of him supposed he should go back out there with his brothers but he knew he didn't want to leave her. Finally he decided he should get her into something more comfortable.

He took off the halter top of her jumpsuit and then paused. He had no idea how to undress her without waking her up. And what if she did wake up and thought he was doing something...

"Derek?"

"Yes. I was trying to make you comfortable," he said. "Not being a creeper."

She started to laugh. "Thanks. Sorry I fell asleep. I know you're not a creeper. However it does sound like your brother might have known a few guys like that."

"It does. He had some wild days in the NFL," Derek said, going to sit down on the other side of the bed and take off his shoes. He heard her moving behind him as he finished getting undressed. He realized this was what he'd been hoping to find with Bianca. There was an intimacy that living together had brought to his life that he'd never had before. Something that he had always wanted but never thought he'd find.

Thirteen

Bianca watched him moving around getting undressed. He took his watch off first and then pulled his shirt from his trousers and toed off his shoes. This was the casual intimacy that she'd been looking forward to in her marriage but that she'd never had. Sex with Jose had always been on his terms and quick. He'd left her when it was over. The one time with Derek—and sleeping in his arms afterward—was the closest she'd come to spending the night with her lover.

Tonight she wanted more. She was tired of waiting and avoiding him. In their conversation earlier, Derek had seemed to suggest that he wanted more from her than just something temporary. She was buzzing from the champagne and the festivities. Tonight had changed everything.

She hadn't felt this hopeful about a relationship since she'd found out she was pregnant and thought that would fix her failing marriage. But this change was inspired by Derek.

He'd missed her.

He'd held her close when they danced, lighting a fire deep inside of her. One that would never be put out.

She stood up to get changed but decided that it had been too long since she'd had Derek. She knew it had been her own fault. But now that they were in this room together again, she wanted him.

And there was no reason she couldn't have him.

She striped down to her underwear. She'd worn a pushup strapless bra under the jumpsuit and left it on now. The tops of her breasts spilled out of the fabric. She wore a matching thong.

She turned to check her lipstick in the mirror, planning to touch up the bright berry color she'd used earlier, but when she looked in the mirror her gaze met Derek's. He watched her. His chest was bare and one hand rubbed down over his stomach. He'd taken his pants off and his erection poked through the opening in his boxers.

She canted her hips back and looked over her shoulder at him.

"See something you like?" she asked.

As opposed to the first time they'd been together, tonight she was herself again. The new Bianca, who had the confidence to know that this man wanted her and she could give him something no other woman could.

He sorted of grunted at her and a smile played around her lips.

She pouted as she turned and walked toward him using all the knowledge she'd gained on the catwalk in Paris. She knew how to move her body to draw attention to it.

"Do you think my lips need touching up?" she asked as she rounded the bed where he stood.

"Hell, no. I'm going to kiss the remaining lipstick off your mouth anyway," he said.

"Are you?" she asked. "I thought I was going to leave it on your skin. I was thinking I'd start here. With a kiss on the side of your neck. And then maybe work my way lower."

She touched him with her fingertip on the spot where his pulse beat rapidly and then walked her fingers downward. She skimmed over his nipple and watched him flinch as she continued moving lower. She stopped when she reached his belly button and swirled her finger around it, dipping her finger inside, and then bent forward to swirl her tongue around it. She felt his erection jump and lengthen against her breasts, which she'd deliberately leaned forward to rub against him.

She stood back up and put her hand on his shoulder, going up on tiptoe to bite the lobe of his ear. "Do you think you'd like that?"

He growled a response that sounded like yes and his hands came to her waist and then moved lower to her buttocks, grasping both of her cheeks and lifting her off her feet.

"Part your legs," he said in that low gravelly tone. "Put them around my waist."

"No."

She slithered down his body and away from him. "You sit down. Wait."

He growled deep in her throat when she leaned forward to brush kisses against his chest. Her lips were sweet and not shy as she explored his torso. Then he felt the edge of her teeth as she nibbled at his pecs.

He watched her, his eyes narrowing. Her tongue darted out and brushed against his nipple. She kept doing that to him and he began to realize where she was going with this. He arched off the bed and put his hand on the back of her head, urging her to stay where she was.

She put her hands on his shoulders and eased her way down his chest tracing each of the muscles that ribbed his abdomen and then slowly making her way lower. He could feel his heartbeat in his erection and he knew he was going to lose it if he didn't take control.

But another part of him wanted to just sit back and let her have her way with him. When she reached the edge of his boxers, she stopped and glanced up at him.

He held himself still, waiting to see what she was going to do next. She grabbed his boxers and carefully pushed them over his hard-on, easing them down his thighs and then leaving him to step out of them.

Her hands were on his erection and then he felt the brush of her lips against his shaft. She stroked him with her fingers and took the tip of him in her mouth. His hands fell to her head as she sucked him into her mouth and his hips canted forward. It had been too long since he'd been with her and he was on the knife's edge of his control.

He pulled her up and she let him. Sitting down on the edge of the bed, he drew her to him. He reached around behind her to undo her bra and when it fell off, he sat back to look at her. She took a half step back and put her hand on her hip, arching her eyebrows at him.

"Like what you see?" she asked.

"Stop teasing me, Bia," he said. "It's been too long and I'm about to lose it."

"Good. You're too controlled. I think you're trying to manage everything about this like you would in the operating room. But this isn't supposed to follow a script. This is supposed to be raw and honest."

"I feel raw," he said.

He pulled down her thong and she stepped out of it. He fingered the soft hair that covered her secrets and then drew her down on his lap, lifting her slightly so that her nipples grazed his chest.

"Now it's my turn," he said.

She nibbled on her lips as he rotated his shoulders so that his chest rubbed against her breasts. She put her hands on his shoulders and arched her back, her center rubbing over his erection.

"This is what I want," she said.

Blood roared in his ears; after months of waiting he wasn't sure of his control. He'd dreamed about this moment every night in the bed where he'd taken her, made her his. She was his fiancée as far as the world was concerned and now he wanted to leave his mark on her.

He was so hard, so full right now, that he needed to be inside of her body. He fumbled for the nightstand and the condoms he'd optimistically put in there earlier in the day. He couldn't get hold of the box but felt her reach around him and grab it.

"Is this what you're looking for?" she asked, holding a foil packet up.

"Yes," he growled.

"Let me," she said, scooting back on his thighs and ripping it open. She put the condom on the tip of his penis and slowly rolled it all the way down. She let her fingers linger lower, caressing him before she looked back at him.

There was a fire in his soul that was being fanned by Bianca. She was everything he'd always wanted but never thought he could have. He pulled her closer, his mouth slamming down on hers. All subtlety was gone. He plunged his tongue into her mouth and tangled his hands in her hair. The pins that held it up fell to the floor. He put one arm around her waist, lifted her up until he could shift his hips and found the opening of her body.

He drove up into her as she bit his tongue. When he was buried inside of her he stopped. He opened his eyes because he wanted to make sure this wasn't another erotic dream that he would wake from feeling frustrated and alone.

Bianca's eyes were open as well and there was fire in her big brown gaze. She shifted up and then slowly lowered herself back down on him. She put her hands on his shoulders as she started to ride him.

He pulled her head down to his so he could taste her mouth. Her mouth opened over his and he told himself to take it slow but slow wasn't in his programming with this woman. She was pure feminine temptation and he had her in his arms. All of the control he'd honed over the years was gone.

He nibbled on her lips and held her at his mercy. Her nails dug into his shoulders and she leaned up, brushing against his chest. Her nipples were hard points and he pulled away from her mouth, glancing down to see them pushing against his chest. Then she arched her back and he felt the brush of her nipple against his lips.

He caressed her back and spine, scraping his nails down the length of it. He followed the line of her back down the indentation above her backside, all the while taking control of the motion of her hips and driving her faster against him.

She closed her eyes and held her breath as he fondled her, running his finger over her nipple. It was velvety compared to the satin smoothness of her breast. He brushed his finger back and forth until she bit her lower lip and shifted on his lap.

He suckled her, used his teeth to tease her and then played with her other nipple with his fingers. She continued to ride him, her pace increasing but it wasn't enough for him. He wanted her.

He needed more.

He scraped his fingernail over her nipple and she shivered in his arms. He pushed her back a little bit so he could see her. Her breasts were bare, nipples distended and begging for his mouth. He lowered his head and suckled.

"You have very pretty breasts, Bianca," he said against her skin. She smelled good here as well, as if she'd spritzed her perfume in her cleavage earlier in the evening.

"Thank you," she said. "I always thought they were on the small side. That's why I wear push-up bras all the time."

He cupped them and looked up at her, their eyes meeting. "They are just right."

She leaned down and kissed him softly and gently. "I'm glad you think so."

He put one hand on the small of her back. With his other hand he pulled the remaining pins from her hair until it fell around her shoulders. He pulled it forward over the front of her chest. She sat straight with her shoulders back, which thrust her breasts up at him. He had a lap full of woman and he knew that he wanted Bianca more than…anything. She wasn't something he could win by working hard and studying, which had always been his way. And leaving her alone hadn't worked, either. It was only now that he had her back in his arms that he realized he was never going to let her go again.

She put her hands on his shoulders and he felt her tighten herself around his shaft as she shifted up on him and started to move again. Her eyes closed and her head fell back. He watched her for a moment until he felt like he was going to explode. But he needed to bring her along with him.

It had been too long and even though he wanted to make this last he knew that he was going to be hard-pressed to do that.

He leaned down and licked her nipple and then

blew on it and saw the goose bumps spread down her body. He loved the way she reacted to his mouth on her breasts. He kept his attention on them. She started to ride him harder and faster as he continued touching her there.

He leaned down and licked the valley between her breasts, whispering hot words of carnal need. She responded by digging her nails into his shoulders.

He bit carefully at the white skin of her chest, suckling at her so that he'd leave his mark. He wanted her to remember this moment and what they had done when she was alone later.

He kept kissing her and she rocked her hips harder against his length. He grabbed her hips and held her to him as he slammed up into her. Then he bit down carefully on her tender, aroused nipple. She screamed his name as her body tightened around his and he lifted his mouth to hers to capture her cries of passion.

She continued rocking against him and he slowly built her passion back to the boiling point again. He suckled her nipple as he rotated his hips to catch her pleasure point with each thrust, and he felt her hands in his hair clenching as she threw her head back the exact moment her climax ripped through her.

He varied his thrusts, finding a rhythm that would draw out the tension at the base of his spine. But she was having none of that and leaned down to whisper in his ear. Telling him how good he felt. And how deeply he filled her. Her words were like a velvet whip on him and he felt his orgasm coming a second before he erupted.

He didn't want this to end. The thought flashed

through his mind that the last time after they'd made love things had gone wrong.

"Bianca."

He called her name as he came. She arched over him again and then they collapsed back on the bed in a heap. He held her close and pretended it was just after-sex euphoria but he knew that she was in his heart now.

There was no leaving her. There was no turning back from this. And though he wasn't as sure of what the future would hold he knew that when the board made their decision about who would be chief of cardiology, he wasn't going to come home and break his engagement to Bianca. He wanted her to be his fiancée for real.

Which meant he was going to have to ask her to marry him.

And that was scary. Because she'd agreed to one thing—a temporary engagement. And the last time when he'd asked her for that, the answer hadn't been as important as it would be this time.

He carried her into the adjoining bathroom and they took a shower together. Neither of them talking.

When they climbed back into bed, he held her to him, cuddling her close and knowing that everything had changed. When they'd made love the first time it had fixed something broken in Bianca. This time it had fixed the pieces of him that had always been out of joint, leading him to an important realization.

That he'd finally found the right place for himself, right here in her arms.

Fourteen

The wedding weekend changed a lot between them but when they got back to their routines it was hard not fall back into old habits. But surprisingly, they didn't. The first morning they were back in the house Bianca went downstairs early to see Derek before he left for work. He and Beni were morning people, and she found them chattering away the entire time. They had started a new routine.

Derek changed a few of his other habits, too. Instead of staying home in the evenings when they went up to the club to play tennis he started joining them. As the weeks went by and the board meeting to name the new cardiology chief drew closer she started to feel like they were becoming a family.

So the day of the big announcement was a big deal

in her mind. She and Beni planned a special dinner for the three of them and she was pretty proud of the way that Beni had helped her decorate the courtyard.

Cobie was even helping them by hanging some lights she'd found online that were decorated with the caduceus, the symbol for medicine and surgery. She looked around the courtyard and knew that many of the most important moments in her life with Derek had happened here.

"Thanks for helping us get everything set up today," Bianca said to Cobie.

"No problem," he replied. "The little dude promised to help me with my Spanish so we're square."

"*Si*, Mama," Beni said. "Cobie is *muy bueno*."

She smiled as the two of them started speaking in Spanish and realized how Beni had really started to bloom here in Cole's Hill and in Derek's house. He liked having all of his stuff out of storage. She and Derek had taken him shopping in the outlets at San Marcos a few weeks ago to bulk up his room. This place was starting to feel like home.

And that felt right to her since Derek was definitely the man she'd fallen in love with. There was a niggling doubt in the back of her mind that wouldn't be eased until she asked him tonight to marry her. It was funny how everything here had started out temporary in theory but from the moment she'd started talking to Derek and they'd moved together, everything had been more real than it ever had been with Jose.

Being with Derek had shown her that what she'd felt for Jose had been infatuation and a little bit of oh-my-

God-I-can't-believe-this-is-my-life. There was none of that with Derek. There was just living in the town she loved and building a family with him and Beni.

She had something she'd never expected to find with anyone after Jose left. A part of her had been afraid that another man wouldn't be able to love her son the way she did. But Derek was really good with Benito. Even when the two of them had been keeping their distance, he'd still made time for her son. It had shown her that Derek Caruthers was a man of his word. And when he made a promise he kept it.

The doorbell rang, and since Cobie was helping Beni to wrap some lights around one of the trees, she waved for him to stay and went to answer it.

She opened the door to see Kinley and Penny standing there. Penny had on a cowboy hat, a pair of jeans and a T-shirt with a ballerina on it.

"Howdy," Penny said.

"Howdy," Bianca responded, stepping back and gesturing for them to come in.

"I got the cake you asked for from the bakery," Kinley said, handing the box over to her.

"Thank you. I wasn't sure I'd have time to get it before Derek comes home."

"Any word from him yet?"

"Nothing. I can only assume he's still in the meeting," Bianca said.

Kinley's phone pinged and she looked down at it. "That man. I told Nate we should turn on Find My Friends on our phones since he drives fast and I was worried about him having an accident on his way from town to the ranch."

"Okay. So what does that have to do with anything?" Bianca asked.

"He can see I'm at your place and wants to know if you've heard from Derek," Kinley said.

Bianca had to smile. One of the things she loved about the Caruthers family was the closeness between the brothers. She was glad that Beni would have more uncles.

"No, nosey, she hasn't," Kinley said out loud as she typed. "Okay, do you need me to help with anything?"

"Not really. I think everything is almost ready. Just waiting for Derek," Bianca said.

She patted the pocket of her pants where she'd slipped the ring box earlier. She had every last detail planned and now all she could do was wait. She decided to text Derek to see if he'd heard any news.

Any word yet?

Yes. Good news. I am the new Chief of Cardiology. Bad news three-car accident on the highway. Going into surgery now.

Congratulations. See you tonight.

Can't wait. <3

"Derek got the chief position," Bianca told Kinley.

"That's great," Kinley said. "Was there a chance he wouldn't get it?"

"Yes. I mean, he's brilliant and everything but he's still sort of young for the position. Plus, Dr. Masters joined the board to oversee the cardiac surgical wing and name the new head, and she and Derek had some past…relations."

"Relations?" Kinley asked with a laugh.

"I know that sounds dumb, right? They dated. And when they broke up she wasn't ready to move on. So she was sort of not happy with him on a personal level. I'm glad she's finally past that."

"Me too."

Kinley and Penny visited for a few hours, but by then, Bianca's elation had turned to worry. There was still no text from Derek that he was out of surgery. Her guests went home, Cobie retreated to the pool house and it was just her and Benito in the house. She tried to distract herself by watching him race his car around the backyard on the cone track that Derek had laid out for him. But when the time for dinner came around and there was still no word from Derek she was starting to despair.

She finally texted him to check if he was out of the operating theater. She got no response. And though she didn't want to be the type of woman who had to call around to find her man—she'd done that with Jose—she finally called the hospital and learned he was in surgery. The receptionist then forwarded her call to the cardiac wing so she could get an update from the assistant.

The fear and doubt that had been building inside of her dissipated as she heard the nurse's reassuring voice. It was hard to think that she was still dealing with trust issues. Derek wasn't interested in another woman. He had dedicated the last two months to her. Even the month when they'd been sort of avoiding each other.

"Could you let me know when Dr. Caruthers is out of surgery?" Bianca asked the nurse after they'd exchanged greetings. The nurse was pleasant and chatty, and Bianca decided she'd been worrying for nothing.

Until what the woman said next stopped her dead in her tracks.

"Ma'am, he left the hospital at least an hour ago."

Derek was exhausted as he and Raine left the operating room and went into the post-op area to clean up. They still had to see the family and talk to the other surgeon who would do the follow-up surgery for the other injuries sustained by his patient. The car accident had been pretty horrible and the medevac had brought three patients to their hospital and airlifted two others to Houston.

It had been a long day and he was looking forward to getting home to Bianca and Beni and having a low-key evening. He'd operated on the six-year-old girl who had been seated behind the driver. The driver was still in surgery. The point of impact had been on the driver's side and those passengers had sustained the most threatening injuries. The mother and two siblings had various fractures and lacerations but weren't being admitted to the hospital. When Derek walked into that waiting room and saw them sitting there, he had a flash of how he'd feel if it were Bianca and Beni in the operating room.

He sat down and updated them on the status of their

daughter and then let Raine take over so he could go home to Bianca. But then he had to answer a text from his brothers and he noticed one from Bianca as well. He told her he'd be leaving soon. He needed to see her and make sure she was okay. He didn't bother with a shower and just went to the parking lot. But he stopped when he saw Marnie leaning against his car.

"I take it your patient is doing well?" she asked as he approached.

"Yes. She'll make a full recovery."

"Good to hear. You really are a miracle worker when you're in the operating room," she said. "Sorry I made you jump through hoops before naming you chief."

"It's okay," he said. Actually, without Marnie's delaying tactics he would have continued on his path, never realizing what he was missing. He'd never have asked Bianca to be his fake fiancée. In a way, he thought he should be thanking Marnie.

"You made me realize how single-focus my life had become. I'm glad you forced my hand," he said.

She nodded and then gave him a hard look. "I hate it that you are marrying someone else."

"That's just because you don't like to lose," he said. "You don't love me."

She tipped her head to the side and studied him for a very long time. "You're right. I don't love you. You're too independent. I guess I tried to make it so you would need me but the more I tried that the farther away you got."

"We just weren't meant for each other," he said. "You'll find someone who will be right for you just like I have Bianca."

She nodded. "I hope so."

"I know so. The right man is going to fall at your feet, Marnie."

She gave him a quick smile. "From your lips to God's ears. 'Night, Derek."

"Good night, Marnie," he said, unlocking his door and getting into the car. As soon as he was behind the wheel, he took a deep breath. He wasn't ready to drive. He sat there, thinking. In the old days he would have gone to see Nate. That little girl had reminded him of Benito and he had never been so scared in the operating room. Once he started focusing on the heart and the operation his mind had cleared but when he'd first looked down at that little body, he'd realized how much his life had changed.

He had a family of his own now and keeping them safe was the only thing that really mattered to him. He took his phone out to text Bianca and let her know he was on his way home and saw he'd missed a text from her.

Where are you? The hospital said you left an hour ago.

He quickly typed his reply.

Sorry, got caught up talking to the family and then Marnie. On my way home now.

There was no further response and he scrubbed his hand over his face. He put the car in gear and drove home as fast—and safely—as he could. Within twenty minutes, he'd pulled into the driveway of his house and then let himself in.

Benito came running up to him and he bent down and scooped the little boy up. He was so happy to see him healthy. He glanced over Beni's head at Bianca and saw that she had her arms wrapped around her waist.

He knew she was upset about something but he only knew that his heart was so full of love for her that he needed to hold her and tell her.

He carried Benito in his arms over to her and hugged her close. She was stiff for a moment and then she relented and put her arms around them. He held these two people who had come to mean more to him than life itself in his arms for a few minutes until Beni squirmed to get down and excitedly told them to follow him to the courtyard.

The first thing Derek saw were the lights and the table. He stopped next to it and realized how very lucky he was to have decided to ask Bianca to be his fake fiancée. The only thing left to do was to make this real. She was already in his heart and in his mind he was planning a wedding for them soon.

Bianca saw the fatigue on Derek's face and she wanted to give him the benefit of the doubt. But he'd told her he had been talking with Marnie instead of just coming home to her. She wasn't sure how much of her jealousy and unease was from Derek and how much of it was left over from Jose.

Plus, what if he'd had to do something else in order to convince Marnie to give him the job? But she knew

Derek. Or at least she thought she had. He wasn't the kind of man who would betray her like that. Was he?

She and Benito led Derek out onto the courtyard patio where they'd set up dinner. The lights were on and the medical paraphernalia that she'd gotten to decorate the table were all in perfect position. She'd blogged about making every little thing in life special and her readers had given her some good feedback but now she was afraid she was a fraud. She was falling apart because her fiancé hadn't texted her right back.

"Wait!" Benito exclaimed. He ran back into the house and Derek looked over at her.

"What's he up to?" Derek asked.

"He has a surprise for you," Bianca said. Beni had wanted to dress like a doctor, like Derek.

"Poppi, look at me," the little boy said when he came back out on the patio. He had on a pair of scrubs and a stethoscope around his neck.

Bianca glanced at Derek and saw that moment of vulnerability and love on his face as her son called him Poppi.

"I'm like you," Beni said.

"I couldn't be prouder," Derek said. He scooped Beni up. The two of them chatted during dinner and Bianca sat there trying to reconcile the two images she had of Derek in her mind: the man who'd spent an hour with his former girlfriend and the guy who was learning Spanish and talking to her son about any topic the toddler wanted to discuss.

That love she felt for Derek grew stronger but her doubts held it trapped. She was afraid to let herself believe in him…believe in them. She watched him for a sign. Something that would show her that he was ready for the change that she wanted them to make as a couple.

At the end of the meal she was still waiting for a sign of what she should do next. She decided to keep the ring in her pocket. Asking a man to marry her seemed like a big risk when she wasn't sure if she'd fooled herself into believing in something that might not be real.

After Beni was bathed and put in bed she went back downstairs to find Derek. He was in the den talking on the phone and she hesitated in the doorway unsure if she should go in or not.

But he waved her inside and she came in and sat on one of the padded leather armchairs while he finished up his call.

"Sorry, that was Nate. He wanted to talk and this is the first chance I had," Derek said. "Did you get Benito put to bed?"

"Yes," she said. "He was very excited for you even though he has no idea what your promotion means."

"He's a sweet boy," Derek said, coming around to sit in the chair next to her. "I am starting to think of him as my son."

Those were words that would have warmed her heart earlier in the day, but now with doubts and old fears dominating her thoughts, it was hard.

"That's nice."

Derek leaned away from her and looked at her out from under that mop of bangs that had fallen forward. She didn't want to be charmed by how he looked but she always was. She always saw the boy who'd been her friend long before they'd been attracted to each other, when his hair was rumpled like it was now. She wanted to trust Derek.

She wanted to believe that he was just talking with his ex-girlfriend for some innocent reason instead of returning Bianca's texts and getting home to her. And a part of her knew all she had to do was ask him. Derek wasn't Jose, who would tell her sweet lies that she'd know better than to believe. Derek was blunt and honest.

"What's up? You haven't been yourself since I got home," he said. "Did something happen today? I'm sorry I've been so focused on my day I didn't even think to ask you."

She had that first inkling that her trust in him wasn't misplaced. "My day was fine. No bad news."

"What is it then?" he asked.

She took a deep breath and knew she had to just say it out loud. Now that she was sitting here next to him she felt almost silly about her suspicions but she couldn't just dismiss them.

"Why were you talking with Marnie?" she asked. "I was worried about you and called the hospital and they said you'd left an hour before you texted me."

Derek rubbed his hand over his face and she studied him. She was looking to see if he'd avoid making eye contact with her or get angry that she'd asked him.

"Sorry. She cornered me at my car. We talked. I realized that if it weren't for her and the pressure I'd felt I would never have asked you to be my fake fiancée. I wouldn't have even asked you out on a date, Bia."

She knew that. They had been friends but she saw now that they both had been careful to keep parts of their lives hidden. It had worked for them for a long time. "I know. Why was that?"

"I think I was afraid to see you as anything more than a friend," he said.

"Me, too," she admitted. "Being friends was so much easier than this. I was nice and safely living my life and pretending that you were still the boy who'd been my friend in middle school. But to be honest I'd noticed you'd changed."

"Same. So what's changed tonight?"

She took a deep breath. "I was jealous when I realized that you were with her."

Fifteen

Jealous.

He looked over at her sitting there in her short-sleeved blouse with the wide-legged trousers and realized how sophisticated she looked. He felt like a country bumpkin next to her.

And she was jealous.

She never had to be. He knew that but Bianca didn't. Could he convince her of that truth?

"Of Marnie? She's completely out of the picture," Derek said.

"I know that here," she said pointing to her head. "But my heart isn't so sure."

He leaned forward, putting his arms on his legs and his head in his hands. "I'm not that kind of guy, Bianca. I mean, I might have never been able to commit to a woman for the long term but I've never been the kind of guy who needed to date more than one woman at a time to prove something to myself."

He suspected her fears were based in her previous marriage and if he were being totally honest with himself he knew he'd contributed a little bit by the way he'd asked her to be his pretend fiancée instead of his real one. At the time he hadn't been capable of doing it any other way but now he knew it had been a mistake. He loved her.

He would do whatever he had to in order to make sure she understood.

"I know that. I mean, there's a part of me that can't believe that I even had to bring it up, but I do. I know it's not fair of me to ask you to pay for someone else's damage—"

"You're not asking," he said. "It's not a problem. I am the one who came over to you at the club that night. I'm the one who changed our dynamic. And I know that I've fallen in love with you."

He shifted around in his chair to face her and then reached over to take her hands. He wanted to make her understand that he was willing to give her as much time as she needed to feel safe with him. To believe in him and the love he had for her. She'd been conned by a world-class Casanova and he didn't want to do anything that would hurt her.

"You love me?"

"Yes. I didn't mean to blurt it out like that but I've known it since you moved in. I missed you every time you were gone, and Beni too. I started to realize what it meant to have a family of my own. But I also know that I asked you to do me a favor and now I'm changing that by telling you how I feel. I don't want you to feel trapped."

"I'm not trapped. I'm sorry about the jealousy. It took me by surprise because a part of me knows that you are nothing like Jose. But then I remembered the big show that our engagement was and how you and I started out as just…"

"Pretend. I think I was lying to myself even then," he said. With Bianca he didn't want to play games. When he'd seen that little girl on the operating table tonight he'd realized how fragile life was. He didn't want to waste another minute of his time with her.

He needed her to know how much she meant to him.

"This isn't going to change," he said, taking her hand and putting it over his heart. "My love for you has been a part of me for a long time. And at first it was the love of friends but it has grown and I want you to be my partner in life. I want to be Beni's father and I want us to give him brothers and sisters. I want everything when I look into your eyes, Bianca."

He felt her hand under his start to shake a little and she gave him the sweetest smile he'd ever seen on her face before pulling her hand free of his.

She stood up, and then went down on one knee in front of him.

"What are you doing?"

"I love you, Derek Caruthers. I never thought I would say this to another man but the last two months have showed me that the dreams I'd had of what life could be were possible with the right person."

"Get up," Derek said. "You've shown the same thing to me."

She shook her head and he shifted until he was kneeling next to her on the carpeted floor.

"What are you doing?" he asked her.

"Something that I should have done a while ago but I wanted to wait until we gave our temporary arrangement a real shot."

"Okay," he said, though he wasn't sure what she was getting at.

Then she reached into her pocket and took out a ring box. He felt his heart melt. The love he felt for her swelled and he couldn't quite believe what he was seeing.

"Derek Caruthers, will you marry me? Will you be my husband and partner and father to my children? Will you love me forever?"

"I will," he said. He leaned in and kissed her. He wanted to keep the embrace light but this was Bianca and they'd just decided to make their engagement real. When he lifted his head they were both breathing heavy. He stood up, drew her to feet and carried her into his bedroom.

He set her on the middle of his bed and remembered the first time they'd made love. That was the moment when he'd realized how much Bianca meant to him and that he was probably never going to be able to let her go.

"Wait a minute. You haven't put your ring on yet."

He opened the box and saw that it was a man's signet ring with a caduceus in the middle and a raised stone with their initials linked together in it.

He put it on his finger and then made love to Bianca. He had thought that his career was the one thing that would define him. But he found that living with Bianca and Beni had shown him who he really was. He was a surgeon yes and a brother and a son, but he was also a father, a friend and a lover. And it was more than he'd thought he'd ever call his own.

* * * * *

Don't miss any of these novels from
USA TODAY bestselling author
Katherine Garbera!

THE TYCOON'S BABY SURPRISE
HIS BABY AGENDA
HIS SEDUCTION GAME PLAN
HIS INSTANT HEIR
BOUND BY A CHILD

Available now from Mills & Boon Desire!

MILLS & BOON®
Desire™

PASSIONATE AND DRAMATIC LOVE STORIES

A sneak peek at next month's titles...

In stores from 10th August 2017:

- **A Family for the Billionaire** – Dani Wade *and*
  Little Secrets: The Baby Merger – Yvonne Lindsay

- **Taking Home the Tycoon** – Catherine Mann
  and **The Heir Affair** – Cat Schield

- **Convenient Cinderella Bride** – Joss Wood
  and **Expecting the Rancher's Baby?** – Kristi Gold

Just can't wait?
Buy our books online before they hit the shops!
www.millsandboon.co.uk

Also available as eBooks.

Join Britain's BIGGEST Romance Book Club

50% OFF your first parcel

- **EXCLUSIVE offers** every month

- **FREE delivery direct** to your door

- **NEVER MISS a title**

- **EARN Bonus Book points**

Call Customer Services
0844 844 1358*

or visit
illsandboon.co.uk/subscriptions

* This call will cost you 7 pence per minute plus your phone company's price per minute access charge.